KT-561-471

AUDREY HOWARD

A Flower in Season

coronet

CORONET BOOKS
Hodder & Stoughton

Copyright © 2002 by Audrey Howard

First published in Great Britain in 2002 by Hodder and Stoughton
First published in paperback in Great Britain in 2003 by Hodder and Stoughton
A Division of Hodder Headline
A Coronet paperback

The right of Audrey Howard to be identified as the Author of the work has been
asserted by her in accordance with the Copyright, Designs and Patents Act 1988.

7 9 10 8 6

A CIP catalogue record for this title is available from the British Library

ISBN 0 340 76935 1

Typeset in Plantin by Palimpsest Book Production Limited,
Polmont, Stirlingshire
Printed and bound in Great Britain by
Mackays of Chatham plc, Chatham, Kent

Hodder and Stoughton
A division of Hodder Headline
338 Euston Road
London NW1 3BH

Each flower blooms in its season

Some bloom early

Some bloom late

Yet all bloom in time.

I

It was the unmistakable thud of a clenched fist striking flesh and bone that attracted his attention, followed by a grunt, whether of pain or satisfaction he could not tell. Pulling on the reins, he brought his tall black mare to a halt, swivelling round in the saddle as he tried to identify from which direction the sound had come then waiting for a moment to see if it was repeated. When it was not he shrugged his shoulders, deciding he had imagined it and if he had not what was it to do with him if two men fought out some grudge among the trees? There was always some chap, probably young, for the young were known to be hot-headed, taking offence at another. He was about to urge on his mount when the sound was repeated and a woman cried out. The black labrador who ran at his heels pricked his ears and sniffed the air, turning to his left. He whined softly.

"What is it, boy?" he murmured, but the dog continued to look uneasily to the side of the lane where a gate led on to a rough track.

He was returning from Penrith where he had instructed his banker in a matter of some urgency regarding shares that he wished to purchase in several railway lines that had been authorised and would be constructed over the next few years. It was the start of the era of what would be called "Railway Mania" and any shares in an authorised new line were instantly snapped up by the astute businessman. The Liverpool and Manchester Railway, opened in 1830, the

Edinburgh and Dalkeith a year later, the line to Clarence
from a junction of the original Stockton and Darlington, the
Durham and Sunderland, already carrying passengers, had
made him a small fortune, and whenever shares came on the
market he bought them, not just in the north but down as far
as the Bristol and Gloucestershire Railway, indeed wherever
a line was to be built. The country from Land's End to John
o' Groats would eventually become a vast network of railway
lines cobwebbing north, south, east and west and he, as a man
of enterprise who saw the potential of adding to his already
considerable wealth, had been in on it from the start.

From where he sat his mare he could see right down the
full length of Lake Ullswater, a distance of five miles, for the
air was perfectly calm, clear and mild. It was autumn and
the glorious changing shades of the trees were particularly
pleasing to the eye, shades of brown and crimson, bronze,
amber and yellow. He could hear faintly from below the
sound of children's voices and knew they would be picking
the ripe, luscious fruits of the season, blackberries from the
hedges along the lane to his house. A squirrel ran across the
path, secure in its mistaken belief that it was alone, a beech
nut in its mouth, and his dog watched it unblinkingly as,
suddenly aware of them, it turned in alarm then scampered
away to safety. The lowering sun was turning the waters
of the lake to flame as it slid down the sky, blurring the
day's brightness to a shaded hue and up on the fells purple
shadows were forming. An owl hooted as evening approached
and even as he lingered indecisively birdsong began to die
down among the thinning foliage of the trees. The lake was
bordered along its winding shores with cultivated land and
wide grassy pastures, some of it his own, green pastures on
which were dotted white farmhouses looking out among the
trees towards the lake. Dry-stone walls divided the fields, in
which cattle grazed, while high up on the fells the grey-white

shapes of sheep could be picked out. The land sloped gently upwards from the shore until it reached the foot of the fells rising in breathtaking magnificence to the broken tops that brushed the sky. He could see Place Fell pushing its bold breast into the lake, forming first a large bay to the left and then bending to the right, altering the lake's shape, but the waters were blue, calm, smooth as a mirror. A cormorant flew low over the shimmering surface fishing, then rose with something in its beak. Gowbarrow Fell reached majestically to the heavens on the right-hand side of the lake and to the left rose Swarth Hill. His land, his place, his birthplace, the inheritance that all the men of the fells and dales considered the best in the world.

His dog looked up at him enquiringly, one paw raised, ready, when given the order, to slip away through the under-growth and investigate whatever had disturbed his master. Where they had halted was a five-barred gate which stood open, rotting on its posts, and the man frowned, for he deplored bad management and neglect. The rutted track beyond the gate led through a strip of woodland towards the River Eamont. He could hear the sound of tumbling waters, never far away in this wet land of the lakes, dashing down steep, rocky slopes, chuckling merrily as it raced towards the lake below. Above the trees of mature oak, ash and beech could be seen a roof which he knew to be that of the Moorend corn mill and from a chimney wisped a thin smudge of smoke.

His mare, an animal of obvious breeding, tossed her head fretfully, wanting to be off, for she had had a long ride and ahead of her lay her stable, the oats she would be lovingly fed by the stable lad and the comforting rubdown that was her due. She became even more irritable when the man on her back turned her in at the gate and proceeded slowly up the track. The dog kept beside him for he was obedient to his master's command. The ground was covered with a mosaic of gold, copper, bronze and flame, leaves that were soft, deadening any sound his mare's hooves might make, wet with the rain that fell so persistently from these Lakeland skies, and when he entered through another gate, equally neglected, into a cobbled yard overgrown with grass at the front of the mill none of those there heard his approach.

A man, big, broad-shouldered, heavily muscled, his face scarlet with rage, had a boy by the scruff of his neck and even as the man on the horse watched, the back of his enormous hand fetched the lad a blow across his face which lifted him from his feet.

"P'raps that'll teach yer ter be more careful, yer idle gob-shite. Dost think I'm made o' money scatterin' Seth Cartwright's corn about as if it were nowt but a handful o' muck from field an' what am I ter tell him when he comes ter weigh it an' finds it short?"

A young girl who had been cowering against the skirts of a woman suddenly darted forward and did her best to catch the raised fist of the enraged man but with a contemptuous flick he cracked her a blow that sent her flat on her back a couple of feet away.

"Nay, Jethro," the woman wailed.

"It was me, Faither," the girl cried out but the man was beyond listening to anyone in his bloodlust.

They were all taken by surprise, even the boy being beaten, by the snarl of cold anger that came at them from the edge of the cobbled yard. The horseman leaped nimbly from his mare which, alarmed by the tension and the thundering of the enraged man, skittered away to a clump of holly beneath a beech tree, and had her rein not caught in a branch would have taken off in mad panic for home. With a short command to his dog to "stay", which he did, dropping down on to his belly, Chad Cameron strode across the yard and, lifting his arm, swung his short riding crop, cutting it about the man's head. The man swore obscenely, dropped the boy and swung round savagely on his attacker with the evident intention of beating him to pulp, and a lesser, wiser man might have backed away.

Not Chad Cameron. Standing his ground he brandished the whip as the big man lifted his fist, ready to aim it into his face. For a moment it looked as though murder might be done, or attempted, but something stopped the brute, perhaps recognition of who the intruder was, even in the blood-red rage of his anger, for Chad Cameron was a powerful man in these parts, but he still could not control his tongue.

"What the bloody hell dost think you're doin', you interferin' bugger?" he thundered, still shaking his fist in Chad's face. "What gives you the right ter come between a man an' his lad? Get off my land unless you want some an' all. Bloody hell, it's comin' ter summat when a man can't—"

"If you raise that fist to me or to that boy again I shall fetch the constable and have you taken away in chains, and you'd better believe me when I say I can do it. Dear God, d'you want to kill the lad, that's if you haven't already done so," for the boy lay where his father had dropped him. His mother had run to him, lifting his head into her lap, putting an anxious finger to his cheek where his father's fist had split it, begging him to tell her he was all right, murmuring those words mothers have for a hurt child in which the only ones recognisable are "there, there". It only served to infuriate her husband, the boy's father, even more.

"Leave him alone, woman. No wonder he's such a bloody milk-sop wi' you molly-coddlin' him every time he gets a knock. He needs a boot up the arse not bloody kisses." He snorted contemptuously but it was evident that his violence was lessening. The girl had regained her feet, her hand to her cheek hiding what promised to be a furious black eye and the one that was visible glared at her father with loathing.

And was it any wonder, Chad thought. He stepped away from Jethro Marsden, his face cold, his golden-brown eyes narrowed and menacing. He was very white about the mouth. The whip he had used on the man flickered angrily against his boot.

"You're a bully and a coward, Jethro Marsden, and I regret the day my father sold yours this corn mill and the land on which it stands."

"Well, that's just too bad, Mr Cameron, but there's nowt yer can do about it now," the miller jeered.

"It's not the first time I've had to speak to you about that drunken temper of yours. You nearly put one of my labourers in the infirmary last year and had it not been for his fear of reprisal he would have fetched in the constable. No matter what I said I could not persuade him to make a charge against you. It's a wonder to me that any man brings his grain to be milled by you. I suppose it's the distance they would have to travel that weighs in your favour. By God, if I could get you out, I would."

"Well, yer can't."

"And these children of yours are not strong enough to do the work you expect of them," he went on, as though Jethro had not spoken, "and neither, I suspect, is your wife. You should employ a man to help you but then that would mean putting your hand in your pocket, wouldn't it, giving you less to spend on ale, and with three pairs of hands to do the job, willing or unwilling, despite their obvious inability to manage heavy work—"

"They're strong enough, an' anyroad, it's nowt ter do wi' you or any man what I do in me own business and on me own land an' with me own children. Lad's lively enough when he wants ter be. Just needs a bit o' . . . correction now an' again."

"Correction! You call opening his cheek to the bone, correction? I've heard tales of that leather strap you keep hanging behind your door and if I was to ask the boy to let me have a look at his back what would I find? And what about your daughter? Does she get 'correction' when she fails to lift a sack of grain that would fell a grown man?"

The girl peeped at him from beneath the tangle of her hair on which a light dusting of flour had settled. It was tied back with a piece of twine, falling in a thick cascade of dark brown curls to her buttocks, and from its unruly appearance had known no recent acquaintance with a hairbrush. She was dressed in what he could only call rags, a short skirt, neatly mended in a dozen places and a bodice to match, poor things the colour of earth but clean, as she was, for the most part. She wore no shoes and her feet were coated with the muck of the yard. She still held her hand to her face, covering her eye and cheek, but the one that peered from beneath the curtain of her hair was the most startling colour he had ever seen. For some reason it reminded him of the wisteria that grew up the front wall of his home, a sort of violet, a purple-blue with tiny specks of gold in it, the pupil coal black to match the long lashes that surrounded it. He could not guess her age, still a child he would have thought, and yet he noticed, and then felt ashamed for doing so, that two small breasts, no more than buds, pressed against the thin material of her bodice.

"Well, will there be owt else, sir?" the last word uttered with a deliberate sneer. "I've work ter do if you haven't."

"You mean your family have, don't you? By God, I wish I had the means to turn you out, Jethro Marsden. What I've seen here today sickens me.".

"Aye, well, happen it does. Gentry's well known fer its weak stomachs an' soft heads. Now get off my land an' try minding yer own business." He turned away and the girl flinched, scuttling to where her mother and brother faltered.

Chad Cameron looked about him helplessly. He studied
the yard and the clearing of rough grass that surrounded it.
Those trees through which he had ridden were split by the
track, the track itself rough and churned up by the dozens
of waggons that passed over it annually. Farmers for miles,
and villagers locally brought their wheat, their oats and grain
to be ground at Jethro Marsden's corn mill and the concern,
though small, was thriving, for, say what you liked about the
miller, he worked hard, and so did his family. Wheat was
cultivated in these parts and indeed in most areas of the
country, its main value as bread flour. To the miller and the
baker its important qualities were its strength, its flavour and
its flour-yielding properties. Ask any farm wife or the wives
of the working men who all made their own bread and they
would tell you that the potency of a flour is in its ability to
produce a well-risen loaf. Barley was not much grown since
its main value was in the brewing and distilling industries and
there were none of those on the shores of Lake Ullswater, but
oats, which were hardy and could be grown in any soil, even
on high land, played a large part in Jethro's milling labour. He
could also be called on to crush peas and beans and gleanings
from the ploughed fields used for animal feed which brought
him in a few extra shillings for his ale.

The main building, the water mill, was built of stone three
storeys high, the bagging and drive floor at ground level and
on the second level which stretched the full length and width
of the building was the "stone" floor where the three pairs of
millstones were located and where the real work of the mill
was done. On the top floor was the family's living quarters,
a bedroom where Emily and Jethro slept and several rooms
used for storage. There was a large fireplace on both floors
at the north end. What might have been a large porch
with a chimney jutted out into the front of the yard on
the ground floor with a door let into the side and this,

Chad happened to know, was where the miller's wife had her kitchen. A cow lowed at the back of the mill, for it was getting towards milking time and a pig rootled around to the side of the building, looking for scraps under the trees. Several hens cackled and pecked at the ground, guarded by an aggressive rooster which was keeping a stern eye on Chad's dog. It was all in good order, apart from the two gates and Chad, had he the right which he hadn't, could find no fault. He had properties of his own, farms that were rented to decent, long-term, hard-working tenants, as were his cottages in which his labourers lived. He had a bobbin factory in Staveley, a pencil factory nearby, for the materials needed in such concerns were all close at hand: lead, coppice woods. His shares in the copper mines over towards Coniston were worth three times what his father had paid for them years ago. Worth a bob or two was Chad Cameron, the men who were in business and did business with him agreed with one another, and their wives, those with marriageable daughters, vied with one another for his attention.

The boy who had been helped to his feet by his sister and mother was limping rather unsteadily towards the doorway of the kitchen. The mother glanced back, doing her best to smile her thanks but it was a sad smile which told him that the moment he was out of sight Jethro would give them what for. He might not hit them again, not with Mr Cameron only just gone, but the rest of their day would be a misery – and what was unusual about that? – until he fell into the drunken sleep that ended it. The boy seemed stunned, inclined to fall over his own feet and was it any wonder, the blow he had received. Blood still oozed from his cheek and dripped from his chin and Chad resolved to send Ned, one of his grooms, to fetch Doctor Travis to him. A stitch might be needed and it would do no harm to let that bugger know an eye was being kept on him, not just by Chad Cameron but by Doctor Travis who was a magistrate.

Jethro stood in the centre of the yard, swaying slightly, his head lowered like a bull about to charge, his bottom lip, full and red and moist, hanging open, revealing his rotten teeth, and in the doorway his daughter hesitated, wanting, it seemed to Chad, to say something but not quite daring. He knew he himself looked somewhat daunting, for he gave the impression of being stern, serious, cold even, which was not the case but he couldn't help his own damned appearance, could he? He returned her look and when she smiled he was quite taken aback by the dazzle of it. It lit up her swollen face and put chips of blue diamonds in her eyes so that he was reminded of a brooch of lapis lazuli his grandmother used to wear. She had removed her hand from her face as she helped her brother to the house but even with the slightly lopsided look he could see she would be a lovely woman if she was ever allowed to reach that age by the brute who was her father. There was something about her, a narrowed gleam to her incredible eyes, a lift to her tousled head, a look of righteous indignation as she cast a malevolent glare at her father. She was a skinny little thing, despite the budding breasts, all hair and eyes, but it seemed her spirit was unbroken by the vicious treatment she and her brother, *and* no doubt her mother, received at the hands of the miller.

He turned to his horse and with a movement of his hand called the dog to him but before he mounted he swivelled back to Jethro.

"Mind what I said, Marsden. I'd not have animals on my land treated cruelly, let alone children. I don't care if they are yours" – as the man would have answered him, no doubt ready to give him a bit of lip – "and I shall keep my eye on the situation. If I see either of them with an injury I shall have the law on you. So think on."

Springing into the saddle, he urged on his mount, first into a canter and then a full gallop, disappearing into the wood from which he had come.

"That bloody swine up at Moorend Mill's been mistreating those children of his again," he told his sister that evening as he shook out his damask napkin. He placed it across his knee before picking up his spoon and appreciatively sniffing the bowl of soup Martha had just placed before him.

"Chadwick, please, you know I cannot abide bad language, and particularly in front of ladies," of whom she was definitely one.

"I'm sorry, Sarah, but it's enough to make any man swear the way that man treats his family. The boy's no more than fifteen and the girl even less and yet he works them like grown men. God only knows what would have happened to the lad if I hadn't been passing. Five o'clock in the afternoon and the sot was—"

"Chadwick, please . . ."

"Well, that is what he is, Sarah, a drunken sot and I've half a mind to have the law on him. If it wasn't for those children . . ." For a moment his eyes became strangely unfocused as though he were seeing something to which the other two occupants of the room were blind. Something that troubled him and yet at the same time gave him a certain amount of pleasure.

"Chadwick?" his sister said questioningly.

With a start he realised that Sarah had addressed him, indeed was staring at him with some perplexity and that Martha, the elderly maid who was serving their evening meal, was tutting since it was not like him to let good food go cold. She had been in service at Longlake Edge for over forty years ever since she had come as kitchen-maid to old Mrs Cameron. She had seen Chad born, watched him grow from a solemn infant to a sturdy young lad and into the mature man he now was, and with the privilege of an old and trusted servant felt she had the right to show her displeasure wherever it was needed. Not always in actual words, of course, though that happened sometimes, but with muttered asides, expressions of disapproval and the odd "tut" or two.

Neither she nor Sarah Cameron was aware that his mind's eye had returned to the scene he had witnessed earlier in the day and in particular to the expressive face of the game and plucky waif who had smiled at him. That was all she had done, smiled at him and inside him something had returned her smile and felt warmed by it. A slip of a girl and him getting on for thirty and yet he had felt drawn to her. Not in *that* way, naturally. Good God, he was old enough to be her father but something vital in her had appealed to him, said something to him, awakened a part of him that he didn't recognise. Silly old fool he was, but she had had a very *taking* way with her and even now, as he raised his spoon to his lips, tasting a mouthful of Mrs Foster's delicious vegetable consommé, she came again to smile at him.

"Chadwick?" his sister repeated coolly.

"Yes?"

"What on earth is the matter with you?"

Standing to his left, her hands smoothing her snow-white apron, Martha would like that question answered as well, the expression on her seamed old face said.

"The matter?"

"You seem to have gone into a daydream."

He smiled. "Really, Sarah, when have you ever known me to daydream?" He took another spoonful of soup and Martha, satisfied, turned back to the serving table. The job of serving the master and mistress should have been the duty of one of the parlour-maids but Martha, because of her long service with the family, ruled the kitchen, even above Mrs Foster, and often took it into her head to take it over, despite her age, and who were they, her minions, to argue? Mrs Foster was cook and did all the ordering of foodstuffs, under Miss Cameron's supervision, of course, but Martha still thought of herself as a kind of housekeeper and general guardian of the Cameron family.

"Anyway, as I was saying, that man will have to be watched. He is a tyrant and a drunkard and I'm afraid the two characteristics put together are very dangerous. Those children of his do the work of grown men and his wife is clearly terrified of him. I sent Ned to ask Doctor Travis to look in. The boy's cheek needed seeing to and it will do no harm to let Marsden know that his treatment of his family is not going unnoticed."

"Chadwick, dear, do you think it's wise to intervene in what is clearly a family matter? If the man feels the need to chastise the boy, who might, for all you know, have deserved some punishment . . ."

Chad looked up from his soup and, though no particular expression was discernible on his smoothly shaved face, the tone of his voice told her of his disapproval.

"Sarah, had you seen that boy's face I'm sure you would not have made that remark. It was cut to the bone—"

"Really, Chadwick, not while we are eating, please." Sarah Cameron made a small moué of distaste. The old maidservant turned from the serving table where Daphne, one of two parlour-maids, had just placed a tray of vegetables and a pile of pork chops under a warming cover which she would serve as a second course, and looked with sharp concern at her master.

"He's a bad lot is that chap," she stated tartly, "an' needs constable fetchin' to him. I were down by't gate t'other day and he were fair wackin' that plough horse of his, poor old thing. It's not fit to be pullin' a gig, let alone plough."

"That's enough, Martha. We were not speaking of plough horses."

"I were just sayin'." And having said it she returned, satisfied, to the task of placing the chops, three for her master and two for Miss Sarah, on hot plates.

"That's what I mean, he has a bad streak in him and needs watching. I shall make it my business to keep my eye on him. Seth Cartwright told me he has seen him fighting outside the Bull at Pooley and had it not been for the restraint several men put on him would have beaten Will Stirling's lad to pulp."

"Chadwick, dear, do you think we might talk of something less violent while we eat? It is quite putting me off dinner."

Sarah Cameron was a woman of thirty-one, a spinster but one who did not wish to change her status though she had received one or two offers of marriage in the blooming of her youthful prettiness, for her dowry had been not inconsiderable. Why should she marry, she said, only to herself, of course, since she had all the advantages of a married woman with none of the, to her, disgusting practices that went on in the marital bed. She ran her own home, Chadwick's home, she had her own carriage, her own circle of friends, her own dress allowance since her brother was a generous man, and her life was one that suited her admirably. Chadwick liked comfort, good service, well-cooked meals, the things a man of refinement and sophistication required in his life and she was well able to provide them. They entertained frequently and were entertained in return, having among their acquaintance men of high office, men of wealth, men like Chadwick himself. She was known for her good works, for her commitment to the church where she and, if she could get him there, Chadwick worshipped.

Brother and sister were not alike to look at. Where Chad was dark, sombre, brown-eyed, unsmiling, inclined toward gravity – which was often misleading, for he kept his sens of humour well hidden – she was fair, her fine hair brushed back from her face into a neat chignon, completely proper for a lady of her years and station. Her eyes were a light blue, her skin pale, for a lady did not go out into the sunshine without the protection of a parasol. She wore gowns of good quality, well made but again suitable for a spinster lady from a decent family. Subdued colours, modest, worn with the jewellery come from her mother when she died. Again, not flamboyant, but good pieces which, had he married, would have gone to Chadwick's wife.

The room in which they dined was of a restrained opulence, a reflection of the large and prosperous middle class who were well able to afford the many quality goods that had once been the preserve of the aristocracy. Silk-covered walls in apple green with draped curtains of the same shade and material at the tall sash windows; a polished table of glowing mahogany with a sideboard to match; brilliant glassware and shining silver; scented candles and bowls of fresh-cut flowers from the extensive gardens and green houses. There was an enormous fire crackling and leaping in the white marble fireplace and all this luxury was set on a richly patterned carpet of crimson and apple green. Above the fireplace was a large gilt-framed mirror and about the room, on the mantelpiece and arranged on small tables and on the sideboard, were ornaments of Sèvres, Meissen and others collected by the previous mistresses of Longlake Edge.

Sarah chatted of this and that, topics more suited to the dinner table in her opinion. The coming ball at Holme Park to which they were invited and to which, so Mrs Armstrong, the vicar's wife had told her, Squire Mounsey had promised to look in, which was a feather in Ernestine Tyson's cap, didn't Chadwick think so? The lecture that was to be held at the Assembly Rooms in Penrith on the subject of the plight of the poor wretched slaves in the southern states of

America to which she hoped Chadwick would accompany her. The forthcoming marriage of the daughter of her dear friend Jessica Gould and her hopes that the weather would not turn nasty, which it was inclined to do up here in the north.

"I think I'll take my coffee in my study, Sarah, if you don' mind. I have some papers to go over before I retire."

"Of course, my dear."

"So I'll say goodnight."

"Goodnight, Chadwick, and please, my dear, promise me you won't lie awake brooding on that dreadful man and his family."

His lips twitched in what might have been a wry smile, for sometimes his sister said the most absurd things. Lie awake brooding! And yet when he finally turned out his lamp the impish face of the young girl with the incredible eyes was the last image that flickered inside his eyelids.

2

"Quickly now, the pair of you. Sadie'll take you in until I come for you which shouldn't be long by the sound of him, the drunken pig. Will you listen to him . . . no, don't, the words are too vile. Mother, please, will you go with Briony. I won't come to any harm. I can keep out of his way until he falls into his usual drunken stupor. Take Sal with you. The last time he kicked her I think he cracked one of her ribs. Please, please, get a move on."

"Son, won't you come with us?" Emily Marsden pleaded. "I'm afeared . . ."

"Please, Danny, come with us." His sister took his hand and tried to draw him towards the river which stood between them and the cottage where Sadie Evans and her son lived but he pulled impatiently away from her.

"If there's no one here you know he'll only come lookin' for you. Please, lass, get on an' stop arguin'. I can hear him from here an' why he doesn't fall in the bloody lake's a mystery. One of these days . . ."

"Don't, Danny, don't say it."

"I wish he would. Now get across the river an' stay with Sadie. Oh, Lord Jesus, how much longer can we stand this?"

The boy turned abruptly and scuttled away towards the back of the mill house, almost in tears, for that was what he was, no more than a boy carrying a man's burden.

Briony Marsden took her mother's arm and began to hurry

through the stand of trees between the mill and the river. The dog, with a sad, backward glance at her young master, reluctantly followed as though she knew full well it would do no good, to her or to him, to stay behind.

Emily limped as quickly as she could beside her daughter, favouring the leg that *he* had kicked and broken in one of his drunken rages and which had healed awkwardly. It was just another of the injuries inflicted upon her by the man she had married seventeen years ago. She had been the pretty, guileless daughter of a bootmaker in Penrith when Jethro Marsden had entered her father's shop to order himself a pair of boots, sturdy knee boots of good quality leather, for even then he was a successful miller with a guinea or two in his pocket. How she had admired the strong, handsome young bull who had courted her so ardently, his dominance thrilling her girlish heart which had known nothing but affectionate cherishing since the day she was born, and how she had begged her father to allow the match. The corn mill above Pooley Bridge was not so far away, she had implored him, well within visiting distance in the gig Jethro had promised her.

It was not until she lay under him that first night while he raped her again and again that the true horror of what she had done become clear to her. In her innocence she had thought his strength to be that of a true man and only once he had her safely within his grasp was his real nature revealed. Beneath his physical strength lay nothing but cruelty and greed, for when her father died, knowing nothing of what his daughter suffered, as it would have been more than her life was worth to enlighten him, everything he had came to Jethro.

She had two reasons for joy in her life. Her children, the two who had survived, for of the twelve she had given birth to in sixteen years, only they had lived. And her second, kept a secret from their father, was something she had vouchsafed only to them. From an early age she had passed on the learning

she herself had been given. Her father, being a progressive sort
of a chap, had insisted, despite her being a mere girl, on a bit
of decent schooling and she had thanked God nightly for
it, though it often crossed her mind that she had little else
to thank Him for. Sometimes it was tricky for Briony and
Daniel since they had to pretend an ignorance of the written
word and scratch their heads over the "sums" Jethro worked
out painfully on a scrap of paper. He could read slowly and
now and again it took his fancy to bring home a newspaper
cast aside at the inn where he drank. He would pretend a
knowledge of the written word which they were forced to
admire and only when he was absent could the three of them
pore over the sentences and gain some comprehension of what
was going on in the world beyond the mill gate. Even as young
children, ten or eleven years of age, Emily had read to them
of the death of the King, George was his name, and of the
new King his brother, who was called William. In June 1837
it had been the turn of the young Princess Victoria when her
uncle William died of pneumonia. She was to be crowned at
Westminister Abbey in June the following year and the nation
would have a queen. Emily, Danny and Briony waited eagerly
for it, praying that their lord and master would bring home
a newspaper with a report of the coronation, for they had
little colour in their lives and surely this would be a grand
affair. They were told of the Duke of Wellington who had
been a brave soldier and great Prime Minister. They learned
of tremendous upheavals in the country, of men turned into
landless labourers by the enclosure of common pasture and
driven to despair by harsh winters and the hunger of their
families. Of unrest in Ireland; of revolution in France, of
the cries for reform and universal franchise. Had their father
known of his children's awareness of what took place, not just
in their own country but worldwide, thanks to their mother,
he would have skinned the three of them alive.

Sadie Evans was not surprised when they knocked on the door of her cottage which stood in a row of others belonging to Mr Cameron. It wasn't the first time they had "called on her" which was their way of telling her they needed shelter for an hour or two. Naturally, this wouldn't happen on a weekday, for the mill did business every day except Sunday and it was on a Sunday that Jethro got *really* drunk, mindlessly, insanely drunk instead of just his usual truculent inebriation.

Briony had wanted to bring Glory, the old plough horse, even the fat sow who was ready to farrow, for her father had been known to belabour his animals if his children were not immediately available, but Danny had been almost hysterical in his need to get her and Ma away before Pa came stumbling up the track to the house.

"For God's sake, you'll be wanting to take the damn chickens next," he exploded, nearly out of his mind in his panic to get his mother and sister to safety. "Just do as you're told and get up to Sadie's. I'll come for you when it's safe."

"I'm afeared he'll—"

"He'll do far worse things to you than he will to the beasts, Bry," he said brutally, pushing her quite forcefully in the direction of the track that led towards the river. There were rough stones jutting from the foaming waters across which it was easy for the youngsters to jump but Emily, with her crippled leg, would need assistance and time was not on their side as the sound of Jethro crashing against the gatepost and the volley of obscenities that followed rose above the trees.

Sadie Evans and her son worked for Mr Cameron which was the reason for the neat cottage she and Iolo occupied. Sadie was a widow, her husband, a Welshman come to find work out of the mines that had wrecked his health, had died anyway of the "black spit" as the miner's asthma was called. Sadie was a laundress known in the parish for the pure immaculacy of her "whites", since she was an expert in the art of boiling, her delicate touch with a "flat iron", her strong right arm to turn the wringer with its rubber rollers, and the mangle which, if used properly, saved an inordinate amount of ironing. She also had the strong back and teeth-gritting determination necessary for bending hour after hour over the wooden washtub. She was tall, broad-shouldered, handsome with ruddy cheeks and the good teeth she had acquired from eating the fresh food she had known as a farm lass in Lancashire. Dai Evans had picked her up on his travels, spiriting her away from the big house where she had been in service as laundry-maid. His whimsical Welsh humour, his merry brown eyes, the goodness of his soul captured her heart and persuaded her to follow him to Longlake Edge where he had worked as old Mr Cameron's cowman. Sadie had been given a trial in the laundry and her superb workmanship had ensured her a foot on the ladder, which she climbed swiftly until she was head laundry-maid with two girls under her. They worked long hours, she and her easy-going Dai but they were, by the standards of their class, well provided for. Their marriage had lasted only five years and he had left her with a heart that, though it was irretrievably broken, was as big as the fells that backed her cottage, willing to do "owt for anyone" and a son who was as good-natured, as merrily inclined as his father whose job, when he was barely as tall as the animals he milked, he took over. Neither of them could read or write but they were well placed with Mr Cameron and felt no lack.

She opened the door and surveyed the sorry pair who faltered on her well-scrubbed doorstep. Briony was wet from the knees down, for it had proved tricky to get her ma across the stream and she had been forced to wade, holding her ma's arm to balance her. Her hair, which had also got a wetting, flowed about her and she had the appearance of a bedraggled kitten. The dog was no better, shivering violently and not just because of the wetting she had received, her ears drooping, her tangled butter-coloured coat dripping on Sadie's clean step.

She opened the door wide without a word and though Briony tried to speak, to explain, to make up some reason why she, her mother and the dog should be dithering on Sadie's rug, no words came. A wooden frame that had been hung with Sadie's own freshly ironed sheets and lace-trimmed pillow cases airing in front of the fire was whisked to another part of the kitchen, and she and Ma were seated opposite each other by the range with a cup of hot, sweet, strong tea – which Sadie considered necessary at times like these – in their hands. Sal was allowed to huddle up to the fire and Sadie, sipping her own tea, questioned neither of them. Jethro Marsden's foul temper and violent disposition were well known in the district and it was a wonder to them all that he had not killed somebody in one of his barbarous moods. If he hadn't been such a good miller, producing flour that resulted in bread that any housewife could be proud of, he would have gone under years ago. His father had been a hard man, but nothing like his son, a man who had kept himself to himself, his family with its nose to the grindstone – almost literally – and it was perhaps his strict upbringing that had set Jethro on the road he now took.

"Another cup, Emily?" Sadie asked. She could see Jethro's wife had calmed down a bit and the girl looked less terrified. She only hoped that lad, that brave lad, was all right. She'd seen the state of him a time or two when his pa had got at him and he had not been a pretty sight. She had smeared her own soothing ointment on his back and had told her Iolo that she'd a good mind to report him to Mr Cameron. Not that it would do much good, for the miller owned the mill and the authorities would only say that a man had a right to strap his own lad. Which she supposed was true but if her Dai had ever attempted it with Iolo he'd have not stood up for a week! But then Emily was not made of the stuff Sadie was and hadn't the strength or courage to defy her man or defend her children. Iolo was Sadie's joy, an extension of the love she still had for Dai. Iolo, though he spoke with the broad vowels of a north countryman was, in her eyes, as Welsh as Dai. Iolo, or Iorwerth, his full name, had been christened such since his heritage was Welsh and it was said that Iorwerth was regarded as Edward in English, Edward being her father's name. So, all very suitable.

Emily accepted another cup of tea and was even tempted to try one of Sadie's jam tarts which had just come out of the oven. Despite the enormous amount of work she got through each day Sadie always found time to knock up a few scones or an apple pie, for her lad had a good appetite.

Sadie Evans's cottage stood in a row of others on a lane that ran at the edge of Chad Cameron's land. It was built of local stone with roof slates of the grey, blue and sea green common to the Lake District. There was ivy climbing the wall and partly covering the roof and in the summer a profusion of pink, sweetbriar roses, past their best now in the autumn. Sadie's was the end cottage and the small garden which her Iolo tended was the best kept of the dozen, though Mr Cameron insisted that his workers preserve a tidy look about their plots. He was responsible for the maintenance of the cottages, which were sturdy and snug, and he expected the cowman, the grooms, the carpenter, the shepherds whose families occupied them to keep the gardens in good order. The kitchens, all of them, had the latest cast-iron ranges installed, with a fireplace beside in which a good fire was kept going night and day, for the weather on the high fells could be bitter. Sadie had a high-backed rocking-chair, hand-made rugs, an old dresser crowded with blue and white crockery and a table in the centre of the kitchen scrubbed to the paleness of winter snow. Upstairs, approached by a narrow, winding staircase, were two oak-beamed bedrooms and at the back of the kitchen was a scullery where Sadie did her own laundering. Water had to be fetched from a pump at the back of the cottages, good, clean water, but it was a back-breaking job when her workload was heavy. Iolo did what he could of a morning before setting off for the milking, carrying bucket after bucket and tipping it into the water butt that stood at her back door from where she had only to carry it to her sink. A hard life but a decent one and she thanked God for it every night before she climbed into her pristine bed.

The tabby cat, which resided in a basket by the side of the fire with her everlasting litter of kittens, raised her head and hissed warningly at the dog who was bothering no one. The kittens wrestled and fell about but every time one tried to climb out of the basket Tabby dragged it back. The room was still but for the crackle and splutter of the fire, the plaintive mewing of the kittens and a canary singing for dear life in a cage by the window.

"We won't bother you for long, Sadie," Emily began but Sadie reared up indignantly, setting her cup and saucer on the table with a crash that startled the dog.

"Bother! What bother? I'm glad of yer company, my lass. Yer welcome at any time. Any time, d'yer hear. I were only sayin' to our Iolo this very morning that I'd not seen yer fer a while. In fact I were goin' to walk over—"

"Eeh, no, Sadie, you must never do that. Not with . . ." She had no need to say more, for everyone knew Jethro's views on visiting and what he called time-wasting.

"But, lass . . ."

"No, no, Sadie! As long as me and Briony can come over here when . . . well, when . . ."

"All right, lass, say no more but yer know yer welcome."

"I know. Thank God."

A movement on the lane at the end of Sadie's garden caught

her eye and she stood up and moved to the window. Briony did the same, picking up the dog, all three of them beginning to smile, Sal included, at the sight of Danny opening the gate. He saw them at the window and waved and they knew that today everything was all right.

Sadie opened the door and dragged him in, pushing him into the rocker from which Briony had just risen and before he could argue a cup of tea was in his hand and a jam tart set out on a plate. His mother and sister sat at the table, both smiling, while the dog rested her head on his knee, her eyes gazing up apologetically at him.

Danny, with the appetite of the young, with Jethro snoring in a drunken stupor and with the crisis over, ate all Sadie's jam tarts and a piece of apple pie she pressed on him. When Iolo came home accompanied by his collie bitch, Poppy, they made a cheerful group, for with the humorous Welsh blood inherited from his father he had them laughing over the antics of old Duddy Morris who, at the age of seventy – or thereabouts, for how the hell could he know his real age, he snorted defiantly – still worked as he had done since he was seven years old and that had been in the reign of George III, the mad king as he had been known. Old Duddy had that morning offered to fight young Ned Turnberry who had tried to get old Duddy to sit down and have a rest and had been roundly cursed for his pains.

Iolo was nineteen years old, and his craggy young face and the dark Celtic eyes he had inherited from her Dai turned again and again to young Briony who was, as she should be at fifteen, a lively, laughing and lovely young girl. Away from her father she flowered like a rosebud which opens in the warmth of the sun. A brute he might be but Jethro did not keep his family short of food and both his children had the glossy hair, flawless skin and strong white teeth of the well nourished. The lad was tall but Briony was a little dab of a thing, slender but with budding breasts that were thrusting against the drab fustian of her bodice. The skirt was short, just touching her ankle bone and her bare white feet were pushed into a pair of black boots, probably once belonging to her brother. Her mass of hair, which had never been cut, was dragged back from her forehead and fastened with its usual length of twine, for Jethro did not hold with geegaws, which a bit of ribbon would be.

It was very evident to Sadie that her lad was taken with Briony Marsden and though she could not quite see the lass tackling the loads of laundry – should she move in with them – that she herself dealt with every day of the week, she would not be averse to a match between them when the time came. And after all, the girl did the work of a man down at the corn mill so she couldn't be as insubstantial as she looked. At fifteen she would soon be ready for marriage and happen in a year or two, that's if they could get Jethro to part with her, Iolo and Briony might make a go of it. And that was where the difficulties would begin: persuading her father to let a valuable and profit-making pair of hands escape him. Eeh, what a hard row the lass, and the lad for that matter, had to hoe, for how were the pair of them ever to lead lives of their own with his hard fist on their necks holding them to him?

Iolo offered to walk them home, ostensibly to give Emily a hand across the stepping stones, but again the horror in all three faces dissuaded him. If Jethro should be about he was quite likely to take to all four of them and though she was as fond of the mother and her children as if they were related Sadie didn't want her Iolo smashed to smithereens by the brute who waited for them at the mill. He might be in the unconscious state he often fell into when drunk but then again he might not.

She and Iolo stood at the door of the cottage as Emily,

Briony and Danny, the cowed dog at their heels, moved slowly along the lane and down the slope towards the fast-flowing stream. Briony turned to wave, smiling with that valiance that tried to tell them, and the world, Sadie supposed, that she and her family would survive. Sadie's heart contracted with pity and she wished there was something that could be done to help the three of them but there wasn't, was there? Turning away, she sighed, leaving Iolo to stand at the door for another few minutes, then he too sighed gustily and came inside, closing the door behind him.

The next time Chad Cameron saw them they were dragging a sledge. The pair of them were harnessed to it like a pair of horses pulling a plough, leather straps about their shoulders and under their armpits, attached to the big sledge which Jethro had himself knocked together for the purpose. Sometimes a farmer required his milled grain to be delivered back to him and for an agreed sum Jethro was prepared to oblige. After the mill was done for the day, of course, and his children had finished their work.

They strained against the straps which cut into their flesh, both of them leaning into it, their feet, wearing clogs today, he noticed, feeling for the snow-covered track that led up to Brett Farm. Despite the cold their young faces were dewed with sweat and the shirts they wore were soaked with it. Danny's hair stuck to his forehead and Briony's, which was tied back from her pinched face with the usual scrap of twine, had tiny beads along her hairline. The sledge was heaped with four enormous sacks of grain. They were both forced to stop when he led his mare in front of them, their breath scraping in their lungs, and Briony leaned even further forward and rested her hands on her knees. Danny wiped his face on his sleeve.

"We can't stop, sir," he pleaded, for he knew how hard it would be to get the thing going again, especially uphill.

"Take those damned harnesses off," Chad heard himself
snarl, without the slightest idea of what he proposed to do.
"You're not beasts of burden. Look at your sister. If I'm not
mistaken those straps have chafed her skin to such an extent
it's beginning to bleed. I know it's not your fault, lad," as the
boy's face took a sullen turn. He got down from his mare and
without so much as a by your leave eased the harness from
Briony's back and set her gently on the edge of the track.

"Sit there, child, and you too, lad, while I . . . while I . . ."

They sat obediently where he had put them, their heads
hanging, their breathing slowly easing as he watched them,
plucking at his lip, a habit he had when he was angry and yet
had no way open to him to ease that anger. He could have had
a donkey sent up, the one that pulled the lawnmower in his
garden or the small farm cart but he knew it would make no
difference to these children's lives. They might have an easier
day *today* but what about tomorrow and the next day? Jethro
Marsden was not breaking the law which, if he had, would
have been easy to deal with. Most children who were born
and worked in the country, and in the towns as well, were
accustomed to hard labour, to performing tasks that were
beyond them. Many were in the hands of men who were not
related to them and who exploited them beyond their frail
strength. None of them attended school, even those who lived
at home, and they were expected to fill their days with any
work they were given, whatever their age or size. But the
father of these two didn't seem to care if he pulled their soft
young bones from their sockets, crippled them, or even if he
caused their deaths. He reduced them to trembling terror and
there was nothing he, Chad Cameron, could do about it.

At a nudge from the boy to his sister they both rose
reluctantly to their feet.

"We'll have to get on, sir, or Faither'll . . ."

"I'll be over to see him about this, lad, and you can tell

him so. He has no right to treat you like this." But he knew he was wasting his breath, at this moment, *and* indeed if he should go and see Jethro Marsden. He could not tear his eyes away from the scrawny girl. Her collar bones, which showed above the neckline of her shirt, looked as though they were about to break through her delicate skin. Her pointed face, from which the black eye he had seen her receive had faded, looked up at him gravely, then she smiled, as she had done on that day and she was suddenly lit with that same incredible loveliness. A strange despair filled him and he wondered at it. He had always had a certain tenderness for those weaker than himself, animal or child, though he kept it well hidden, and this girl's fragility and the way she was treated touched a raw nerve somewhere in his chest.

He turned away, ready to mount his mare but the boy's apologetic voice stopped him.

"Sir . . ."

"Yes?"

"Could you . . . you see we can't set the sledge to move without . . ."

What a bloody fool he was. Without being harnessed into the damned contraption and given a heave to start it these two children could not get it under way.

"Please, sir. We shall be in trouble if . . ."

Grimly, without a word, he hooked the leather straps to them and putting a shoulder to the back of the sledge gave it a mighty push up the slope. Even then he couldn't let it go and the cowman in the yard at Brett Farm was astonished to see the old sledge belonging to Jethro Marsden, his two children harnessed to it as usual, being shoved into the yard by the immaculately dressed and commanding figure of Mr Chadwick Cameron of Longlake Edge.

3

It was Chad Cameron's old granny who had put the family on the road to prosperity, for it was she who had the sound business sense that her engaging and handsome husband had lacked, but which, fortunately, her son and grandson had inherited. Of course she had not been old then. She had been Miss Margaret Chadwick, the only child of a small but prosperous yeoman farmer with a thriving farm to the east of Penrith on the fertile plains surrounding the River Eamont. When it was obvious that she was all he was to have, Frank Chadwick, lacking sons, had sighed, made the best of a bad job and taught the lass all he had known. And not just about farming.

He had been owed a bit of money. The chap who owed it couldn't pay so he had asked Frank if he'd accept some shares in a mining company and though they weren't worth much Frank had agreed. Then, to his astonishment and the chap's chagrin, they had suddenly become valuable and the one hundred and thirty-three pounds grew into several thousands. This had whetted Frank's appetite and, in a small way, since he was a cautious man, he began to buy shares in this and that, to invest in this concern or that, sharing his knowledge and his foresight with his Maggie.

Maggie was a bonny lass, added to which she would come into money and property when her father was six feet under, and there were many young men, particularly among the farming community, who courted her. But her heart was lost one lovely day in May when dashing Archie Cameron rode into her father's yard and politely asked the lad who was grooming one of the great Shire horses that pulled the plough if he might have a drink of water for his own smart grey.

Maggie had been in the dairy. She wore a snow-white apron over her serviceable grey cotton dress but she had pulled off her cap and her dark glossy hair tumbled about her face and down her back. She was the personification of robust country comeliness, rosy-cheeked, tall, full-breasted, and when she smiled her good white teeth gleamed in her honest face. Archie was enchanted. He himself came from what was known as the squirearchy. His family owned a manor house, once a small farm on the edge of Lake Ullswater built in the mid-sixteenth century by his forebears, much extended and improved but now falling into disrepair. Let it be said that he did not specifically marry Maggie for the wealth she would bring with her but it certainly helped to settle his mind. He was twenty-eight years old and she was twenty-four and by the time their first child was born two years later Maggie had pulled together the family fortunes, brought the house back to its former glory and begun building the small empire which her son and grandson strengthened even further. Archie was a good husband, merry, loving and faithful and when, ten years after they were married, he broke his neck in a fall from his grey she was devastated.

But Maggie Cameron, as she was now, was not one to brood over what could not be mended. She had kept the farm her father left to her. She could often be seen riding over there, skirting the town of Penrith, in her small gig to check on its progress under the agent she had put in to run it.

The house at Longlake Edge was surrounded by four and a half acres of formal terraced garden. Beyond the garden was extensive farming land, moorland, and the high peaks of the fells which all belonged to the Camerons. There were farms rented to tenants, some handed down from father to son, begun in the days of old Maggie: Brett Farm, Mell Farm and others, and the money inherited from her thrifty father multiplied again and again. She had invested in many of the industries of the Lakeland, copper and lead mining, slate quarrying, bobbin mills, since bobbins were much in demand in the textile industry of south Lancashire, several coppice woodlands, and when her grandson, Chad, named Chadwick after her side of the family, took over after the death of his father the Camerons were considered to be the wealthiest family in the district. Maggie lived to be sixty-one and there was not one day when she did not miss her husband who had gone before her twenty-seven years earlier. There was a streak of tenacious devotion, a faithfulness, a predisposition for loving only once in her life, something she had inherited from her father who mourned her own mother until the day he died. It was a characteristic passed on to her son and grandson, though as yet Chad Cameron had found no woman to whom he could devote himself. That is until he met Briony Marsden!

She was in the strip of woodland that stood between the corn mill and the start of his own land. The bluebells were a lake of azure and she was lying in them, thinking herself alone but for the dog beside her. Her arms were outstretched, her head thrown back, her knees bent, her skirts up above them, her eyes closed, and had it not been for the sudden stiffening of the dog, would have remained in this position. His mare's hooves made no sound in the spring undergrowth and his dog, trained to stay by his side, did so, but the yellow mongrel stood up bravely and growled.

She sat up, hastily pulling at her skirt and he had time to note that the tiny buds which he had noticed last autumn had become rounded breasts, small, peaked and pushing out the front of her tight bodice. Her hair, which he had previously seen tied back with a bit of string, was loose and fell over her shoulder in a tangle of brown curls, glossy with a recent washing he thought, and her amazing blue eyes widened in consternation at the sight of him.

She scrambled to her feet as he dismounted.

"Please, don't get up, Miss Marsden," he heard himself saying formally just as though she were a lady of some consequence he had come across, perhaps on her own immaculate lawn. "The bluebells are very fine, are they not, and you look very comfortable among them."

"I'm sorry, sir," she stammered. "Am I trespassing? I didn't know, you see, and when Faither took Danny to Penrith . . . it's the county fair . . ."

"Yes, I know. I've just come from there but—"

"Danny was to drive the cart back with the livestock and other stuff while Faither—" She stopped abruptly but Chad could have finished the sentence for her. "While Father took himself off to the George Inn."

"So you are playing truant, are you, Miss Marsden?" Aware that it was ridiculous to be calling this young girl from a different class than his own by the formal "Miss Marsden" but appallingly he was suddenly conscious that he did not know her name, her given name! And perhaps she was not aware of the meaning of the word "truant" with which the working classes would not be familiar.

It seemed she did. She smiled shyly and nodded. "Yes. Mother said I was to go. She knows how I love this time of the year . . . the bluebells, the trees coming into their finery. Spring is the start of the year, at least I think so but . . ." It was as though she suddenly realised, at least in her mind, that she was saying too much in the presence of this gentleman who was so far above her in station. She bobbed her head and her hair fell in a flowing curtain of shining silk across her face and he was quite enchanted. How pretty she was and how she had altered in the last few months. He had thought her to be about eleven, he remembered, since she was so small but he could see now that she was older. Her figure, even in the remnant of the bodice and skirt she wore, was rounded, slender, perfectly proportioned, a tiny waist with gently curving hips. Her skin was fine, without a blemish, smooth and the colour of pale honey, and he concluded she must spend time out of doors. The full coral pink of her mouth was startling against it. He stood before her, quite fascinated as the thick lashes about her eyes spread a dark fan nearly to her cheekbone and almost touched her eyebrows above. She blinked and a strand of her silky hair caught in them and without thought he lifted a hand and gently pushed it back, tucking it behind her ear. Her lips parted and she stood perfectly still and, at least for him, the moment was defined. He should mount his horse and ride away, he was perfectly well aware, for any man of his class knew where this sort of thing could lead. The gentleman and the milkmaid! The old story of the upper class exploiting the lower and, even as these thoughts twisted themselves around in his head, ridiculous thoughts since he had no intention of harming this young maid, he resolved to mount his mare and leave.

"Shall we sit down?" he said instead.

Obediently she sat. The turf was dry and mossy and the air pleasantly warm. The leaves on the trees, oak and beech and hornbeam, were pale and green, ethereal in their loveliness, the translucent light of spring giving them a beauty that would not be equalled throughout the year. Small woodland animals moved cautiously in the undergrowth but the dogs, who might have been expected to investigate, stayed where they were. They lay companionably together, their muzzles on their paws, their ears twitching, their eyes watchful, and he sun spangled between the branches of the trees fell on he smooth, well-cared-for coat of Chad's dog, giving it an extra polish but highlighting the unbrushed state of the yellow mongrel.

There was a light breeze which moved the tremulous leaves and for several moments nothing was said, for neither knew where to begin. She was the miller's daughter, young and unworldly in the presence of a man from another level of society, or indeed with any man for she had known none but her father and brother. She was ignorant of what gentlefolk spoke about and in a way he was the same though in reverse. He was twenty-nine, a man of sophistication well used to the company of women. Two sorts of women. Those who dined at his home and in whose fathers' homes he was entertained. They were well bred and were treated with the respect their husbands or fathers demanded. The other sort were vastly different but always available to a man with money. When he needed it he could purchase anything he wanted to cater to his own masculine needs. He was known to be somewhat reserved, haughty even, but he was much in demand as a guest, for not only was he wealthy but he was a bachelor. Now he wished he had that facile ease with words that some men possessed, though why in God's name he should need it now and what the devil he was doing here, trying to think of something to say to this young girl, was a mystery to him.

He sounded almost angry as he spoke. "And how is your mother, Miss—?" He broke off sharply and she turned in dismay, thinking him to be annoyed. "I'm sorry, but I don't know your name."

"It's Briony." Then she smiled and he could feel the lurching of his heart as it missed a beat. The last time he had seen her smile it had caused the same reaction. He didn't return it, in fact he frowned and her smile slipped away.

"Briony."

"Yes." Her voice was hesitant, since she thought she had in some way unknown to her offended him. "It's a plant."

"Really."

"Yes. Mother says there is black briony and white briony. I am white, she told me, though how she knows . . . well, they grow in hedgerows and . . ."

"Really?" he said again.

"Oh, yes. They're very pretty." She tried another smile.

"So are you," he declared harshly, then sprang to his feet with such force she stared up at him in amazement. And could you wonder, he thought, as he reached for the rein of his mare which was quietly cropping the grass beneath the tree. His dog leaped up and so did hers, bristling, both of them in surprise. Why had he made that remark about her loveliness? What the bloody hell was he doing here anyway, he asked himself again as his mare, startled like the two dogs, moved in a nervous circle. He had one foot in the stirrup as he did his best to throw his leg over her rump, hopping about in what he knew was a foolish fashion. He was furious with himself, knowing he had been ready to while away the afternoon like some country bumpkin beneath the trees with a wench beside him and if any of his acquaintances had come across him they would have believed their eyes were playing them false. He was, for some reason, in a great rage and the innocent reason for it sat among the bluebells and watched him, bemused. What a bloody fool he was, he thought. Chad Cameron, the largest landowner in the district, a man of some consequence dallying with a country lass and the sooner he got on his horse and rode away the better.

She got to her feet. "Can I hold your horse, sir?" she asked him politely, and when with a muttered oath he got himself into the saddle and galloped off she stared after him in consternation.

"Now what was all that about?" she asked the dog. "What

did I say to make him so mad? One minute he was polite and talking as nice as you please, next he's off like an arrow from a bow. I like him though. He thinks I'm pretty, Sal. What d'you think of that? A great man like him," she continued confidentially, lying back among the bluebells, putting her arm across the dog's back as she lay down beside her and yawned. Briony yawned with her and the two of them began to doze and then, as the quiet hum of the woodland soothed them, both fell asleep.

She awoke with that slow dreaming the warm sun, the quiet companionship of the dog had induced in her, then, with a great start, sprang to her feet. She needed no watch, indeed she did not possess one, to tell her that it was late.

"Sweet Jesus," she whispered as she began to run like the wind in the direction of the mill, dodging among the tall trunks of the trees, leaping across fallen logs and swathes of fern, the dog beside her. "Oh, sweet Jesus, don't let him be back . . . please, don't let him be home yet." But Jesus didn't listen to her and she could hear the commotion as she reached the gate, her breath sawing in her throat.

"What the bleedin' hell d'you think this is," her father was thundering, and, like a sparrow twittering in terror beneath the menace of the hawk, her mother was doing her best to protect her child, to explain that it was *her* fault that Briony was not there doing something, *anything*. Jethro considered that unless his children were in their beds asleep they should be occupied with some task and to find that his daughter was not where she should be when he came home had flung him into a livid rage.

"I don't keep the lot of yer to loll about in idleness," he roared, accompanying his words with a slap about his wife's face.

"I know, Jethro, I know, and I wouldn't have let her go but she'd done all her jobs and—"

"Done all her jobs! There's a dozen jobs about the place she could have been at and what I want to know is why you didn't get her to do 'em. I dunno, I'm away from't place for an hour or two an' when I come home I find the pair o' yer actin' like bloody ladies. You on yer bum by't fire an' 'er ladyship gone God knows where and with God knows who—"

"Oh, no, Jethro, she's not with anyone, only Sal."

"Don't you interrupt me, yer daft bitch, an' you," swinging round to his son who stood by the cart ready to lift down the crate of young chickens and the roll of plain grey cloth purchased in the market from which Emily was expected to fashion their outfits. There were reels of cotton, a packet of needles and pins and several other articles such as a new pair of tongs and a copper kettle, for no matter how careful Emily was these things did wear out and needed replacing occasionally. Danny had unhitched the horse and put him in the stable but Jethro's unexpected arrival had caught them unawares. They were not to know that, after insulting several of his customers and threatening to knock Joe Blamire's bloody head off, the landlord of the George, with some help from Joe and the insulted customers, had thrown him out and barred him from returning. His mood could not have been more vicious.

"What the bleedin' 'ell d'yer think yer doin', hangin' about like a half-wit waitin' ter be told what ter do?" he snarled at his son. "Get that cart unloaded an' look sharp about it."

Suddenly he saw Briony creeping through the gateway, doing her best to escape his notice, the dog slinking at her heels and his face lit up at the sight of her. Emily moaned deep in her throat and Danny's mouth, which already was beginning to set in a permanent grimace of anxiety, tightened into a white line.

"So, madam, yer've decided to come home, have yer? Now, isn't that good of yer." He began to smile, a smile of ruthless anticipation and Emily made some small movement, though what she meant to do could only be guessed at. Danny felt something tear inside him, as he knew his sister was in for some terrible punishment and though he didn't want her to suffer it he hoped it was only a beating. He had seen the way his father had begun to look at her and his young manhood knew what that look meant. He was seventeen now, a tall boy but lean, strong enough to lift the sacks of grain and manhandle the tools and goods of their trade but without the physical or mental capabilities to stand up to his father.

"Right, miss, come over here where I can get a good look at yer. What yer been doin' then, an' who with?" He meant nothing by the last few words for he knew perfectly well there was not a man in the district who would dare even to *speak* to his lass but for some reason his daughter's face flushed, the dough-like paleness of her terror turning to a rosy pink. At once Jethro Marsden sprang forward and grasped her by her forearms, shaking her like a stuffed doll so that her head flopped on her slender white neck and her tangled hair, still loose after her wild dash through the woods, fell about her in a curtain.

"Yer bloody dirty bitch, yer've been wi' someone, haven't yer? Yer've been messing about in them woods wi' some man an' by God I'll find out who it is if I have ter take the skin from yer back. See, get inside. No, not you," he snarled when his wife and son made a move to go with him as he dragged at the almost senseless figure of his daughter. "You two can get on with your work while I see to this idle little bitch." From the expression on his face they were both made aware that he was going to enjoy it. "I'll teach yer to—"

"No, you won't."

For a moment it seemed the very birds had stopped their murmurings. The chickens which pecked and strutted about the cobbled yard came to a standstill, or so it appeared, the dog cocked her head then slunk down on her belly and Emily

turned her face to the wall in despair, for what she had feared
for a long time was about to happen and surely murder would
be done.

Jethro turned slowly, still holding Briony by the arm. Her
feet barely touched the ground and she seemed to hang
awkwardly in mid-air but her eyes, which had been glazed
with terror, became sharply focused, fastening on her brother.
He had a pitchfork in his hands and though his face was as
grey as the ash in the fire bottom his eyes were alight with
something none of them had ever seen before.

"Let go of her, you brute, or I swear I'll kill you. Oh, yes,
I'm well aware that you can take this pitchfork off me now
and beat me to bloody pulp but I'm warning you that if you
don't let her go you'll never have another night's sleep. I'll
stick this in your chest" – brandishing the pitchfork – "when
you're in your bed and gladly swing for it."

Jethro was so amazed he actually let go of Briony's arm
where five bruises from his thick fingers were already showing.
She fell to her knees then scurried on them to her mother who
picked her up and held her close.

"Well, bugger me if the lad's not got balls after all, but yer
know what? Yer going ter pay for this, my son. Oh, how yer
going ter pay fer it. A bit of correction is needed, I can see
that so put that bloody pitchfork down an' come over here."
He laughed with pleasure, distracted from his "punishment"
of his daughter by the thought of the hiding he would give
his son and *then* he would attend to her.

Danny made a tentative threatening movement with the
pitchfork but it was plain to see that the fire had gone out
of him and he was terrified of the enormous brute who was
advancing on him.

Jethro laughed more loudly and the birds and small animals
who lived in the trees and undergrowth about the mill cowered
back and were totally still and silent. The dog whimpered in

the back of her throat and so did Briony, but something teased her memory and it came from the half-hour she had spent with Mr Cameron. Mr Cameron was an important man in these parts. Mr Cameron had said she was pretty and though she didn't know why he should think so, or even say so, he was a man who could be trusted. He had come to their rescue once before and even her father had been wary of him. Mr Cameron . . .

"If you touch our Danny I'll run for Mr Cameron, Faither. I was only speaking to him this afternoon. Yes, he was the man who . . . and he asked me about you," she lied desperately, "and . . . well, he said if ever you beat me or Danny again I was to run for him. Doctor Travis is a magistrate and a friend of Mr Cameron's and . . . well, you'd better let Danny go."

They all three turned to stare at her, their mouths open, their eyes wide, and for once Jethro was stunned to silence. He swayed slightly, turning his head from his daughter to his son, ignoring his wife who was ready to faint in terror. In a maddened sort of way he was secretly proud of his children who had, for the first time, dared to stand up to him. Naturally there was something of him in them which explained it but until this afternoon they had never displayed it and he was nearly ready to smile and praise them. Of course he wouldn't, for it didn't do to let them get the upper hand, which is what they would think they had achieved if he allowed it. But just the same it had taken the edge off his rage and there was always another day. He thought he might just get out that bottle of brandy he had in the cupboard and have a little drink and then, when all this was put to one side and the three of them thought it was over, he would take the lad, strip him and leather him with the belt until his back bled. Then he would get the lass and . . . yes . . . Something pleasurable stirred in his crotch and he began to smile. Yes, he might just strip her and . . . what? What would he do to her? He didn't know yet but he'd like to find out.

"Bloody hell," he exclaimed mildly, "as I live and breathe, two little doves turned hawks. Who would have believed it? We'll have that soft dog o' yours snarling and turning wild next an' happen yer spineless mother standin' up fer herself. Wouldn't that be summat ter see." He smacked his thigh in what seemed to be high glee but his eyes were as cold and grey as the lake in winter. Not a prick or a gleam of light, just flat and blank and what his children knew was a terrible menace. They were well aware, as was his wife, that they would not be let off. That this would not be forgotten. He would get drunk now, blind and senselessly drunk, fall into his bed and sleep all night but tomorrow he would wake and remember. God help them.

4

The dining-room looked splendid and Sarah Cameron felt a smug pride fill her, for it was all down to her. The table was a triumph, set with porcelain fashioned by Josiah Spode, so fine the light could be seen through it and hand-painted with gold swags around its edge and the letter "C" done in intricate curlicues in the centre. Margeret Cameron, once Chadwick, with the impeccable taste unusual in a simply bred country girl, had had it made specially, for she was proud of her alliance with a family from the gentry and had felt the need to display it. The cutlery was silver, eighteen places each flanked with an array of gleaming knives, forks and spoons and four delicate cut-crystal wine glasses. Snowy napkins, Sadie's best work, were arranged in wings from which bloomed a fresh pink rosebud. There were flowers everywhere, hothouse roses decorating the length of the table between each scented candle and swathed at each corner in an arrangement of fern and ivy. The room was bathed in a subdued glow, from the candles which spaced the table and the polished sideboards, and from the fire, despite the season, which glowed on the hearth.

Sarah sighed in satisfaction, moving one of the exquisite finger bowls a fraction, careful not to spill the orange-scented water it contained. It was all perfect and she reflected on the outcome she hoped for. Their guests were men with whom Chadwick did business and their wives on whom she "called" and who called on her and it did no harm to let them see how successful her brother was, but there was another purpose to the dinner party. She was aware that Chadwick had no need of her help in finding himself a wife, for really he could have his pick of the suitable young ladies in Cumberland, but the one who had been invited this evening was suitable not only for Chad but for herself. She was realistic enough to know that one day Chad must marry if the line was to be perpetuated but it would make all the difference to *her* if a bride could be chosen who she herself could manage.

She straightened her already straight back and her lips thinned as she considered what this evening – and the months that would follow it – would mean to her. She had looked after Chadwick's household since the age of nineteen – twelve years now – ever since her grandmother had died, her mother and father having gone two years earlier in a typhoid epidemic. She was the first lady of Longlake Edge and had no intention of giving up her authority, even when Chadwick married, and so the choice of a wife, the *right* choice was imperative. She had no intention of being pensioned off to what might be described as a "dower house", relinquishing her position to some little madam who would demand the keys that had hung on Sarah's belt for twelve years, who would give orders to Sarah's servants, who would make decisions which might ripple Sarah's very pleasant life. The young woman, the child really, who had been invited, with her parents, this evening, admirably fitted the bill.

There was only one flaw in the perfection of her plans for the evening and that was Chadwick's stubborn refusal to allow her to employ a butler.

"What the devil do we need a butler for, Sarah?" He had frowned. "We are adequately served by—"

"By old Martha! By Daphne and Gladys!"

"They are well trained, by you, and Martha" – who had been ten years old when she came to Longlake Edge – "was taught by old Granny Cameron herself. If you wish you may employ more maidservants but I will not have flunkeys hanging over my shoulder while I dine. We have never had menservants, except outside and I have no intention of starting now. The chap up at Ravensworth Park that Bernard and Jessica employ gives me the jitters in his preposterous wig and velvet jacket. It's all for show and—"

"It is only keeping up a standard that the Goulds are accustomed to . . ."

"No, Sarah, I won't have it and that's an end to the matter," and she had had to give in though it infuriated her to do so.

Martha entered the room with Daphne behind her carrying what was known as a "tazza" on which was piled an elegant pyramid of fruits, all grown in the Cameron gardens and hothouses. Nectarines and peaches, glossy plums, figs and pears and apples, all of which Sarah herself had arranged.

"Where d'you want this, Miss Sarah?" Martha asked and then directed Daphne to the side table which Sarah indicated, where its magnificence was placed between two silver candlesticks.

Martha stood back and so did Daphne, gazing in satisfaction at the display, for you had to give Miss Sarah her due. She certainly knew how to do things properly.

"It looks a fair treat, Miss Sarah, a credit to you."

"Thank you, Martha. Now I think you and Daphne and Gladys had better go and change. Our guests will be here in half an hour. Gladys can take the ladies' wraps and show them to the room where they can attend to their toilette and Daphne can serve the drinks while you supervise in the kitchen, Martha. Mrs Foster has everything under control?"

"Oh, aye, she has that. Minnie an' Mabel" – who were kitchen-maids – "are good lasses and I'll mekk sure there's nowt goes wrong."

Sarah sighed. Martha, with the privilege of an old, long-serving retainer, was given to making remarks that a butler, or footman, would not dream of making and at the wrong time. She might take it into her head to ask one of Sarah's guests if they'd enjoyed a certain dish and even, if she felt the need, to offer the recipe for it.

It was all a huge success. The gentlemen were resplendent in the identical uniform of full black and white evening dress: a frock coat with white satin waistcoat and a white satin cravat, narrow-legged black trousers and black evening pumps. The ladies were in a variety of colours and styles befitting their age and marital status. Mrs Madge Seddon, a handsome woman in her early forties and the mother of the girl who stood shyly at her side and of whom Sarah had such high hopes, was married to George who was only a little less wealthy than Chadwick. Mrs Seddon was quite superb in rose-coloured terry velvet with a turban on her silvery hair to match. It was twisted into a complicated shape and had a plume a foot tall, nodding in the direction of the person with whom she conversed. Mrs Jessica Gould, Sarah's dear friend, had brought her newly married daughter Judith and her son-in-law, Marcus Arbuthnot, who was, to Jessica's great satisfaction, related distantly on his mother's side to a baronet. Mrs Gould wore pale green crêpe decorated with gold embroidery, a hat of the same shade and material, worn at an angle and turned up from her florid face, with a trimming of fly-away ostrich feathers. Mrs Freda Garlick wore blue grenadine, Mrs Tyson was majestic in mulberry-coloured silk, and Mrs Mary Armstrong, the vicar's wife, was subdued in dark brown. The younger ladies, Angela Tyson and Judith Arbuthnot, were in primrose yellow and the palest blue. Their bodices were close-fitting and Judith's, since she was now married, was extremely décolletée as was the fashion, the waist pointed in front, the skirt very full and gathered or pleated. They were of a length to display the ankle, just touching the instep with a small bustle of frills cascading at the back. Their waists were like wasps, drawn in by stays made of light whalebone.

To make up the numbers Ernestine and George Tyson had also brought their twenty-year-old son Percival, and Mary and Julian Armstrong their Gilbert, an earnest young man who was about to act as his father's curate.

But all the ladies, young and old, were put in the shade by the exquisite Miss Adeline Seddon. She was sixteen and pretty as a picture in a dress of palest pink gauze, its flounced skirt strewn with knots of silver ribbon and sprays of pink flowers, and in her silver-gilt hair were pink rosebuds tied with silver ribbon. She carried a posy to match. She was agreeable, well brought up, socially acceptable and perfectly trained in the art of being the wife of a rich and successful businessman. She was seated next to Chadwick and it was believed by her mama and by Sarah that they made a handsome couple and judging by the attentive way Chadwick conversed with her a match would soon be forthcoming. They were not to know that Chad Cameron was bored beyond measure, by her and by the occasion.

The talk was of the latest theatrical performance in the Assembly Rooms of the George Inn at Penrith, the extreme youth of their new Queen, the popularity of Wordsworth who lived, as it were, among them in Lakeland and the publication of Mr Charles Dickens's latest book, *The Pickwick Papers*, among other topics which might be discussed in mixed company. After dinner, of course, when the ladies retired, leaving the gentlemen to their port and cigars, they would talk of things that concerned them, business matters, the expansion of the railways, the state of the colonies and the problems of Ireland.

All very pleasing and, as she stood arm-in-arm with her brother at the front door of Longlake Edge watching the carriages carrying their guests down the gravel drive towards the road at the edge of the lake, Sarah sighed in satisfaction. A little push from her, several meetings already privately arranged by herself and Madge Seddon to show off the perfection of Miss Adeline Seddon would be followed by a late autumn wedding, she was sure.

Earlier in the evening Danny and Briony had been dragging the sledge along the lower lake road in the direction of Mell Farm taking Farmer Stephens's ground oats back to him when the first carriage passed them, throwing up a cloud of white dust, for it had been a dry summer. It turned in at the gates to Longlake Edge and as they reached the gates a second, coming from the opposite direction, did the same.

It was going on seven o'clock and being only just past the middle of summer, still light. A crimson sun hung in the sky above Gowbarrow Fell, the sky itself shaded from orange and pink to the palest lavender. The trees stood black and maroon against the sinking sun and behind the two youngsters the waters of the lake were pink and rippled with gold. Home-going birds flew across the streaked sky and a line of ducks cut a serene swathe through the reflection of the shore on the water. Except for the soft clop of the horses' hooves on the dusty road and the swift passage of the carriages the evening was quiet, still, empty.

"They must be havin' a do at Mr Cameron's," Danny said with little interest, for he was tired and had only one thing on his mind: getting Farmer Stephens's ground oats to him, dragging the empty sledge back home and falling into bed. He had been working beside his father for the past twelve hours and though the load they pulled was comparatively light, indeed he had protested he could manage it alone, it was a fair walk up to Mell Farm.

"Can we stop and watch, Danny?" Briony pleaded. From the open gateway they could see up the drive to the front door of the house where the first carriage had pulled up and with a flurry of colour and flounces a lady was being handed out by Mr Cameron.

"For God's sake, Bry, we've been at it for twelve hours," Danny began to protest, but his sister was already easing the leather harness from her shoulders and moving towards the wide-open wrought-iron gates. He sighed, but really could he deny her this little diversion in her drab and hardworking life? Their father would be up at the Bull in Pooley Bridge and would not be home until dark. A few minutes would make no difference.

"Look, Danny," she whispered as though those alighting into the beautiful garden, preparing to enter the beautiful house, could hear her. Her eyes were lit up like violets in a sunbeam behind the thick fringe of her lashes and her lovely face was flushed and pink as though she were one of the guests and could barely wait for the excitement to begin. "There's Mr Cameron and Miss Cameron. They must be having a party." A young lady had just stepped out of her carriage, followed by an older lady and gentleman and for several minutes both Danny and Briony were awed to a reverential silence, since neither of them had ever seen anything quite so beautiful as Mr Cameron's young guest, nor the gown she wore. She must be someone special the way Miss Cameron fussed about her, leading her up the steps and into the house. Even though it was not yet dark every window was a blaze of candlelight. A big black dog came from round the corner of the house, its tail whipping in a frenzy and there was some laughter which floated down the drive as Mr Cameron took it by its collar and handed it over to an embarrassed servant.

Briony watched and slowly the excited smile slipped from her face and some dark thing inside her dragged at her delight. She hadn't the faintest idea what it was. She only knew that the pleasure she had felt at being a spectator to the splendour of Mr Cameron's party guests arriving had slipped away and a feeling of sadness had taken its place. And yet it was not just sadness. There was something else and she was bewildered to discover that what she felt was anger. She was angry and she didn't know why, or what at! What had all this to do with her? Why should she feel sad and angry unless it was because her life, which was as far removed from that of the pretty girl as it was possible to be, should exist as it did in fear and trembling of one man while this girl was so cherished. Not just by her parents who had alighted from the carriage with her but by Mr Cameron and his sister.

Then it came to her like a flash of lightning before the rumble of thunder. She was jealous, not just of the girl's obviously fortunate way of life but of her association with Mr Cameron! She had crouched in the grass beside the gate, frowning furiously at the sight of his hand reaching out to the pretty girl in the pink dress and had wanted to stand up and shout some obscenity, one of those used by her father, and yet at the same time she felt a desperate need to turn and run.

There were other carriages bowling along the road now, each turning in at the same gateway, and for several more minutes the son and daughter of the miller crouched down beside the stone gateway and watched. Mr Cameron was there to greet them all, taking the ladies' hands and bringing them gallantly to his lips, shaking those of the gentlemen, and though she could not hear what was said she knew as though she could see inside his mind that he was playing a part. A part he did not relish and she wondered dazedly as she and Danny stood up how she knew. She had seen him riding past the gate to the mill, stark and serious on his ebony mare. He had sometimes nodded to her, unsmiling, aloof, and it was not until he had come to her and Danny's rescue last year that she had actually heard him speak. They had met again in January when she and Danny were pulling the sledge up to

Brett Farm and he had given them a hand and in the bluebell wood, and that was all. And yet, just as if she were inside his head and his voice was speaking to her, she was certain that tonight, though he was welcoming courteously the men and women who entered his house, his heart wasn't in it and inexplicably she was glad. *Dear life, she was glad!* The pretty young lady had smiled at him, shy as a fresh new rosebud, and he had returned her smile and it had struck at something in Briony's chest but it had meant nothing to him. He knew it and she knew it and when she got to her feet at Danny's irritated insistence she was persuaded to resume their journey on to Mell Farm.

"What's up with you?" he wanted to know as they fell into step together and put their shoulders into the harness.

"Nothing."

"It doesn't look like nothing to me. You've a face on you like thunder."

"No, I haven't."

"You can't see it from where I see it."

"I can feel it and it's not like thunder so stop going on at me."

"What the hell's got into you?" He was quite amazed.

"Nothing, so be quiet."

They dragged along in silence for a while, turning in at the gate to the track that led up to Mell Farm, then Danny stopped, removing the harness and leading Briony to a large flat stone which lay at the side of the track and sitting her on it. He sat beside her.

"Don't fret, Bry," he said bravely, for who was he to see into the future which looked bleak for them both. "We'll be all right, you know. When he's gone."

"I know," she answered equally bravely.

"We'll have a big house like Mr Cameron and give – I don't

know – parties and balls and you'll have a grand frock and I'll be dressed up in a black suit like his and . . ."

She put her hand in his. "I know, Danny." Though, of course, they both knew they wouldn't. The trouble was they neither of them could see a time when their father would not have total control of them. He was strong, strong as a bull and would go on for ever, intimidating them, exploiting them, treating them like the black slaves they read about who were transported from one side of the world to another, working without wages for cruel masters. But surely there could be no more vicious master than the one they had?

"We could run away," Briony whispered hopelessly.

"What about Mother?"

"We could take her with us."

"She's not strong, Bry. She couldn't . . . couldn't manage it. We couldn't leave her."

"I know." She wanted to weep. She felt so strange. The sight of Mr Cameron with his hand held out to the pretty girl had, for some reason, upset her and so had the picture of the beautiful house and garden, the glimpse of how other people lived, safe, secure, and compared to her life it had seemed like a peep into paradise.

"Cheer up, Bry," Danny said anxiously, putting a comforting arm about her shoulder, strangely moved by his sister's dejection. She was always the one who cheered them up, him and Mother, with her cheerful disposition and smiling, optimistic spirit, but tonight she seemed to be swamped by something that drowned her brightness and though he was aware it was something to do with the Camerons he didn't know how to make it better.

They rose together and yoked themselves into their harness and began the long trudge up the hill to Mell Farm. Jacky Sidebottom, Farmer Stephens's cowman, another who had an admiring eye on Jethro Marsden's bonny daughter, was there to open the gate for them and to help Briony off with her harness. After that they were rewarded by Cissie Stephens with a long draught of milk which was still warm from the cow and an enormous slice of her clapbread still warm from the oven and spread thickly with her butter.

"Poor lambs," she said later to her husband, her kind face indignant, "'aving ter traipse all the way up here at this time o' night. It's a cryin' shame an' it's time someone let on ter the authorities." Though she knew as she spoke that no one would for they were all afraid of Jethro Marsden.

The summer moved on and the fear that dominated Emily Marsden's life, not for herself but for her daughter, grew and festered inside her. She could not explain what she meant by festered. It was as though some injury, some wound that had been inflicted on her simply would not heal but instead grew more and more infected, turning rotten, turning to something that kept her awake at night as she lay beside the snoring, muttering hulk who lay scratching and picking beside her. He wore a short nightgown under which his hand was always sorting out his private parts, even in sleep. Sometimes it would wake him and he would reach for her and inflict cruel indignities on her recumbent body, the smell of him, since he rarely washed his body below his neck, a stench in her nostrils which made her gag.

The truth of it was that she was afraid to leave her daughter alone with her father. She was like a flower growing on a dung heap, a lovely flower that bloomed more brightly every day, one that all the men who brought their business to the corn mill could not fail to notice and it made Jethro wild.

"Get yer gone, girl," he would snap at her when a cart drew up the track towards the mill. "Go an' help yer mother in't kitchen an' don't come back till yer fetched. You, boy, turn that grain that's drying in't kiln," which was what Briony had been doing. Even Jethro was aware that his daughter, slender as she was, could not manhandle the filled sacks, so Danny was taken off the work he shared with his father and given Briony's task. In the preparation for milling the wheat, oats and corn there were many tasks that his daughter could manage. Spreading the grain for drying in the kiln was one of them. Another was manipulating the sieve which removed "dirty" grain, the dust and straw, and hand-picking the small stones that often got into the grain when the crop was cut.

But though he had not as yet laid a hand on the girl, except for the almost daily cuff about the head which he thought was necessary to get his children to their manual labour, his eyes would follow her slim figure about the kitchen, lingering on her small peaked breasts and the tender whiteness of her neck where her hair fell in curling confusion. Her skirt was short, for the material he fetched from the market was never quite enough to make it the length decency demanded and her ankles and narrow feet were studied with narrowed eyes.

If only she could get the lass away, Emily agonised. Perhaps in service to some decent household like the Camerons or one of the gentry who lived hereabouts. But if she did approach Miss Cameron or Mrs Armstrong, the vicar's wife, and if they did agree to take on Briony, she knew as sure as the sun rose in the east and sank in the west that Jethro would go round and demand his child back which he had a father's right to do.

She had, one day, almost confided in Sadie but at the last moment she had bitten her tongue, for who knew where it might lead if she divulged her fear to someone else. Sadie was as frightened of Jethro as all the folk in the valley but she might take it into her head to go to Mr Cameron or Doctor Travis and then where would they be? Jethro was careful now of where he hit his children, making sure their faces were unmarked and it could hardly be proved that he was beginning to take an unnatural interest in his daughter's young comeliness, could it?

So she watched and prayed and tried to keep her daughter close by her, which was tricky since Jethro insisted he needed her in the mill. She was quick, deft, and if there were no tasks immediately to be done in the practice of milling she could be put to sweeping or some other work that would keep her under Jethro's sharp eye.

So Emily worried and watched and prayed, sometimes in the tiny church of St Michael's in Glebe where Mr Armstrong preached, when she could slip out on a Sunday morning while Jethro slept off Saturday night's excesses. She felt that perhaps actually in a church God might hear her more clearly as she asked Him for protection for her girl, but it was all a waste of her long dragging walk across the fields, her leg hurting like toothache. A waste of her hours on her knees, a waste of her breath as the icily cold day in November was to prove.

5

Briony crept to the back of the loft and buried herself and the trembling yellow mongrel beneath the loose pile of hay that her father stored up there to feed Glory, the plough horse. She could hear the animal now, chomping on the mouthful from the pile Danny had tipped into his manger, his old teeth making the best it could of the meal. He snorted and seemed to sigh, like an old man past his peak who is being asked to labour beyond his ageing capabilities but keeps struggling on. She had no idea how old the horse was, only that he had been there when she herself had first toddled out of the mill house into the yard. Even then she had been put to work, throwing handfuls of meal to the hens and collecting their eggs, and woe betide her if she should break one. She had staggered on her infant legs, heaving the bucket of scraps for the pig, tipping it into the trough, the task almost beyond her small strength so that she often had difficulty in not falling in with the swill!

Her father owned a couple of fields which his father had purchased, along with the water mill from old Mr Cameron and in them he grew, or rather his family grew and tended, potatoes, beetroot, carrots, cabbage, grass for the animals, oats for porridge, whatever he could squeeze into the couple of acres, wasting not an inch. Again, as soon as she could walk she had been thrust into the field, picking stones and scaring the rooks who did their best to feed on her father's growing produce. There was a small apple orchard that provided them with fruit and it was this good food, cultivated by Emily and her two children, which enabled them to become the healthy, hardworking beasts of burden Jethro needed to prosper. All the produce was stored in the loft of the cruck barn which was built into the slope of the bank at the rear of the mill and where Briony was now hiding.

It was said there had been a mill at Moorend for over five hundred years but the present one had been built in 1625 or thereabouts and for the last forty or so it had been in the hands of the Marsden family. The wheel which gave life to the mill lay to the left-hand side of the building and at the rear lay the mill pond, fed by a man-made channel eight hundred yards long which itself was fed by a tributary of the river. The wooden wheel was what was known as "overshot", which meant when a valve was opened the water, directed by a spout, collected in buckets round its edge, the weight of the water in the buckets turning the wheel. When not in use the water that turned the wheel returned to the river through a tail race tunnel below the mill yard. Until quite recently, certainly in Jethro Marsden's time, the industry had been run on a system known as "toll grinding" and was the bulk of the miller's trade. It was a steady trade, consisting for the main part of one sack for each customer, a farmer or a villager bringing their single sack and taking away that same sack of ground wheat or animal meal for their stock. For his part of the labour the miller received one-sixteenth of the value of the grain milled. Jethro had built up his business in order to meet the demands of the ever expanding merchant milling, in a small way, of course, but he was an ambitious man and with the help of his growing son, and his daughter who would do her share, he meant to extend even further.

Briony burrowed deeper into the hay, she and the dog shivering in unison. Despite the sound of the tumbling water which swept over the wheel she could hear her father's voice raised in furious rage coming from the mill and she and the animal cowered further and further into the hay.

"Don't let him find me, please, please," she whispered imploringly into the dog's rough coat, not awfully sure to whom she was addressing her plea, "and keep our Danny safe." She shivered even more, with the cold and with the remembered horror, not just of what had taken place tonight but of the previous evening when her father had staggered in from his nightly trip to the Bull. He had taken them by surprise, arriving home earlier than he normally did, for Jethro never moved from the bar until closing time or until the innkeeper threw him out. Well, he wouldn't exactly *throw* him out, for there wasn't a man in the parish who would dare lay hands – without the help of half a dozen others – on Jethro Marsden, especially when he had been drinking. He was not what could be described – far from it – as a "good-natured" drunk, one of those who are merry and amusing to others. His normal truculent belligerence, which meant you had to be careful what you said and how you said it, turned to what the men who drank beside him called "nasty" if he was crossed. If he took exception to a careless word spoken in jest, to a look he considered offensive, or even to the colour of a man's waistcoat, he was known for his killing temper.

They had been sitting round the dying fire in the kitchen, her mother, Danny, herself and Sal, Danny's dog, for, despite the intense cold, they were afraid to apply any more wood lest it bring some fearful retribution about their heads. They would normally have been in their beds, Mother in the one she shared with Father at the back of the top storey of the mill house, Briony in the small truckle bed pushed into a corner under the rough, ladder-like stairs and Danny in what was no more than a cupboard built into the kitchen wall. The cupboard had a sort of shelf in it on which was laid a thin palliasse. The doors could be shut on it during the day but at night they were left open, that is after Jethro had gone upstairs, for not one of them could sleep while Jethro was awake. Sal slept in there with him, the pair of them huddled uneasily together until all was quiet.

The night before, Jethro had brought home a meat pie bought over the counter at the Bull and wrapped round it were a couple of sheets from a newspaper. It was dated last July but Emily had carefully hidden it away after the pie was wolfed down – solely by Jethro, naturally – and this evening while he was out the three of them had spread it out on the kitchen table and read every word printed on it.

It made exciting reading. They knew, naturally, that their young Queen had been crowned in June, June 28th to be exact. They had not known any of the details but here, in this old, stained newspaper was a full report of the magnificent event. The procession through the streets of London which afforded the common people the opportunity to enjoy the ceremony, the crowds that had poured into the city, the salvo of artillery from the Tower and the Queen herself in the state coach. The National Anthem, the new Royal Standard on Marble Arch, the uniforms, the regalia, the cheering when the crown was placed on Her Majesty's head and the near catastrophe when Lord Rolle, who was nearing eighty, stumbled and fell on the steps. The Queen immediately stepped forward, the entranced readers learned, and held out her hand to assist the aged peer. And when the Queen appeared wearing her crown, her jewels and the royal purple, followed by the fireworks at night, the people had gone wild with excitement; it was all here in the words written in the newspaper.

He must have crept up across the cobbled yard, for not even the sharp-eared dog heard him and when he burst in with a roar of laughter at what he saw as a fine joke, they all leaped to their feet, the dog included and began to run about the room like chickens with their heads cut off, or so he described it, inordinately amused at the rumpus he had caused. That is until he saw the crumpled newspaper spread upon the table. In his small, porcine eyes a suspicious gleam began to shine and his face, which had been laughing in grotesque glee, drooped into a ferocious frown.

"What the bloody 'ell's this?" he roared and for a moment Briony believed her mother might simply faint away or fall to the floor in her terrified confusion. But in a way that astounded her and Danny, Emily spoke up bravely. After all, Jethro knew she could read and though she was aware he wouldn't like it she could only own up to telling her children what was in the old newspaper.

"It's the Queen, Jethro," she faltered.

"The Queen? What in hell's name are yer talkin' about, woman?"

"It's in the newspaper . . ."

"What is?" Briony and Danny hovered at the side of the fireplace, both of them longing to protect their mother but knowing the inadvisability of opening their mouths, for it would do no good in the end.

"It's the coronation . . . in the newspaper. I was telling the children . . ."

"Telling the children! *Telling the children.* D'yer mean ter say yer've nowt else ter do but sit on yer bums and read rubbish like that? I've never heard anythin' like it, and" – catching sight of the dog cowering at the back door – "what the bloody hell's that beast doin' in 'ere?" ready to pick on anything in his rage. He turned round so quickly he nearly toppled across the table. The dog, witless with terror, did her best to slither under the closed door. Briony and Emily clung together against the chimney breast while Danny, who had moved towards Sal, looked as though he would like to plunge a knife deep into his father's chest.

"How many times have I ter tell yer I'll not have that bloody animal under me feet?" He aimed a heavy fist at his son who dodged nimbly, opening the door, but Jethro drove his huge hobnailed boot into her side as the dog streaked through. She yelped and Danny twitched, his face as grey as the ash that had collected in the fire bottom. At seventeen he was tall, rangy, still a boy with bones that stuck out all over the place, at his shoulder blades, his elbows, his big, knobbly hands and wrists. He would make a big man when he was fully grown, probably as big as his father but now he was inclined to fall over his own feet as boys of his age do. He knew only too well that if he made one wrong move towards him he would be lifted from his feet by the whole weight of his father, eighteen stone of muscle and bone. And the thing was, his father was not *really* angry, as he had seen him angry in the past. He was just having what he liked to call a bit of fun. The newspaper and the reading of it was nothing. The dog was nothing but he had drunk half a dozen pints of ale, which was less than usual and had had the sudden fancy to come home and torment his family.

He sat down on the bench beside the table. "Right, woman, get me summat to eat an' then take yerself off ter bed. It's enough to put any man off his grub havin' to look at a face like thine so bugger off. No, not you," he told his cringing daughter. "You can stay an' talk ter me. Tell me about this bloody coronation which is so interestin' ter the lot of you. Go on, tell me what yer mother's bin stuffin' yer silly head with. See, sit here by your old pa," patting the bench and eyeing her neat waist and breast as he did so.

"Faither . . . I'm not sure what . . ." Briony began to quaver and by the door her brother strained to keep his place, swallowing his boy's big Adam's apple. Emily placed a plate of cold meats, cheese, fresh bread and pickled onions on the table in front of her husband, shrinking away from him but reluctant to leave her children. Particularly her girl!

There was absolutely no way she could protect them, though she had done her best ever since Daniel was born. She had marks on her body to prove it, marks she would have been ashamed for another human being to see and in places she could not even mention.

She threw her leg out when she walked, the limp caused by the old break which had healed awkwardly.

"Jethro, will you not come to bed?" she pleaded, her very soul withering at the thought of this man lying beside her, doing the things he liked to do, most of them cruel and inhuman, but she was uneasy. She did not like the way he was looking at Briony. *Talk to her!* What did he mean, he who never talked to anyone except to give orders and certainly never listened. Dear sweet Lord, what did he mean? Danny would kill him if he hurt Briony, not with his fists, of course, since it would be like a fly tackling an ox, but with the carving knife, her sewing scissors, the pitchfork in the barn, any weapon that lay handy, so not only was Briony threatened but so was her son.

"Get away with yer, yer daft bitch. Go on, get ter yer bed, and you" – turning to grin wolfishly at his son – "into that yard an' chop some wood fer't fire."

"I've done it, Faither. A great pile."

"Then do another, yer soft little sod. See if yer can grow a muscle or two on them things yer call arms."

He picked up the crust of bread and sank his teeth into it, then put a whole pickled onion in his mouth, crunching it with great enjoyment.

He stopped for a moment. "Well, what yer waitin' for?" he snarled at his son, his mouth full of food, some of which dropped on to the table.

"Faither . . ."

"Jethro, will you not come up?" Poor Emily, thirty-five years of age, looking twenty years older. Once as pretty as a hedge rose, she tried her best to look as she did then when her big husband had swept her off her feet and into his bed with great enthusiasm. It was quite pitiful, that coyness, that desperate attempt to beguile her husband away from what she feared.

He stood up with a voice like thunder so that even the horse in the barn stamped uneasily.

"Bugger off, woman, and you, boy, get inter't yard. Now then, girl, come here an' sit yer down. I tell yer what, why don't we be right cosy. You come an' sit on yer pa's knee and tell me all about, what was it . . . the Queen." He reached out a hand to Briony, his thick fingers ready to close round her arm and draw her on to his lap but Danny had heard and seen enough. His mother had crept hesitantly up the stairs with a look on her face like death and his own was the same.

He opened the door with every intention of removing himself into the yard as his father had ordered, but as the cold November air seeped into the room he began to shriek.

"Run, Briony, run for God's sake . . . run." And before their father's amazed and furious gaze his son and daughter fled into the night.

They had stayed there, cowering together, first in the bit of woodland that stood between the mill and the road. At last, after shouting what he would do to them when he found them, he had gone upstairs, blundering through the kitchen and up the ladder to his wife's bed where he had given her "what for". Later they had crept into the loft and, with the dog for warmth, slept uneasily beneath a pile of hay and a tattered horse blanket.

This morning, before he was even out of his bed, they were in the fields, picking stones, weeding the recently planted potato patch and with a bit of ingenuity, in which they had plenty of practice, they kept out of his way. He was his usual self when they crept into the bagging and drive floor of the mill where it was Danny's job to adjust the gearing to the correct speed for the millstones on the floor above. He appeared to have forgotten what had happened the night before and they breathed a sigh of relief in unison.

He was busy all day attending to the villagers who brought their single sack of grain to be milled, to the waggons piled high with local farmers' grain which pulled up outside the big door let into the ground floor of the mill. When he shouted out of the window for the pair of them to come and give him a hand, they scuttled across the yard and flew up the ladder hoping to God that last night's episode had been forgotten as often it thankfully was when the drink wore off.

One of the pieces of whirling machinery in the mill consisted of a main shaft to a crown wheel from which power was taken off to a further series of shafts. One of these led to the line hoist which lifted the sacks of grain to the top floor where they were stored until their contents were milled. It used the power of the water for its movement and operated through a series of trapdoors, one to each floor. It was Danny and Briony's job, with their combined weight, to lift the heavy sacks off the hook and the line which had brought them up. When the grain had been milled and the sacks refilled, the whole process was done in reverse.

At their father's command they clambered down the ladder to the loading ramp then lifted the sacks of ground corn, between them straining their young bodies, sweat pouring off them, staggering across the ramp to the waiting waggon which today belonged to Seth Cartwright.

"Eeh, tha' shouldn't be carryin' weights like that, lass," Seth had protested, just as though she, or Danny, had any choice in the matter but they merely smiled politely. Danny touched his forelock and watched the farmer drive away shaking his head.

But their hopeful belief that Jethro had forgotten the events of the night before were to be sadly smashed, for as soon as they had finished what Jethro called their tea, instead of setting off on his nightly sojourn at the Bull in Pooley Bridge, he settled down in his chair by the fire, lit his pipe and turned to Danny with what passed for a jovial smile on his mottled face.

"Right, lad, I want yer ter get over to Seth Cartwright's an' tell 'im I can't manage that animal feed I promised fer termorrow after all. I'm fair pulled out wi' work but if he fetches it over the day after I'll do me best to oblige."

Danny licked his lips, looking from one face to another, his eyes slipping desperately from Emily to Briony as though deep in his heart he knew this was some trick but how was he to elude it? Emily, though she couldn't quite put her finger on it, or at least did her best to avoid it, knew deep inside that there was some horror waiting for them and Briony felt the pulse at her wrist, her throat, wherever a pulse beat, come to a sickening stop.

"But, Faither, will it not wait?" Danny began.

"No, it bloody well won't an' unless yer want a taste of the buckle end of me belt yer'd best get over there."

"But . . ."

"Would you defy me, boy?" Jethro roared and all three flinched as though he had struck them. With a despairing look at his mother, one that begged something of her, Danny slipped from the kitchen and set off at such a rate up the slope at the back of the mill even the lean dog couldn't keep up with him, turning back into the yard and cowering under the pig trough.

Emily turned to the range and began soundlessly to move things about, trying to look busy without drawing attention to herself but it did no good.

"Get yerself off, woman," he growled.

"I'll just finish these—"

"I'll finish you in a minute. Yer always complainin' yer tired so get to yer bed an' have a good night's sleep. Perhaps yer'll shut yer gob then."

Briony stood blindly, numbly, hopelessly beside the table and when he caught her by the wrist and drew her on to his enormous knee across which his breeches strained and the thick shape of his genitals heaved, she had no option but to let it happen. She sat rigidly, trying not to look at his stubbled face, his rotting teeth, his red, lustful eyes, trying not to catch his breath which was foetid with decaying food. His hands began to move over her and his foul mouth fumbled into the soft flesh of her neck and at the top of the stairs her mother moaned soundlessly in her throat. Briony began to lose her senses, transfixed by fear and horror as his hand slipped under the hem of her skirt and crawled like some foul slug up the slender curve of her calf to her knee.

"Lovely . . . lovely little lass . . . sweet," he was slobbering against her cheek.

When she fell to the floor she did not immediately realise what had happened. Her father was still in the chair but he was beginning to slide downwards and behind him her mother still held the heavy frying pan with which she had hit him. Had it been something sharp, an axe, or even the heavy poker in the hearth, she would have staved his head in, but the flat bottom of the frying pan merely stunned him and even as Briony scrambled to her feet and began to back away he was coming to.

"Run . . . run, Briony," her mother was screaming as Danny had done the night before, herself turning to the ladder down which she had just scrambled and even as she did so she knew she had made a mistake. The ladder went to the upper floors and nowhere else and though there was nothing more he wanted than to have the feel of his daughter's young body under his hands, first Jethro needed to deal with this screaming shrew who had just hit him.

Briony obeyed her mother. She was almost senseless, her fear and revulsion so great that for a moment or two she stood dithering in the yard and when the dog's nose touched her hand she was ready to scream. But it brought her back from the mindless terror her father's hands and mouth had flung her into. Followed by the dog she ran into the barn and, heaving Sal with her up the ladder, dived, sobbing harshly, into the hay where she pleaded with someone, anyone, not to let her father find her.

It was no more than a minute or two later when she heard the thudding of boots on the cobbles and ventured a peep out of the high "letting-in" door of the barn and in the light that streamed from the open door of the kitchen watched as Danny streaked towards it, his hair standing straight out from the back of his head with the force of his movement.

Knowing some dreadful, appalling thing was about to happen to a member of her family but ignorant of how she could stop it, she pushed the quivering dog to one side and before her nerve failed her climbed down the ladder, hurtling from the barn to follow her brother, neither of them making any sound.

There was a cry from somewhere in the mill and then silence. Danny's long legs had covered the cobbled yard in a couple of strides, then he was in the kitchen and springing for the ladder that led to the floor above. Again he seemed to have wings in his heels. There was no fear in his set young face. It was as though he were moving to some command that only he could hear, some sense that was telling him what he should do, where he should go, and why.

When Briony reached them, her mother, her father, her brother, her breath rasping in her throat so that each one hurt her, they were on the stone floor, the first-floor level where the millstones were located. Strangely, for the last thing her father did when the final customer had gone was turn the valve to shut off the flow of water, the water wheel was still revolving. The drive to the millstones was still powered and the millstones themselves were still revolving.

Her mother lay on the floor, her head turned to one side and she seemed to be looking at her daughter, for there was a light in her eyes as though she smiled. Her neck was angled unnaturally so that her ear almost touched her shoulder and had it not been for that Briony might have believed that her mother had merely lain down for a rest. She was sprawled somewhat as though she had tripped but she hadn't, of course, her father's livid expression told her that. He was glaring about him, not exactly confused, for when had Jethro Marsden ever been confused, but wary, an animal caught in a clearing by a hunter, not afraid, for, again, when had Jethro Marsden ever been afraid, particularly of his own son who confronted him.

"Bloody bitch asked fer it," he was muttering, his great fist, the one with which he had knocked the life out of her, clenching angrily. "She clouted me one with the fryin' pan. An' what you lookin' at, yer soft sod," to his son who was moving slowly towards him.

"Nothin'," Danny whispered in the back of his thoat, "absolutely nothing." Then with a sudden deliberate heave, catching him unawares, he pushed Jethro Marsden into the slowly moving machinery which turned the two enormous millstones used for grinding the animal feed. For a moment Jethro teetered and then, as his balance went and he put out his arm to steady himself, it caught and was slowly drawn between the stones. Briony heard the bones of his arm crunching. The blood spurted in a great gout, the stones which would not allow for the passage of anything more than grain of corn came to a shuddering halt and her father began to scream.

His great body hung there, his feet scrabbling the floor but he was caught like an animal in a trap.

Briony ran to her mother, lifting her poor battered body into her arms, cradling her tenderly but Danny continued to stand watching his father screaming and bleeding to death then said, conversationally, "I set the wheel going, Faither. I just wanted you to know. I didn't go to Farmer Cartwright's. Well, I couldn't, could I, not with you mauling our Briony. I wanted to get you up here, you see and into the stones. I didn't know how but it seems my mother did that in the end, God rest her soul. I knew it was the only way to get rid of you, and fitting too. Aye, scream, scream, like you made my mother scream and now you've killed her and for that alone you deserve to die. I hope you rot in hell . . ."

His eyes were as hard and cold and passionless as stone, and yet his voice had a dreaming quality as he watched with great interest his father's blood drain away across the floor and begin to drip through the floorboards. Briony rocked backwards and forwards, her mother in her arms and watched mindlessly as Danny shuffled towards the stairs.

6

She sat in Sadie's kitchen rocking-chair, motionless, doing her best in the silence that seemed to have taken over her life to get herself back to reality. Ripples of something she could not call sea-waves, since she had never seen the ocean, washed against her, swamping her thoughts, leaving only one and that was that she was doomed to spend the rest of her life in Sadie's chair with her father's blood on the hem of her skirt. It seemed inevitable but then, when the ripples eased and she became aware of herself as Briony Marsden, she wished she could have remained where she was in that comforting silence, with her body turned into some inanimate jointed thing and her mind ceasing to function. But it did not last.

There were people around her. Sadie came to peer at her, red-eyed, uncertain, it seemed to her, of what to do with her.

"She'll not let me near her," she said to someone and Briony wondered idly who it was.

"But she can't stay there. Look at the sight of her with all that . . . that blood. Shall I fetch some hot water?"

"No, let her be for a while. The doctor said . . ." The rest of the sentence faded away as though Sadie had wandered off into her scullery. Someone held her hand and she let it be held, a young man she thought might be Iolo who sat in the chair opposite, the chair where, not so long ago, her mother had sat and drunk Sadie's tea and nibbled at one of Sadie's jam tarts.

At some point a dog thrust its cold, wet nose into her hand which hung over the arm of the chair and when she turned her head, slowly, which was the only way she appeared able to move now, she saw it was Sal. Sal's eyes were puzzled as they stared unblinkingly into Briony's but Briony turned away listlessly. The dog licked her hand, searching for comfort in this strange world that had come upon them and Briony smoothed her head, comforting herself more than the dog.

Then, suddenly, *he* was there. The room was filled with him, and the others, the drifting shadowy figures who had surrounded her, slipped away and she was alone with him.

Though she did not know of it he had been forced to quarrel quite violently with Sarah on the subject of going to the aid of the Marsden girl whose brother had killed his father and, who was to know, perhaps even his mother!

"Don't be ridiculous, Sarah. No one has the slightest idea what happened at Moorend Mill but I mean to find out. I cannot turn my back on those two youngsters. No man of conscience could." But it was not his conscience that was shouting orders to Ned to saddle his horse, and deep in his heart where his feeling lay hidden he was well aware of it.

"But Mrs Evans and her son are there to . . . to do whatever is necessary for the girl. So we were told . . ." For news of the dramatic events at the mill had spread like wildfire through the community. "I don't think it would be prudent for you to be involved."

"Prudent! Dear God, Sarah, this is not the time for being prudent. There has been some terrible . . . well, let us call it an accident for now at Marsden's place and someone must find out what there is to be done."

"Chadwick, I must insist that you keep out of this . . . this scandalous affair."

"Don't be ridiculous," he told her flatly, flinging on his coat.

"I am not being ridiculous, Chadwick. The law will deal with whoever has—"

"I appreciate that but the child, the girl, must have someone to . . . to . . ."

"To what, Chadwick?" Sarah's eyes narrowed suspiciously. She didn't even know what reason she had to be distrustful, she only knew she didn't want her brother to be mixed up in this sordid business. After all, the Camerons were one of the first families, high in the social register in these parts and though, naturally, she would do her Christian duty by the girl, send a basket of food, perhaps clothing or blankets as one did to the poor, she felt that to become more actively involved might compromise her own status. She didn't quite like the look of her brother, the furious speed with which he was heading for the stable yard, nor the desperate look in his eye as he did so and once again she did her best to restrain him.

"Why don't you send Ned, Chadwick? He can ascertain what is . . ." Her voice followed him into the yard and the women in the kitchen exchanged looks. They all knew of the brute who lived up at the mill and the way he treated his children and his animals, not to mention that poor crippled wife of his, and if someone had done him in, well, it seemed to them the world would be a better place for it.

Sarah would not have recognised him as he approached Briony Marsden. His voice was stern and yet his eyes were a soft brown, warm with some emotion that comforted the girl in the rocker.

"Briony." He pulled Sadie's low footstool towards him and sat down on it, facing her, taking both her hands in his, and though again she felt a sense of comfort and security she also felt the stirrings of alarm at what she saw in his face.

"You can't stay here, child," he said. "You must be very tired and Mrs Evans tells me there is a bed waiting for you upstairs. Won't you let her put you in it? Your mind's in a muddle, so go to bed, lass, it's the best place for you. See, there's hot water by the fire to . . . to clean your . . . your . . . to wash in and when you've had a sleep I'll come back and we can talk."

"I'll just wait here for Danny, sir, if you don't mind," she heard the crumpled doll in the rocking-chair say ever so politely, and Mr Cameron leaned forward and shook his head.

"No, lass, it's best you get to bed. You can't sit here."

"Why not?"

He smiled then and she thought she had never seen him smile before and how handsome he looked.

"Because I say so."

"But what about Danny? I must wait."

"Danny's had to go somewhere . . . to talk to some people and until he returns it's best you get some sleep. Please, won't you do it for me? Let me take you upstairs and then Mrs Evans . . ."

He lifted her easily, turning to Sadie who was hovering in the doorway, holding her tightly so that again she had that feeling of security, of being safe. When Sadie followed him upstairs she was delivered to hot water, clean sheets, an enormous nightdress that smelled of lavender and a deep night's sleep, courtesy of the draught Doctor Travis – who had appeared from somewhere – had given her and which it seemed sensible to give way to now that Mr Cameron had said so.

She awoke to a warmth, a comfort, a cleanliness she had never before known. Mother had done her best with the few bits of things Father had allowed but the sheets and blankets on her truckle bed had been thin and worn and not always as clean as they might have been. Mother had been forced to make her own coarse soap by boiling animal fats and soda and as for warmth in the winter Father had scarcely allowed them enough fuel to keep in a bit of fire except for cooking or when he lolled before it.

The light was brightening slowly, turning from the greyness of a winter dawn to a soft glow that heralded the sunrise, and the silence gave place to the familiar sound of birds awakening, to the barking of a dog somewhere on the fells and to the cackling of hens.

She stretched and yawned and burrowed further beneath the colourful quilt. She had no inclination to leave this comfortable haven. Something had happened, something that squirmed at the back of her conscious mind and she had no wish to disturb it, for she knew it was something she wasn't going to like.

The room she was in was small and sparsely furnished. There was a simple pine washstand embellished with an embroidered runner. A pretty cream-coloured ewer and jug decorated with a painted blue bow stood on the runner and on either side was a candlestick-holder to match. An oval mirror hung on the wall and against the far wall a pine wardrobe stood, polished, like the washstand, to a honey glow. The floor was bare polished wood and next to the bed was a rag rug made from every scrap of material that had once been garments Sadie, Dai and Iolo had worn. It was a history of Sadie's life, for in it was a scrap from the pretty rose-coloured dress she had worn on her wedding day, pieces from Dai's shirts and a cotton scarf he had worn knotted at his neck, bits of Iolo's baby clothes, and it was one of Sadie's most treasured possessions.

It felt lovely just to lie here and peer sleepily out of the square of window to where the bare branches of an apple tree wavered beyond the glass, but a rough tongue explored her face and there was Sal staring down at her, which was unusual in itself for Sal always slept with Danny.

Danny! She sat up in bed, flung back the covers and swung

her feet to the rug beside it. There was a fire burning in a grate, before which stood a rocking-chair, twin to the one downstairs. The fire's warm orange flames flickered and reflected on the whitewashed ceiling and in the polished wood of Sadie's furniture and she longed to lie here and drowse for the rest of the day, but though she shivered at the thought of it she knew she must face up to what lay in wait for her. Sal slipped quietly to the rug and stood, her head on one side, waiting for her, her eyes sad and bewildered.

"Oh, Sal," she murmured, then, lifting her head bravely, she crept across the polished wooden floor of Sadie's bedroom – knowing where she was now – and holding the tent-like nightdress with one hand so that she would not trip, the dog at her heels, she moved noiselessly down the stairs and into the kitchen.

He was there sitting before Sadie's fire, a cup of tea in one hand, his other fondling the head of Iolo's collie bitch. Sadie could be heard in the little scullery to the rear of the kitchen talking in a quiet voice to someone, the sound of water being poured into the shallow sink accompanying her voice. Iolo answered her and she shushed him.

It was Poppy, Iolo's dog, who alerted the man to Briony's presence. Though she was in evident rapture under the caressing stroke of his hand, she turned and stood up, growling softly, not at Briony but at Sal who did not belong on Poppy's territory.

Chad Cameron looked round swiftly and for several seconds could not look away, nor indeed did he want to. She looked so comical in what was evidently Sadie's nightgown and yet so frailly lovely, his heart caught in his throat and he could not speak. It was, despite its size, a pretty nightgown, for Sadie was an expert needlewoman and had liked to please her man in their bed years ago. It was made from fine lawn and about the wide neck Sadie had stitched what was known as drawn threadwork, fine and lacy. The sleeves were long and full, as was the nightgown and on Sadie it was a perfect fit but on Briony it floated like white smoke, the neck drawn to one side and hanging off her smooth white shoulder. Her hair was tangled into a curling mass halfway down her back, a long tendril falling across her shoulder. There was a small window at the head of the stairs and the light from it fell at her back and through the gown her slender, perfectly proportioned figure could clearly be seen.

He stood up slowly. The two dogs approached one another warily and again Poppy growled then they were nose to nose but in the way of good-natured animals their tails began to wag. The noise of Poppy's growl brought Sadie and Iolo from the scullery and at once Sadie gasped with horror. Iolo's mouth fell open and on his face was the same rapt expression that clothed Chad Cameron's.

"Briony, chuck . . . nay, what yer thinking of comin' down like that? See, Iolo, run an' get the . . . the quilt . . . owt ter cover 'er with. Mr Cameron," she said in a reproving voice, for it was obvious to a blind man on a galloping horse, as her mam used to say, he couldn't take his eyes off the poor child, and her in such terrible trouble an' all! As if the death of her mother and father and what had happened to their poor Danny made the expression on Mr Cameron's face even more appalling. But then he was a man and the lass was so pretty and so innocent.

Only when she had made all decent, with Briony in the rocking-chair wrapped up like a parcel in the quilt Iolo had dragged from his mam's bed, was Sadie satisfied.

When Briony was seated Chad returned to his own chair. Sadie took his cup from him and hovered next to the child, as she still called her though it was obvious from the way the nightgown had fallen about her that the term was no longer apt. She knew that Mr Chadwick had returned half an hour ago because he wanted to talk to the lass but first she must make sure Briony had something to eat. Iolo had gone, taking Poppy who herded his cows for him, both of them reluctant since Poppy liked the feel of the stranger's hand and Iolo liked the sight of Briony Marsden's young beauty on display.

"Now then, my lass, yer'd best have summat to eat," she said briskly, bending to lift a kitten which was wavering across the floor and dropping it back, protesting piteously, into the basket which was once again filled with one of Tabby's frequent litters.

"I'm not hungry, Mrs Evans, thank you," Briony told her, her eyes on Mr Chadwick who must have something to tell her about . . . about Danny.

"I don't care whether yer are or yer not, yer havin' summat to eat." Sadie's voice was firm. "I'm not havin' tha' fadin' away to nowt for want of a bite."

"No, thank you, really, I couldn't eat. I just . . ."

"Briony." His voice was deep, soft, concerned, and he leaned forward as though to emphasise the importance of what he was about to say. "You must eat. Mrs Evans is right and I insist on it."

"No."

"I say yes." He turned to Sadie. "A cup of tea, I think and then . . . ?" He waited for Mrs Evans's superior knowledge of such culinary things as she thought appropriate.

"I could do 'er a scrambled egg on a bit of toast," Sadie said hopefully, turning to smile at Briony.

"That would do nicely, Mrs Evans, and when she has eaten she and I will talk."

"I shan't leave her, sir," Sadie said sternly.

"Of course not, Mrs Evans, I would wish you to stay." For Briony would need the warm motherliness of this kind woman when she heard what he had to tell her.

Sadie had been preparing a good wholesome meal before

Briony came drifting down the stairs. Her Iolo needed a decent feed at dinner-time and the lass would need something to keep her strength up for the ordeal that lay ahead of her. And then there was Mr Cameron! Was he to eat with them? A nourishing Lancashire hotpot would seem to be just the thing, the one her mother had taught her how to make before her Da had come along and swept her off her feet, and if Mr Cameron was to stay it could be made to go round. He seemed to be right mithered by the lass's plight and had hardly been off her, Sadie's, doorstep since Danny had appeared on it yesterday.

She would never forget the sight of him, no, not if she lived to be a hundred and her shriek of horror had brought them all out from the cottages in the row where Sadie lived. Covered in blood he had been, so that at first she and Ethel Hodgson, who lived next door and was married to Mr Cameron's hedger and ditcher, thought it was Danny who was hurt. He was literally *dripping* with it. They had hurried him over Sadie's doorstep, her and Ethel, shouting to Jenny Turnberry to fetch hot water but when they managed to get a coherent word from the lad it seemed all he wanted was for somebody to fetch Mr Cameron. One of Dorry Blamire's lads, one with summat about him who could be trusted to deliver a sensible message, had set off wild with excitement, and within minutes, flinging himself off his mare, Mr Cameron was there and it was him who had got the full and terrible account of what had happened up at the mill from the frozen-faced lad.

"I did it, Mr Cameron," he kept saying. "It was me. I pushed him. Well, I had to, you see. I couldn't let him . . mess with Briony, could I?"

The women who crowded into Sadie's kitchen had gasped and flinched, for they all knew exactly what Danny meant but there was more to come.

"He killed my mother, Mr Cameron." Dorry Blamire put her hand to her mouth and began to cry, for she was known to be soft-hearted, but Sadie gave her a stern look as this was no time for tears.

"She did her best to . . . to protect our Briony," Danny went on, "so he killed her. I had to stop him, didn't I? I pushed him into the stones. He's still there with Briony and Mother. He's dead and I killed him. I did it. It was me . . ." And he started all over again, repeating patiently the horror of what had happened. It was all said in the high toneless drone of deep shock as though the lad's mind had escaped somewhere safe and the thin voice that came from him was not his own. He would have gone on and on, saying it over and over had not Mr Cameron sat him down in Sadie's chair and chucked a great swig of brandy from a hip flask he had in his pocket down his throat, which cut off the horrendous flow of words. Women were sent running here and there to fetch men, to fetch the doctor, to fetch the constable while Mr Cameron flung himself on his mare and galloped off in the direction of the mill.

When he returned he had the still, silent, blank-faced figure of Briony Marsden before him on the saddle. He handed her down to the women then galloped off again without a word.

Sadie had slept in her son's bed last night, leaving open the doors between there and where Briony lay drugged so that if she should wake she would hear her, but to tell the truth she only dozed, for the vivid pictures Joe Blamire and Ned Turnberry brought back with them of Jethro Marsden trapped by his arm and of his blood which flowed across the wooden floor to the very hem of his daughter's skirt were enough to keep sleep from even the most stout-hearted.

Now, at Mr Cameron's words, a strange, thin, cat-like sound escaped from Briony and she began to scream, a scream of absolute terror when he told her that Danny had been arrested for the murder of his father and taken to a temporary prison in Penrith.

"*No . . . no . . . no . . .*" She shook her head violently from side to side, her hair swinging out like a glossy cloak, and Sadie stood up uncertainly. Sal backed away from the rug where she had settled and the mother cat hissed warningly as the dog collided with her basket. "Not Danny . . . not Danny. It wasn't his fault, he was defending me and my mother. Not Danny . . . Please, Mr Chadwick, tell them . . ."

The quilt was flung to the floor and she threw herself at his feet, clutching at his hands, Sadie's nightgown dragged down so that the tops of her small breasts were exposed. Her face was like paper and her eyes were enormous shadows of dark purple, the colour that seeped into the mill pond at the back of the mill as dusk fell. Sadie was quite horrified, as much by her reaction to Mr Cameron's words as the revealing of her white breasts which no man except a woman's husband should see. Mr Cameron saw them though and his face closed up as he reached for the quilt, dragging it roughly about the girl's shoulders.

"Stop it, d'you hear me. Stop this noise at once." He shook her a little as she knelt before him but Sadie could see the fearful weight of anxiety that showed in his eyes.

"It will all come out, Briony, everything that happened. What was done to you and your mother by . . . by your father. Danny was protecting you and that will be taken into account. No, no, stop it now. Sit back in your chair and listen to me. Procedures have to be followed. Danny has . . . he has . . . it all has to be investigated and though Danny may have to remain in prison for—"

"No, please, sir, don't let them keep him in prison. It was not his fault." She leaned forward and again the quilt slipped but this time Sadie, who crouched at her side, was ready for it, tucking it modestly about her.

"I know that, Briony, and so does Doctor Travis who will vouch for Danny. Speak up for him and tell the . .

well, when the time comes let it be known that your father ill-treated you all, threatened your lives, which makes what Danny did an act of self-defence. Do you understand?" He leaned forward and seemed as though he wanted to get hold of her hands to reassure her but they were well wrapped up by the vigilant Sadie.

"I wanted to tell you myself what was to happen and beseech you not to worry, but I must get to Penrith and make my statement on Danny's behalf. There are gentlemen with influence who . . . well, I shall leave you in Mrs Evans's good care."

"Oh, indeed, sir," Sadie said, patting the bundle that was Briony.

"And I shall be back as soon as I can."

"Will tha' not tekk summat ter eat, sir," Sadie begged him, for the delicious fragrance of her hotpot was beginning to fill the kitchen.

"No, thank you, Mrs Evans." He hesitated, then, surprising Sadie for what else would she do, he asked, "You'll take care of her, won't you, Mrs Evans?"

"I cannot for the life of me understand why you have to be involved in this, Chadwick. It is not as though they were your people. I mean by that, workers on your land. The mill was not your responsibility, nor the family who live in it."

"*Lived* in it, Sarah."

"Pardon. I'm afraid I don't—"

"Two of them are dead. One is in prison and the other in a dangerous state of near dementia."

Sarah curled her lip. "Really, Chadwick, I think you are exaggerating somewhat."

"Which part, Sarah?"

"The girl is surely not in a state of . . . whatever it was you used to describe her. And if it's true that the boy killed his father surely he is in the best place where he can be a danger to no one. So what is there for you to do, tell me that? Why must you go galloping here and there? You say the girl—"

"Briony, that is her name."

Again Sarah's lip curled in disgust. "Chadwick, please, the girl—"

"I haven't time to be standing here debating a point with you, Sarah, so I'd be obliged if you would get out of my room and allow me to change. I still have blood on my—"

"So I see and I must protest—"

"Protest all you want but I am riding into Penrith at once."

"But why?"

"I must speak to Bernard Gould who is a magistrate and might have some influence if it comes to trial."

"*If*! The boy is a murderer."

"And to Doctor Travis who has seen the results of Marsden's cruelty to his children. And I, of course, mean to be witness as to the boy's good character."

"Chadwick, please," his sister wailed. "For my sake, don't get involved."

"I am already involved, Sarah." But he didn't mean it in the way his sister imagined. Chad Cameron had a trick of wiping all expression from his face when he wished and he used it to best effect now.

7

The gig drew up at the door of the cottage with a flourish. The cottage door opened and Briony and Sadie stood there somewhat uncertainly, for neither of them had ridden in a gig before and were not awfully sure how to enter the thing.

"Hop in, ladies," Joe Blamire said cheerfully from his seat behind the pony, turning to wink at them, then, remembering the circumstances, wiped the expression from his face and did his best to look serious. The occupants of the other cottages in the row crowded on their doorsteps, for it was not often such an equipage was seen in their lane. Most of them were women and toddlers, the men and older children being at work, though Joe did notice Blacky Blackhall poking his nose out of his doorway. Having another day off work with his "bad" back, he supposed absently, wondering why Mr Cameron kept him on. He was a damned good carpenter when he could be made to get off his backside, and the intricacy of his carvings were a sight to behold so Joe supposed that was the reason.

Joe, sensing the anxiety of the woman and the girl, poor lass, climbed down and guided the pair of them round the rear and heaved them up over the wheel and into the gig, then ran round the back again, climbed up and squeezed in beside them. The small, well-kept vehicle was used only by Miss Sarah who drove it herself, though there was room for two. Three was a bit of a squash but the lass was only a little slip of a thing and didn't seem to mind. Well, if he was honest, she didn't seem to notice and could you wonder after what had happened. She seemed to be in a daze as though she wasn't awfully sure where she was going, or why and when Joe had left the house Miss Sarah had been the same.

The argument between her and Mr Cameron had been heard from the stable yard where Joe had been harnessing Roddy, the docile Welsh cob that pulled the gig.

"I'm sorry, Chadwick," she could be heard saying in that imperious way she had, "but I shall need the gig today. I promised Madge Seddon that I would go over and . . ." If the truth were known Sarah was still piqued by Chadwick's total indifference to the charms of Adeline Seddon who had, by one means or another, been thrown in his path by herself and Adeline's mother whom she had intended visiting today. They were not yet about to give up on the idea of a match between the pair, and Chadwick's high-handed intention of taking the gig for the use of the girl from the mill infuriated her.

"Well, my dear, if you must go use the carriage. Ned can drive you."

"Chadwick, it is hardly worth getting up the carriage just to go to—"

"Then perhaps you can go another day. Send a message to Mrs Seddon. I'm sure she won't mind."

"But I do. In fact I strongly resent this, Chadwick. That gig is for my use and why you should feel the need to send it over to . . . to Mrs Evans is beyond me."

"How do you suggest that she and Briony get to Penrith, Sarah?" Chad's voice was patient but those of his servants, most of them long serving, recognised what was in it even if Miss Sarah didn't, or perhaps she chose to ignore it. Miss Sarah was enough to try the patience of a saint with her high-falutin' manner and her absolute determination to have her own way. In most things, things they knew didn't matter to him, Mr Chadwick allowed it, but he seemed to be absolutely resolute in his commitment to helping the Marsden family in any way in his power. Riding about the countryside, it was said, calling on men who might be of some help to the lad in gaol, employing the best counsel in the county to defend the boy and sending the gig, *Miss Sarah's* gig, which was making her wild, to take Sadie Evans and the lass into Penrith. To get her some suitable clothing, Daphne had repeated to those in the kitchen, having heard the master and mistress going on about it over dinner last night, for she could hardly go to her mother's funeral in those rags Jethro Marsden had considered good enough for his daughter, that's if he had considered it at all.

"Surely some suitable garments of the servants could be made to fit her. To send her into Penrith for brand-new clothing seems somewhat extreme to me. Whatever will people say?"

"Really, Sarah, does it matter what people say?"

"It does to me and it *should* to you. I cannot imagine what Miss Pendleton will think when Mrs Evans and that girl—"

"Briony."

"Oh, for goodness sake, Chadwick. Anyone would think the girl was related to us, the fuss you are making. A new gown and to acquire it she must ride in *my* gig. There is the farm cart, the one that is used for—"

"The farm cart! Sarah, I'm surprised at you. The girl has suffered a terrible tragedy, losing all her family in one day and you suggest I send her and Mrs Evans into Penrith in the cart that is used about the farm."

"Why not? It has a bench seat in it and they are hardly used to driving about in a carriage, are they? Blamire can take them in, and that is another thing. Who is to pay for these garments this girl is to have? I presume she has no money of her own."

"You presume correctly."

"So?"

"I will pay for them, Sarah. And I hardly think—"

"That is your trouble, Chadwick. You hardly think! Our position in this community—"

"Oh, for God's sake, Sarah. Where is your Christian spirit which flaunts itself every Sunday in church but begrudges Briony Marsden a decent gown to wear to see her mother buried?"

"And that is another thing—"

"I'm sorry, Sarah, but I haven't the time to stand here arguing with you." And he had walked out into the yard, leaped agilely on to his mare's back and dashed wildly through the yard gate and on to the driveway that wound round the house. The stable lads watched him go, as amazed as Miss Sarah at the stand Mr Cameron was taking. The lass was to be pitied and indeed they all felt sorry for her, and for her brother, but still! There was a limit to charity.

Sadie was to say later she felt like the Queen in her royal coach as she and Briony bowled along the narrow road to Penrith. For the first mile or two they ran beside the river, the water bubbling and chattering joyfully over the stony river bed on their right, travelling sedately through the village of Stainton where the fells began to smooth themselves out into the Vale of Eden. Joe was enjoying this unusual day out and the change from his duties about the stables and paddocks at Longlake Edge and, despite the sadness of the circumstances, so was Sadie. Out of consideration for the lass, though he would have liked to since he was a gregarious man, Joe did not try to engage Sadie Evans in conversation, but he could see the widow was made up with riding in the gig and as they approached the outskirts of the little market town travellers on foot became more frequent.

"'Tis busy terday, Mr Blamire," Sadie ventured, looking about her with great interest. Those on foot were for the most part country folk dressed in hodden-grey, the men's trousers tied with string below the knee, the women in white aprons and bonnets, the men in a soft hat with a drooping brim. They all, men and women alike, wore home-made stockings and sturdy, wooden-soled clogs on their feet, the distinction between the men and women being that the women's clogs had brass clasps rather than iron. They all turned to stare at what they considered to be the "grand" folk in the gig and Sadie smiled graciously, inclined, like Joe, to enjoy herself on this unexpected outing. Briony, wearing the shawl that was Sadie's own and which she had tucked closely about her, sat between them, pale-faced, eyes unseeing, until Joe drove with a smart turn into the market-place and drew up at the monument in the centre. The clock stood at ten minutes past twelve.

"It's market day, tha' see," Joe said as though in answer to Sadie's previous remark and even Briony came from her spell to stare round at the cheerful bustle of the crowds who swarmed about the stalls. Joe helped them down from the gig, ordering them to stand well to one side while he unhitched the cob, leaning the gig on to its shafts in a line of others at the side of the cobbled square out of the way of the heaving crowds, then led them and the horse to the George Inn behind which a dozen or so others, mostly stout farm animals, were safely stabled.

"Now, my lasses, you go off an' get what yer need an' I'll wait fer thi'."

"Nay, Joe Blamire," Sadie protested. "Yer never goin' ter wait in't public 'ouse. Mr Cameron'll not be right pleased if yer get tipsy an' us on such a ..." She inclined her head in the direction of Briony who stood like one of the carved statues in Mr Cameron's garden, only her eyes moving as they took in the lively crowds into which she and Sadie were about to plunge. Sadie did her best to indicate to Joe that this was an unhappy mission and not one for merrymaking.

"Nay, Mrs Evans, I'll just 'ave me a meat pie an' a pint of ale. No chap can get tiddly on that. Now off tha' go an' remember what Mr Cameron said. Nowt off market stall." The previous evening Joe had been there at the front door of the cottage he shared with Dorry, smoking his pipe, when Mr Cameron had told Mrs Evans she'd to shop at Miss Pendleton's which was where Miss Sarah had her own clothes made.

"I understand that a gown could not be made to measure for Thursday" – which was the day of the funeral – "but I happen to know that Miss Pendleton has several dresses already made up which can be altered for customers who are in need. Mourning and that sort of thing. Tell her Mr Cameron wants the best and something . . . well, smart. She will know what I mean. And a bonnet. One that will not swamp her."

They had all overheard the conversation and been open-mouthed in wonder, for what the hell did it mean? *Swamp her!* Well, this Miss Pendleton would know, they supposed, and the lass could hardly go to the funeral in what she had on, nor to the trial of her brother. And it occurred to them to wonder how the master knew the inner working arrangements of an establishment such as the dressmaker's!

At Miss Pendleton's request Briony obediently shed Sadie's shawl and stepped out of the skirt she had worn for the last six months. Miss Pendleton was a picture of unshockable composure as she helped her with her bodice but was forced to avert her eyes from the skimpy undergarments Sadie had washed and ironed with scrupulous care the night before, since they revealed so much of her customer's smooth white flesh. Mr Cameron had made it quite clear when he had called into her smart little shop that Miss Marsden, *Miss Marsden, if you please*, was to have the very best. Miss Pendleton dressed most of the ladies in the district and, having been warned, so to speak, by Mr Cameron, had hurried the two women, both wearing *shawls*, into a private room at the back of her establishment, for if Mrs Seddon, or Mrs Mounsey, wife to the squire up at Manning Green, should enter and find her in attendance upon women of the lower orders there was no doubt they would walk right out again and give their business to the newcomer who had opened up at the top end of the market. An attractive young Irish woman who, it was said, had a rich admirer and was a cause of some worry to Miss Pendleton.

"I think a chemise and drawers, in fact two of everything, don't you agree, Miss . . . er . . ."

"Mrs Evans," Sadie told her curtly, determined not to be overwhelmed by this disdainful, frozen-faced spinster, a clever dressmaker and milliner it was said, though Sadie knew nothing about such things.

"Very well, Mrs Evans. Mr Cameron, who it seems has taken this young person under his wing" – turning a shrewd eye on the young person in question, wondering, no doubt, Sadie was sure, exactly what the relationship was between them, as indeed would other folk hereabouts – "has stated that no expense is to be spared in fitting her out. A funeral, he said—"

"Aye," Sadie cut in quickly before the woman, who must have known what had happened at Moorend Mill, could elaborate on the event. She would not ask, naturally, for was she not, in her own eyes, discreet, at least with those whom she served, but this young girl was not one of those and a bit of probing, a bit of gossip to be passed on would not be unwelcome.

"Aye, Thursday, so 'appen we could get on." Sadie's voice was sharp and, to Miss Pendleton's annoyance, she sat down on one of Miss Pendleton's immaculate velvet and gilt spindle-legged chairs. Sadie had been somewhat perturbed by the fact that Mr Cameron was to pay for *their* Briony – as she now was to Sadie since there was no one else to claim her – to be kitted out in the best money could buy for her mother's funeral but now she decided the lass might as well take advantage of it. Not that Briony was in a fit state to take advantage of anything at the moment. She was pushed and prodded and pinned and, when they emerged from Miss Pendleton's two hours later, might have passed for the daughter of one of Miss Sarah's fine friends. The dress was simple. Black, of course, in a fine broadcloth suitable for winter, the skirt full and gathered about a narrow waist, the bodice high-necked and pointed at the front, the sleeves ballooning from the shoulder to a tight-fitting cuff. It was in the fashion of several years ago, one that Miss Pendleton had had in stock for a while but these two country yokels would hardly know that, would they? They didn't. A small brimmed bonnet, very demure and unadorned, a woollen pelisse, also no longer fashionable, and Briony's outfit was complete.

Except for the clogs she still wore!

"I believe there are stalls in the market square which will help you there," Miss Pendleton remarked coldly, "since I do not sell shoes."

And with that Sadie had to be satisfied. She led the wordless, one might almost say stupefied figure of Briony Marsden from the shop, carrying the prettily wrapped parcel of new undergarments Miss Pendleton handed to her and, holding Briony's arm, led her back towards the George where Joe lolled against the wall.

His face told its own story, for in the two hours since he had last seen her Briony Marsden had been transformed from a whey-faced foundling to a young lady of fashion. Though she was pale her mouth was a rich, ripe poppy and her eyes, despite their lost look, were still the incredibly vivid blue which had so startled Chad Cameron. The small brimmed bonnet covered her hair which Miss Pendleton had wound into a high chignon. The only inconsistency in her new image were the clogs!

"Well, bugger me," he stammered, his eyes widening in amazement and his smile widening in appreciation, but the rest of his pronouncement was interrupted by a clatter of horses' hooves and the sound of Mr Cameron's voice.

"Miss Marsden, there you are," the voice said and the two women stood back against the wall while Joe automatically reached for Ebony's bridle as Mr Cameron jumped to the ground. His startled eyes, in a way he later realised was extremely rude, swept up and down Briony's changed appearance, and his mouth fell open. Only for a moment and neither Sadie nor Joe noticed, for they were, like him, looking at Briony.

Regaining his composure, he addressed her as though what he had to say was of no more import than a remark about the weather. It was the only way he could deal with the sensation in the middle of his chest which was a mixture of so many emotions he could barely name them. He longed to put his arms about her, draw her into their circle, soothe her, comfort her, tell her that she had nothing to worry about for he was here to take the burden of grief and anguish from her, and because he could do none of these things he sounded cool, distant, almost disinterested.

"I thought I might catch you, either here or at the dressmaker. I have arranged for you to see your brother before he is taken to Carlisle."

She barely felt Sadie's hand on her arm nor heard the hiss of dismay from Joe but the terror of Mr Cameron's words ran through her, turning her blood to water and her legs to jelly and she was glad that she had the wall at her back or she would have fallen. Ever since she had watched with horrified fascination the waves of her father's blood creep towards her and listened to his screams; ever since the warm comfort of this man's arms had been wrapped about her, taking her away from the horror, she had felt that he would make sure that Danny, who was not to blame since he had been defending her against her father's cruelty, his cruel *perversion*, would come to no harm. Certainly he must be questioned by whoever it was whose job it was to see to such things but, after a night, or perhaps two in the gaol at Penrith, he would be released. On Thursday they were to bury their mother and naturally Danny would be there beside her but . . . but . . . Her mind seemed unable to function and her already pale face changed to the colour of unbaked dough.

"Carlisle . . ." she managed to whisper. "But why? when?" She put out a small, black-gloved hand to him and for a moment Chad felt he would break. He had already revealed too much of himself to Mrs Evans and he was aware that his actions had aroused amazement and consternation among his friends and servants but he must pull himself together. He had to remember that he was a gentleman, a man of some standing in the community and, apart from the kindnesses one showed to those less well favoured, it would not do to help this family more than was necessary.

"Perhaps Mrs Evans would accompany us." For with Mrs Evans there he would have to resist the temptation to take her arm and convey her across the square as though she were some tender frond of womanhood which might droop and fall without support.

She seemed unable to comprehand the meaning of what he had told her and Sadie held her more tightly, putting her arm about her waist.

"But Carlisle . . . why?"

"Let's get over to the gaol, Miss Marsden," he said briskly, his face a mask of tight muscles, a deep frown dipping his eyebrows. "The man in charge is expecting us and—"

"But when is he to go? It is the funeral on Thursday."

"Yes." He could think of nothing else to tell her, at least not here in the crowded market square. When they were safe from curious eyes, perhaps back at Mrs Evans's cottage, when she was sitting down and with Mrs Evans close at hand he would say what had to be said.

"Watch the mare, Joe," he commanded the spellbound groom. "We won't be long and when we return I shall need you to drive Mrs Evans and Miss Marsden home."

"Yes, sir." Joe touched his forelock, at the same time keeping a tight hand on Ebony's bridle, for the horse, as were most thoroughbreds, was inclined to be skittish among a crowd of people. He watched as the strange trio threaded their way through the rows of stalls and the press of people who crowded round them. Stalls on which anything from a dozen eggs to a yard of what purported to be French lace was sold. As Mr Cameron, Briony Marsden and the stout figure of Sadie Evans disappeared down a side street where the town's gaol was situated he debated on whether it would be worth the risk of tying up Ebony at the back of the inn with the rest of the horses and slipping inside for a pint of ale, then, regretfully, decided against it. Ebony, unlike the other animals stabled there, was a valuable piece of horseflesh and if anything happened to him Mr Cameron would have his, Joe's, hide, then sack him! He sighed, then settled with his back against the wall to await his master's return.

Though Chad Cameron's money had provided Danny with all the comforts a prison can offer, the cell could not be disguised as anything but what it was. There was a dank odour, a dampness that seemed to rise from the old stones that lined the floor. The cell was small, the stone walls seeping some liquid which none of the three visitors cared to examine. The meagre light that fell about the place and the air the prisoner was forced to breathe came through the slatted door which gave on to a dim passage. There was no window. To give the place its due it was meant only as a holding cell for those who broke the law before they were sent on to the county gaol in Carlisle or, in the case of minor infringements, were put up before the local magistrates. There was rarely more than one prisoner and that was the case today. Danny Marsden sat on a mattress, fouled and grey, which had been thrown on a plank bed. There was no other furniture in the cell except for a bucket in the corner. The stink was overpowering. He was manacled.

Sadie had been directed to wait outside by the warder since she was not a relative and only some coins slipped to him by Mr Cameron, who was well known in Penrith, allowed him to accompany Briony into the prisoner's cell.

When she saw the manacles about her brother's ankles a thin, anguished sound escaped from Briony's lips. The door was closed and locked behind them but at once Chad Cameron was hammering on it, bringing the surprised warder back with his keys.

"What the devil d'you mean keeping this lad in manacles? I was told that they would be removed. And what is that in the corner?" he thundered, so that even Briony and Danny shrank away from him.

"Why, 'tis bucket, sir. Prisoner 'as ter—"

"Remove it and empty it at once. And unlock those manacles. What d'you think I pay you for, you lazy—"

"But, sir, the prisoner be off—"

"Empty it at once but don't come back until I call for you. Miss Marsden and her brother—"

"But, sir," the man began to protest but he did as he was told.

It was Briony who was the strong one and though he stood at the door, doing his best to give the brother and sister a small degree of privacy he could not help but overhear their whispered conversation.

"Danny, sweetheart, don't fret, please, don't fret. Mr Cameron will have you out of here before you know it." His heart sank and he bowed his head against the greasy woodwork, for he knew he had no influence in the assizes in Carlisle. Not even to make the life of this poor lad a bit easier with a bribe or two as he had done here.

"But I'm to be taken to Carlisle, Bry." It was obvious the boy was weeping. Dear God, he was barely into his young manhood, Chad sorrowed. All his life he had known nothing but depraved cruelty, hard work that would have felled a grown man, nothing but violence and exploitation beyond his years, sharing it with his young sister. Now, for doing his best to protect her, and his own mother, he was to be conveyed to Carlisle where he would be tried before the judges for murder. Neither he nor Briony knew the full horror of what was before them.

"Danny, really, it won't be for long, love. Mr Cameron will soon have it all sorted out. He'll make them see what happened, what we suffered and then they'll let you out and we can go back to the mill. You and I'll run it. We know how to do it. We should. We've been at it long enough. We'll need a strong man, a good man. Mr Cameron'll know of one and then . . . Danny, we're free . . . free of him. Mother . . ." She began to cry, mingling her tears with her brother's and at the door Chad felt his heart break and he wanted to groan out loud. "If only Mother could have been with us. No, don't cry, love. Be strong and have faith. Just bear up and as soon as you're out we'll start again. I'm staying with Sadie so you mustn't worry about me. Promise me. Promise me."

"Oh, Bry, I'm that fright."

"I know, I know, but it won't be for long. I promise you."

They stood up and put their arms awkwardly about each other, standing thus for several minutes while Chad Cameron leaned his forehead against the door and did his best to pray to a God he was not awfully sure ever listened.

8

Briony lifted the flat iron to within a fraction of an inch from her cheek to test its heat, then, satisfied it was just right, began to smooth it up and down the back of Mr Cameron's shirt. It was a fine shirt, its material one she had never known before she came to Longlake Edge. It was called cambric, Sadie had told her, and was lovely to touch. She ironed it reverently, taking the care Sadie had taught her.

The pale washed spring sunshine filtered through the high window on to the table beneath it where she worked. It was a big table used not only for ironing but for folding linen and at the moment was covered with a coarse ironing cloth topped with a clean calico sheet. Beside her stood a large iron stove on which were several flat irons, "sad" irons, as they were called, sad coming from the word "solid". As the iron she was using cooled it was replaced on the stove and the next one taken up, all done in strict rotation. To achieve perfect smoothness the bottom of the iron was coated with beeswax. When the plain ironing was finished, a "goffering" iron would be used to perfect the frills on the front of Mr Cameron's shirt – his evening shirt – but this was a delicate job and one at which only Sadie was accomplished, though Sadie had told her that at the rate she was going it wouldn't be long before she could be trusted with the special task.

The laundry room, which had a stone-flagged floor with good drainage since the moving about of washing tubs caused a deal of spillage, was at the rear of the house backing on to the big kitchen and scullery. It had its own cold water supply, with three sinks and water taps. A boiler in the corner was built into its own housing of bricks and next to it was a range for heating water. A very modern laundry was the one at Longlake Edge with every convenience for the benefit of the laundry-maids. Mr Cameron was known for his consideration to his servants, whether indoor or out. It was a large room, for a lot of space was needed to accommodate all the paraphernalia of washing, the assorted irons, drying frames, sticks for stirring the clothes, washboards and wicker baskets. High up near the ceiling were other drying frames that could be lowered by a rope over a pulley but these were only used on wet days or to "air" the ironed garments, bed or table linen.

A door that led from the room in which coal was stored opened with such force it clattered noisily against the wall and a lad of about twelve entered carrying two great buckets filled with coal. Following him, as though she had been waiting patiently at the door for the opportunity, was Sal. Poor Sal who pined uncomprehendingly for Danny and in consequence did her best to stick to Briony's side as the only one she knew in a world gone mad. The servants in the kitchen were sick to death of her, they complained, always hanging about at the back door instead of remaining in the stable or the yard where she had been put with Mr Cameron's dog. Looking for Briony, she was, hoping probably that where Briony might be, her young master would suddenly appear. She could be heard howling dismally at the laundry door, giving Mrs Foster the creeps, she said, and if the master didn't do something about it, she would! She was not specific as to what that might be.

"Where dost want these, Mrs Evans?" the lad called cheerfully, huffing and puffing dramatically in an effort to impress the occupants of the laundry with the difficulties of his labours. He had coal dust on his hands and face and on various parts of his person and Sadie glanced at him, tutting irritably.

"Well, yer can get rid o' that animal fer a start," she pronounced shortly as Sal huddled against Briony's cotton skirt. "This is no place fer a dog an' if she comes in here again I shall tekk her out an' tie her meself to the ring in the stable wall. And where d'yer think the coal should go, yer daft 'apporth? In't copper with the whites?"

For a moment the boy's mouth dropped open, then, realising that he was being ridiculed, for Mrs Evans's tongue was known to be sharp, he grinned appreciatively at the joke. He set the buckets down beside the range. Briony had bent down to soothe the dog, stroking her head and pulling her ears, and Sal whined sadly. Her old life had been one of cruelty with many a kick she had not deserved but her love and loyalty for Danny, and his for her, had made it worth while. Now he was gone and her canine mind was filled with misgivings. She was kindly treated and well fed each night alongside Iolo's collie bitch when she went back with Briony to Sadie's cottage, but her world was not the same without her master.

Sadie was filling a huge wicker basket with neatly folded freshly washed sheets which she meant to carry round to the rough bit of garden beyond the stables where her washing lines were placed. It was a fine day with a nice breeze, a good drying day, which meant that the drying frames close to the ceiling would not have to be lowered. She turned to Briony, watching compassionately as the girl put her face close to the dog's, holding the animal's head between her hands and gazing into her eyes. She murmured something and the dog wriggled closer, while the boy, who was a good, kind-hearted lad, cocked his head on one side, his expression sympathetic, for everyone at the house knew Briony Marsden's sad tale. Dicky was officially known as the boot boy and, indeed, he cleaned all the boots and shoes in the house, including those of the maidservants, but he also did any odd job that came to hand, such as carrying the coals to supply the laundry.

Suddenly, as though making up her mind about something, Sadie said, "Get yersenn a wash, lad. No, not in't kitchen" – as Dicky turned away towards the door – "there, in't sink. There's hot water in plenty, then yer can help Briony ter tekk washin' inter't garden as long as yer promise not ter touch owt. They'll not mind in't kitchen but this 'ere basket's too heavy."

Briony stood up and, lifting an iron from the stove, turned to face her. "I've not finished the ironing yet, Mrs Evans," she said anxiously. She always called Sadie Mrs Evans in the laundry or the kitchen where they ate with the other servants. "I was just going to start on the table napkins."

"Never mind them, lass. Jenny can do them when she comes in. 'Er Alfie's a bad chest, Ned said, but she'll be 'ere soon. So get yersenn outside. These sheets is ready ter go out while there's a bit o' wind and a breath of fresh air'll do yer good, an't dog. Dicky can carry the basket."

"I can carry it myself, Mrs Evans, but I'd rather finish these napkins."

"I know you would, an' yer a good girl but we've nearly finished this lot," indicating the neatly folded piles of laundry which were waiting their turn to be put out to dry. "You've been at it since six this morning."

"And so have you, Mrs Evans."

"I'm used to it, an' there's not a lot left ter do so off yer go."

"Please, Mrs Evans, I'd rather—"

Sadie's tone was tart. "I know you would but will yer fer once do as yer told an' stop arguing." For the girl would work until she dropped if she wasn't checked.

Briony Marsden had been working in the laundry for the past five months, ever since her brother had been taken to the assizes in Carlisle to await trial for the murder of his father. Mr Cameron had explained carefully to her what was to happen when he followed them into Sadie's cottage on the day they had gone to Penrith to purchase her an outfit suitable for the funeral.

"He is to go to Carlisle gaol, Briony, where ... No, no, you must not distress yourself. You know I shall do everything to make sure he is not ... not mistreated. He shall be decently fed and be given the best a prisoner can be given. I have some influence." Meaning, though she was not aware of it, that whatever his money could buy for the lad would be bought. Bribes to gaolers ensured that decent food was brought in. That as far as possible his cell would be cleaned out frequently, indeed that if there was such a thing he would be put in the *best* cell available and not with much of the riff-raff who filled its walls while waiting for the circuit judges. Of course minor offences were dealt with by the magistrates but there were those imprisoned with Danny who had been involved in violent crimes, the penalty for which could be hanging or at the least transportation. Briony would visit him whenever it was possible, he told her. He himself would take her, or, if that was not possible, knowing his sister as he did, though he did not voice this last, he would send her with Joe or Ned in the carriage.

"The only problem is ... well, the circuit judges, which means the judges who travel about the north from court to court where trials are to be held, only come to Carlisle twice a year and unfortunately they were there this month. They will not be back until the summer."

Briony stood up violently, the hoops of her new dress swaying dangerously close to the open fire, her face contorted in anguish and at once he rose from his chair so that they were as close to one another as a couple about to embrace. At the door to the scullery Sadie watched anxiously. Sal was at her feet, shivering, for the atmosphere frightened her as once Jethro Marsden had frightened her.

"Please, Mr Cameron, he can't be kept there. Not for six months. He's done nothing wrong. Tell them. You saw how my father was that day you . . . Danny was defending us, my mother and me. Is it wrong for a man to defend his family which was what Danny was doing?"

He did not mean to do it, for he knew he must keep the feelings he had for this young woman under control in the private realm of his heart, but he caught her hands between his own and held them to his chest and if his sister had seen it she would have been filled not only with consternation but furiously angry. Sadie watched. Watched and, at last, understood what was in this man. And was alarmed. She had lived in the gentrified world – in it but not *of* it – ever since she was thirteen and had left her father's cottage to work at a big house near Chorley. A good-looking maidservant had caught the eye of the master's son and like a fool she had given in to his blandishments. God only knew if the naïve lass thought he would marry her but, when it was discovered she was in the family way, she was turned out without a character and only the good Lord knew what had become of her. Surely Mr Cameron wouldn't . . . wouldn't . . . not with their Briony in such a defenceless state. Well, not exactly defenceless, for Sadie Evans would fight tooth and nail to make sure she was safeguarded against any man who tried it on!

"Briony, hush . . . hush, now. It will be all right. I know it's a long time, six months, but I shall do everything in my power to make his incarceration . . ." Then wished to God he had minded his tongue, for the word brought a further spasm of terror to the girl's appalled face. *Incarceration!* Surely he could have found a less graphic word to describe what the boy had to endure. He looked appealingly towards Mrs Evans who bustled forward and did what he longed to do. She put her arms about the shivering girl and drew her into their comfort.

"There, lass, don't tekk on so. Mr Cameron'll see that Danny's comfortable an' well treated, won't yer, sir? See, sit thi' down an' I'll fetch a cup of tea and then we'll decide what's ter be done while yer wait fer 'im ter come home. I'm sure Mr Cameron'll find yer summat."

"Of course. There is no need for you to worry about money."

"And you shall live 'ere wi' me an' Iolo until Danny comes 'ome. You shall 'ave Iolo's room."

Briony could feel herself drifting off into the terrifying state that had overtaken her at the exact moment she lifted her mother's lolling head into her lap. For most of the time since that horrific day she had been fully aware of where she was and what had happened to her family, but every now and again she whirled away as though her dread mind could no longer cope with it all and wanted nothing more than to escape. Even back to what her life had been before Danny . . . before her father . . . It had been a hard, merciless life but it had been a familiar one. It had had a routine, some form to it that she had recognised and accepted, but now her days were distorted, still full of fear and, the worst of all, *it was unknown*. She didn't know where it would lead her and though she knew Mr Cameron was kind and could be trusted she was deadly afraid of what was to come.

But on that day she allowed herself to be placed in the chair where she had been sitting beside the fire. Sal sidled up and laid her head on her knee and she put her hand on it, finding a small amount of comfort from the feel of the tangled yellow fur. She and Danny had often tried to brush the dog, when Father wasn't about, of course, laughing quietly – which was how they had learned to laugh in their oppressed lives – at the impossibility of turning the animal into the handsome creature that was Poppy. Poppy's coat was smooth and gleaming, with a long full tail, small tipped ears, eyes almond-shaped and dark. She was dignified, intelligent and faithful. The last two words could be used to describe Sal but there the similarity ended, for Sal was scruffy, with ears that hung down dismally and a short stump of a tail that looked as though it had been cropped. But she was gentle, affectionate and both she and Danny loved her.

"I don't care about me, Sadie," she said in a muffled voice. "I just want Danny to come home where he belongs. He and I can run the mill with the help of a strong man. You'll know one, won't you, Mr Cameron?" turning to put her free hand on his knee, not noticing the way he flinched, her brilliantly blue eyes brimming with tears. Her face was as pale as a lily and as delicately beautiful and Chad Cameron swallowed painfully, for the only thing he wanted was not talk of mills and prisons and funerals but to lift this frail creature up and carry her home where to the end of his days he would care for her, and never let her be hurt again.

"You mustn't concern yourself about the mill, Briony. That can wait for a while. Let's get Danny's trial over and then we'll see." And if he had his way, which he usually did, this lovely young woman would never set foot in that bloody mill again. It belonged now to her brother and when he was released he, Chad Cameron, would ensure that it would all be in working order so that, as Briony said, with the help of a reliable man, he could resume the business his father had so abruptly relinquished. Trade would be won back. Farmers and the villagers who had once come to Jethro Marsden had been forced to take their grain to the mill at Little Salkeld, which was a fair tramp, grumbling at the time it took but that would be put right when Moorend Mill was reopened.

But first the girl. She must be provided for. It was then that Mrs Evans spoke up, not meekly, not humbly, respectful, yes, but with a firm belief that what she was about to suggest was right.

"I need a lass in the laundry, Mr Cameron. Besides Jenny. Daisy Medcalf's in the family way and was ready to give her notice so if Briony's no objection . . ."

Briony turned to Sadie and for the first time a light shone in her face. It seemed to both of them that this was the answer to one of Briony's problems, neither of them considering that the job of laundry-maid was not Sadie's to hand out willy-nilly. The mistress of the house employed her own servants and if not the mistress, then the housekeeper or cook. A laundry-maid was of the same status as a kitchen-maid and must be of good character with proper references. Briony was not even trained in laundry work!

"Oh, yes, thank you, Sadie, that would be wonderful," she said. "I'm used to hard work and—"

"Oh, no, I don't think so." Chad frowned, his eyebrows swooping fiercely, for he had pictured this young woman sitting . . . where, for God's sake? Doing embroidery as his sister did? Was he mad? Did he imagine that Sarah would calmly accept into her home the low-born daughter of the murdered miller, a young woman whose brother was in prison for that very murder? So where was she to be put? In this cottage, perhaps, where she would be warm and safe and well looked after. Mrs Evans evidently was fond of her and . . . and . . . God, he didn't know where his thoughts were leading him. She must not be worked hard, as she had been before the death of her father, but he could hardly expect her to sit in front of the fire and be waited on which was exactly what he *did* want for her. The idea of her in the laundry with her arms up to the elbow in soapy water was anathema to him, perhaps on her knees, a bucket beside her, scrubbing the flags or whatever it was laundry-maids did. Oh, no . . . no . . .

He actually felt himself beginning to shake his head in denial before his normally clear and well-ordered mind took over. The cool, sharp-thinking mind that had been his before he had seen that translucent smile light up this young woman's eyes. There was something inside him that he had not known existed, not in himself, at least. Other men might know it, experience the joy and pain of it, but not level-headed Chad Cameron. He realised now, of course, that it had always been there ready to be awakened but it needed the right woman to bring it forth, and up to that day he had never met her. What he felt for her had sprung into life then. Not there one moment but there the next, as if it had always existed; as if, unknowing, he'd spent his life waiting for it.

Both women looked at him in surprise and, making a great effort to appear normal, he turned away and picked up his greatcoat which he had taken off in the warmth of the kitchen. He made a show of shaking it out and then pulling it on, reaching for his hat, his gloves and riding crop.

"I don't think Briony is . . . I imagined she would rather remain at home until . . ."

"At home, sir?" Briony looked around her. "I have no home, only the one Sadie has offered me until Danny is released." She squared her shoulders and her rosy mouth thinned to a determined line. "But I cannot expect Sadie to keep me for what you tell me might be six months. I must work and to be . . . to be beside Sadie – Mrs Evans – would make me . . . She has been so good to me, as you have, and I would feel safe."

Her incredible eyes were enormous in her face, too big for it, but it was not that which pierced Chad's already badly stricken heart. To be bracketed with Mrs Evans in her gratitude, in the emotional turmoil of her life was something that was hard to swallow and yet what else could he expect? She had not the slightest conception of what was in him and never would. He must step warily or there would be talk in the valley; probably there already was, for he had gone out of his way to help her brother, doing more than any other man in his position would be expected to do. He must draw back before he made a fool of himself, not only in her eyes, for at her age she must think of him as elderly, but in the eyes of the community among whom he lived.

He bowed courteously, the very gesture highlighting the difference in their status, for no man of her class would do such a thing. Both she and Sadie bobbed a small curtsey as a servant might to a master and with a cool nod he strode across the lane to where his mare was tethered.

He was about to turn and inform them that the gig would pick them up on Thursday in time for the laying to rest of her mother when his last thoughts slipped back into his mind and he strangled the words in his throat. There would only be gossip – further gossip – about Chad Cameron's peculiar concern for the Marsden children. The church where Emily was to be interred was not far and in Cumberland, where superstition and death were an inseparable part of folklore, traditions must be upheld. The funeral procession, which included the family, would walk to the church. Representatives from every household would attend the funeral. The body of Emily Marsden had been watched over by the women of the community since she had been put in her coffin. Sadie and Briony had sat together, Briony's hand in Sadie's, looking down at the peaceful face, for though she had died in violence her features in death had regained their youthful comeliness. The mangled remains of the man who had murdered her had been taken away and disposed of by Mr Cameron and Doctor Travis, and Briony had not asked, nor indeed cared, where that might be.

The day of the funeral was wet, not a steady downpour but a misty drifting curtain of rain that parted now and again to reveal the high peaks and dewed the black bonnets and bare heads of the mourners. Briony walked between Sadie and Iolo, both ready to catch her should she falter but, with her eyes on the obscure heights of Little Mell Fell, she walked steadfastly up towards the church. Men from Mr Cameron's estate carried the coffin while the "passing bell" tolled six times as was the custom for a woman. There was no need for the bearers to pause at the "resting stones" as they might do if they bore a weighty corpse. Poor Emily, as light as thistledown, was carried shoulder-high until the church was reached.

Standing with the working men, the labourers, the farmers, the men who had had dealings with the miller but who had come in respectful sympathy for the family, was Chad Cameron. He kept his eyes on the straight-backed, slight figure of the daughter of the woman being buried that day, giving the appearance of a grim-faced tiger on a leash, ready to leap forward in defence of the lass, those with imaginative minds thought, though why they should do so was a mystery to them. His face was without expression. He had removed his hat and his hair was dewed with the fine rain. It hung on his eyelashes and he was seen to blink, as was the daughter of the woman who was being laid to rest but she did not cry. She held Sadie's hand and when the earth began to fall on the coffin she turned her head away and looked northwards, over the heavily wooded area that surrounded the church, over the high fells, and only Chad Cameron knew that her brilliant violet-blue eyes were seeing not their gauzed beauty but a cell where her brother wept for his mother, for his freedom and for the dream that he and his sister shared.

Since that day he had barely spoken to her. A polite "good morning" should she be crossing the stable yard towards the washing lines at the rear of the outbuildings when he was mounting his horse. She would be carrying a basket of washing. On her feet were clogs and about her waist a snowy apron and her abundant hair was completely covered by a frilled cap, the sort servants wore. She *was* a servant and he could do nothing about it as she paused to bob a curtsey. She was pale, bowed down, not by the hard work she did, but by what her brother was facing and her dread of the future. Her lovely eyes were dimmed now, the life gone from them, but she was well cared for, well fed – he made sure of that with the extra coins he pressed into Mrs Evans's hand. She had a warm bed and a decent roof over her head during that bitter winter while they waited for the circuit judge to reach Carlisle. He knew she went whenever possible to visit Danny Marsden who lived out his miserable existence in a tiny cell, taken the thirty miles to Carlisle in Sarah's gig, driven by either Joe Blamire or Ned Turnberry. Despite the good food she lost weight, for the decent dress supplied by Sarah to all her servants hung about her slender figure like a sack. He wondered that Sarah did not notice that he himself had become somewhat gaunt as both he and Briony Marsden waited for June and the trial of Danny Marsden.

9

The trial took place on June 30th.

A cold, uncomfortable wind, a rheumatic wind which affected Duddy Morris's old bones though he wouldn't have dreamed of saying so, blew right through from February to April and here it was the end of June! They called it a "helm wind" in the Eden Valley. A biting, blustery, easterly wind which rattled windows and whirled the dead leaves across the lawns at Longlake Edge. Duddy shook his head and told anyone who would listen that the owl which nested in the strip of woodland at the back of the stable had been calling "t'wet" for over a week, which heralded rain, and rain it did so that on the day Briony, Sadie and Mr Cameron drove into Carlisle the closed carriage had to be used, much to the disapproval of Sarah Cameron. She could see no reason to send the sister of a murderer in a carriage, she said tightly to her brother, let alone travel with her and was most put out when Chadwick turned on her with controlled fury.

"It has not been proved that Danny Marsden is a murderer, Sarah. You have heard of the saying 'innocent until proven guilty' I assume. I am hoping for a suspended sentence. An acquittal, or a lighter sentence on the lesser charge of manslaughter."

"He confessed to it, Chadwick." Sarah tossed her head in high dudgeon then, noticing that Gladys, who was serving luncheon, was all ears, sent her from the room with a nod of her head so Gladys could report nothing further on the argument to the rest of the kitchen servants. Raised voices continued to come from the dining-room but even with the kitchen door slightly ajar they couldn't quite hear what was said. Nevertheless the closed carriage was brought round to the front of the house the next morning at seven o'clock! The master climbed into it, his face sombre to match his apparel, turning away from his sister who glared at him from the window, hoping, no doubt, that at the last minute he might come to his senses and let the Marsden family solve their own difficulties.

The carriage's shining splendour, despite the rain, caused a stir in the cottages where the menfolk were just setting off for their day's labour. Briony looked a real lady in her black gown and bonnet, their wives told one another, but they noticed that she was as pale as the driven snow, even her lips white and compressed, and that Sadie held her arm until Mr Cameron got a grip on her, holding a large black umbrella over her, almost lifting her into the carriage.

They did not speak on the journey. Mr Cameron had explained the procedures of the court to her, doing his best to alleviate the terror that had hung over her for the past seven months. This day would be formidable for on it hung Danny's life, she was aware of that, but Mr Cameron's quiet confidence had gently settled into her own heart and though it beat like a drum in her chest as they entered the town just having him beside her gave her courage and comfort.

The town was packed and Ned had great difficulty forcing the carriage through the throng that had come to see the trial. Carlisle had once been a border fortress and there was still a strong military presence with a garrison which had grown in the early part of the century. Another important building was the new Citadel, or Assize Court, designed by the architect of the British Museum and following the pattern of Henry VIII's old Citadel, an imposing structure in front of which was great confusion as avid sightseers struggled to gain access.

It was a crowded list today and for the rest of the week, since the last time the circuit judges had been in Carlisle was November. The gaol was jam-packed with felons and the hotels and lodging houses filled to the attics with litigants and witnesses. At the entrance to the Assize Court there was a list pinned up of the cases that were to come this day before the Honourable Mr Justice Bowyer.

Regina versus Jenkins for fraud.

Regina versus Mossop for riot and assault.

Regina versus Holme for receiving stolen goods.

Regina versus Marsden for murder.

Regina versus Garnett for theft and assault.

Briony had not slept the night before, dozing to awake with nightmares leering at her from every corner of Iolo's small room. Shadows in which her father drifted, huge and menacing. She had left her bed and gone downstairs to huddle over the fire with Sal shivering up against her knee and had been ready, washed and dressed long before Mr Cameron rapped at the door. They had sat side by side on the long journey through Penrith and north to Carlisle and she had had the strange feeling that she would have been glad of his hand to hold. His arm and shoulder were warm and steady against hers and she leaned on him a little. What would she have done without him, she thought, over these last dreadful months. He was not a man for show, for fulsome reassurances on the outcome of the trial as some were. He did not tell her that it would "be all right", but she was aware that he had gone out of his way to get the best counsel he could for Danny.

The cell at the gaol had filled her with horror when she had first visited, bare, cold, damp with nothing in it but the barest necessities. A bucket and a plank bed, but at least Danny had been allowed the warm blankets she and Sadie had taken in to him. In the cell with him there had only been one other prisoner, an elderly man, a well-educated man who had helped her brother in many ways though his own predicament was not of the best. He had talked to Danny of his life and experiences, acting as a tutor, not from books but from his own retentive memory. It had helped both of them to get through the weary months of waiting and she knew Danny had been glad of him. Other cells along the stone corridor of the gaol had been filled to overflowing with noisy, shouting men and as they had passed the doors the terrible stench that came from them had almost overwhelmed her. Danny's cell, thanks to Mr Cameron, was not as bad as that though the smell was noxious and they had been able to sit side by side on the bed and hold hands while they talked of what they would do when he was freed. On the far side of the cell Mr Jenkins had done the same with his two children, a youth and his sister who clung to him pitiably. Briony would have liked to question Danny about them but it seemed unfeeling to talk of someone else's troubles when Danny had such an enormous one of his own.

As they descended from the carriage they were jostled by the crowds who seemed in a merry mood as though the trials were to be a play by William Shakespeare or some French farce. There were pedlars selling oranges and chestnuts and buns and even an organ-grinder playing a cheerful tune to which a pathetic monkey capered.

"Great God," thundered Mr Cameron, fighting a way through the multitude, his arm about Briony's shoulders, and Sadie, incensed by the mockery being made of a good lad's life, or death, hit one chap on the side of his head with Mr Cameron's umbrella.

"Get out o' me way, tha' daft lummox," she fumed at him, watching Briony anxiously, but by now, as though some being from outside herself was watching over her, Briony had retreated into a place that enclosed her in a protective blur through which, though she could see where she was going and hear people speaking, she could feel nothing. What she did hear most distinctly was the voices of Dorry Blamire and Jenny Turnberry still ringing in her ears, wishing her good luck and telling her that she and Danny would soon be home.

"We'll 'ave us a right merry neet then, lass, with plenty of powsowdy" – a mixture of ale and rum – Jenny's cheerful voice from her doorstep had told her as she waved to the carriage when it made its uncertain way down the narrow lane and Briony clung to that image and those words as she was led into the courtroom.

Places had been saved for them at the front of the room which was already crowded when they took their seats. Guards and jurors and witnesses filled the spaces immediately before the high bench where the judge would sit, while barristers and the prisoners' counsels talked loudly and milled about as though it were a market-place. Behind Briony, Mr Cameron, Sadie and various other folk whose relatives were on trial, including the young girl and youth whose father had shared Danny's cell, were the public who had come to see the fun.

The clerk of the court rapped with his hammer and everyone stood up and the Honourable Mr Justice Bowyer came in, bowed solemnly to the court and sat down. The first trial began and Briony retreated even further behind her protective shield. She heard names being called, and from behind her someone sobbed. Sadie smoothed her hand and sat so close to her she could feel her shoulder trembling against her own. Or was it *her* shoulder that was trembling? She could feel nausea rise in her, for it was hot and stuffy and the smell of unwashed flesh filled the ill-ventilated room. What went on as prisoners were marched in to face their various charges and then out again passed over her in a sickly haze.

Suddenly there was a great stirring in the court. Mr

Cameron whispered to her and when she looked up at him he smiled.

". . . next . . ." she heard him say and then, there was Danny, standing in the box. He wore leg-irons and deep inside her Briony moaned silently. Tall and thin he had always been but now he was like a scarecrow, emaciated, gaunt, his eyes haunted, his big knuckled hands trembling on the edge of the box. He looked at her and tried to smile and it was then that she struggled to escape the fog she was in, for here was her brother, her beloved brother who had looked out for her as best he could ever since she had been a toddler.

There was a great deal of talking by several learned gentlemen, which went on for a long time but she and Danny continued to look at one another as though this were really nothing to do with them and she supposed in a way it wasn't, for Mr Cameron had hired the gentlemen to speak for them. And then it was her turn. She barely remembered stumbling to the witness stand where she swore to tell the truth, the whole truth and nothing but the truth, which she did, about what had happened that horrific night, one of the gentlemen leading her through what she herself had seen and all the time she kept her eyes on Danny for surely all he wanted to do was to forget it, wipe it from his memory as she longed to do.

Then it was over and she crept back dazedly to Sadie.

"Does the prisoner wish to say anything in his own defence?" she heard someone ask and she realised that Danny was barely aware that they were referring to him. He did not speak.

The judge tried again. "Have you anything to say before the sentence is passed?"

Danny looked at him and moistened his lips. "No, sir."

"Very well then."

Mr Cameron got to his feet, looking very stern, respectable, very obviously a person of importance and the judge and jurors looked at him in some surprise.

"If I might crave the indulgence of the court."

The judge studied him through the dust that seemed to float above the peering, muttering assembly and the clerk of the court glanced at the clock on the wall.

"You have some evidence you wish to . . ."

"Only of his good character, sir, if I may."

The judge pulled a face and the gentleman who had, so Briony realised, spoken for Danny, sighed gustily. The crowd shifted so as to get a good look at the man who had stood up and Danny stared mutely, hopelessly, it seemed, at Chad Cameron.

"Very well."

"My name is Chadwick Cameron and I have known Daniel Marsden all his life. No doubt you will reason that this young man who is accused of killing his own father, who confessed to killing his own father, is beyond putting up a good defence in his own favour. Only his young sister. But I think the circumstances, which you have gone into at great length, should be taken a step further. Jethro Marsden, as many witnesses today have testified, was a cruel man who tormented his family beyond endurance. His wife, who he killed, his young daughter, his son who did his best to protect them both though he was but a lad. Jethro Marsden was a brutal, ill-balanced tyrant and, had he lived, would have been hanged for the murder of his wife."

"That is not proved, sir."

Chad Cameron continued as if the judge had not spoken. "This, surely, should be taken into consideration. This boy has never before committed a crime. He is honest and decent and I beg you to find him not guilty. I personally will vouch for him and guarantee his good behaviour. He has a steady job, a trade, and I give you my word he will never break the law again, if indeed he has broken it now."

He sat down in total silence while Danny continued to stare at him as though he were God come down from heaven to say a few words on his behalf. Briony could see him relax visibly as though surely it would be all right now, for Mr Cameron, the most influential gentleman Danny knew, had spoken up for him. Never mind lawyers and barristers who, though they had talked at great length to Danny in his cell, he did not know, but Mr Cameron was important, really important.

An hour later the jury brought in its verdict: guilty of murder. The judge agreed with their recommendation that he should be lenient in view of the accused's age and exemplary record and the circumstances of his life under the cruelty of his father. He was not to hang. They sentenced him to seven years' transportation.

He was led away dragging his chains, straining to look over his shoulder at her, bewildered, she could see that, and though her own heart was breaking she managed to give him an encouraging smile as though he were not to despair, for surely Mr Cameron would find some law, some loophole through which Danny might slip.

It was not to be. The next hour passed in a daze of pain and disbelief as it seemed she had to say her fare-wells to her brother right away, for the transport was wait-ing to take away those prisoners who, like Danny and the elderly gentleman, had been sentenced to transportation, some for life. Mr Cameron had made arrangements for her to see him once more before they took him on his journey to Liverpool and the ship that was to sail across the world. He wore not only leg-irons but chains on his wrist now, for he was a convicted felon and of the two of them, she was the stronger. There was no privacy, since the gentleman with whom he had shared his cell for the past seven months was making his own farewells to his children.

Danny cried like a child who has been unjustly punished, holding out his chained hands, and though she was so much smaller than him Briony cradled his head against her shoulder and hushed him as her mother had once done.

"You will do very well, Danny, and I shall be here when you come home. You *will* come home, love, believe me, and your mill will be waiting for you. I'll keep it going. Mr Cameron will help me. And I have friends: Sadie and Iolo. They say the climate in Australia is warm, and the sunshine will do you the world of good. Be strong, love. Keep strong, for you will need your strength when you become the new miller at Moorend. I love you, Danny. I'll take care of everything."

She did not weep on the homeward journey and Chad Cameron and Sadie Evans watched her anxiously, waiting for the collapse they expected. She had seemed so frail, so defenceless on the way to Carlisle, ready to lean on anybody who held out a sympathetic hand. Her hands had plucked at the hem of her glove and worried the small black reticule in which Sadie had put a beautifully laundered white square of cambric. It had lace round its edge and was embroidered, white on white, with her initial, a beautiful thing that Sadie had treasured since her Dai had bought it for her on their wedding day. If the trial had not gone well, as Sadie had privately believed, she had expected tears of despair, and Dai, who had been a kind-hearted chap, would not have objected to the gift he had given Sadie being used to mop them up. Briony had not used it!

Chad watched her, doing his best not to appear to do so but her eyes were blind and she did not see him, nor the wild beauty of the fells about them. The rain had stopped while they were in court and there was sunshine, fluffy clouds drifting across the sky, the leafy lane along which they drove laden with wild honeysuckle and the distant prospect of purple heather. To their right was the Hesket Forest and to their left the stone-scarred heights of Lazonby Fell dotted with the slow-moving, grazing sheep, but Briony seemed unaware of anything but her own deep, sad thoughts. Even when Sadie spoke, declaring they would soon be home and she was looking forward to a decent cup of tea, Briony did not respond.

Chad found his own thoughts darting like swallows above a roof-top, busy with what he intended to do about the silent girl opposite him. Though it had still shocked him that Danny was to be transported he had been expecting some form of punishment for the lad. Perhaps a spell in gaol or . . . well, he had no idea really what he had hoped for but something must be done for this girl. She could read and write, he knew that, so perhaps a post might be found for her as a governess though a family who would be prepared to take in the sister of a condemned murderer might be hard to find!

Turning right in the market square at Penrith, the horses did not need Ned's urging as they approached the familiar wooded slopes of Ullswater.

There was no wind and the lake was as unruffled as a stretch of silk. Long shadows fell across the subtle colouring of the Lakeland hills and a star pricked the soft blue of the sky. It was getting dark, the slow falling towards night which occurs in mid-summer but Joe Blamire and Ernie Benson were in their small gardens at the front of their cottages, ostensibly turning over the soil to prepare for planting runner beans, sowing celery, leeks, turnips and Brussels sprouts for the winter. Most of the men were encouraged to grow what they could in their small plots though some were more assiduous than others. Blacky Blackhall, with his "bad back" giving him "gyp", sat on his doorstep, puffing on his clay pipe, and when the carriage drew up at the front of Sadie's cottage all three men straightened up. There were faces at the windows. Sadie's door stood open, for it was a warm evening and as Chad helped Briony down from the carriage, then turned to do the same for Sadie, Sal flew out with Iolo so close on her heels he almost tripped over her. He looked, his gaze agonised, at Briony, then over her head to his mother who shook hers sadly.

"Will tha' come in, Mr Cameron?" she asked politely, but he refused, just as politely, telling her he would be over in the morning to . . . well, to see how . . . He nodded at Briony's back as she disappeared into Sadie's cottage and Sadie understood.

"Am I not ter come ter . . . ?"

"No, Mrs Evans, stay at home for a few days. Give her time to . . ." Get over it? Pull herself together? Get used to the idea? Come to terms with the fact that there was a good chance she would never see her brother again? Keep her out of the way of curious – kindly but curious just the same – stares and questions? If he had his way she would never return to the laundry and what Sarah would have to say when he told her that her laundress was to have a few days off didn't bear thinking about. He would deal with that when it came up but as yet he could think of no alternative employment for Briony. He knew she was strong even if she didn't look it. She had had to be to survive the hard work and ill-treatment she had known under Jethro Marsden, but surely there was something more . . . more suitable for her. More suited to her delicate loveliness, her air of breeding, of refinement, for that was what she had. Refinement. He had not known how to explain to her that with her brother convicted of murdering her father, the mill was now Briony's property. If Sarah was half the Christian woman she pretended to be he might have asked her for advice about how to protect the new heiress, for that was what she was, but Sarah had already taken against the girl because of the way in which he, Chad, had helped her over the last few months. Shown her up, forcing her to employ the girl, making a fool, as she thought it, of himself and the Cameron name among the people she called friend. Perhaps the vicar's wife might know of an appropriate position?

"I'll see you get your wages, Mrs Evans," he added softly so that none in their gardens could hear.

"Nay, sir," Sadie bristled. "Dost think I care about—"

"I know that, Mrs Evans. Nevertheless, you shall have them, and so shall Miss Marsden. You both need a rest after what you have been through. She depends on you and I rely on you to take care of her."

He peered in what Sadie could only call a desperate way into the dimness of the firelit kitchen where Briony was just removing her bonnet. She had spoken no word since they had left the Assize Court in Carlisle. Sadie studied his face which was as pale and gaunt as Danny Marsden's had been as they led him from the court and Sadie made so bold as to put a sympathetic hand on his arm but his face closed up and he took a step away from her. The words of comfort that she would have given to any man in the same tormented state dried up on her tongue. This man had feelings for Briony Marsden that he would allow no one to see, let alone speak of them to *her*. His deep brown eyes, so golden and soft a moment ago, became as bleak as the storm clouds that would often build up over the heights of Gowbarrow Fell. He was telling her that she was to keep her place as he would keep his. His involvement with the Marsden family was no more than any decent man would have done, for though they were not among his workers, those who were *his* responsibility, they lived on the edge of his land and he could not see two young people go under for want of a helping hand. Or so he would have her believe. Sadie knew better. She had seen that softness in the eyes of another man. That certain expression which had crossed her Dai's face when he looked at her. Chad Cameron might fool himself but he couldn't fool Sadie Evans.

"Thank you, sir," she said and bobbed a curtsey, then stood to watch him, his face expressionless, as he climbed into the carriage.

"Straight home, Ned," she heard him say, but she was aware that though he had been born at Longlake Edge and had lived there all his life the woman in it did not make it home for him.

She lay in her bed and wished she could weep. There was a knot inside her which would only loosen if it was released with tears but it seemed to be frozen solid in the middle of her chest. She could see Danny's face, his face as once it had been as a small boy and Father had thumped him for some imagined misdeed – imagined by Father, that is – and the unfairness of it had been more than Danny could bear. As he grew he had become adept at seeing the blows coming and sometimes had even been able to dodge them. With his young body often black and blue, his young face discoloured with a bruised eye, he had overcome, borne up, and they had looked forward, hopelessly she now knew, to a future without Father. His young spirit, simply because it was young, had managed to find a bit of hope, and amazingly they had survived. Now, his expression had told her as he was led away there was no hope, only the fear of what he was to go to, of the unknown and he had become a frightened child again. And there was no one, *no one* to help him get through it. He was alone in a terrifying world, an unknown world, and if she could have gone with him on the prison ship she would gladly have done so.

But there was the mill! It belonged to Danny now and when he came home he would need something to help repair the damage done him by Father and by the unfair justice that had been meted out to him. She would write to him – Mr Cameron would know how to arrange it – she would write every week and tell him, *encourage him*, to get through this and at the end of the seven years the mill, a shining star in the dark of night, would guide him back from whatever trials he was to suffer in the penal colony.

She turned in the bed and stared out through the open window to the dark blue velvet of the summer sky and the thousands upon thousands of stars that were scattered across it. Sal lifted her head from where she lay beside her and looked into her face, then licked it gently and the feel of the rough tongue on her cheek and the rough fur under her stroking hand comforted them both. She was lucky. She had Sadie and Iolo and the folk in the cottages were inclined to be friendly to her. She had Sal, who was a link to Danny, but who had Danny got to help him through . . .

Suddenly a face imprinted itself on the darkness beyond the window and though she had really not looked at it, for her whole being had been concentrated on her brother, it came to her now. A sad, deeply lined face but with kindly eyes and a lift to the corners of the mouth which told of a nature that was ready to smile on others. It was the elderly man. The one who had shared Danny's cell. The gentleman, for he was that, who had kept Danny's spirits from flagging during the months they awaited trial. He was to sail to the far side of the world with Danny and perhaps, with him beside him, Danny would have a friend to get him through. The thought comforted her and she fell asleep.

IO

She awakened as the misted orb of the sun rose in a potpourri of peach and orange, pale green and daffodil yellow over Arthur's Pike on the eastern side of the lake. The summer dawn came early, painting golden shadows overlapping lazily with rippling apricot across the lake, the tiny breeze washing the waters against the shore. The sky was the palest blue, pricked here and there by a star and by the thin sickle of the fading moon, no bigger than the crescent of a baby's fingernail. A dog fox, making its way home, barked shortly and Sal lifted her head while in the trees an early bird twittered sleepily.

She lay for a while, watching the morning brighten through the open window, watching the breeze lift the curtains and knew that she had returned from that place where she had drifted for so long. The place where no effort had been required, where nothing had changed from one day to the next. She had existed where it had been enough to be warm, to be sheltered and fed, waiting for the day when Danny would be returned to her, but it had not happened and now that day was to be so far off she must wake, delay no longer since there was much to be done.

She was up even before Iolo who was one of the early risers at Longlake Edge, the cowshed at the back of the stables his destination. He would wear a greasy hat that he pressed well into the side of the cow, Daisy or Clover or Buttercup – avoiding Clover's tail with which she liked to give him a clout – while his hard hands brought forth milk in steady streams, as once his father had done. The milk was used only for the household's consumption but it was his job to deliver it at the back kitchen door before seven. Mr Cameron insisted upon perfect cleanliness, even in the cowshed and it was another part of Iolo's job to keep it so. The animals had to be taken to the field where they fed all day on rich, clover-stitched grass and then brought back for their evening milking. In between he turned out the cowshed then put his hand to any labour that needed doing, in the stable yard, the kitchen garden, the forge, Blacky's carpenter shop or even a bit of dry-stone walling. Since Briony had moved into Sadie's cottage he had slept on a truckle bed in the kitchen but he was never there when Sadie and Briony started their day.

She wore a plain grey cotton dress, the skirt just touching her instep, the sleeves rolled up to her elbow, the top button of the bodice undone, for already it promised to be a hot day. Sadie snored musically in her bed as she tiptoed past her door. Iolo's mother was glad, Briony thought, of the rest Mr Cameron had insisted upon. Sadie had borne the burden of Briony's fear and dread, her grief for her mother and her loneliness for Danny for the past seven months, and she was no longer a young woman. She was strong, reliable, used to working hard, inclined to be affectionate and good-humoured but Briony's troubles had weighed heavily on her and she deserved a release from them now that the trial was over, and she needed this rest before she resumed her duties. No doubt Miss Cameron would be fuming up at the big house at the absence of two of her laundry-maids, for despite the shadowed world Briony had existed in ever since Danny was hauled off to gaol she was aware that Mr Cameron's sister was not the lady bountiful she thought herself to be.

Making no sound, she crept past the truckle bed where Iolo slept. He was on his stomach, his brown, curly head resting on his forearm which was flung up on his pillow. It had been a warm night, the fire was still smouldering ready to be brought back to life by Sadie's bellows, and the bedcovers had slipped down to his buttocks. For a moment she was surprisingly diverted by the broadness of his naked muscled back, the shapeliness of his waist and the cleft where his buttocks began. He was a good-looking young man and she had seen the way the housemaids eyed him, giggling together, especially Minnie the kitchen-maid who was herself a pretty girl. But her interest did not last long as, surprising her, a pair of luminous amber eyes surrounded by long brown lashes swam into her vision and a stern face frowned in disapproval. Strangely the image gladdened and strengthened her, but then hadn't he always had this effect on her? Hadn't he always been able to take away her fear and desolation, ever since that day he had come into the mill yard and stopped her father from beating Danny? She would always be grateful to him for that and for what he had tried to do since.

Putting him from her mind, she turned away and bending to pick up her clogs which she had left by the door she called Sal to her with a movement of her hand. Quietly she lifted the latch and let herself out into the dewy morning. There was nobody about except the tabby who had been on night business of her own and was waiting on Sadie's doorstep.

Despite the weight of sadness that still bore her down and the dreadful certainty that it would never leave her, not until Danny was returned to her, she lifted her head and sniffed deeply, taking pleasure from the fragrance of the flowers along the lane. The air, though warm, was sweet and swallows swooped in elegant flight above the roofs of the cottages. She knew they nested in the rafters of Mr Cameron's barn and she stood for a moment and listened to their churring trill, amazing herself that she could derive pleasure so soon after what had happened only a few days ago. Still, she must get on, get on to this new beginning that was to be her future until Danny came home.

There were a few primroses in the shade of the dry-stone wall and a clump or two of stitchwort which was beginning to fade in the dry ditch to the side of the lane. Wild columbines were coming into their summer beauty, clustered with blue speedwell, the red of campion and the yellow of buttercups, a tumbled ribbon of colours reaching for the sunlight. Sal sniffed her way among them, looking for a likely place to relieve herself, then did it delicately at the corner of Clem Hodgson's wall as though she knew he had no care for such an impertinence.

At the bottom of the lane she turned left away from the lake, moving off the track and into the bit of woodland. She trudged slowly across the mossy carpet under the dense summer canopy. The glades were cool, restful, but though she had steeled herself for this moment her clogged feet became hesitant and Sal, who had been investigating familiar scents along the path, crept close to the hem of her skirt, looking up anxiously at her.

"I know, girl, I know," Briony murmured to her, stopping for a moment to rest her hand on the dog's troubled head, "but it has to be done. There's only you and me now so we must do it together. It will get easier with time."

The mill had a lost and deserted look about it. The grass had grown through the cobbles in the yard and was waist-high against the windows which were dirty and laced with cobwebs. Mr Cameron had done all that was necessary in clearing the wheat, oats and animal feed that had been awaiting the miller's attention on the day he died, contacting the farmers and villagers to whom it belonged, arranging to have it picked up. The rickety cart had been dragged into the barn and the horse which pulled it put to graze in the meadow with his own horses where it had grown fat and sturdy. The hens had been disposed of, she didn't know where. There would probably be vegetables thriving in the fields but she would look at those later. First she must pluck up her failing courage and enter the building where her father had killed her mother and where her brother, in trying to protect her, had killed her father. She was vaguely aware of having heard murmured remarks about "cleaning up" and though she had turned away from the very thought, she knew what it had meant. She prayed that it had been done. She imagined it would have been, for Mr Cameron was a thorough gentleman who allowed no essentials to be overlooked. He would have seen to it all, she was certain, then locked the door, pocketed the key and ridden away with his duty done. It seemed no one had been near since.

She found the spare key on a hook just inside the barn door where it had always been kept and with Sal's nose attached to her heel, or so it seemed, she crept quietly across the yard to the front door, so quietly it was as if she were afraid to disturb those who had died here. Not her gentle mother, for her ghost would be a sweet and patient one, a threat to no one, but what of her father? Well, damn him to hell and back, which was surely where he belonged. She was not going to allow him to frighten her again!

She drew a deep breath, straightened her back, lifted her head, turned the key in the lock and for the first time in eight months stepped over the threshwood of her old home. Sal hung back, one paw raised, her short tail as far between her legs as its length allowed. She whined disconsolately, the expression on her face almost human in its anxiety, then, though she had been taught to be timid by Jethro Marsden, she took courage from Briony and followed her into the house.

The pale morning sunlight did its best to gain entrance through the small mullioned windows of the kitchen, emphasising the dust that had gathered over every piece of furniture.

Someone had evidently done their best to clean up what had been the last meal her family had eaten together, putting the frying pan back on a hook but not the one where her mother had been accustomed to hang it. The plates and cups and spoons, four of each, had been washed and left on the table, and the bench where she and Danny had sat to eat had been pushed neatly underneath. On the bare wall there were no pictures, only a sampler worked by her mother when she was a girl. "God seeth thee", it said, which Briony doubted for surely He would not have allowed Jethro Marsdsen to be so evil. Beneath it was her mother's name: Emily Middleton. The date stitched on it was 1813.

The ashes had not been cleared from the hearth though they had been brushed back beneath the iron bars of the fire-grate, and her father's chair, the most comfortable, had had its cushions plumped up as though even in death he was believed to be important.

Trailing her fingers across the table, she moved into the scullery where again there had been an attempt by someone to clean the place up a bit. Sal followed close to her skirt and when she opened the back door skittered through it and out to the edge of the mill pond. The water was still, as was the wheel. She stood for a moment in the shade cast by the mill house and in her mind's eye she saw Danny romping for a moment with Sal. Throwing a piece of stick for the dog to fetch, wondering as she had not done then – when she was a child – at the resilience and bravery of the boy Danny had been.

But this would do no good, she thought resolutely. She must get on, go over the mill, the bagging and drive floor, the stone floor, the top storey, see what needed doing and start on the fearsome task ahead of her. Moving back into the kitchen she climbed the two sets of stairs to the bedroom her mother had shared with her father. The bed had been stripped and when she opened the carved oak press her mother had brought as a bride from Penrith she saw that the bedding had been scrupulously laundered, probably by Sadie, scattered with lavender and folded neatly into the chest along with her mother's beautifully stitched quilt.

Carefully she lifted the bedding out of the chest and placed it on the bed, then, kneeling in the dust, she opened the lid of the box that was hidden at the bottom, a tin box with the picture of a castle on it, and looked inside. She considered its contents, her face expressionless, then closed the lid, returned the bedding on top of it and lowered the lid of the chest. She remained kneeling for a minute or two as though in prayer then got to her feet and looked about her.

On the wall were wooden pegs on which her mother's hodden-grey winter cloak hung. Pressing her face in its folds she smelled the aroma of herbs and fresh bread, of clean linen and lavender, smells that were associated with the work her mother had done unremittingly in the service of her family. There was an old bonnet but every trace of her father, his clothing, his boots, his wide-brimmed hat had all been removed. On the wide windowsill was a flowered earthenware ewer and jug, the roses painted crudely, but she knew it had been dear to her mother, and beside the bed on the side where her mother had slept was a small table. On the table lay her mother's Bible. Despite all that had been done to her, the suffering she had known for years at the hands of her vicious husband, she had still believed in God and had often read to them and had them read to her from the good book.

The memory scalded her. She wanted to weep then but that would not do. Not now. She had things to attend to, plans to make and her mother knew, wherever she was, that her daughter grieved for her and that tears were not needed.

Sal had not come upstairs with her. The habit of a lifetime

ingrained in her while Jethro had been alive would not allow her to ascend the stairs and she had lain down, shivering slightly, at their foot.

"I won't be long, Sal," Briony had told her when all her attempts to get the bitch to follow her had failed. When Sal began to bark, a loud, defiant bark that told Briony she was very afraid, she flew down the stairs to see what was wrong. A rat, perhaps, or something in the undergrowth that was crowding up to the back door which she had left open.

For a moment her own heart lunged, then rose and began to beat frantically, for standing in the yard were two figures, a man and a woman, both of them tall, evidently just come from the barn, the door of which was now wide open. Sal continued to bark hysterically, then ran back to Briony and leaned against her as though her store of courage was suddenly used up.

The woman put out a trembling hand, a beseeching hand and on her face was an expression of dread, of shock and dismay, and yet across her plain features lay something that might have been hope. The man, or youth, was broad-shouldered, well made, or might have been if he had not looked as though he had not had a square meal for months. His clothes, a crumpled jacket, a pair of corduroy breeches and a grey flannel shirt whose frayed cuffs stuck out below the sleeves of his jacket, hung on him and the wide-awake hat, evidently not his, sat on his ears looking as though it might slip down over his eyes but for their support. The young woman was not much better, wearing a much mended dress too short in the skirt, a bonnet of cotton and big black boots very much the worse for wear.

"Oh, dear Lord," the woman whispered, taking the man's hand between her own and Briony noticed they were none too clean. "I'm so sorry, Miss Marsden. We did not mean to alarm you but we thought the place was empty, you see. We were told you were living elsewhere. Not that that is any excuse but . . . well, we were coming to see you and last night we were so tired and the barn was . . . Do forgive us." She smiled hesitantly and the young man, taking his cue from her, did the same.

Briony put her hand on Sal's head and at once the dog stopped her racket. In fact she began to wag her tail and with an aplomb that amazed Briony she strolled across the yard and pushed her nose into the youth's hand. At once he grinned and hunkered down, stroking the dog's head and pulling her ears.

"Good doggy," he said, "good doggy." Sal was in heaven and Briony stared in wonder, for not since Danny had gone away had Sal shown the slightest interest in anyone, not even Iolo who was willing to make a fuss of her.

"I'm sorry but . . ." she stammered and though she had been badly startled by their appearance she found that they were vaguely familiar to her. She had seen them somewhere but for the life of her she could not have said where.

"Please, Miss Marsden," the woman hastened to add, taking another hesitant step forward, a step that was not threatening. The man, or over-large boy, as he appeared to be, was still squatting down with Sal who had rolled on to her back so that he might tickle her belly. "Don't be afraid. I appreciate that we are trespassing on your property but . . . well, we could think of nowhere else to go. Our home is – was – in Keswick but since Father was taken we have lived in lodgings in Carlisle. I worked in . . ." She shook her head. "It really does not matter but now . . ." Her voice petered out sadly and she lowered her gaze to the ground. Briony thought she might begin to weep but she looked up again bravely and tried her best to smile.

Her property! Yes, she supposed it was her property until Danny came home. The thought uplifted her and she studied the girl and it was then that she recognised her. She saw the cell where Danny and the old man had languished through so many months and, on several occasions she remembered that there had been two visitors, two young people, and though she had taken little interest in their appearance she suddenly realised that these two were they. The old man's children. The old man whose name had been at the top of the list on the day of the trial. Regina versus Jenkins. Fraud!

Recognition and understanding must have shown in her face, for the girl sighed sadly. "Yes, our name is Jenkins and Edwin Jenkins was our father. Still is, of course," she added bravely, "and we are hoping that . . . with your brother to be his friend he might survive. We don't expect to see him again but at least with Daniel beside him he might find peace of sorts. We know nothing of the penal colony but he and Daniel seemed to take to one another. Oh, Lord, Miss Marsden, please forgive me but . . ." With a grace that belied her height and breadth she sank to her knees, bowed her head and this time allowed the tears to come.

Briony sprang forward and so did the youth, both of them lifting the weeping girl, who had evidently come to the end of her strength, to her feet, their arms about her.

"Lizzie, don't cry," the boy begged her. "You've still got Thomas. Thomas is here, Lizzie." And to Briony's amazement he also began to cry, blubbering like a naughty schoolboy, and at once Lizzie took a deep breath, wiped her hand across her wet face and turned to him, taking his hands and kissing his cheek. She had to stretch up to do so.

"I know, Thomas, I know. Don't cry, there's a good lad. Now go and play with the doggy" – she turned enquiringly to Briony who supplied her with Sal's name – "with Sal, while I talk to Miss Marsden."

They sat at the table in the kitchen, the tragedy they shared drawing them together as no other circumstance could. There was a spoonful or two in Emily's tea caddy and some sugar in a tin above the mantel, but no milk, of course. They did not speak while Briony brewed the tea but when they were both seated, their hands cupped round the welcome mugs, one being received by Thomas at the back door, they studied one another, taking stock, liking what they saw and Lizzie Jenkins began to speak.

"I know your brother's story since my father told me about what had happened. I'm so sorry for your loss. I know your brother loved you and your mother and what your father did to you was unforgivable."

Briony felt the first pinprick of shame pierce her, for in all the time she had sat with Danny she had never once enquired about the family of the man who had shared his cell. This girl's father had divulged to her the horror that had befallen the Marsden family but Briony, in her deep self-absorption, her desperate anguish over her mother's death and Danny's plight, had not returned that compassion as the father of this girl, and this girl herself, had.

"Your father . . . ?"

"My father was a clerk in an accountant's office and when my mother fell ill he took money, manipulated the account books so that it was not noticed. We were poor and the doctors bills were . . . ." She shuddered and the tea in her mug spilled over a little on to the table. "My mother died and the falsification in the books was discovered and my father was arrested."

She was calm now, her eyes looking over Briony's shoulder into the calamity that had overtaken them. "And there was Thomas, you see. He is still a child though he is eighteen and no one will employ him. Unless I am with him he is afraid, so I have to take him everywhere I go. It was difficult during my father's time in gaol but we managed. Now we are destitute so I need to work. A job where Thomas can be by my side. Though he is only a boy in his head he is enormously strong. As I am. With me to tell him what must be done he . . . oh, Miss Marsden, I'm sure we could be of great help to you." Her gaze returned to Briony and she spoke passionately now, the monotone of her voice rising to a spirited, hopeful crescendo. "We – my father and I – heard you telling your brother that you would keep it all together for him, his mill, I mean, until his return and we are here to help you. And ourselves, naturally. We need no wages, just a roof over our head, food, safety for Thomas. We know nothing of milling, but you do. With your experience and brain and mine and Thomas's strength, surely . . . ?"

Again as it had done before her voice petered out and she hung her head in desolation. "I know it's asking a lot but . . ."

"Miss Jenkins."

"Lizzie, please."

"Lizzie. Have you any idea what your arrival means to me? Have you? I was determined, *am* determined to get the mill working again but quite simply I had no notion where to start. I had the vague idea that Mr Cameron – that's the gentleman who brought me to the trial – might advise me, help me to look for a strong man to do the lifting, the heavy work but now . . ."

Lizzie Jenkins raised her head and the pale neutral of her grey eyes had turned to a brilliance which lit her plain face and gave it a beauty that was almost mystical. Her features were very ordinary. She had a wide mouth, full and pink, and good teeth. Her hair, uncovered when she removed her drab bonnet, was a nondescript brown, dragged back into a heavy chignon, but it was her eyes that revealed her inner strength. She was probably five feet ten or eleven, with wide shoulders, a full breast and good hips, a womanly woman, and at least a good six inches taller than Briony.

"Miss Marsden . . ."

"Briony."

"Briony, do you mean . . . ?"

"I do. I had begun to disbelieve that God existed, that if He did he had deserted me and my family but surely He must have sent you and your brother to me this day. I never thought . . ."

"Neither did I."

"To find exactly the right people on the very day . . ."

"I know, I know. When we were walking I kept saying to Thomas that we'd be all right when we got here but it was to make him feel better. I had no real hope."

"You walked! You walked from Carlisle?"

Lizzie lifted her head and grinned, and her whole face creased into an expression that was lovely to see, revealing the humour that had been buried by what had happened to her family. "I told you we were strong."

"You must be famished."

"Well . . . well, yes, we are a bit."

Briony jumped to her feet and whirled around as though searching for something with which to feed this marvellous young woman, a crust, anything, but of course there was nothing. But she knew where there was food and she knew, thanks to Jethro Marsden, she could pay for it.

"Call Thomas and let's go to Sadie's." She was ready to laugh and cry at the same time and so, it seemed, was Lizzie.

"To Sadie's?"

"Yes, she'll feed us, and I must tell her what we mean to do. She won't be pleased."

And she knew someone else who would not be pleased, wondering as the thought came to her why she should think so!

11

She was right. He was not pleased. In fact the force of his anger astonished and frightened her, so much so that she stammered and stuttered as she did her best to explain what she had planned.

They were in his study at Longlake Edge into which the amazed Gladys had shown her, Gladys not knowing whether to ask her what the dickens she thought was doing, demanding to see the master, the cheek of it, or leave her on the back step while she ran to Mrs Foster to seek her advice. Maidservants didn't speak to the master of the house. The correct procedure, if she had to address someone in authority, was to approach the mistress, who was, of course, *Miss* Cameron, but no, the cheeky madam asked for *Mr* Cameron.

"You'd best wait here," Gladys sniffed, indicating a spot by the kitchen door while Mrs Foster, Martha, Daphne, Minnie and Mabel stared, open-mouthed, their hands stilled, the tasks they had been performing left untended. Only Dicky, who had been sharpening the knives in the scullery, gave her a smile. They had all heard, naturally, that her brother had been shipped to the penal colony at Botany Bay, not awfully certain they even knew where that was, and they were sorry for her. She'd worked like a good 'un in the laundry for the past six or seven months and had sat beside them at mealtimes but she'd had little to say for herself. She and Sadie had, amazingly, been given a few days off, leaving only Jenny Turnberry in the laundry, which had meant extra work for Minnie and Mabel since the mistress, who had been furious and determined to take it out on someone, had whipped them away from their kitchen duties and left Mrs Foster short-handed. Now, here she was, the girl whose brother had killed her father, having the nerve to ask to see the master *privately*! That's what she'd said. Privately. They'd have given a week's wages to know what it was all about! And to top it all when she had been shown into the study, the master had rung the bell and ordered *coffee* just as though she were a *proper* caller.

He had actually laughed when she told him what she intended. She'd never seen him laugh before. Smile, yes, a smile that had altered him almost beyond recognition, lighting his face, lifting it from its normal sombre graveness, revealing his good, strong, white teeth, curling his lips, crinkling his eyes, warming them from a dark brown to the richness of a polished chestnut. But his laughter was astonishing. She was fascinated and quite, for the moment, diverted from the purpose of her visit. It came out of him in a shout of amusement as if he had never heard anything quite so hilarious in his life, then, as suddenly as it had come, it vanished, and his eyebrows dipped menacingly.

"Really, it's out of the question, surely you can see that. How on earth do you expect to do the work, the *physical* work your father did? It needs a strong man to shift the sacks and—"

"I know that and that's why I'm to employ—"

"And the farmers won't like it. A woman in a man's job? Ridiculous. And the physical side to the business of milling is not all. There are accounts, money to be handled . . ."

"I can count and my father didn't keep—"

"No, Briony, it really won't do. I thought you would have had more sense than to think that you could keep the place going until Danny comes home. Oh, yes, I heard you promise him that but I thought—"

"You thought I was just saying it to make him feel better?" Something inside her was beginning to clench into a tight ball which so far she could not recognise. At the start of the ... well, she supposed she should call it an interview, she had thought she would be overwhelmed by the sheer magnificence of this house, the hall through which Gladys led her, the sweep of the graceful staircase which flowed up to the bedrooms, the highly polished furniture, the sonorous tick of the tall clock which chimed as she passed it and then this room where Mr Cameron managed his business affairs. Where he retreated for privacy and relaxation.

Two walls were lined with bookshelves containing what must be hundreds of books. The third wall was dominated by an enormous fireplace and above it was a gilt-edged mirror which reached the high ceiling. There were guns in a case, fishing rods leaning in a corner, a decanter cabinet standing on a table, a rich Turkey carpet on the floor, and in the centre of the room looking towards the window and the exquisite picture of the garden it framed was a large desk littered with papers, pens and inkstands. There were sporting prints on the walls wherever there was a space. The wide windows looked out on to the long stretch of immaculate lawn, acres of it with terraces dug out of the sloping land to the edge of the lake, beds filled with flowers, roses, sweet william, peonies and pinks, wallflowers and Canterbury bells all arranged so that the tallest made a frame for those at the front of the well-tended beds. There was an arbour at the side of the house – she had seen it – at this time of the year a mass of honeysuckle and climbing roses, paved areas cut out where wooden seats were placed so that one might sit and feast one's eyes on the beauty of the lake, with stone steps leading here and there right down to the water. It was quite, quite breathtaking, that panorama beyond the window and the lake itself on which several small sailing boats skimmed like dragonflies about to take wing.

The room was uniquely masculine, as might be expected, and Briony suspected that it was the only room in the house, with perhaps the exception of this man's bedroom, that was totally without the influence of his sister. On the rug before the unlit fire lay the big, black labrador that had been with him the day he had accosted her father. His tail moved slowly when she entered and his eye winked as he studied her but he did not get up.

Mr Cameron waved a dismissive hand and the knot inside Briony tightened further. "I suppose I did, and believe me if I thought there was any way it could be done I would help. I suppose, if you didn't want to sell the business, I could put in a man, rent it to him for a period of, say, seven years, until your brother returns." Though privately Chad Cameron thought there was little likelihood of that. From what he had heard of the penal practices very few felons survived the harshness, the climate, the brutality of the system, let alone returned to their homes. They were there not just to help carve out a colony for the enterprising English but to be punished for their crimes and the lad would not be treated gently.

He studied the straight-backed figure of the girl who sat on the opposite side of his desk. The sun shone through the window and though she wore the rather fetching small bonnet he had bought her for her mother's funeral, curly wisps of her hair had escaped at the back and about her ears and the bright light burnished the rich brown to a shade almost coppery. She had sipped her coffee politely but now she leaned forward and put the cup and saucer on his desk. Her wrist was narrow, the features of her pointed face fragile, her throat slender, her shoulders delicate and she looked as vulnerable as a child, which she wasn't. The lift of her budding breast testified to that. He almost laughed again, ready to curve his mouth in a smile at the absurdity of this lovely creature working in her brother's mill and when she exploded the dog lifted his large head and stared at her and his master almost fell off his chair.

She had not known she possessed a temper! It had never advertised itself when her father was alive. It would have been more than her life was worth to show spirit so, she assumed, she had kept it on a tight rein, so tight it had never escaped. Now it did.

"How dare you! How dare you condescend to tell me what I am to do with my brother's property. You have no right. None at all. I am answerable to no one and if I wish to set up in business then I shall do so. *You* will sell it. *You* will rent it to a suitable tenant just as though the mill belonged not to Danny, but to Chad Cameron."

He did not correct her. If she knew that the mill was her own, to do with as she wished, there would be no curbing her madcap scheme.

She stood up and so did the dog and, when he had recovered his breath, so did Chad Cameron though he was not sure what he was to do. She began to swirl about the room, her skirt brushing the dog's nose and he backed up and sneezed. She was so fierce, so furious and the funny thing was Chad was delighted. Not that she should be angry with him but that her spirit, that lovely shining spirit she had shown him a time or two with her smile when he had first noticed her, was not broken. It was totally inappropriate that she should run the mill, of course, and he would point it out to her shortly but really, her shining violet-blue eyes, the flush in her cheek, the snap in her voice was sheer joy. God, he felt he could reach out for her and swing her round the room in a polka, laughing like a schoolboy, which was sheer bloody foolishness since he was a man of thirty and she was no more than a young girl. But a young girl who had come to this ridiculous decision and must be stopped, persuaded – that was the word he must use, the method he must use to end this nonsense. Run the mill! Take over the business where her father had left off when her brother had killed him! She must be made to see that her place was not at the mill but . . . but . . . and that was where his mind ran into a blank wall, for where *was* her place? What was she to do? She had worked in his laundry for the past seven or eight months and he had not liked that, he was not sure why; but if not back in the laundry where she was at least under the kindly authority of Mrs Evans, then where? She could read and write as well as his own sister. He knew because she had borrowed books he had picked from his shelves when he found her reading a penny novelette belonging to Cook, and her vocabulary was wider than Sarah's despite her years with the governess his parents had employed. She was comely and had what he could only call *breeding* though where it came from he couldn't imagine. So what was her future? Dear Lord, he didn't know, but one thing he was sure of and that was it would not be running the damn mill at Moorend.

He was just about to tell her so, to repeat what he had already said, sitting down behind his desk and indicating that she was to be seated, when she swung round and began to make her way to the door.

He watched her, his mouth open, looking foolish, he knew, and he did not like it.

"Briony . . . Miss Marsden, may I ask where you think you're going? This has to be decided . . ."

She flung open the door. "It has already been decided, Mr Cameron. I was merely doing you the courtesy of informing you of my plans but you seem disinclined to listen so I will take my leave and say no more except that I shall always be grateful for what you did for my brother."

God's teeth, what had she been reading, he had time to

think. She spoke like a lady. At least the words were those of an educated woman though her voice still contained the sounds of the Cumberland where she had been born and reared. Different districts spoke in different tongues. The servants and those of the lower orders spoke in the old dialects of Cumberland to one another but they invariably had to "translate" it for foreigners. The accent of the dales of the Lake counties was soft while out on the west coast it was harsh, but Briony Marsden had that soft slur which was attractive but sounded unusual in the wording and the correct grammar she used.

The kitchen servants, crouched behind the half-open door, turned to look at one another in amazement and Minnie whispered to Mabel it was a good job mistress wasn't in before pressing her ear more eagerly to the door.

"Briony, will you stop this nonsense and come back. We will discuss this sensibly and between us I'm sure we will find a solution that will—"

"There is no solution to find, Mr Cameron." She stood with her back to him, half in and half out of the room. "I have made my mind up and nothing you say will change it. I told you when Danny was sentenced – well, I told Danny – that I would run the mill until he returned and that is what I mean to do. I have employed two people."

"What?" He stood up and his voice thundered round the study, escaping along the hallway so that the maidservants felt inclined to scuttle back to their work. In fact Minnie, being the youngest, did so, attacking the pile of potatoes she had been peeling with renewed vigour.

"I have found two people. A man and a woman who are to work for me."

"What did you say?"

"I believe you heard me. A strong young man—"

"A strong young man?" He advanced towards her with

every intention of dragging her back into the room, it seemed, to where he could keep a firm grip on her madness, her future and anything else to which he felt entitled. The thing was that for so long he had gently led her, advised her, arranged her life so that she was safe and sheltered. He had taken care of her, protected her interests and her brother's and in the process had become accustomed to her dependency on him, to her gratitude, and here she was telling him that she no longer needed it, or him. She was to be independent, which was absolutely ludicrous, a little bit of a thing like her, and when he had finished with her she would realise how very foolish this all was.

"A strong young man and his sister," she went on.

"His sister? I can't believe that you would employ total strangers."

"They are not strangers. You have met them. They are the children of the man who was in prison with Danny. They have nowhere else to go and so they walked from Carlisle."

"And you are to take them in, is that it? I presume they are conversant with the running of a water mill." He had not meant his voice to sound so sarcastic but that was the way it came out and he was not sorry. He ran his hands through his hair in a distracted manner, which was not at all like him but he was disturbed to such an extent his normal grave and urbane demeanour had totally forsaken him.

She whirled to face him. "No, they are not but I am, Mr Cameron. My father saw to that and though he did it with harshness he taught me well, something . . . the only thing I have to thank him for. He was a hard taskmaster but it made me what I am. Lizzie and Thomas Jenkins will live with me at the mill and I will teach them what my father taught me. I don't know what the farmers and those who brought their grain to Moorend will think of a woman running the business but I imagine they will be glad to relinquish that tramp to Little

Salkeld. I felt it only polite to let you know that I shall no longer be in your employ and thank you for what you tried to do for Danny. I shall—"

"Money, Miss Marsden." His voice was harsh, angry, and she was again surprised by it. "I take it you realise that money will be needed to start—"

"I have money, Mr Cameron. My father was kind enough to leave his savings hidden at the mill, which, though I know they legally belong to Danny, I shall keep in trust for him, with his mill. The money will get me started and keep us until the work comes back. Now, I think that's all for the moment so I'll bid you good-day."

Before he could utter another word she closed the door quietly behind her, leaving him to sink back in his chair, his normally amber-tinted face pale and strained. There was a look about his mouth and in his eyes which suggested he was in wild pain and was furious at feeling it which was hard to understand. He was a strong man and yet he felt vulnerable, weakened by a slip of a girl; no, she was a woman now. Even as he leaned back in his chair something inside him began to shiver, to tremble and to his own consternation he began to laugh, to laugh so loudly they heard him in the kitchen. She, the miller's daughter, had not come back through the kitchen but, amazingly, had let herself out of the front door and was, the servants presumed, striding down the front drive towards the gate and the lane that led to the mill, and now here was the master laughing his head off.

He laughed until he felt tears come to his eyes and as suddenly as his laughter had begun it stopped and his own damnation struck him with the force of a sledgehammer.

He loved her! He wanted her for his own! He had been fighting it for months now, telling himself she was too young, or he was too old. That she was not of his class, that he was merely sorry for her, poor child, but she was not a child, she was a woman, with a woman's mind and a woman's body, slender as it was. She was to be independent, so she said, but even as the laughter died in him something else took its place and a certain peace invaded him.

He sat back in his chair, steepling his hands and putting his fingers to his lips. His eyes stared unseeingly through the window and down the garden to the lake. They were narrowed, the heavy lids giving him a deceptively sleepy look but the emotion inside him was far from sleepy. He knew what he wanted. He had accepted it and with acceptance had come the knowledge of what he meant to do.

There was much the same reaction at Sadie's cottage. Sadie was enjoying these few days that Mr Cameron had so generously allowed them but she and Briony must get back to their work tomorrow. Jenny had been in complaining of the lackadaisical way in which the kitchen-maids were helping out, if you could call it that, she said, for neither of them knew how to mangle, let alone iron even the simplest garment. Them ruffles on the master's shirt were a right bugger to do and – wistfully – when did Sadie think she'd be back?

Jenny had gone, thank the dear Lord, or it would have been all over the county by nightfall, and so had the lass and her half-witted but gentle brother. Sadie had fed them with generous portions of creamy porridge, bacon, eggs and fried bread with steaming cups of hot, sweet tea. They'd wolfed it down, the lass casting apologetic looks at Sadie as if to say how sorry she was to be so greedy and then the pair of them, with polite words of thanks, had simply disappeared. Now, here was *her* lass saying the daftest things and at first Sadie couldn't believe it. She'd sat there, the tabby on her lap, her face as white and shiny as candle wax, her hand smoothing the rich black coat of the animal until, with an oath which her Dai would not have believed her capable of, she'd sprung to her feet, toppling the cat almost into the small fire.

"Yer what," she shrieked, "yer goin' ter do what?"

"I think you heard me, Sadie. I'm going to open the mill again. Lizzie and Thomas will help me. Well, you saw the size of Thomas so with their—"

"Over my dead body. A slip of a girl like you, an' all on yer own."

Briony sighed patiently. "I won't be on my own, Sadie. Lizzie and Thomas will be there and with my experience and their strength we shall manage very nicely until Danny comes home."

"Don't talk soft, girl. Yer'd think Danny'd gone down ter Lancaster or somewhere and'd be 'ome by't weekend. Seven years, lass. 'E'll be gone seven years. 'Ow yer goin' ter manage fer seven years? Yer only sixteen."

"I shall be seventeen in October and I'm quite capable of making my own decision about what—"

"Don't you get a cob on wi' me, my lass. 'Oo's had the lookin' after yer these last months an' seen what it did to yer. Yer not able to see ter thissen, never mind run the mill, an' what these folks are ter do – this Lizzie an' Thomas – oh, aye, I know 'oo they are an' I'm sorry for 'em an' for their pa, but that don't mean you 'ave ter tekk 'em up. Let 'em find their own way, just as you 'ave to."

"That's just what I intend doing, Sadie, don't you see. Ever since I could walk almost, I have worked in the mill. Though my father didn't consciously teach me the business, I learned it nevertheless and though I can't do the heavy work that he and Danny did, Thomas can. I intend looking for a strong boy to help him. Perhaps you might know of someone. And with Lizzie to make it all . . . all, well, proper, I intend to build up the business until it is as prosperous as in my father's day. More so, in fact."

"Never you mind about another strong boy, lady. Yer not doin' it an' that's my last word." Sadie's face had turned a mottled purple and she seemed to sag and at once Briony was across the room, gently pushing her into her chair where, for a moment, she was convinced she was about to weep. She put her arm about her shoulders and her cheek on Sadie's greying hair, then moved to sink down at her knee, taking her hands which were twisting in her apron.

"I must do it, Sadie, don't you see? I promised Danny." She looked up pleadingly into Sadie's agitated face.

"Yer reckon lad'll be back then?" Sadie's voice was harsh and Briony reared back, then, understanding the pain of what Sadie saw as her own desertion, she reached up, put her arms about her and kissed Sadie's cheek.

"Sadie, you know what you mean to me, don't you. I . . . I love you. You have become a mother to me and I wouldn't hurt you for the world but this is what I have to do. Not just for Danny but for myself. I'm not cut out to work in a laundry for the rest of my life."

"Like me, yer mean?" Sadie sniffed but her face had returned to its normal colour and her expression had softened. "What's up wi't laundry?"

"I . . . well, it doesn't *challenge* me."

"What the 'eck's that supposed ter mean?" Though she knew full well. The lass could write and read and do sums. She had a thinking brain, she'd proved that time and time again and just look what she'd gone through yet she hadn't gone under as many might. That brother of hers hadn't deserved the sentence they'd given him and she didn't deserve the hard row she'd have to hoe to hold on to what was rightfully theirs. Hers and Danny's. But she'd damn well try. Sadie herself was right disappointed at the upset to all her own plans: she and Briony working side by side in the laundry; Iolo and Briony, thrown together in this cosy home Sadie had made, a match between them and, of course, the babies, the babies that Sadie longed for. She and Briony got on like a house on fire and to have her as a daughter-in-law would have been the fulfilment of all that Sadie had dreamed of. But still, it wasn't far to the mill and if Iolo could be given a shove here and there happen his courting of this lovely girl would continue. Not that it had really begun but Sadie knew what was in her lad's face every time it turned in Briony's direction.

"Well," she sighed, "I suppose I'll 'ave ter get used to it though what Mr Cameron's goin' ter say I shudder ter think."

"He's already said it." Briony planted another kiss on Sadie's cheek then rose to her feet.

"Yer've never told 'im already." Sadie was shocked.

"I thought I'd better get it over and done with. Lizzie and Thomas are already down at the mill arranging for somewhere for us to sleep."

"Eeh, lass, can yer not sleep 'ere?"

"I'm already putting Iolo out of his bed and—"

"'E doesn't mind." But Sadie knew she was beaten. She stood up and reached for the tea caddy on the shelf above the range. Again she sighed deeply. "Well, if yer've medd yer mind up there's no more ter be said. Come on, lass, let's have a drink o' tea."

12

Sadie had a saying she had brought from Lancashire, which her own mother had taught her. When a Lancashire house-wife gave her home a good scrubbing and scouring she called it "fettling". It was at such an occupation that Chad Cameron found Briony Marsden on the day he rode over to Moorend.

She had scoured the threshwood at the entrance to the kitchen. She had cleaned and polished every window in the building, black-leaded the grate and "turned out" the bedroom in which her mother and father had slept, and in another part of the mill Lizzie was similarly occupied. In the fields Thomas was hard at work clearing weeds and rescuing any vegetables – having been shown by Briony which was which – with Sal beside him. Sal had attached herself to Thomas and went everywhere with him, sleeping beside him in the same cupboard bed that had once been occupied by Danny. It was a tight squeeze but neither the youth nor the dog seemed to mind. The boy, as both Lizzie and Briony thought of him, was made up with the animal, and Sal, as though she had to have some male to whom she could give her devotion until her master returned, and sensing with that instinct animals have that Thomas was not quite as other men were, never left his side.

Lizzie, not having known either Emily or Jethro Marsden, and being the practical young woman she was, had suggested that she took over their bed while Briony, who could not face the prospect of sleeping in it, for the time being at least, again slept on the truckle bed tucked into a corner of a storeroom on the top floor. They meant to make two of the partitioned storerooms into extra bedrooms so that they might each have one but until the place had been fettled, with coats of whitewash applied to every wall, inside and out, they made do with the temporary arrangements. Later, Lizzie said sensibly, when the room shared by Briony's parents was refurnished Briony would settle in the bedroom which was the largest and therefore should be hers by right. New curtains and mattress and perhaps a pretty pine chest of drawers would transform the room. With a washstand on which to put her mother's ewer and basin, a pine wardrobe in which to hang her best outfit and the others which Lizzie optimistically forecast she would undoubtedly have, perhaps a rocker to place before the small fireplace, Lizzie was sure Briony would feel able to sleep in what Lizzie always called her mother's room. She never spoke of Jethro.

She had just filled her bucket with hot water from a kettle heated over the fire in the range and was carrying it, its weight dragging down her left side, towards the scullery whose stone-flagged floor she was about to scrub when there was a peremptory knock on the kitchen door, it opened and he walked in. Strode in was how she would have described it, with a certain arrogance she did not like. At once she put her hand to her hair which was tied up with a strip of cloth torn from an old apron she had found hanging behind the scullery door and from which curls escaped, drifting across her face and down her neck. Woman-like, and furious with herself, she was conscious of her appearance in the cotton skirt and bodice – the skirt too short and the bodice too tight – she had brought with her from her days in the laundry. He was, as usual, immaculate in a plum-coloured coat and dove-grey trousers, a white, artfully tucked and pleated shirt and a snowy cravat, perfectly ironed, and she had time to realise that Sadie must be back at work!

"Joe Blamire's wife told me I'd find you here," he said without preamble, eyeing her outfit and the heavy bucket she still held with great disapproval. "I see you have decided to ignore my advice on the matter of running the mill on your own."

"I am not alone," she managed to gasp, wondering why she felt so out of breath. "Lizzie is upstairs and Thomas is out in the field. They are both earning their keep."

"Are they indeed." He frowned, his eyebrows dipping ferociously. "And could you not put that bucket down. It's far too heavy for you to be—"

"I am about to scrub the scullery floor so how do you suggest I get the thing over there?"

"Couldn't this Lizzie person do the hard work, that's if you insist on this madness? You are not fitted—"

"Not fitted! Dear God, what do you imagine I did before my father died? Believe me, scrubbing a floor is child's play to—"

"I know that, damn you, but as I've said before there is no need for it. Oh, for God's sake put that bloody bucket down or am I to take it from you?"

Slowly she lowered the bucket of water to the floor, wiping her hands down her skirt. She watched him suspiciously, wonderingly, the expression on his face not only surprising her but filling her with alarm. He was so *angry* about something and what she herself was experiencing puzzled her.

"What is it you want, Mr Cameron?" she asked him quietly. "We had this discussion only the other day. I told you what I intended to do and you told me you thought it was madness. Despite that I am here making a start so why do you feel the need to . . . to . . ."

"Interfere?"

"Yes, I am hurting no one. I am not breaking the law. I must have something to occupy me until Danny returns and this is all I know how to do. I promised him that the mill will be here, a working mill, when he comes home and—"

"And so it will be," he interrupted with a fervour that was so unlike him her mouth dropped open in amazement. "Let me get a man in. I'm sure there would be many, experienced, strong, reliable, who would be glad of employment. There is no need for you to do this on your own."

"I have told you, I am not on my own. Lizzie and Thomas need work."

"They could still be found work, I don't know, somewhere. I would employ them. Perhaps the lad could remain here and—"

"He is not able to function without his sister. They cannot be separated."

It was his turn to be surprised. "Why not? He's a big enough chap. How old is he?"

"Eighteen; eighteen in age but his mind is younger."

"Younger! You mean he has not all his wits?"

"Yes."

"God's teeth, woman. You mean to tell me you are to work this mill with a woman and a half-wit?"

"Don't call him that. He is big and strong. He is capable of anything with his sister beside him. He is gentle, kind."

He turned from her in exasperation, pushing his hand through his hair, then whirled back so precipitously he almost knocked over a chair. He steadied it and himself, speaking slowly, doing his best to suppress a great need to tell her to behave herself and do as she was told. She was a woman and women should be guided by a man, though why he should think so was a mystery to him when he remembered his old granny. The last time he had seen the defiant young woman who glared at him from across the kitchen, though he had known then that it wasn't necessary since he'd made up his mind, he had decided to "sleep on it" as Granny Maggie used to say. He *had* slept on it and he was here just the same.

"Will you, please, give up this nonsense and allow me to find a man – on your behalf, of course," he added hastily, "a man of whom you approve and who will be in essence in *your* employ."

"And do what? Return to your laundry?" She lifted her head imperiously as though to say she was better than that and so he too believed.

"No, not the laundry." He regarded her almost coldly, his eyes steady, his mouth in a grim line.

"What then?" She clasped her hands in front of her and her chin rose even higher.

He had meant to tell her that he could buy the mill from her, giving her enough money to live without working. Instead, he found himself saying, "I wish you to become my wife."

The silence that followed was long and hollow, with echoes of his words slipping in and out of her head, confusing her and at the same time thudding deafeningly in her chest with what seemed to be delight! Her heart stopped beating, or so it seemed, and she thought she might stop breathing with the shock of it. Or she might start to laugh! To laugh at the staggering amazement of his words and at her own reaction to them. *Delight!* Did she mean that? Did he mean what he had said? Or did he mean it as a joke, a stupid and cruel joke? Surely he could not be serious; surely . . . Her mouth had dried up and she could not speak even if she had known what to say, how to answer him . . .

She put out a trembling hand and placed it on the back of the chair in which her father had once lounged, licking her lips, her face like paper, her eyes almost a blue black, and upstairs she heard a crash as though Lizzie, who was moving things about in the storerooms prior to giving the floors a good scrubbing, had dropped something.

He broke the silence. "I see you are somewhat . . . surprised. Yes, I can understand why," as she still did not speak. "But you must see that you cannot possibly work here, not as you mean to do. You say what else can you do so I have found you an . . . alternative."

"An alternative?" Her voice cracked and her hand clung to the back of the chair, for in truth she felt her knees buckle and was afraid she might fall.

"Briony, you are too . . . fine for this. I can look after you. As my wife you will be protected from . . . well, from all the hardships and troubles you have known in the past. You will be respected. You will be Mrs Chad Cameron and—"

"And what will you get, Mr Cameron?"

"You are a beautiful young woman, Briony, and a clever one. You will soon adapt to being my wife."

"You do not speak of love, Mr Cameron."

"Do you want me to?"

"No, not if it's not felt."

"Do you love me?"

She began to laugh then, a hysterical laughter, for inside her was an excitement, a knot of something pleasurable, something that made her want to sing, but as quickly as it came she quenched it, for really had she ever heard anything quite so ridiculous?

He watched her and the tiny bud of hope he had cherished as he saw the confusion in her face, shrivelled and died. He had thought that for a moment she might consider his mad proposal, which was how she would see it, as everyone in the district would see it. Not that he cared about them. He was too wealthy, too powerful to be affected by what people thought of him. His influence in the community would guarantee complete acceptance of whoever he chose as a wife. His many business interests would continue to flourish with or without their approval but it seemed it did not matter, for this lovely young girl considered the matter so comical, so ludicrous, she could not hide her vast amusement.

"I take it you do not like the idea so I'll bid you good-day," he said, turning away and putting out his hand, which he noticed was trembling, to the door latch.

"No, wait, please," Briony was amazed to hear herself say. She studied the strong curve of his back, the breadth of his shoulders, the lean hips and long legs in their perfectly fitting trousers. She noticed his heavy, chocolate-coloured hair was in need of a trim, for it hung over the collar of his coat. His boots were highly polished. Everything about him was fine and when he turned, his eyebrows raised enquiringly, she saw for the first time how very handsome he was.

"Yes?" He gave her a cool, appraising stare.

"Well . . ."

"Yes?"

"I'm . . . you've taken me by surprise. I . . ."

He smiled, a smile with no warmth in it for he knew that if he let her see a fraction of what was leaping and banging inside him she would be alarmed.

"Perhaps you would like time to think it over. I realise that this . . . this idea has come as a shock to you. I'm somewhat shocked myself." He allowed a ghost of a smile to lift the corners of his strong mouth. "But it seems to me to be an admirable solution for us both."

"For us both! What would it benefit you?" She moved towards the range and picking up the poker gave the fire a stir. Not that it needed it but it gave her something to do, something that would allow her to escape his keen gaze, his apparent indifference to her answer, and to calm the turmoil that raged inside her. He wanted, for some reason known only to himself, to marry her. To take her up to Longlake Edge and make her mistress there and the thought terrified and excited her equally. He was a kind man. His actions since Danny had been arrested proved that. A generous man, a wealthy man and . . . and a very attractive man. So why should he pick her? There must be a dozen young women of his own class who would give their souls to marry him and yet . . . Dear God, he wanted her.

"I asked you what you would get out of it. Will you answer me?"

He smiled then, a wide smile since he had his feelings well under control now. "I need a wife. A young wife who will . . . I beg your pardon if this offends you, but one who will give me children. My sister" – he paused – "my sister is . . . she is somewhat difficult to live with and I believe the small house at . . . the Dower House, she calls it grandly, will suit her admirably. As my wife you would be an asset—"

"I am a miller's daughter. The sister of a man transported for murder. Do you honestly believe that your friends would welcome such a woman into their society? How can I possibly be an asset to a man such as yourself? I know nothing of entertaining or the life you lead. And then there is—"

"Briony, please, allow me to know what is best for myself. There is plenty of time for you to decide and for arrangements to be made for the mill and for . . . Lizzie, is it, and Thomas, to be settled into work that will suit their circumstances. Just promise me you will consider my offer."

Turning, with nothing more than a slight, formal nod, he opened the door and moved out into the cool, windless day.

She sank bonelessly into the nearest chair which happened to be her father's and, with the part of her mind not whirling round and round the fantastic proposal she had just received from Mr Cameron, she made a mental note to get rid of it. She rose again and blunderingly moved towards the scullery, almost tripping over the bucket she had placed on the floor an hour ago, an era ago, aeons ago and again with that portion of her mind that would keep getting away from her she whispered silently that there would be no more scrubbing for her. Not now. *Not now!*

He let a month go by, a month in which not one farmer, not one villager brought their grain to be milled by the miller's daughter at Moorend Mill.

Though she did not appear to be doing so she waited for him to come. She had told no one, not even Lizzie on whom she had become increasingly reliant, of his proposal since quite honestly she did not know what to tell her, how to explain it, nor even how she was to answer him. Surely, she said to herself as she lay on her truckle bed at night, if she meant to refuse him she would have done so at once but she hadn't. She was dithering, half drawn to the idea and half dismayed by it, so she said nothing, did nothing. In fact she threw herself even more urgently into the business of regaining the customers lost with her father's death and with the re-making of her home, of the home she meant to share with Lizzie and Thomas.

The cart was dragged out of the barn and, displaying a talent even he had not known he possessed, Thomas sawed and hammered, mending broken wheels and generally putting the rickety old thing to rights. Glory was reclaimed from Mr Cameron's paddock, sleek, sturdy and handsome, and put between the shafts and the three of them drove into Penrith on market day where two brass beds and three mattresses were purchased. At the second-hand dealers in the market square they found a couple of simple pine chests of drawers – Thomas could make do with the old chest – a pine wardrobe and three worn but comfortable bentwood rocking-chairs with upholstered seats, suitable for the kitchen. On a market stall they bought plain white cotton sheets and pillow cases, warm blankets and two hand-made quilts; on another rolls of pretty material from which to make curtains, and on a third several rugs though Lizzie proposed that she should begin the task of hooking several others from the old clothes she and Thomas had worn for the eight months of her father's imprisonment and which, with the purchase of new from the market, she and Thomas had now cast off. A sensible gown of dark blue cotton, a bonnet to match, sturdy shoes and a cloak Briony had insisted on buying her, with nankeen breeches, two shirts and a corduroy jacket for Thomas.

"I'll pay you back, Briony, I promise I'll pay you back," she reiterated as she smoothed the fine cotton of her skirt and then turned to Thomas, pulling his jacket more securely about him as though he were a small boy.

"I haven't bought them, my father has," Briony answered her shortly, "and the work you have done and will do in the future will amply repay me."

Wearing their splendid new garments which were, after all, no more than working clothes, Briony in her grey cotton skirt and bodice which had been let out at the seams and fitted her more modestly, she began the task of training Lizzie and Thomas to the working of the mill, the overshot water wheel, the valve that controlled the supply of water, the buckets that moved the wheel and the tail race tunnel below the mill yard. She explained the gearing which drove the millstones at the correct speed, controlling her need to shudder away from the ones that had trapped and killed her father. She showed them how to work the sack hoists that lifted the grain and emptied it into large wooden bins, and instructed them about every working part, though of course it would be much easier to teach them exactly how it was done when the farmers began to fetch their corn and animal feed. They would need another lad. Sadie had one in mind: Billy, the twelve-year-old brother of Dicky Williams who, as boot boy and general servant of all the other servants, had shown himself to be hardworking and reliable and she was sure Billy would be the same.

For the first week they caught up on all the many tasks that had been neglected since Jethro's death. Though it was late in the year they planted seed potatoes and carrots which needed deep cultivation, Briony explained, the ground being well tilled and cleaned first, which was Thomas's job. They prepared the soil for turnips and swedes and cabbage. They had bought hens and a rooster at the market and here Thomas proved invaluable in repairing the hen-house. They discussed the possibility of rearing their own pig as Emily once had done and perhaps a cow could be put in the bit of field where Glory grazed. It kept them up at nights, discussing the possibilities open to them, though at times Lizzie wondered whether she was imagining Briony's air of distraction, just as though her mind were not always fully occupied with this great adventure the three of them were embarked upon. But then her mind was probably far away in the Australias where her brother and Lizzie's father had been sent, Lizzie told herself, that's if they had arrived there yet, or at all. Lizzie had heard of the brutal treatment on the prison ships and the long journey to the other side of the world.

On the Monday of the second week when not one farmer had availed himself of Briony's newly opened mill, she decided to walk up to Mell Farm and speak to Mr Stephens, to Brett Farm where Mr Stirling worked a couple of hundred acres, to Mr Carey at Bramble Farm and, just in case they hadn't heard, let them know that Moorend was once more open for business.

"Oh, aye," they all three said, and the others on whom she called. Aye, they'd heard, they told her but just at the moment they were satisfied where they were. 'Appen in the future. They'd just got used to the miller at Little Salkeld, they mumbled, somewhat apologetically, but just for now . . .

It was the same wherever she went.

"But just think of the time you'll save, Mr Cartwright," she had pleaded with the farmer who had once told her that a little lass like her shouldn't be lifting the heavy sack of grain with which she and Danny were struggling. "And I'm sure, seeing that you're an old customer, I could arrange a special price for you."

"Nay, lass, I'll stick where I am. Besides, a lass like you . . ."

"Yes, a lass like me?" She lifted her chin and looked as though she might punch his, he was to say to his Alice later.

"Well, what wi' thy pa gone and thy Danny away, it don't seem right ter . . . Tha're no more'n a slip of a thing."

"I have help, Mr Cartwright," she told him eagerly. "A strong lad."

"Aye, I've 'eard." His voice had grown truculent, for he didn't like being tormented by this little butterfly which would keep darting at him.

She trailed back down the track that led from Mr Cartwright's farm to the road that edged the lake and was not privy to the argument that took place between Seth Cartwright and his Alice in the dairy at the back of his farmhouse where Alice was viciously turning the churn, though the butter had "come" minutes before.

"'Tis not fair nor proper, Seth Cartwright, an' well tha' know it. Little lass's doin' 'er best ter get on 'er feet an' there's you doin' tha' best ter stop 'er. I'm right ashamed, lad, that's all I can say."

"Now you listen 'ere, Alice Cartwright. I'm only a tenant on this bloody farm an' if 'e ses jump I've ter bloody jump. Don't send yer grain there, 'e ses, not until I tell thi' and what 'e ses goes. Now don't ask me why 'cos I don't know."

"Poor little lass, as if she 'asn't 'ad enough ter purrup with wi'out 'im makin' it worse. An' 'e were so good ter them both when—"

"Will yer be quiet, woman." Seth was beside himself, not only with anger and frustration, but with shame, but had he any option, he kept asking himself as he whistled up his dogs and stumped off up the fells to inspect his flock.

Three weeks later she sat with her head in her hands and would not be consoled by Lizzie's soothing comments about being patient, it was only four weeks. There was still plenty to do, the curtains weren't finished yet and she hadn't even started the hooked rugs. Give it time, she said, which could be well used in the fields and had she noticed the leak in the far storeroom on the top floor? Never mind, it would give Thomas something to do.

"And what will *we* do, you and I, Lizzie? There are only so many times one can scrub the kitchen floor and polish the windows."

"You could go round the farmers again, go further afield, perhaps, and what about the villagers in Pooley Bridge and others hereabouts? They all have small crops of oats and animal food to be ground. I'll come with you."

"They've set their minds against me, Lizzie. Because I'm a woman and the men are too . . . too, oh, I don't know, too thick-headed to deal with a woman."

Lizzie sighed. "Well, that's men for you, and talking of men, here's Mr Cameron riding up the track. What d'you think he wants?"

Briony lifted her head, then stood up, smoothing her skirt, wondering why it was that every time Mr Cameron chose to visit she was wearing her old working clothes.

13

He bowed courteously in Lizzie's direction, no more than the shadow of a smile about his lips and it was very obvious that he wished her far away.

Briony's heart was pounding so loudly that she was sure the other two could hear it but she managed a polite nod as she stood to greet him. She knew none of the ways of genteel society but her natural good manners and surprising refinement in view of the way in which she had been brought up by her coarse father gave her dignity.

"Good morning, Mr Cameron. This is my friend and partner, Miss Lizzie Jenkins. Her father was ... is ..." She faltered then, and Chad felt the muscles in his stomach clench in his need to go to her, to hold her in his arms, tuck her head beneath his chin and smooth her hair, but he stood impassively, aware that the two young women must think him a cold bastard. He thought she had never looked more lovely and wondered that each time he saw her he had the same thought. She had lost that wan, despairing look. Her porcelain skin had regained its lustre, clear and almost translucent. When she stood up he saw she had regained her grace, she was lithe and supple, the dragging apathy that had been hers for months totally gone. Her small jaw was thrust defiantly forward, her incredible eyes flashed with lavender-blue brilliance, her lips, full and coral-tinted, were parted as she drew a deep breath as though to brace herself in readiness for argument and her small breasts rose and peaked against the plain grey bodice she wore. He dragged his eyes away before she noticed the intensity of his gaze.

"Yes, good morning, Miss Jenkins. It's a pleasure to meet you in more . . . congenial surroundings," then could have bitten his tongue since he did not want to remind her of the dismal surroundings in which they had last met.

"Thank you, sir." Both the women sat down, their hands folded in their laps, waiting. Briony, though she had spent no more than a few weeks in Lizzie's company, had picked up unconsciously some of her mannerisms, for though Lizzie's mother and father had been poor they had come from the middle classes and had taught their ways to their children.

"May we offer you some refreshments, Mr Cameron?" Lizzie asked him after he had lowered himself into the third chair which rocked alarmingly, startling him.

"Thank you, no, Miss Jenkins. I just wanted a word with Miss Marsden. A private word."

Lizzie made as if to rise but Briony put out her hand to stop her. "Mr Cameron, whatever you have to say may be said in front of Lizzie. She and I have no secrets."

"Really?" His voice was ironic.

"No. Besides, we are very busy."

"Really?" The irony in his voice increased and he glanced about him. "I saw the young man in the fields turning over the soil with great vigour but I cannot hear the sound of the water wheel."

"No, well . . ." She bit her lip and he wondered at his own cruelty but he must do this thing if he was to . . . to have her. He had not realised how love could force a man to such extremes and he did love her, wanted her, desired her above any woman he had ever met but he would not have dreamed of telling her so. It did not occur to him that it might be the best course!

"Where are your customers, Briony? The ones you swore

would come back to you when they realised the mill was reopened?"

"They will come, Mr Cameron."

"Could you not bring yourself to call me Chad?" he said unwisely, for both Briony and Lizzie looked at him with astonishment.

"Chad!"

"That is the name my friends call me and I hope you and I are friends. Now, as you seem unable to hear what I have to say in private I must repeat my offer in your friend's presence."

"Your offer?"

"Come, come, Briony. Don't pretend you don't know what I mean."

Lizzie's head turned from one to the other, her face a picture of puzzlement.

"I'm afraid . . ."

Chad turned politely to Lizzie. "You must wonder what is going on, Miss Jenkins, so I will put you in the picture, so to speak. A month ago when Briony told me what she intended to do with this mill I . . . well, I disapproved and offered her another solution to her problems. She needs protection, a proper home, a proper life more suited to a woman like her. In fact, I offered her marriage. Yes, you may gasp, Miss Jenkins. Not that I, a man of means and position, would be prepared to marry a young woman who many would consider to be – I hate the word – *beneath* me, or beneath my class but that I should be so presumptuous as to believe that such a beautiful young woman might consider a man she does not love. But I believe we would suit one another. She has—"

"Mr Cameron, Briony is my friend, I hope, and I'm sure would be considered fortunate to be offered marriage by a man of your standing, but you yourself admit that she does not love you and I'm sure – from your attitude – that you don't love her."

"I have a high regard for her, Miss Jenkins. She has shown herself to be exceptionally brave, loyal and—"

"Might I say a word here," Briony interrupted harshly. "You two seem determined to discuss my future as though I were a child or as if I can't make up my own mind. Lizzie, I should have told you what happened between me and Mr Cameron—"

"Chad."

She turned on him in fury. "Oh, don't be so ridiculous. I can't marry you, I told you that then and I'm telling you again now. I don't trust you, despite what you did for Danny and me. *Why* do you want to marry me, for God's sake? I can offer you nothing."

"Briony . . ."

"No, no. I am determined on my course. I and Lizzie and Thomas and Billy Williams will work this mill—"

"Billy Williams, and who the hell is Billy Williams?" His face was drawn into a tight mask and Lizzie caught a glimmer of something in his eyes she could not quite put a name to, but he and Briony seemed to be locked in some . . . something that was nothing to do with her even though it might affect her and Thomas's future.

"Lord, does it matter? Now, if you don't mind, Lizzie and I have work to do and we would like to get on." She rose imperiously to her feet and he thought he had never seen anything quite so magnificent as this fragile and yet strong young girl whom he loved with a passion beyond his own understanding.

He rode away unaware that as his mare moved through the trees to the side of the mill Briony Marsden was crying bitterly in the arms of Lizzie Jenkins. It might have lifted his own spirits if he had and yet he felt that he should not lose hope entirely. It was barely a month since she had set her feet on this road she was determined upon and from what he had gathered from her hints and remarks that had been made she had a small reservoir of cash from her father which would probably see her through a month or two. She and the young woman, with the lad driving, had been seen with the cart bringing back items of furniture from Penrith so she was evidently using what money Jethro had left to furnish her home, but unless the mill's business returned it would not last long. God almighty, he felt so bloody dishonest doing this to her but he could see no other way. No one would suffer, he would see to that. The mill would thrive when he put in a reliable miller and would be waiting, a viable business when Danny Marsden came home, if he ever did. He would see that the Jenkins couple had decent work and . . . and *she*, this young woman with whom he had fallen so completely and inexplicably in love, would lead the sort of life that should be hers. She would be in his safe-keeping. She would be loved and protected. Jesus God, how she would be loved, but he must be patient.

He found himself on the road that ran round the lake, on his right the sloping hill of land on which Longlake Edge stood. There was no one about, for the afternoon was running into evening and he was reminded that the road would soon carry the splendid carriages of the guests Sarah had invited to dinner. Miss Adeline Seddon for whom Sarah had had such high hopes would not be among them. She had been snapped up by a young sprig of the gentry, her blonde ringlets and large dowry having attracted the attention of the second son of a baronet with an estate in Lancashire. Mrs Seddon had made it plain that she – and presumably Adeline – could wait no longer, but he had been made aware that another charming child was to be trotted out for his perusal this very evening.

On an impulse he dismounted and tied his mare to the gate

that led on to the drive up to the house, then, removing his jacket, threw it carelessly across his saddle. Sighing deeply, he wandered down the grassy slope, under the stirring trees, which led to the edge of the gleaming lake and sat down on a rough, moss-covered rock. The grass was starred with wild flowers, the vivid yellow of buttercups and their cousins, marsh marigolds, water crowfoot, white-flowered; the purple blue of violets which reminded him of *her* eyes, wood anemones, all persuaded to bloom so close to the water. A flight of swallows swirled above his head making for the barn where they nested but he scarcely noticed, so deep were his thoughts. It was suddenly dusk and the sky had turned to the colour of a duck's egg, an exquisite pale blue with long, trailing streaks of ivory clouds edged with a pure, pearl grey. Above Gowbarrow the sun was drifting towards the horizon and the clouds which wisped across it were a vivid gold, though he did not see the beauty as he stared, his eyes unfocused, across the lake. He saw only *her* face in all its many expressions. Defiant, determined, sorrowful, smiling hopefully, angry, resentful, haughty, but always with that sweet beauty which had caught at his heart almost two years ago. He sighed deeply then smiled wryly, shaking his head, for he seemed to be doing a lot of that recently. Sighing, his heart heavy with longing and sometimes despair!

As he crossed the road and untethered his indignant mare who was in a stew to get to her stable which was so near, the first carriage approached and drew in through the wrought-iron gates and the astonished face of Bertram Addison, a new acquaintance and the father of the sixteen-year-old who was Sarah's hope for his future, peered from the window. Chad waved and grimaced in apology as though to say he had been held up, then sprang into the saddle, racing towards the back of the house, knowing he was in for trouble from his sister.

He was right. As he flew through the kitchen, watched by

the open-mouthed servants, and into the hallway, Sarah was just about to move out on to the steps to greet Mr and Mrs Bertram Addison and their delectable daughter who were descending from their carriage.

"Where in heaven's name have you been?" she hissed, even in this extremity avoiding the "language" she would have liked to use in her fury. "Our guests are here."

"I know, I'm sorry, I'll explain later. I'll go and change while you make my apologies."

"If you've been with that . . . that girl I'll . . ." For Briony Marsden was still a bitter bone of contention between them.

"Later," he managed to whisper before bolting up the stairs.

The evening was as he had expected, a repetition of so many that had gone before. He did his best to be polite and interested in the impossibly named *Pansy* Addison whose mother explained, simpering proudly, that she had been christened so because of her eyes which had indeed the colour and loveliness of the flower. He chatted amiably with the gentlemen over port and cigars when the ladies left the table and bowed most courteously over the hands not only of Pansy and her mama but of the other ladies as the guests took their departure.

Hoping for a reprieve, he entered his study but Sarah had not yet had her say and she followed him in, closing the door behind her so that the servants would not overhear the dressing-down she meant to administer. She had not seriously believed that he had been with "that girl" as she always called the miller's daughter, the girl who had been a constant thorn in her side ever since the brother had murdered the father. Chadwick had spent far too much of his time and attention on the family and she had told him so a score of times. She had even, despite her protestations, been forced to employ the girl in her own laundry but that, thankfully, was over and she had gone back to the mill where, it was said, she was to operate as her father had done. Good riddance to bad rubbish, she had said, for the taint must be in the family and she was relieved that at last she, and Chad, could put it behind them. It had infuriated her that they had lost Adeline Seddon but Pansy Addison was just as sweet and malleable and she had high hopes of a match.

"Well?" she exclaimed. "Have you an excuse for the unpardonable bad manners you displayed in being late for your own dinner party? Our guests—"

"*Your* dinner party, Sarah." He took a cigar from the box on the desk and with a taper which he lit in the fire, put it to the cigar, drawing the smoke deep into his lungs. He put one foot on the fender, an arm on the mantelshelf and leaned on it, staring down into the glowing coals.

"Don't be ridiculous, Chadwick. They were your guests as well as mine and I was mortified . . ."

He sighed and she stopped as though some instinct told her something terrible was about to happen, to be said. And when he spoke the words she began to shriek so that in the kitchen Minnie dropped a saucepan she was drying with such a clatter all the maids squeaked and huddled together as though a band of marauders were about to attack the house.

For a moment Chad thought he might have to restrain her, then as suddenly as she had begun she stopped. Her face was bone white and her hair had become disarranged but she spoke calmly.

"Have you gone quite mad?"

"No, I haven't. I mean what I say and as soon as it can be arranged . . ."

"Don't talk such nonsense. The girl has bewitched you in some way but if you must have her then go ahead. I'm sure she will have no objection to being your whore if she is paid well enough and as—"

"You have a foul mind and a tongue to match it, Sarah, and I demand you retract—"

"Don't be ridiculous." There was sneer in her voice. "She is no more than a—"

"She is a young woman of great intelligence and integrity."

"How many other men has she been involved with, tell me that, before she got her claws into you? Dear God, the creature is depraved if she thinks—"

"She thinks nothing. She is an innocent girl who knew nothing of my intentions towards her and I will not have her name besmirched. Now, if you will excuse me I have papers to look at." He moved towards the door and opened it, holding the handle politely but his expression was hard, cold, telling her she would be wise to hold her tongue. Sarah had never seen him lose his temper and had no idea how close she was to the explosion. Even as a boy, she had always known him to be polite, cool, reserved, but if she had looked closely into his tawny-coloured eyes she would have seen the hot coals of his rage.

"I refuse to leave until this has been resolved," she declared, as cold now as he was and just as determined on her own way.

"There is nothing to be resolved, Sarah, so I must ask you to excuse me. And I think it advisable to keep this to ourselves for the moment." He had pushed the door to as he spoke, for he did not want it known all over the district that he had an interest in the Marsden girl.

"Believe me, Chadwick, your sordid secret is safe with me. Do you seriously imagine I want it known among our friends that my brother has lost his mind and has designs on the sister of a convicted murderer? I shall pray for you, pray that you will come to your senses and put this . . . this fanciful whim behind you."

She turned, her head held high. She picked up her wide skirts waiting for the door to be opened for her, then swept through it and up the stairs.

They got through August and September. They planted more vegetables. Thomas had repaired the plough which had been a fragile thing to begin with, since Jethro was no carpenter and would not pay out good money to Blacky Blackhall to have it mended, and with Glory plodding patiently along the rows of thin soil – since this was not really arable country – the top field was made ready for planting. They bought a pig which they fattened and a cow and with the help of Dorcas, the dairy-maid from Longlake Edge who gave up several of her Sundays when Sadie begged her, learned the craft of butter- and cheese-making, hoping, when they were more expert, to sell the surplus at the market. They had Billy to feed now, since they had hired him on the understanding that he would become an integral part of the team that would grind the corn, the oats, the animal feed at Moorend Mill. Four mouths to feed, two of them with the voracious appetites of young, hardworking boys and the money which Jethro had put away, not much for he had drunk most of it, was dwindling fast. In the belief that they would earn more in the mill, they had spent on furniture and materials for curtains, on clothes and boots. Thomas had moved upstairs into the made-over bedroom, one that had once been a storeroom, and Billy took his place in the cupboard bed in the kitchen, but Sal went with Thomas, sleeping on his bed in the bare room which contained nothing else but the chest that had once been Emily's.

Still they did not come, the farmers and villagers, and winter was ahead of them. October was a lovely month, almost like summer with mild but shortening days. They picked apples and blackberries and made jam, they preserved fruit which

Lizzie's mother had taught her how to do. They pickled the eggs they did not use. They made chutney with the chopped-up pieces of vegetables, sour apples and tomatoes bought cheaply at the market and they baked their own bread, buying the flour from the same source, Briony bemoaning the fact that a year ago her mother had it free from the sweepings in the mill. They killed the pig, or Ned Turnberry did it for them, for even Thomas, though willing, could not bring himself to slit the squealing animal's throat. Following Sadie's directions they preserved the cut-up joints, removing the ribs for immediate eating. The legs were reserved for curing, the meat from the shoulder blade salted and cured for bacon. The cured pork, now called hams, Sadie told them, hung from the beams of the kitchen ceiling and the two young women were satisfied that they would not starve through the coming months since they were self-supporting. They had made rushlights from the pork fat and great stacks of wood, sawed and chopped by the two boys, were piled in the yard. And soon the men would bring their grain to be milled by the new miller at Moorend Mill and their sadly depleted funds would be replaced. They said this to one another frequently.

It snowed in January, hesitantly at first, surprising Briony, though why it should she didn't know for she had been brought up on the fells. By nightfall it had become a slanting curtain which hurled itself against the windows and doors as though doing its best to get in where it was warm and cosy. There was a simmering "tatie-pot" on the fire and the two boys – for what else could you call the childlike Thomas? – arm-wrestled on the kitchen table, oblivious to the creeping worry that invaded the two young women.

It stopped snowing in the early afternoon of the next day and when they opened the kitchen door the drifts against the door were four feet high. The beauty of the landscape was quite breathtaking, the brilliance of the immaculate snow, across which nothing moved, hurt the eye. It sparkled in the sun which shone from a sky the colour of a cornflower, cloudless and serene. The woodland between them and the road carried its burden of snow, black and white and silver against the placid lake. The air was sharp, clean, inclined to hurt the lungs if a deep breath of it was drawn in, but the boys floundered out, laughing as children do, making for the barn where the flat wooden spades were kept for this particular purpose. They would soon clear a path down to the road, they shouted, but the women were silent as they turned back to the warmth and the cheer of the spotless kitchen. There was nothing for them to do. The two of them had spent the last months cleaning and polishing and scouring. There was bread and to spare in the crock. The hens had to be fed and their eggs collected and in the barn the cow, who had been brought in last night, needed to be milked. Lizzie threw on her shawl and donned the stout clogs which they had bought in the market at the beginning of the winter and, when the boys had cleared the rough path to the barn, moved quietly into the yard, shutting the door behind her. No word had been spoken.

When she returned Briony was at the table, staring sightlessly at the small pile of coins which were counted out neatly before her.

"Four and elevenpence halfpenny," she muttered, putting her head in her hands. Lizzie removed her clogs which were clotted with snow and moved across the kitchen to put a hand on Briony's shoulder.

"Briony, we'll manage somehow until . . ." she began.

"Until when, tell me that? It's been six months."

"I know but we mustn't give up. I'll find work. Now that Thomas is settled I could leave him with you. Don't despair, love. We have our health and enough to eat growing in the ground and I'm sure when the farmers get over their antagonism towards a woman miller they'll—"

Briony stood up so violently the bench on which she sat fell backwards. She listened to the excited shouts of the boys in the yard then turned her set face to Lizzie.

"I have to go out. I won't be long."

Lizzie was aghast. "But the snow, you'll never get through."

Briony's answer was to fling her shawl about her head and shoulders, strap on her clogs and open the door wide. Sal peeped out from behind her skirts, sniffing the air, then scurried back to the comfort of the hooked rug before the fire which Lizzie had made. The yard was almost cleared and a path had been made through the trees as far as the barn. Under the trees the snow was not so thick, protected from the worst of the blizzard by the thick trunks of oak, horse chestnut and yew. The river was in full spate and the stepping stones were slippery but when she reached the other side and the row of cottages she found that some enterprising cottager had cleared a path. Probably Iolo, she thought absently as she knocked on Sadie's door. It was getting dark and the rushlights in the window looked very welcoming, and soundlessly she whispered a little prayer that within she might receive the answer to the impasse in which she found herself.

14

Sadie radiated that special warmth and yet common sense that was particularly her own, a warmth that had comforted Briony on so many occasions and a common sense that had guided her through the past year or more. At the same time as she welcomed her she scolded Briony roundly for gallivanting about on such a day. That was the word she used. Gallivanting, just as though Briony were wandering about enjoying herself, which was what the word meant where Sadie came from.

"Yer must be a gobbin" – another Lancashire expression – "comin' out on a day like this. 'Ere, tekk that shawl off an' yer clogs and get thi' ter't fire. I've just got these scones outer th'oven, see, they're still warm. Now wait while I fetch butter, or 'appen some o' me strawberry jam and a splodge o' cream. I've just mashed tea and we'll get summat inside thi' an' then tha' can tell us what's to do."

"No, honestly, Sadie, I'm not hungry, really. I just wanted to—"

"Eeh, lass, yer must be frozen, not ter mention clemmed," Sadie remonstrated. "Wilta have some soup, then? 'Tis fresh made an' wouldn't tekk but a minnit ter warm up."

"No, Sadie, please, I just wanted to have a word."

"I dunno, tha' were always faddy wi' tha' food. Tha'll 'ave a cup o' tea though, fer I'll not let yer go until yer do."

Briony accepted the tea – strong and sweet, for if she couldn't get food into you Sadie's panacea for all ills was a cup of tea – and listened passively to the flow of Sadie's voice. Iolo was still up at the house, she explained, for hadn't that there Clover decided to produce her calf this very day and the lad was convinced that if he wasn't there at the birth the thing would be born with two heads or some such daft notion. She herself had just spent ten hours at her washtub, her mangle and ironing table, along with Iris, the new laundry-maid who was turning out to be a bit nesh, and with Jenny, for today was the day when every bed in the household was stripped and the sheets and pillow cases laundered. She did not mention the length of her working day to Briony. She was dog-tired but the little lass obviously had something on her mind and if Sadie could help her, even if it was only with a bit of advice, that was what she was here for. Sadie had heard all about the dismal failure of the corn mill despite the lass's hard work. She had been told that Briony had tramped about the district trying to drum up work, begging the farmers and the like to send their corn and oats and such to be milled, but despite the couple who had moved in with her, a sensible young woman Sadie had thought her to be on the few occasions they had met, they had been dogged with ill luck.

Her voice was soft and compassionate as she did her best to recall bits of gossip that might bridge the gap until the lass told her what was up. "D'yer remember Daisy what had the bairn? Aye, course yer do. You took over when she left. Well she brought it round, a lovely little lass for us all ter 'ave a scen. Master's away somewhere, down London 'tis said, and not ter be back until Thursday. An important man is Mr Cameron, so they say, an' it'll be summat ter do wi' 'Er Majesty's weddin' I'll be bound." Sadie had an inflated belief in her master's importance. "Mind thi', I'm not that sure I fancy th' idea of a German king but if that's what Queen wants 'oo are we ter say 'er nay."

"Of course not." Briony's unblinking eyes stared into the

fire as, for a few minutes, she let go of the terrible burden under which she and Lizzie struggled. Sadie was . . . well, she hardly knew how to describe the soothing effect Sadie had on her, had always had on her, and for just this moment she let her drone on until she suddenly realised that Sadie had asked her a question.

She turned and smiled. "Pardon?" She did her best to appear interested but failed dismally.

"I said, what's ter do, lass? I know yer 'avin' a hard time of it down at mill but if there's owt I can do tha've only ter ask."

"Oh, Sadie, what are we to do? The money my father left – not much in all conscience – has nearly gone. Oh, no, Sadie, no. I haven't come to borrow," as Sadie opened her mouth to speak, "but Lizzie and I need to work. I'm sure that soon, perhaps when the weather gets better," sticking stubbornly to her dream, though what the weather had to do with it Sadie couldn't imagine, "the farmers will start to bring their grain but until then we must have work. I don't know exactly what Lizzie has in mind. Probably scrubbing or, or sewing. She's a fine needlewoman, but the only thing I know is laundry work and I meant to ask if you'd speak up for me with Miss Cameron" – she turned to stare disconsolately into the crackling fire – "but it seems you already have enough laundry-maids. I wasn't aware that she'd taken on another when I left. I suppose I was so wrapped up with my own affairs . . ."

Her voice trailed off. The canary sang its heart out in its cage and the tabby groomed her latest litter of kittens. The fire flickered cheerfully, casting orange and gold shadows on the ceiling between the heavy oak beams and across the whitewashed walls, and Sadie's heart ached, for she knew just what that dragon up at the big house would say. Hadn't those in the kitchen heard her and the master going hammer and tongs about this very child and her brother who had been torn from her through no fault of his own, poor lad. Yes, he'd killed that old sod who had tortured – you could use no other word – him and this sad young woman since they were no more than bairns. He'd defended her and his mam and for his brave action, at least them round here thought it was brave, having come up against Jethro Marsden in the past, he had been taken from his sister, his home, his country and shipped off like an animal to the far side of the world. New South Wales – the name had stuck in her memory because of her Dai who'd been born in Wales – and it was from there that wool came, or so Briony had told her, and it was reported that it was as good as the best wool from Saxony. So happen the lad would be working with sheep, which would be good for him bearing in mind his background up here on the fells of Cumberland.

But in Sadie's sad opinion there was not a hope that the mistress would take the lass on again. She had been slipped in, if you like, by the master, almost behind her back the last time but she'd not stand for it again. The lad had been in gaol then but not sentenced. Now he was a convicted felon, a murderer, and Sarah Cameron would not dream of having the sister of a convicted murderer working in *her* laundry.

"Well, I could ask her, lass, but I don't rightly know. Well, what wi' Iris an' Jenny . . ."

"Shall I come up and speak to her? There might be something in the kitchen or even the dairy with Dorcas. I know about dairy work, or perhaps Miss Cameron might know of something in the kitchen of one of her friends? She knows a lot of people, but I'd rather work with you, Sadie, if at all possible. So, if you get an opportunity, will you ask her and also about Lizzie?"

Sadie avoided Briony's pleading eyes, for she knew that in her own would be the hopelessness of persuading Miss Cameron to take on not only this girl but her friend who also had a relative, her father, who was a convicted felon. In fact there were very few, if any, of the high and mighty folk in the district who would be charitable to that extent. Bad blood, they would say and even if they should hesitate about it Miss Sarah Cameron would soon see that they changed their minds.

"If she won't, or can't, Lizzie and I might find work at the inn at Pooley Bridge. I've heard they're always looking for barmaids and strong women to scrub."

"Eeh, nay lass." Sadie was horrified. The very idea of this dainty little creature behind the bar of the inn at Pooley Bridge would not bear thinking about. All the rough labourers in the district drank there – including her own father when he was alive – and they would not consider moderating their language because of her. She would be leered at, joked about, insulted by the coarseness of their talk. Barmaids had to be thick-skinned, give as good as they got, be lively, pert, and this child was none of these things. Spirited, oh aye, but in a refined sort of way. No, she'd best tackle Miss Cameron though the thought dismayed her.

She thought Miss Cameron was going to strike her the next day when she put it to her, or rather humbly begged employment for the miller's lass who was having a hard time of it since . . . well, since her brother had been sentenced to transportation. She could hear herself babbling, her heart beginning to pound, for the look on Miss Cameron's face was enough to make the most stout-hearted quake in her clogs. She didn't mention Briony's friend for fear her mistress might have an apoplexy. Her face was already crimson with indignation. Her light blue eyes seemed ready to pop out of her head and her mouth had thinned to a pinched and dangerous line.

"How dare you come to me with this," she hissed, "though I dare say that . . . that harlot—"

"Nay, Miss Cameron," Sadie cried, shocked beyond measure. "She's never—"

"Harlot I call her and harlot she is." Had not the hussy set her sights on Sarah's own brother, for Chadwick himself had told her so. At least not in so many words but it seemed he was charmed by her, bewitched by her and if Sarah could do her harm she would. *Employ her!* She would rather employ old Cissie Hartley who for a shilling, or even less, would deliver a child or lay out a corpse and hadn't removed her clothing for so long her stink went before her.

"She's a dab 'and with a gofferin' iron, Miss Cameron, an' knows 'ow ter shape 'erssen wi' owt in't laundry. She works right—"

"That is enough, woman. I don't care how clever she is or hardworking I will not have her in my house. Besides which we have enough laundry-maids and need no more—"

"She'd do owt, Miss Cameron, scrubbin', scullery work," Sadie went on desperately then stepped back hastily as her mistress stood up so violently the table at which she sat shook and a milk jug fell off, spilling milk on the pretty flowered carpet.

"Don't you interrupt me when I am speaking and if you don't watch your tongue I might even consider replacing you. Now get out of here and back to the laundry and don't let me hear another word, d'you hear."

"And did your business go well, my dear?" Sarah asked her brother as they sat at dinner a few nights later. She was not particularly interested in what his business in the nation's capital might be, since she was not a knowledgeable woman and was concerned with nothing that did not take place in her own small sphere. She believed that it was a lady's duty to enquire though, to make polite conversation, to show interest even if one did not feel it. She would, as the meal progressed, tell him of the events of the neighbourhood, perhaps mention Pansy Addison, ignoring the terrible fright he had given her before he went to London regarding *that* girl, and bring up the question of the invitation she had received from the Addisons to the ball they meant to give for their precious daughter's seventeenth birthday. It was to be a grand affair attended by the wealthiest in the county and beyond. She was well aware that Chadwick had no love for such occasions but she meant, by fair means or foul, to get him there.

"Yes, I was able to buy shares in several railways which are to be incorporated this year and I was approached to put money into a company which means to sink mines in Cornwall. Tin mines. That was the main reason for my visit."

"And will you accept?" Sarah asked the question automatically, since she had no feelings on the matter one way or another.

"Possibly." He sat back and patted his lips with the snowy napkin Sadie had ironed only hours earlier. Martha removed his soup plate and turned to Daphne at the serving table where a succulent loin of pork awaited.

"Is'ta ter carve it, then?" she hissed at the girl and Daphne started in apprehension, for it was not her job to carve the joint.

"Nay, tha' usually do it, Martha," she whispered, while Chad turned his head and looked in their direction. Sarah tutted irritably, glaring at the two maidservants.

"Tha' knows I burned me 'and on the stove, tha' daft gowk. I told thi' tha'd 'ave ter manage ternight but no, tha' were too busy at back door tellin' that there lass ter gerroff 'ome an' not ter bother—"

"What is going on, Martha?" Chad asked irritably. He had had a long and tiring railway journey on the Great Western Railway first from London to Birmingham, then from there to Preston and Lancaster where he had transferred to a coach. The proposed line from Lancaster to Carlisle was several years away!

"Nay, maister, I did tell the lass she'd ter carve joint ternight on account o' me burnin' me 'and but she were gossipin' at back door—"

"I were't gossipin', maister," Daphne protested. "I were only doin' what mistress told me—"

"That's enough, Daphne," a sharp voice from the table told her. "Now, if neither of you feels able to carve perhaps Mr Chadwick could . . ."

But Chad Cameron, for reasons he could not explain, was not prepared to let the matter go.

"And what girl is that, Martha?" His voice was quiet and Martha, at first anxious, took heart from his calmness.

"It were't girl from't—"

"Martha!" There was warning in Sarah's voice and Martha looked anxiously from one to the other.

"Well, I dunno . . ." She was flustered, that was obvious, and Daphne stood like a guardsman ready to be marched off by a superior officer.

"Martha."

Martha, who was an old and trusted servant, suddenly took heart from the fact, for it was not her fault and she didn't see why she should be put in this awkward position. They had all heard Master Chad going on the other night and they all knew of his interest in the girl and her family. Mistress wouldn't like it, that was for sure, but that was nowt to do with her.

"It were that lass from't mill," she said, darting a glance at her mistress.

"What did she want?" And they were all aware, even Daphne who didn't know what the dickens was going on, that *something* was.

"Chadwick, I hardly think it's necessary for us to be concerned about this just now. Let us get the joint carved and have our—"

"What did she want?" His voice was like ice and poor Daphne, for some reason, began to snivel though she'd done nothing wrong.

"She wanted work, maister," Martha quavered, suddenly afraid, suddenly conscious of how old she was and how difficult it would be to find another job at her age. The mistress could be a terror when she was crossed and she was being crossed right now. Her expression told them so and the two maidservants shuffled their feet uneasily.

They were astonished when the master suddenly sprang for the door. His feet could be heard pounding up the stairs and then, after a moment, down again. The front door opened on the cruel and biting wind which seemed to herald more snow, then banged to behind him.

The three women were silent. Martha and Daphne waited for orders but the mistress simply sat at the table and stared at something she didn't seem to like.

The knock at the door startled them, for they hadn't heard a horse approaching but then the snow still cushioned the ground despite the path that had been dug by the boys. Sal raised her head and began to bark and Briony and Lizzie exchanged uneasy glances.

"Open the door, Billy," Briony told the lad, but she knew in her heart who it was, for this was Thursday and hadn't Sadie told her he would be back on Thursday. For some reason, though she knew who it was and why he had come, she felt a strange lessening of tension in her, a kind of sighing relief, a sudden tranquillity at the inevitability of it. For six long months she had striven towards the goal, the dream, if you like, of returning her father's mill to its former status, spurred on by the thought of Danny who would, she had convinced herself, one day return to take up his rightful heritage. When he did, as compensation for what he had suffered, it would be here for him to take up. She had written of it to him in one of her regular letters – to which as yet she had had no reply – hoping to put heart in him during his exile. Dear God, she had tried. She and Lizzie and Thomas, and during that time she had shut this man out, denied something inside her, a small kernel of sweetness that had armoured her in the battle she and Lizzie had fought but now, even before Billy opened the door, she knew the outcome. At the acceptance of it, and of her defeat, her body seemed to melt and she sighed as though putting down an enormous burden at the end of a long and arduous journey.

His bare head, on which a few snowflakes rested, almost touched the heavy wooden lintel above the door and his boots were crusted with frozen grey mush from the yard. It was evident that he had walked from Longlake Edge.

The two young women rose to their feet and the dog wandered across to him and sniffed the hem of the long merino wool overcoat which reached his ankles. He bowed courteously but Briony noticed that his face was without its usual amber tint and, because of it, was somewhat gaunt.

"Good evening, ladies. I hope I am not interrupting anything." Though it was evident from the bareness of the table they had finished their meal. He wondered in that part of his mind not swirling round the possibility that lay ahead of him what they had eaten. If she was reduced to begging for work at Longlake it can't have been much.

"Mr Cameron." The tall girl – he was damned if he could remember her name – was the first to speak.

"Yes, good evening, Miss . . ."

"Jenkins, Elizabeth Jenkins."

"Of course. I hope I find you well, Miss Jenkins."

"Very well, thank you, Mr Cameron."

"Good, good. And you, Miss Marsden . . . Briony?"

"I am well."

"Good, good." It all ground to a halt then and Billy Williams, six years younger than Thomas in age but years older in wisdom, stared curiously from one face to another while Thomas lifted Sal into his arms and cuddled her close to his face.

Lizzie cleared her throat. Briony and Mr Cameron were looking at one another, their faces as white as candle wax, their eyes unblinking and when she turned and began to gather the boys to her, drawing them towards the narrow stairs that led up to the stone floor, they were both bewildered and inclined to argue.

"We will say goodnight, Briony. Mr Cameron," making no pretence of doing anything other than getting herself and the lads out of the way for Mr Cameron to do, or say, what he had come for. Neither of them answered.

The silence lasted for several minutes, for though Briony knew why he was here and what her answer would be, *must* be, she was not going to make it easy for him.

He smiled, that wryly humorous smile that she had seen so seldom, a lift of the corners of his rather nice mouth that revealed the white slash of his teeth. Why doesn't he smile more often, she remembered thinking, for it warms his face and puts golden lights in his velvet-brown eyes, then was amazed with herself. Velvet-brown eyes, indeed! What on earth was the matter with her? She watched as his eyebrows lifted questioningly and knew the moment had come.

"You know why I'm here, Briony?"

"Yes." Her voice was cold.

"You understand what I want?"

"Yes."

"And what have you to say to me?"

"I thought you had something to say to me."

"Ah, yes." His smile did not exactly falter but it dimmed a little. They were both still standing facing one another, she with her hands folded primly in front of her. She still wore the same black gown he had bought her for her mother's funeral and he noticed that it seemed somewhat big on her. She had worked hard and long these last months tramping from farm to farm, sometimes for miles, pleading with the farmers to bring their grain to her for milling. She had restored this mill, with the help of the couple she had taken in, scrubbing, scouring, whitewashing the place and the outbuildings inside and out. He had seen her in the fields and in the woodland gathering wood and his heart had flinched at what he was doing to her, but, by God, he'd make it up to her when she was his wife. That damned frock, for instance, would be replaced with gowns of a richness and elegance not seen outside Paris. Furs, jewellery, a life of luxury, servants to do her bidding and he would fold her in his heart and protect her so that no man would ever hurt her again. Her mill would become a working mill again and he would use his considerable influence to find out what state her brother was in at the penal colony in Botany Bay and when the lad came home – and if it was possible he would make sure he did – the mill would be there for him.

"Do you want me to say the words, Briony?"

"If you please."

"Very well. Will you marry me?" His voice was soft and he leaned forward and took one of her hands, holding it, limp and lifeless, cold as ice, between his warm, strong fingers.

"I don't love you, Mr Cameron. You must know that. And I would be grateful if you could explain to me why you want me. I can bring you nothing. Nothing but trouble, for you must know your sister and your friends will not like it."

"I will like it, Briony, and won't you call me Chad?"

"I . . . I'm not sure . . ."

"What is it you're not sure about?" He nearly added, "my little love" but knowing it would amaze and alarm her he bit the words off hastily.

"I don't know. I only know that this is the only way I can keep the mill working for my brother. I must be perfectly honest with you, Mr Cameron."

"Yes, I suppose you must." Though he wished with all his heart that she might have been less so. Slowly she withdrew her hand and let it fall lifelessly to her side, then turned away and he was not to know that it had taken a great deal of effort on her part not to leave it there, for it felt so . . . so safe and yet safe was not exactly the word she was looking for. She *did* feel safe with him and at the same time she, who demanded honesty, knew there was more to it than that. He really was very handsome, so endearing when he smiled and his eyes had something in them she found exhilarating. He was rich and had great influence and with this combination what might he do for Danny who would need a man of influence to guide him when he came home. He could help Lizzie and Thomas, give work to Billy and he had promised her that she would have the choosing of a decent miller to keep the whole thing going until the mill's rightful owner was home again.

She turned back to him and squared her shoulders like some young warrior queen about to take up her sword and shield in defence of her realm.

"Very well, Mr Cameron, I will marry you."

"Good," he said briskly, as though they had just conducted a business transaction agreeable to them both. "I'll make the arrangements. Now, I'll bid you good evening." He nodded his head, turned on his heel, opened the door and let himself out. When he was safely outside in the dark of the night where no one could see him he turned his face to the wall, resting his forehead on his raised arm and let out his breath on a long-drawn-out sigh.

15

"The moment that whore moves into my home I move out of it."

"That is for you to decide, Sarah. What you grandly call the Dower House can easily be made ready and perhaps it might suit you better to be mistress of your own establishment rather than take a lesser role—"

"I *am* mistress of my own establishment. Longlake Edge has been my home since I was born and I refuse to be thrown out like a garment for which its owner has no further use."

"Don't be ridiculous, Sarah. No one is throwing you out."

"So what do you call this . . . this farrago you seem intent on creating? I am to be evicted, sent to some piddling little cottage in order that that harlot can queen it in my place. Well, I tell you now, Chadwick, I won't have it. I do not intend to leave."

"That is for you to decide. Perhaps Briony would be glad of a guiding hand until she has—"

"Are you mad? Do you honestly believe that girl can take my place?"

"No, she will not take your place, Sarah. Your place in this house is as my sister, my unmarried sister. Briony will be my wife and she will take her own place. She is a decent young woman who will quickly learn—"

"Well, you may be assured that I shan't teach her."

"So it seems. In that case you had better make your

preparations to move to the Dower House. Feel free to spend what you need to make it into a home where you can still entertain your friends and, naturally, your allowance will continue. Take what servants you want, for my wife might wish to employ her own. I will pay all the household bills and—"

"Dear God, Chadwick, please, please don't do this thing." Sarah began to weep, genuinely distressed at what she saw as her brother's insanity. She actively loathed the girl from the mill who she saw as a scheming hussy who would ruin her brother and destroy the good name of her family. It would change her own life for ever and that was enough to desolate any woman, but in her own way she loved Chadwick and wanted only the best for him. And that meant the best wife, one she herself could ease into the position of rightful mistress of Longlake Edge. This girl, this common, working-class girl, would alienate him from his own society, for not one member of the "good" families would entertain him, or her, in their homes, nor enter Longlake Edge. The gentlemen who did business with him would probably continue to do so, for where money was concerned they were hard-headed, practical and not inclined to do anything to jeopardise the making of it. But not their wives!

Chad's face softened, for though she frequently infuriated him he was fond of his sister who had, for years, been a splendid hostess in his home. He had known, for he was a realist, that the chances of Sarah and Briony settling down together in harmony was just so much vapour on the wind, but, man-like, he had hoped for the best. Whether Sarah imagined he might turn about and give up the idea if she threatened him with leaving, he didn't know. Naturally, he would do no such thing. The wedding was to take place next month, March, and already Briony was busy with the young seamstress and milliner from the top end of the Market

Square in Penrith. Miss Avery had been employed to stitch his bride-to-be into the crêpe-de-chines and gauzes, the taffetas and brocades and velvets that would equip her to be his wife. There was no female in Briony's life who could advise her on what wardrobe she needed to become such an important person but Miss Avery knew, for hadn't she been dressmaker and milliner to ladies of fashion in London and even for a spell in Paris. She knew exactly what the wife of a wealthy and substantial gentleman would be required to wear in the life she would lead and had been informed that no expense was to be spared. It would do her no end of good to be the dressmaker to the young wife of Chad Cameron and with her flair and experience would not fail the woman he was to marry.

He could not honestly say Briony acted like a young bride-to-be, for she seemed to be in a world of her own, bemused, dazed, and who could blame her? He had to admit to feeling the same and on the occasions when he called at the mill, for there was much to be arranged, they were stiff and awkward with one another. She was cool, distant, ready to argue with him over the cashmere shawls, the hooded velvet evening cloaks, one to match each elegant evening gown, the morning dresses, the day dresses, the trimmings of which must be in the latest fashion, the pelisse-robes, the peignoirs, the riding costume, for naturally she would learn to ride, the bonnets and petticoats that Miss Avery insisted she would need. And of course, her wedding gown! Words were bandied about such as "princess robes", "chemisette", "gilet corsage", "bishop sleeve", "organ pleating", the meanings of which were a mystery to her and which filled her with a kind of contempt, for what could it all possibly mean to her who was doing this for one reason only, or so she told herself.

The only time she took an interest in what he had to say was when mention of the man who was to be employed to

run the mill was raised and she was strangely evasive when it
came to it. There was plenty of time, she said, for the farmers
and villagers who had once been her father's main customers
must first be persuaded to return with their business. Who was
to say they would and it seemed to her that they had best wait
until their intention was certain. Yes, she agreed, the men,
millers with experience, who had shown an interest in leasing
the mill for a period of seven years seemed, from what he told
her, to be decent, hardworking men who would build up trade
but she must be sure, for Danny's sake, that the man who
took over was the right one. There was Thomas to consider,
and Billy, who must be allowed to continue as employees at
Moorend though Lizzie would, naturally, be coming with her
to Longlake Edge. He did understand that, didn't he? she
asked him coolly. About Lizzie? He did understand that she
could go nowhere without Lizzie, and Chad, obsessed with
his love for her and willing to promise anything to have her
as his wife, agreed.

He did not know how to reach her and so he was just as
cool, just as businesslike. He longed to drag her into his arms,
to laugh and soothe her, to kiss her tight-lipped defiance away
but she kept him at arm's length with her young dignity. She
made it quite plain that she was doing this for her brother
who, defending her, had lost seven years of his life. She would
keep her part of their bargain, she let him know, however
unwilling she might be, but he must not expect her to play
the blushing bride.

The turbulence that blasted along the valley and up into
the outlying farms on the fellside when the news reached
them could not have been more electrifying if their young
Queen had announced herself eight months pregnant and her
married a bare month! They had all known, every farmer and
his shepherd, every gentleman and his family, of the unusual
concern Chad Cameron had shown for the two young people

at Moorend Mill and they had not blamed him, for what had happened to them was tragic, but the news that he was to marry the girl was beyond believing and at first they did not believe it. Not until Sarah Cameron, called upon by her dear friend Jessica Gould who was eager to hear if the dreadful rumour was true, collapsed in painful tears against her shoulder.

"He's lost his wits," she moaned. "He's out of his mind and over a girl not fit to clean his boots. She worked in my own laundry and now she's to be mistress of this house. *My* house. The home I have made for him all these years and I'm to be turned out, forced to live in that . . . that cottage on the edge of the estate. No more than a dining-room and a parlour and two bedrooms above. No stables or coach house, and a bit of a garden that is hardly bigger than those of our own workers. It's not to be borne, Jessica."

"But surely he doesn't mean you to *live* in such a place, my dear. Can you not stay here at Longlake?"

"And live with that slut having the ordering of *my* servants, brazenly putting on airs over *me*? Can you imagine it?"

And Jessica couldn't, as she said to Bernard later that evening at dinner, and if Chad Cameron thought that she and her coterie of friends, *Sarah's* friends, would entertain the creature in their homes or accept any invitation she might be impertinent enough to extend, then she could . . .

She was surprised and more than a little put out when Bernard turned on her with an expression she could only call menacing. Her sons, Wilfred and George, who were dining at home, fell back in amazement and she was only glad dear Judith, who was now married, was not there to hear her father's words.

"You will do nothing, madam, *nothing*, d'you hear, to alienate Chad Cameron. Good God, I do business with the man and if he was to be offended and withdraw his support, I, and many others, would be in queer street, I can tell you."

"Queer street?" Jessica quavered.

"Yes, bloody queer street, woman, so if you have to accept some baggage Cameron has taken a fancy to, though God knows why he couldn't just bed her like other men do . . ."

"Bernard!" Not only Jessica but her sons and the butler who was serving them gasped in horror.

Bernard ignored them. "You'll treat the woman with civility, d'you hear. You'll start by calling on her. Leave cards or whatever tricks women get up to in these circumstances."

"But I've already refused their wedding invitation."

"Then you'll just have to write and explain that we find we can attend after all."

"But what about Ernestine and Madge Seddon and all the—"

"I think you'll find, my dear, that they will all be there in the church. There are not many men in the district who dare cross Chad Cameron and their wives will do as they're told. As you will."

Bernard Gould was right. The church, St Michael's at Glebe where the Reverend Julian Armstrong had buried her mother nearly eighteen months ago, was crammed with not only the servants from Longlake Edge and all the folk who knew Briony Marsden and her tragic circumstances, but with the "best" people who could not afford to displease Chad Cameron. They sat at the front as was their right, dressed to the nines in their good broadcloth, their silks and satins, the working classes at the back of the church in their drab Sunday best, respectable but determined to see the good fortune that had come to one of their own.

The only one not present was Sarah Cameron who didn't give a damn whether Chadwick was displeased or not.

She wore the white dress Miss Avery had thought suitable for a young virgin bride, for there was no doubt that Briony Marsden was virgin. Mr Chadwick had accompanied his future wife on several occasions, to ensure, Miss Avery supposed, that his money was being spent properly and that the lovely young girl was being tricked out in the best Miss Avery could provide. He was stiff-necked, expressionless, arrogant, with none of the emotion, the warmth one might expect in a bridegroom, and the bride was the same, the pair of them barely speaking, to one another, or to her. Miss Marsden obediently stood or walked or turned this way and that, and Mr Chadwick, though showing no particular expression, seemed satisfied. As for affection, or any kind of intimate bond between the two, there was none.

Her dress had a high ruffled collar, a bell-shaped skirt ending in twelve rows of deep, lace-edged frills, with simple white rosebuds to hold her veils which fell to her knees, and high-heeled slippers which raised her to the lobe of Chad Cameron's ear. Nobody walked behind her, for her only friend was Lizzie, considered too tall by Miss Avery who was determined to show off this delicate loveliness she had created to its best advantage. And what else could you call the sight of the exquisite creature drifting all alone up the aisle to her dark groom, since there was no one to give her away. There was a hush as she did so and then a murmur, a tribute to the fragile, lovely symbol of virginity which her appearance depicted.

Chad waited at the altar, as handsome as she was beautiful with a white rosebud in the lapel of his dove-grey jacket, a white brocade waistcoat, the white frills of his immaculate cravat testifying to Sadie's handiwork, his dark hair brushed back but already inclined to curl over his forehead. His hand reached out at once and captured hers and it was then that she came out of the strange, trance-like state she had been in all morning. Lizzie and Miss Avery had dressed her. The young woman who had been employed to attend to her hair had swept it into a glossy coil to the crown of her head, tipping it back, and she had climbed into the Cameron carriage like a young queen, with Lizzie beside her. An unfamiliar Joe Blamire, done up like a bloody footman – his words – in a coachman's uniform found only God knew where, had handed her in with a wink, the last he was to give Briony Marsden, the miller's daughter. The carriage was lined with white satin and decorated with white rosebuds and ribbon and drawn by two white horses hired for the occasion.

It had gone by her in a dream and it was not until Mr Cameron's warm hand took her cold one that she came out of it. The hand was somehow comforting, and though he did not smile his eyes said something that reassured her. She could feel the hostility at her back, coming from the rows of Mr Cameron's friends and she had time to wonder why they had come, since she knew full well they did not approve. She had heard of Miss Cameron's move down to the cottage on the edge of the estate, and recognised the whispers that stopped abruptly when she entered the kitchen. Miss Cameron hated her, and would do anything she could to hurt her and could you blame her, for she, Briony, was the cause of her being turned out of her home. Just the same, she was glad that she had gone, for though she hadn't the faintest idea how to run a house like Longlake she was sure it would be easier without Miss Cameron forever at her elbow. Lizzie would help her and it was this that got her through the weeks leading up to this day. She had been up to the house, as its future mistress, and she could imagine what was being said up there, but it didn't matter, for what she was doing guaranteed Danny's future when he came home. Mr Cameron had promised her that he would use his influence to ensure Danny was as well treated during his sentence as his money could buy and as

she dreamed of the day Danny would be home she missed
the first few words of the wedding service. When she came
out of her reverie the Reverend Mr Armstrong was telling her
that she must obey Mr Cameron, that she must honour him
and love him and though she was not sure about the last she
made her vows in a clear voice, for she was determined to do
her best.

She had entered the church the low-born daughter of a
common working man, one who had been murdered by his
own son, her brother, but when she walked back up the aisle
her hand was held in the crook of her husband's arm. The arm
of Mr Chad Cameron, one of the most influential gentlemen
in Cumberland.

Due to the circumstances a large, elaborate reception was
not held, just a small wedding breakfast at Longlake Edge
attended by Chad's friends, though none of the bride's – that's
if she had any – were present except the tall, broad-shouldered
young woman who, it was rumoured, also had a relative
transported to the Australian colonies. Dear God, what sort
of a predicament had Chad Cameron got himself into, his
guests whispered among themselves, though the men were
inclined to envy him the night ahead, which he would spend
with the delicately lovely young woman who stood silently at
his side.

They were all there, on sufferance, of course, though
Briony was not aware of it. The Seddons with their Adeline
and her betrothed whom she was to marry in June. The
Addisons with Pansy who had had high hopes of the stern
bridegroom for herself. Ernestine and George Tyson with
Percival and Angela, the two young people inclined to look
down their noses at the upstart and view with astonishment
their father's insistence that they attend the wedding reception at all. The vicar and Mrs Armstrong did their best to
show their Christian charity, swelling the numbers with their

family of four. Among them, the parlour-maids, Daphne
and Gladys, who had declined to leave Longlake Edge with
Martha and Mrs Foster and move with Miss Sarah to the
Dower House, helped to serve the guests with the assistance of
two housemaids who were known to Miss Armstrong. Daphne
and Gladys, who were sisters, personally had not been aware
that the cottage went by such a grand name as the Dower
House, but that was what Miss Sarah had called it when she
informed them that she was off and asked, or rather ordered
them to accompany her. When it was pointed out tartly – by
Martha who felt she was entitled to say such things – that
there wasn't enough room for them all, Daphne, Gladys,
Minnie and Mabel were relieved to be able to stay where
they were. The new mistress would no doubt find a cook
and whoever else she felt necessary to staff the house, though
how a plain miller's daughter would know of such things
remained to be seen. What an upheaval! Rather exciting in
their opinion, their dull lives infected with the intoxication of
it all. Fancy Briony Marsden, who had sat at the kitchen table
with them, her hands red and sore with being in the hot water
of the laundry bucket, now being their mistress. And when
it got dark, which it would soon since it was still March, she
would get into their master's bed and have things done to her
they themselves, despite being country girls and used to the
farmyard, could really only imagine.

It was Lizzie who helped to undress her. Lizzie had been
given one of the guest bedrooms, one of such sumptuous
luxury she had hardly been able to believe her eyes when
Daphne had shown her to it. Surely, as a servant, which
was what she believed herself to be, she was not entitled
to sleep in a room such as this, but Daphne insisted that
Mr Cameron had ordered it. She would use it for now,
she told herself, as she removed the rather smart bonnet
Mr Cameron's generosity had allowed her to purchase from

Miss Avery, but when they had settled in, she and Briony, she would perhaps find herself a room in this great house that was not quite so grand, she told herself as she hurried along the broad landing to help Briony.

The room that was to be Briony's – and Mr Cameron's – was even more luxurious and, though neither of them knew of it, one that had been completely redecorated and refurnished by the master of the house for his bride. The one he had slept in since he was a boy was not, in his opinion, suitable for her, since it was a boy's room, a young man's room, masculine and somewhat spartan, but this, Lizzie thought, as she glanced round it, was the most beautiful room she had ever been in. To her it spoke of the love a man has for a woman and it confirmed her suspicions that Mr Cameron felt more for his young wife than he allowed anyone to know. It was soft, warm, feminine, the colours a misted rose, a pale, pale green, the carpet almost white. The curtains drifted in a lifting swirl of white muslin as Lizzie opened the door, a great fire flickered in the marble grate, reflecting, mirror-like in the pale, polished wood of the dressing-table, the delicately carved wardrobe and the cheval mirrors that stood on either side of it. There were framed pictures on the wall, small prints in delicate colours to match those of the room, of flowers and birds. The bed was draped with the same muslin curtains as at the windows and covered with a quilt of rose and cream, embroidered, she noticed with amazement, in lover's knots with the intials C and B entwined in them. Dear God, he *did* love her, and the thought filled her heart with thankfulness, for so did Lizzie Jenkins.

By the fire, in a position of total exhaustion, sat the bride. She was still wearing her wedding finery, staring into the flames of the fire and seemed unaware of her lovely, tranquil surroundings.

She did not turn round, for she seemed to know who had

entered the room. "I was thinking of Danny. I wonder where he is now? It's nine months and still I've had no letter. Mr Cameron said he'd make enquiries . . ." Her voice trailed off and she sighed tiredly.

Lizzie stood for a moment by the door. "Come, love, let's get you out of that dress," she murmured, stepping across the deep pile of the velvet carpet. "It's time you were in bed." She meant nothing by the remark, nothing to do with what was to happen in it, but Briony flinched and turned huge, deep purple eyes towards the bed.

"Yes, I suppose so." And obedient as a child she stood up and allowed Lizzie to undress her, then, when she was naked, lift the exquisite, almost transparent nightdress Miss Avery had personally stitched for her over her head. Lizzie brushed out her hair, turned back the covers and watched as Briony climbed into the bed, her own eyes downcast, for she could not bear to see the stricken look on Briony's face.

"Lizzie . . . ?" she appealed but Lizzie could not help her.

"It'll be all right, love. Mr Cameron is . . . is kind . . ."

She was sitting up in bed when he entered the bedroom, her hair hanging down her back as it had been when he had first seen her but now it was brushed and shining, the tangled mass of curls smoothed out to the texture of silk.

His heart contracted and his mouth was so dry he could hardly swallow, he who had known many women and was now as nervous as a raw boy with his first love. How could he do this to her who looked like a child, a frightened child? How could he take that demure nightgown from her, uncover her young body, allow his man's eyes to roam over it and his man's touch to violate that innocence? He didn't think he could. He loved her, God knew he loved her. He had desired her for months, longing to do what he was now legally allowed to but those eyes, that pale, exquisite face unmanned him and he was ready to turn, to murmur about leaving it for now, she must be tired, the day had been long, but he knew he must not. This thing must be done and done quickly, this hurdle climbed if they were to build any sort of bond between them, forge the trust he longed for, make the marriage which would be as strong and loving as his own parents' had been and, he had been told, his grandparents' too.

Her eyes continued to gaze watchfully at him and their expression reminded him of the day when he had caught her father beating her brother. They were almost haunted, as they had been then. Not exactly frightened but filled with a cautious wariness, like a small animal ready to leap away at the slightest movement from him. She would do what she had promised him. She was ready to fill her part of the bargain they had made, if it could be called such, but it was not of her choosing, he was made very aware of that.

He smiled with what he hoped was reassurance and began the long journey across the room to the bed and he was pleased to see that she did not flinch.

"I won't hurt you," he told her simply, wondering as he said it how truthful that remark was. "I think it best we . . . well, how much do you know of . . . of marriage, of what happens between men and women in . . ."

"My mother and father slept together. I often heard her cry out." Her voice was flat.

He turned away and walked to the window, looking out into the night, his heart saddened and sickened, for how was he to teach her that men were not always cruel to women? Returning to the bed he sat down and put a hand on her shoulder and still she did not flinch as he had expected her to. It seemed he had underestimated the strength and resolution of this bride, this child bride as he saw her, who was determined to see this thing through. His hand ran down her arm and back again to her neck, settling under her hair.

He drew her forward and put his lips to hers, their first kiss. It was soft, deep, caressing, his teeth teasing her bottom lip and he felt her withdraw slightly, in astonishment, he thought.

"You're really incredibly lovely," he murmured, his mouth still against hers then his hand went roughly into her hair. His arm went about her and drew her down in the bed. The covers were thrown back and with an oath he fumbled at the edge of her nightgown.

"I should wait, I suppose, but I can't, damn it. It must be done so let's get it over, shall we?"

"The candles . . ."

"Damn the candles. I want to see you." And see her he did as he lifted her nightgown away and began the slow and dreaming process of making love, as he knew it, to the beautiful young girl in his arms. She would have been glad to have it over and done with. To do whatever it was he wanted of her and then sleep, sleep off this nightmare that had come upon her. But Chad Cameron was a man in love, a lover who needed the woman he loved to take the same pleasure he did from this act. He would have been best served to simply take her, penetrate her, get it done with as she wanted, at least for this first time, but his senses demanded that he took possession of her slowly, his lips and hands smoothing every part of her body, her breasts and pink nipples, the satin of her belly, the sweet swell of her tight buttocks, the dark bush between her legs, her thighs and ankles and toes. Though she made no move to stop him, for she understood now what it was he had always wanted of her, she was bewildered and thankful when at last he shuddered and fell upon her passive body with a gasp.

His own body was beautiful, long, lean, muscled, his chest deep, his skin the colour of amber in the candlelight. She had not known a man could be so beautiful, her mind whispered strangely, but even as the thought drifted by a bruised and battered core inside her told her that soon it would be over and that every time she did this it brought the day when Danny would be returned to her that bit nearer.

When he had entered her she froze for a moment in the agony of it then he had called out her name and that wounded core of her had eased a little.

Later, as he slept with his cheek against her breast, she wept silently, brushing away the tears so that they would not fall on him.

16

The man's name was Jacob Kean. He was about thirty years old, tall and thin and gaunt, with a prominent Adam's apple which moved up and down in his throat as he swallowed nervously. He reminded Briony of Danny in some way and because of it she was disposed to approve of him. He was dark, his hair lank and already thinning, but his eyes were blue and frank and his mouth was gentle.

She sat at the table in the kitchen of the mill and Mr Cameron, as she still called him despite what he did to her each night in their bed, lounged against the wall beside the open door, his arms crossed on his chest. Jacob Kean had been asked to sit opposite her, which he did reluctantly since it seemed to him that he should stand in the presence of this beautiful and beautifully dressed young woman whose mill this was. Well, it belonged to her brother, he had been told, but she was looking after it until he returned, though from what he heard that would be a long way off, if ever, which was one of the reasons he had applied to have the leasing of it.

"Perhaps you could tell us something of yourself, Mr Kean," she asked him politely, speaking like a lady but with the definite accent of the fell country in her voice.

He cleared his throat. "Well, ma'am, I've bin a miller since I were a lad. Me faither were one an' 'e taught me all 'e knew until 'e died. 'E slipped under t'wheels of a cart loaded wi' grain. It took off one of 'is legs an' 'e bled ter death afore tha' could say knife. I were fifteen. Eeh, I beg tha' pardon, ma'am," suddenly aghast at his own insensitivity in mentioning such a thing to this gently bred young woman, as he believed her to be, but she waved her hand dismissively.

"Please do not concern yourself, Mr Kean. I am interested to know if you have ever worked in a mill of this kind and also why you are seeking to take over this one. Why did you leave your last position? Have you a family and if so . . ."

He was eager to tell his life story to this gracious young woman, though he did wonder why it was she and not her husband, or so he had been told, who questioned him. The mill his father had worked had not been his own. He had been a tenant until he died and since then, unable to take over the tenancy, Jacob had been employed by a miller near Croglin. Fifteen years he had worked for him, doing his gritty best to accumulate the necessary wherewithal to purchase a property of his own. He was a good miller, a strong and honest man, but time was passing and when he had heard that the tenancy of Moorend was being offered he had asked his Betty if she was prepared to move away from her family down to what was foreign parts to them who had never gone further than the next village in their entire lives. She had agreed and here he was. It was said without a pause.

"Yes, here you are, Mr Kean, but may I ask how you heard of Moorend?" Briony asked him while Chad stood and watched her and said nothing, for this is what he had promised her. She had done what she had promised. She had become his wife and if she seemed, as yet, to take no pleasure in it, she lay in his bed at night and allowed him to love her body, to do as he liked, to gaze at her in the golden lamplight, to turn her this way and that for his own pleasure, making no objection to his demands which, since he was a normal man, were many and varied though not perverted. He was patient and loving, she was patient and passive and one day, he was convinced, he would make her love him as he loved her. She did not, of course, know how he felt!

"I were on an errand fer t' maister an', well . . ." He looked somewhat sheepish but Jacob Kean could not tell a lie, since he had been brought up in the Methodist persuasion. "I shouldn't a' bin there, me being Methodist but it were a longish journey an' I stopped at the Farmer's Arms at Renwick fer a tankard of ale. This 'ere chap were goin' on about the miller at Little Salkeld an' 'ow 'e were pulled out wi' work on account o' this place at Moorend bein' closed like but it were goin' beggin' fer any chap what would work. An' that's me, ma'am," he finished simply.

There was a silence in which the sound of the flock of starlings swinging over the roof was distinctly heard. A ewe called to her lamb on Chad Cameron's intake land and a dog barked, probably Sal who was out in the field with Thomas and Billy.

Chad pushed himself away from the wall. He remained for a moment, tall and brooding, then, seeming to shake himself, he moved to stand behind his wife, putting his hands possessively on her shoulders, resisting the temptation to smooth them, to run his fingers across her white neck, to bend and kiss it. He wanted her badly with none of the fleeting passion he had felt for other women but with a sharp, almost painful desire that was becoming an obsession with him. Briony lifted her chin and felt a strange need to stretch under his touch, but Jacob Kean was waiting for her to speak, his plain, honest face clamped into a grim expression in which hope did its best not to flare. He was surprised that such a young lass had a husband so much older than herself but then that was the way of the gentry. They did not need to marry young, as he and his Betty had, since with their wealth women were available to them when and where they wanted them. The only way men of his class could get their hands on a woman was by marrying her. Not that that was the reason he had married Betty. They were right fond of one another but it was hard for them to get on when Betty would keep having bairns one after the other. Seven in ten years of marriage and another on the way. If he didn't get this mill . . . Well, it would be the will of God and they'd have to accept it but it was hard.

If he had known of the thoughts that were swirling round and round in the young head of Mr Chadwick's wife his hopes, those he did his best to keep damped down, would have flared into a fire of exultation, and thanks to his God.

"Perhaps we should think this over, my dear." Chad's voice was husky and he did his best to clear it, make it firmer, but even now he found it hard to touch his wife and not feel the need in him, the hot, explosive passion flood his mind and his body. He was in thrall to her and it was a bloody good job that all his affairs were in such perfect order, working smoothly in the pattern he had set them, or the whole sorry lot would come tumbling down about his ears. When he was away from her, perhaps for only a day in Penrith or Carlisle, he found that his mind would slide backwards to that moment the night before when he had stripped her in the firelight, then, naked himself, he had placed his mouth on her taut belly and . . . and . . . Dear God, he loved her.

"We have other applicants," he continued, but Briony stood up and began to stride about the small room, swinging the full bell of her skirts as she turned. It was early June and for the first time she wore the silk gown Miss Avery had created for her in spring. It was the palest dove grey decorated with bands of peach, the bodice well fitted, the skirt full. Her bonnet framed her face, again a pale dove grey to match her gown with ruched peach muslin under the brim. She wore pale grey kid gloves and boots and carried a parasol of peach muslin. She looked exquisite and was often pleased and surprised by her own appearance but she felt it was really nothing to do with her since Miss Avery did it all. She chose the styles, the colours, the fabrics, the bonnets, the high-heeled boots and, putting them all together, turned Briony Marsden, the miller's daughter, into Mrs Chad Cameron, the stylish young woman she had become since her marriage.

She liked Jacob Kean but, more to the point, one hidden from Mr Cameron, she felt that she would be able to manipulate him. By that she meant he was unlikely to object to her interference in the running of the mill. And she intended to interfere, oh, yes, indeed. This man would be meek, humble, grateful and, as far as she could ascertain, not a particularly good businessman or by now, in all these years he had been a miller, he would have moved further than working for another. He would pay her rent for the tenancy of the mill and to pay that rent he would need to work hard and have a hard head. He *would* work hard, she was sure, his honest face told her that, but would his head be hard enough to make the profit she needed, to build up the business, to regain what had been lost when her father died so that when Danny came home it would all be there waiting for him? She didn't think so and anyway, what did it matter? She would be there to make sure that the business prospered. Jacob Kean was just a figurehead. She had known from the beginning that Mr Cameron would not allow a wife of his to be the miller in her brother's place but, as Sadie was so fond of saying, there were more ways of killing a cat than stuffing it with cream!

The miller stood up uncertainly, one hand on the table, the other holding his battered hat. He had walked here from Croglin, he had told them, tramping the sheep trods across the fells to Kirkoswald, down the valley to Edenhall and on to Penrith. He had slept in a stable at the back of the George and been given his breakfast by the landlord in return for cleaning out after the horses. She could see from the state of his worn boots that the miles had been weary ones and though she might argue with Mr Cameron over this, for he was a businessman and would need a good return for his money – her money – she meant to have him. There might be others more suitable – she was sure Mr Cameron would say so – but this one served *her* purpose. Already Billy had told her that there had been a tentative enquiry – Billy had not used those exact words – on the possibility of bringing his corn to be milled from some farmer over Penruddock way, and if one came perhaps she would regain the trade that had vanished when her father died and Danny was sent away.

"When can you start, Mr Kean?" she asked him abruptly, ignoring Mr Cameron's warning exclamation and the frown which dipped his eyebrows.

"Eeh, missis," Jacob Kean spluttered, forgetting his manners which told him he should address this lady as "ma'am". "Dost mean tha'll tekk me on?" He was ready to jig about like a child and his artless face split into a wide smile which revealed the poor state of his teeth.

"I do, Mr Kean." Briony could feel the doubt emanating from her husband and, knowing he was about to object, for he was a man of hard-headed business and such a man would not rush impetuously into an agreement, she turned and bestowed a wide smile upon him. Her eyes were the loveliest colour, that blue which was not really one shade but a mixture of sweet violet, of pansy and of lavender, and yet a lilac purple. They changed colour, lightening or darkening with her mood and now, as her delight shone from them, her excitement at the knowledge that at last, almost a year after his departure, her plans for Danny were about to be put in place, they were the clear and shining colour of lilac in spring. She had received a letter from him, and Lizzie one from her father, crumpled things which must have passed through many hands and had returned on the ship that had taken them out. Danny's had said nothing more than that he and the old man, Mr Jenkins, had arrived at this place called Botany Bay and were both in good spirits. It mentioned nothing of the horror of the journey, the filth and degradation they had suffered, the rats, the meagre and rotten food, the diseases which had finished off scores of their fellow passengers but, probably because they had both begun their journey in relatively good health, they had survived. Only just in the old man's case, though he did not say so. He was waiting anxiously to hear from her but he would not worry, for he had perfect trust in Mr Cameron.

She and Lizzie had wept over the grimy notes and both of them, Briony to Danny and Lizzie to her father, had sat down and immediately replied, putting their letters, as they had done for the past twelve months, in Mr Cameron's hand in the sure belief that he would see that they got to the two men on the fastest ship that was to sail there. She never once questioned her perfect trust in this man who was her husband, never doubted that he could, and would, find a way to make Danny's exile as easy as his money and influence could manage. He knew people in high places and though he had been unable to alter the course of justice, or justice as the law saw it, and keep Danny from his appalling sentence, she believed utterly that he would make it as painless as circumstances allowed.

"Briony, I would be glad to have further discussion with you on the matter before we decide to give Mr Kean the job. It seems to me that we should at least see the other men who—"

"Oh, stuff and nonsense, Mr Cameron, I believe Mr Kean to be the perfect man to run the mill and can see no purpose in wasting our time or his on further—"

He raised his hand and in his narrowing eye was a gleam which, until now, she had never seen. It had been there when he had restrained her father from beating Danny to pulp. Then it had been a full explosion of flashing rage, but now that glitter heralded his displeasure, not only at her arguing with him but in doing so in front of the astonished Jacob Kean. He was not accustomed to being told that what he said was "stuff and nonsense" and though his face wore its usual lack of expression, he could not control the bright glint in his eyes.

"Do you not?" His hand was poised and for a horrified moment both she and Jacob thought he meant to strike her but instead it took hold of hers and drew her towards him and Jacob Kean watched in fascination until, with a polite nod, Mr Cameron asked if he might leave himself and his wife alone for a moment.

When he had gone, Briony's face a picture of wary consternation, he put his arms about her and with a savagery she had never before been subjected to, he took her lips and ground his own against them. Her arms dangled at her side and her bonnet tipped to the back of her head but she could feel the violence of his teeth against hers as her lips parted and her tongue inched to meet his. Her heart began to pound and something like fire ran through her veins as her body pressed itself against him – or did his press against hers? – even more closely.

It lasted no more than ten seconds but when he let her go she swayed against him and almost fell. He was smiling triumphantly, for it was the first time that he had felt the response in her but it did not last long.

"What the devil was that for?" she gasped. "I was doing business with—"

"Were you, my pet? Were you indeed? Well, that may be so but in future if you should ever decide that you can make a fool of me before someone who may, or may not, become an employee, or indeed anyone at all, please remember that it is I who have the final word."

"Really!" Her breath was raw in her throat as she gasped out the word. "Well, let me tell you that I shall—"

"You will do nothing unless I approve of it, my dear wife. I don't think you understand. Moorend Mill was your property, not your brother's: he forfeited all right to it when he was convicted of your father's murder. Now I am your husband I have control of it, of any profits it might make. Now I am quite happy to see that it makes a profit and I promise you that when your brother returns to England I will make it over to him. But what I am not happy about is your belief that it is you and not me who is to make the decisions. Dear God in heaven—"

"But you said we had a bargain. If I was to marry you—"

"I would keep the mill going until Danny returns. I intend to do so."

"But what about me?"

"You are my wife."

"Only because you forced me."

She did not see him flinch nor the spasm of pain that twitched his face as he turned away casually to the window, where beyond it the anxious figure of Jacob Kean idled.

"You are my wife and I expect you to act out the part, no matter how abhorrent it may be to you."

"Why did you kiss me like that?"

He turned to smile at her. He did not tell her that it was the only way, through physical strength, that he could dominate her, that he could force her to *his* will. Instead he told her, "I happen to like kissing you, my pet, and it seemed as good a way as any to distract you from your bull-headed determination to have Mr Kean as the new miller. You see I'm not convinced he is the right man for the job. He is too . . . I hate to use the word *soft*, but it needs someone with a hard head to run—"

"Like my father, you mean?"

"I did not say cruel, Briony, only a man with a bit of resourcefulness, even cunning, one who would not be averse to outwitting a customer if he could get away with it. I'm sure Jacob Kean would be an honest man but is he—"

"I want him." She lifted her chin. Her shoulders squared stubbornly and she glared at him. Her eyes flashed a deep, offended purple and she stepped back as though she would accept no more kisses, nor indeed anything unless he bent to her will. She was like a young puppy which growls in play, which jumps and leaps on its prey in the firm belief that it is quite capable of attack and is unaware that one swipe will have it spinning away into a corner. He wanted to laugh, to drag her towards him, to kiss her into submission, to have her bend her body against his, to laugh softly in return in the playful love-making he longed for and if Jacob Kean had not been lurking about beyond the door he might have lifted her to his chest, carried her up the stairs to the room that had once been her mother's, and then hers, and made love to her until she wept with the joy of it. A dream! A dream he harboured but which, since it was no more than nine or ten weeks since their wedding day, he still had high hopes of.

Well, he supposed he could let her have her way if it made it easier for him to achieve what he yearned for. After all, he was here to watch over the man, to make sure he made a bob or two, or three or four; to make sure the business flourished under his guidance. No enterprise or investment he had ever had a hand in had failed and this one would be no different; and if he could keep that look of gratitude on her face; perhaps have her more passionate instead of just compliant in his bed as he had sensed just now she might be, then it would be worth the risk.

"Come here," he told her, but her bottom lip sprang out and she continued to glare at him.

"Come here and kiss me and then, who knows, if you are grateful enough, and show it I might . . ."

She grinned then. Dear Lord, how easy it was to twist this man about her finger, she thought, as she sauntered across the space between them, standing before him, not touching him but letting him see that he could touch her, which he did, but not as she had expected. With deft fingers he undid the top buttons of her bodice, turned her round so that her back was to his chest and slipped his hand inside, cupping her breast. She was so surprised she did nothing, but her nipples rose instantly into hard peaks and when his mouth smoothed the flesh under her ear she arched her back and a small cry sounded in her throat.

"You like that?" he murmured, joyful in his success but she whipped herself away and hastily buttoned up her gown. Her cheeks were rosy and though she pretended offence he had felt her response again and was satisfied.

"Lord, the man's just outside the window," she whispered.

"You'd best call him in and tell him the good news then." He grinned, turning to ease the discomfort in his breeches.

Jacob Kean and his wife Betty, with their seven children and one on the way, moved into Moorend Mill the following week and barely before their cart was unpacked and their few possessions stowed away in the mill house, Seth Cartwright's waggon was at the ramp that led into the bagging and drive floor. With the help of Thomas and Billy to manhandle the sacks on to the hoist, the water wheel, which, like the rest of the machinery, had been kept in good working condition for the launching of this day, began to turn.

"Eeh, Jake," his Betty said, her rotund figure bustling out into the yard to exchange pleasantries with their first customer, "it's goin' ter be grand 'ere. Look at them bairns," watching her offspring with a good-natured, easy-going eye as they rolled about the grass at the edge of the woodland where once Danny and Briony had cowered in fear of their father. Alfred, who was ten years old, a serious lad like his father, was giving a hand to Thomas and Billy, learning the business as his pa had done, and when the grand lady strode into the mill yard its occupants turned to stare, Seth Cartwright more so than the others.

"Good morning, Mr Cartwright," the grand lady called out. "And how are you this lovely day? Is Mrs Cartwright well?" She smiled her vivid smile in his direction and you could have knocked Seth Cartwright down with a feather, he told his Alice later. There she was, Jethro Marsden's little lass, all tricked up to the nines in a handsome outfit of good blue broadcloth just like *real* ladies wore. Pretty as the cornflowers in the meadow, a dashing bonnet on her head with a veil curling about its brim, a basket with a parcel of some sort wrapped in a snowy cloth and polished boots you could see your face in despite the walk across the fields.

She held out her gloved hand for him to shake, which he did. He was fascinated by the change in her. It must be getting on for a year since her brother had been sent away to his fate and in that time she had been transformed from a whey-faced child into this incredibly lovely, softly rounded young woman, and he could only suppose it was Chad Cameron who had worked the miracle. "Summat" suited her, he told Alice, winking lewdly, earning a slap against his chest from Alice, though she couldn't help but smile.

"So, you have decided after all that you will have your wheat milled at Moorend, Mr Cartwright?" Mrs Chad Cameron said, a certain irony in her voice, and honestly he didn't know where to put himself, he told Alice, for hadn't Mr Cameron been up to the farm only the other day to tell him that from now on the mill at Moorend was in full production. Will

Stirling at Brett Farm, Jack Carey at Bramble, Len Stephens at Mell Farm and a score of others, farmers and villagers, had been paid a similar visit and would, bit by bit, bring their business back to Moorend, which was a bloody good job in his opinion for that walk up to Little Salkeld had been a waste of his good time and money. Mr Cameron would make it worth his while, he had been told, perhaps an easing of his rent to make up for it, though this lass was not to know. Really, it was a bloody mystery, he had told Alice, what Mr Cameron had ordered them all to do; something to do with Jethro Marsden's lass, that was bloody obvious, but she seemed to be thriving on it.

She walked across the cobbled yard which needed weeding, a job Betty Kean meant to put her children to as soon as they had settled in. Them two lads who they were to take on to help Jacob, or so Mr Cameron had told them when they had finished with the corn, were to be out in the fields doing only they knew what, for though Betty was a country lass she knew nothing about growing things. Her pa had had a small garden where he grew a few potatoes and carrots but the big field was bursting with vegetables, with good grass to be turned into hay to feed the animals, they had told her, so there would be plenty of good, fresh food to put on her table. She was made up, was Betty, though she'd miss her ma and her vast family back in Croglin.

She bobbed a curtsey to Briony, wiping her hands on her apron, then indicated that the wife of the greatest landowner in the district should enter her kitchen, oblivious, or perhaps not yet quite understanding that this had once been the home of the grand lady who hesitated on her threshwood.

"Wilta tekk a seat, Mrs Cameron," she offered, hastily picking their Belle from her cradle. At six months old the baby was making a great caterwauling for the breast which flowed with Betty's copious milk and which for the past ten years had hardly had a chance to dry up. "'Appen a drink o' tea." She put the baby on her hip from where she stared with wide-eyed interest at their guest, but Briony shook her head, smiling. She meant to make a friend of this woman, for if Briony had her way, which she meant to, she would be spending a great deal of time with her. Well, not with her particularly, for the domestic arrangements of the mill did not concern her. Only its workings and the amount of business it would do.

"I just wanted to make sure you had everything you needed." She looked round the familiar kitchen which was bright, shining, spotless as Minnie and Fanny had left it, at the cheerful fire which flickered and glowed in the copper pans lining the walls. Her mother's pans, her *grandmother's* pans which Emily had brought with her when she married Jethro. For a moment she felt her mother's gentle, damaged spirit drift through the room, quiet, submissive, as her life had been before her violent death. Then the children erupted into the room, cheerful, vigorous, bursting with life and at once Emily was gone and Briony sighed with deep satisfaction, for it seemed the ghosts of Moorend Mill were laid for ever.

17

As Lizzie entered the kitchen of Longlake Edge it suddenly burst into a frenzy of stirring, chopping, whisking and kneading, giving the appearance that there were at least a dozen maids all tearing themselves to shreds in the preparation of a banquet. The new cook, Mrs Minty was leaning over the range, the wooden spoon with which she had been stirring gravy to her lips, on her face an expression of deep concern, while Minnie stood beside her anxiously awaiting her comments. Daphne was chopping parsley, her face screwed into lines of acute concentration, and Fanny, also new like Mrs Minty, but merely a scullery-maid, was attacking something in a large baking bowl. Dicky could be seen polishing knives in the scullery as though his life depended on it and all this activity Lizzie knew was for her benefit. It was three months since she had taken over the task of what she supposed she could call "housekeeper" at Longlake and she was well aware that the servants, old and new, had been gossiping before she entered the room and at the sound of her approach had sprung into action. They could not quite get the measure of her, she was well aware. She was the friend and companion of their mistress, the new Mrs Cameron, and therefore did not quite fit into the role of servant, as they did, and yet she had, in the chaos that had reigned after the departure of Miss Sarah, Mrs Foster, Martha, and Mabel, taken over the running of the house.

From the rumours that had flown about the place for

weeks after the amazing wedding of their master to Jethro Marsden's lass, it had gradually come to light that Miss Jenkins, who was the daughter of the man transported with young Danny Marsden, had some claim to breeding. Her father was a scholar, a man come from a good family, and her dead mother a relative in a roundabout way of gentry in the Midlands. It appeared that Miss Jenkins knew the right way to go about things, things being the way to run a house such as Longlake Edge, and it had seemed only sensible, or so the master thought, that Miss Jenkins should stand in for the mistress, teaching her what she herself knew, until Mrs Cameron could take over.

What a day it had been when Miss Sarah had moved out! The farm cart, pulled by a plough horse, had made a dozen journeys between the big house and the Dower House, taking Miss Sarah's possessions – a great deal of them and would they all fit into the Dower House, Martha was heard to say. It would be a bit of a squash for the servants, she and Mrs Foster, who had had their own rooms at Longlake, having to share one tiny bedroom in the roof and Mabel, who had decided finally to go with her mistress – the devil you knew being better than one you didn't – with the new scullery-maid, Livvy, in the second. Mr Cameron had been heard to say to Miss Sarah that he would employ a builder to extend the small, square house to make further rooms but if she was intent on going now she must put up with the lack of space for the time being.

"I'd rather live in a chicken shed than share my home with that slut," Miss Sarah hissed.

"But do you need so many servants to look after your needs, Sarah?" he had been heard to ask patiently, ignoring the slur on his wife-to-be. It appeared that the mistress did not care who overheard her remarks about the girl their master was about to marry and you could see he was not ready to quarrel with her on the very doorstep. He had that shuttered look about his face that told them, and her, absolutely nothing about his feelings.

"I am used to certain standards and I will not lower them. I shall be entertaining as I have always done and besides, my servants are accustomed to working beside decent, respectable women."

"My wife will not be working in the kitchen, Sarah."

But Sarah continued as though he had not spoken. "And to serving ladies, not guttersnipes like . . . like that girl. They wish to come with me and I cannot deny them."

On the day following the wedding those who were left, Daphne and Gladys and Minnie, hung about in the kitchen and waited for orders. Waited for their new mistress to come and tell them what she needed doing in the way of menus for the day, and, more to the point, who was to do the cooking. They might manage a bit of breakfast, bacon and eggs perhaps for the master, but the luncheon, the dinner, not only for today, but for ever, they presumed, was another thing. Could *she* cook? Even if she could it was hardly likely the mistress of the house would don an apron and set to at the range. Daphne and Gladys, who had been trained by Miss Sarah, had risen early as usual, taking up hearth-rugs, sweeping the breakfast-room, the dining-room, the master's study, the drawing-room, cleaning out grates, disposing of the cinders, laying fresh fires, dusting and polishing the downstairs rooms before starting on the stairs, waiting for the master and mistress to show themselves when they could then turn out the bedrooms.

Miss Jenkins was the first to appear, descending the stairs where Daphne was just removing her housemaid's box.

"Good morning, er . . ." Miss Jenkins said smilingly, enquiringly, nervously, though Daphne was not made aware of it.

"Daphne, miss," Daphne murmured, unsure whether to curtsey or bob her head as she might to another servant.

"A lovely day, Daphne."

"Yes, miss." Then Daphne fled down the stairs and into the kitchen.

"She's up," she hissed at Gladys who was about to move into the breakfast-room to lay the cloth for breakfast.

"Who? Mistress?" Gladys opened her eyes wide and grimaced as though imagining the change they might see in the insubstantial waif who had wandered up to her room last night, still in her wedding dress. The waif who was now in charge of them, amazing as it seemed.

"No, t'other 'un. What shall we do?" They were whispering as though "t'other 'un" could hear them through the thick walls. Minnie, who had only remained because she had hopes of Iolo who often sat in the kitchen with the maidservants at dinner-time, watched them with an open mouth, for they were all unsure what was to happen in this . . . well, they didn't really know what to call this *thing* that had come upon them. A catastrophe, perhaps, or maybe, with a young and ignorant mistress, it might turn out to be a holiday from now on compared to the strictness of Miss Sarah.

They were soon enlightened. Had it not been for Lizzie, with her strong will, her knowledge of housekeeping learned from her mother, her sense of her own self-worth and certainty of how to display it, Chad Cameron would have had to put up with a general tumbling into slipshod ways.

Breakfast that first day was a bungled affair of burned bacon, spilled coffee, cold plates, overcooked eggs and Minnie's inclination to scream and hand in her notice, for she was a scullery-maid not a cook and had never made coffee in her life. Aye, she'd knocked up a greasy plate of bacon and eggs for her pa in the cottage in Howtown from where she had come at the age of twelve, but in five years at Longlake she had not done much more than scour pans, scrub floors, peel potatoes and clean windows and anything else the others ordered her to do.

Since Mr Cameron and Briony seemed disinclined to speak let alone look at one another, it was left to Lizzie to take matters in hand. Mr Cameron wore the dazed look of, well, she couldn't put a name to it never having seen a new bridegroom the day after his wedding night, but she supposed it was something to do with what he and Briony had just shared, and as for her friend it seemed to her it took her all her time to lift her eyes from her plate.

"This won't do, Briony," Mr Chadwick said at last, eyeing the piece of blackened toast on his plate then turning his sombre, brooding look on his bride. "I appreciate that it is not your fault that half the servants have left with my sister but more must be engaged. A cook and . . . well, whatever maids are needed."

"And how is that done, Mr Cameron? How does one employ a cook?" Briony's voice was crisp.

"I'm not sure. I've never had to deal with such—"

"And neither have I," she retorted coldly. Briony had realised during the painful night she had just endured with this man who sat glowering opposite her that she was to pay a high price to save her brother's mill. She would do it, of course, for she had given her word but the indignities he had heaped upon her last night had humiliated and shamed her, not to mention *amazed* her. Besides the painful penetration of her body that she had suffered, the sheer indignity of the act, the contortions and noises Mr Cameron had made seemed to her to be quite extraordinary. But she had gritted her teeth and remained passive under his ministrations. She did not believe he deliberately hurt her and when, this morning, to her consternation he had done it all over again, she had to admit it had not been quite so painful. He was a mature man and had, she supposed, done this many times and as a woman, a *wife*, she had no grounds for complaint, nor indeed had she any choice! She had entered this of her own free will and she believed in and trusted her husband. She always had. She might not love him but she trusted him. He had done all he had told her he would in the best interests of Danny and would continue to do so, she was convinced of that. And really, was it any hardship to live in this lovely house, in the luxury and comfort and warmth she had never before known? So if she had to put up with Mr Cameron's nightly embrace then so be it. She was strong and resolute and it would all be worth it when Danny came home. A year had already passed and look what she had achieved and would continue to achieve at the mill. But Mr Cameron seemed to be telling her something, asking something of her to do with Longlake and the servants, which she had not even considered in her ruthless drive to resume trade at Moorend.

"This meal we have just eaten is not what I'm used to. I know you are not . . . have not been trained to run a house like this, to interview servants, but it must be done. We shall be expected to entertain."

"Entertain?"

"Of course. I think I might honestly say that within a few days you will be receiving callers" – since Chad was well aware what the attendance of polite society at his wedding meant – "and when they have left their cards—"

"Cards? Callers?" Briony was appalled. She had thought no further than the wedding, the night she had just spent with Mr Cameron, the bargain she had negotiated and which in her opinion had been completed, and it had made no mention of cards and calling and employing staff. Indeed she had not the faintest conception of how to run a great house and would, besides, be too busy keeping her eye on Danny's inheritance to bother herself with the trivia expected

of the wife of a man of influence as it seemed her husband was.

Lizzie cleared her throat and they both turned to her,
Chad with surprise since he had not expected to find her
at his breakfast table this morning, far less take a part in this
conversation, and Briony with hope.

"May I make a suggestion?" Her plain, pleasant face smiled
from one to the other and Chad listened, his dark face
expressionless. He was appalled by the chaos that appeared
to reign in the kitchen and yet could he be surprised, for had
not Sarah run the house like clockwork? Now that she was
gone how could he have expected it to go on as it had always
done, even in her absence? In his eagerness to get Briony to
the altar and then into his bed he had given no thought to the
domestic life at Longlake Edge and how it was to continue
without Sarah. Even now his body throbbed with the memory
of the night he had spent with Briony and with the anticipation
of having her naked in his arms as soon as was seemly. Dear
God, *seemly*! Did he care whether the women who lived under
this roof considered him to be an ardent bridegroom or a cold
fish or indeed *what* they thought? But he was also aware that
this domestic hotch-potch must be sorted out and as soon as
possible. Briony looked the part in her elegant morning gown,
her hair a tumble of curls tied up in a careless ribbon, quite
glorious, in fact. The lady of the house at breakfast opposite
her husband but she was not the mistress of the house in the
true sense of the word. She would learn. She *must* learn. To
be a hostess, to entertain his friends and acquaintances but
who in God's name was to teach her?

He looked politely at Lizzie Jenkins and waited.

"Might I make a suggestion, Mr Cameron?" she asked
again.

"Of course."

"I have some experience of . . . well, my mother came

from a home something like this." She glanced about her at the comfortable breakfast-room. "My father also but he was the fourth in a family of sons and when they married, my father and mother, there was nothing for him. He was a scholar, a teacher, a man clever with words and figures and so they moved away from the family and set up on their own. I will not go into detail." She ducked her head as though at some remembered sadness. "My mother was frail, my father took a post in an accountant's office and, well, you know the rest. But I am conversant, since my parents kept their way of life, in a small way, of course, in how to deal with servants, the way things are done in a house such as this and if you agree, until Briony is capable of doing it herself, might I offer myself as a kind of housekeeper? I could advertise for a cook and whatever staff is needed in the kitchen."

Briony burst into life, rapturous, enchanting, her smile slicing at Chad's heart, since it was not for him she smiled.

"Oh, Lizzie, could you? I really had no idea that you were a lady." She grinned engagingly. "I don't mean that as it sounded but you know that I'm not, don't you. The laundry is about the only place I know here and Sadie is in charge there so that will continue to run efficiently. The kitchen is another matter, so if you could take over I would be eternally grateful."

Chad frowned. "Miss Jenkins is not to take over, Briony. She is to teach you how to run this house—"

"Oh, of course," she said impatiently, not even turning to look at him, her whole being concentrated on Lizzie. "But in the meanwhile . . ."

"Yes?" he said ominously, his hands busy crumbling the burned toast that remained on his plate. Briony did not see it but Lizzie did and she frowned and shook her head.

"If I am to be housekeeper, Briony, which you will need, it must be on a proper footing."

"Of course." Though she had no idea what that might mean.

"I shall need my own sitting-room and a wage, a house-keeper's wage," turning to look at Chad Cameron.

"Naturally, that will be all right, won't it, Mr Cameron?" Briony turned her vivid smile on her husband. The relief of knowing that Lizzie was to take up the reins of this house, leaving her free to do as she pleased intoxicated her and her smile was, for the first time, directed at him, a true, warm smile, a grateful smile and he felt the loveliness of it uncurl some hard knot that persisted in his chest. If only she would smile at him for his own sake and not because he had allowed her her way but surely, that would come soon. When she had settled in to her new life, become used to the luxury, the reality, the pattern of being his wife and mistress of Longlake Edge, then she would . . . would what? Be as he had dreamed of her being? His wife in the true sense of the word. His lover. His friend, or was he just grabbing at mist, doing his best to hold a handful, which every fool knew was impossible?

He smiled his courteous smile, a smile which hardly ever reached his eyes and did not do so now, and Lizzie Jenkins watched him and knew that the hurt inside was tearing him to shreds and would never be mended until his little bride could love him as he loved her.

She spent much of those first weeks living the life that her husband wanted her to, performing her duties diligently under Lizzie's tutelage, biding her time, though neither Lizzie nor Chad knew it. Her house became orderly and well managed, because of Lizzie who rose early with the servants and retired late. Lizzie had been taught to be frugal but there was no need of it at Longlake Edge, for Mr Cameron was used to luxury, good food and wines, efficient service and was prepared to pay for it.

Because she was a new wife and therefore a person newly arrived in the neighbourhood, so to speak, cards were left by Mrs Seddon, by Mrs Addison, by Mrs Tyson, by Mrs Gould, each card bearing her and her husband's name, all of which confused Briony, for what did it all mean and what was she supposed to do, if anything, with these fanciful bits of cardboard?

"It means they will call on you," Lizzie explained, "and that you will return their calls."

Briony sprang to her feet and began to swirl about the drawing-room, ready to kick the small tables, covered with the exquisite ornaments in which the previous mistresses of Longlake had taken such pride, to the far side of the room.

"Good God almighty, what next? I haven't the slightest intention of having these high and mighty women condescending to come driving over here in their smart carriages in order to queen it over me and even less intention of going to their houses."

"They will remain no more than fifteen minutes, Briony. They won't even remove their bonnets. They are just visits of courtesy which will, hopefully, merge into visits of friendship."

"Don't talk such rubbish, Lizzie. How can I possibly be friends with these women when they are all intimates of Mr Cameron's sister who hates the very sound of my name?" Briony's voice was flat and cold. "I have only one friend, no two, you and Sadie and she seems to be uneasy when I call."

"Can you blame her, Briony? You're no longer the laundrymaid who helped her with the mangling. Look at you. You're the wife of the most influential man in the district."

"But I'm no different, Lizzie." Briony's voice was passionate with sadness, for at the moment she was neither flesh, fowl nor fish. Somewhere between changing her name from Briony

Marsden to Mrs Chad Cameron she had lost herself, her true self, and until she could settle into this life she had chosen she wandered desolately between the two. Her days were filled with what she called domestic trivia, walking a few steps behind Lizzie in superintending her servants, interviewing and employing a new cook, a scullery-maid, both recommended by Mrs Armstrong, the vicar's wife, upon whom Lizzie had called for advice on the matter. The tradespeople with whom she came in contact, who knew the neighbourhood and who might be looking for new situations, had been helpful, as had Mrs Armstrong.

So, Mrs Minty and young Fanny had been employed and the house, under Lizzie's watchful supervision and Briony's surly indifference, ran smoothly again. Each night Chad Cameron made love to his wife, and several times on a Sunday afternoon, when he had caught her unexpectedly in their bedroom. He had removed her clothes in broad daylight and laid her on the bed, ignoring her heated objections that Daphne or Gladys might come in.

"Let them," he murmured as his tongue glided across her flat stomach and down into the dark bush of hair between her legs. "We are married, my pet, and this is quite legal."

"Surely not in broad daylight," she answered primly as she lay back. If she was honest, which at the moment she was not prepared to be, she rather enjoyed what this extremely attractive man did to her, now that she was used to it. He made her stretch and sigh and though whatever it was that made her act as she did continued to elude her, she was willing to oblige him.

It was on one such occasion as she lay against the pillows, with his head beside hers, both of them still naked, he smoking a cigar, that he told her lazily that he had a present for her.

"A present?" She was still child enough to take an eager interest in the frequent gifts he gave her, mostly jewellery, diamond earrings, a brooch of amethyst to match her eyes, a gold bracelet set with pearls. She sat up, her small, coral-tipped breasts falling forward, her hair rumpling about her shoulders and down her back. He cupped one breast, then pushed back her hair and smiled.

"Aye. Would you like to see it?"

She shrugged with pretended indifference.

"Very well, if you're not interested . . ."

"I didn't say that."

"I have one stipulation." His eyes were a luminous amber as they looked into hers.

"Really, and what is that?" Her voice was cool, for she imagined he was going to demand something of her that would tie her even more closely to her duties as his wife when all she longed to do was go down to the mill and see how Jacob Kean was getting on. From what she had heard business was brisk but she wanted to get a look at the books, at the state of the machinery and buildings. Make sure that Danny's holding – for she could not quite admit to herself that it belonged to Chad Cameron – was being looked after.

He reached up and kissed her, his lips lingering on hers and she wondered at the sweetness and gentleness with which he sometimes treated her. Often his love-making was fierce, even cruel. He seemed to use her, force her, subjugate her to his harsh will as though he needed something, something she had not given him and if she would not give it willingly he would crush it from her, ravish her almost until she responded.

"That you call me by my Christian name instead of this ridiculous habit you have of addressing me as though I were the local preacher. I realise that some older women, in public, still call their husbands by the formal *Mr* whatever, but I wish you to say my name and my name is Chad." He smiled and she felt herself responding. He really had no idea how difficult it was for her to get used to the perception that this man was her husband. He had been Mr Cameron ever since she could remember. Mr Cameron of Longlake Edge. Almost, one could say, the Squire of Pooley Bridge and the area surrounding it, and even in the tumult of their physical union when her senses seemed to reel away in some strange way, he was still Mr Cameron. A man from a different class than her own and therefore to be addressed formally.

"Well," she said doubtfully, frowning like a child giving its whole attention to a worrying problem.

"Try it. Go on, say it. Chad. That's not so hard, is it?"

"Yes, is is, Mr . . ."

"Say it. And then I'll tell you what I have bought for you."

She drew a deep breath. "Very well." Her voice was prim. "Chad. Will that do?"

"Say it again."

"Really, this is ridiculous." Like many of the things you say and do, she wanted to add, but the narrowed warning in his eyes stopped her.

"Chad, there."

"And you will continue to address your husband thus. That is an order." She wanted to giggle but instead gave a squeak of surprise when he sprang from the bed, naked as a newborn babe, as she was, wrapped her in a blanket and carried her to the window.

"Mr Ca— Chad!"

"Look." He stood behind her, gazing downwards over her shoulder, his arms wrapped about her and obediently she turned to look in the direction of the gravel drive at the front of the house. Joe Blamire was there walking the daintiest little horse she had ever seen. A chestnut horse with a coat as polished as the glossy brown fruit, the conkers that fell from the horse chestnut tree in autumn.

"Her name is Gypsy," her husband murmured in her ear,

"and you are to learn to ride her. You must have Miss Avery make a riding habit for you—"

"Oh, Lord, for me, for me? She's lovely," she interrupted him. Her face was rapturous, her eyes shining with the misted lavender of her tears, then for the first time she turned and spontaneously kissed her husband.

She was a natural, Joe Blamire said with pride, watching with his master as the mistress cantered round the paddock. He preened as though her ability to ride the gentle little mare was all down to him.

Chad would not let her out of the paddock until Joe told him she was ready and then she was to be accompanied by either Joe or Ned, he proclaimed, but on the morning she rode over to Moorend Mill and slid down from Gypsy's back into the welcoming arms of a grinning Thomas she had given both of them the slip. The mare, much admired by Thomas and Billy, was tethered to a ring in the wall where she began to graze on the grass which Briony noted had not yet been cleared.

There was a great deal of activity in the yard. Several waggons were loaded with filled sacks awaiting their turn to be lifted on to the ramp and men in caps and waistcoats, collarless shirts, and trousers tied beneath the knee, steadied the great glossy horses. In greeting they aimed their fingers in the general direction of their ear, staring curiously at her, for they knew who she was and one, Farmer Stephens from Mell Farm, bade her a cheerful "good morning".

She smiled then knocked on the door of the house that had once been her home.

18

The kitchen, which had been a picture of cleanliness when last Briony saw it was no longer so! Betty Kean surreptitiously dusted the kitchen chair with the corner of her apron. Their Jess had been climbing on it only minutes before to reach one of the apples in a bowl on the table and after a morning "plodging" in one of the dirty pools of water that collected in the yard, had put her bare, muddy feet on the seat and she could hardly ask the elegantly dressed lady who came into Betty's kitchen as if she owned it to put her bum on it.

The apples were a rare surprise found in the far storeroom at the top of the house, presumably left there by this very lady who had, it transpired, lived here before she married Mr Cameron. That in itself had been an amazement to Betty who had thought Mrs Cameron came from one of the grand families who lived hereabout. She and Lizzie, whoever that was, with the lads, Billy and Thomas, had gathered the fruit last back end, Billy had told them, while Thomas, the simple one who was bigger and stronger than any man Betty had ever seen, had smiled and nodded as if to say he had helped. The small dog in his arms, called Sal, he told them, looked up at his face adoringly, watching his lips move as though his every word and action was a marvel to her.

It had been a bit of a facer to learn that these lads were to be part and parcel of the deal her Jacob had struck with Mr Cameron. Where were they to sleep, she had wanted to know, for with seven bairns and one on the way they would need every inch of space they could find. The barn, which was a sturdy building, repaired only recently to keep out the weather, seemed a likely place and so a corner of the loft had been transformed into comfortable quarters above Glory's stable, with two beds and a chest of drawers, some rugs fetched over from Mr Cameron's place with a dozen blankets. She was to see to their laundry but as Mr Cameron was to pay their wages she had made no objection. They would certainly be a godsend to Jacob like all the other benefits that seemed to be part of this good fortune that had come their way.

The apples were not the only produce, for in a corner of the barn were potatoes and turnips, the turnips piled in cone-shaped heaps, a thick layer of straw on the bare ground to protect them from mould, a three-inch covering of straw to keep them from the frost and a round of turf to cap them. The potatoes had been set in a pit about six inches deep and covered with good wheat straw to the depth of about a foot. As a country lass Betty was impressed by the efficiency with which the storage had been obtained and was even more delighted to hear that there were more potatoes ready for lifting in the fields. What with the fruit that had been gathered from the small orchard beyond the mill pond and this harvest that had been left behind by Mrs Cameron she and her family would not go hungry for many a long day.

"Will tha' tekk a cup o' tea, Mrs Cameron?" she asked politely as one should a personage of such high standing.

Briony smiled and declined the seat and the cup of tea. She had not come on a social visit and she wanted the Keans to understand this and that they would be seeing a lot of her from now on. She was pleased to see that business appeared to be brisk. She had every intention, now that she and Lizzie had brought order, or at least Lizzie had, to Chad's home, an order he seemed to find satisfying, of beginning the work that was hers here at the mill. The work of guarding Danny's inheritance. For the past three months she had brooded on it but had had no option but to bow to Chad's will.

The worst moment of those three months, repeated half a dozen times, had come when Daphne had put her head round the drawing-room door and asked, "Are you in, madam?" There had been a certain irony in her voice.

Briony had glanced up from the housekeeping book Lizzie had put in her hands and told her to have a look at, an expression of astonishment on her face.

"Of course I'm in. Who the dickens d'you think this is sitting on the sofa?"

Daphne adjusted the look on her face and did her best to be patient. "No, madam, are you in to callers?"

"Callers?"

"Yes, madam." It took all Daphne's willpower to call the daughter of the miller "madam", but she bore the tribulation with calm, as they all must, for it was their job. "It's Mrs Gould. Shall I show her in?"

It was here at last, as Lizzie had told her it would be. The arrival of the first of the callers women in her position were expected to receive. The cards had come and here was the first old busybody following to see how the miller's daughter was managing. Come to poke and pry and question her, ready to snigger behind her hand at the ineptitude of the wench who had set herself up to be the wife of one of *them*. To be the wife of a gentleman, and what the devil was she to say to her? Give her tea, that's what Lizzie had said. She would remain no more than fifteen minutes, Lizzie had said but where *was* Lizzie to get her through these damn fifteen minutes? Mrs Gould was presumably kicking her heels in the hall, waiting to hear if she was to be allowed to enter and Briony had not the faintest notion what she should do next.

"Where is Miss Jenkins?" she asked Daphne, her voice abrupt and yet inclined to tremble.

"She was in't kitchen last time I saw—"

"Ask her to come here."

"But what about Mrs Gould, madam?" Daphne said, smiling somewhat maliciously. It could not be said any of the servants had been overfond of Miss Sarah but at least she was a lady and they were used to serving ladies. She could hardly leave the drawing-room and speed past Mrs Gould who was waiting to see if the mistress of the house was "at home" while Daphne continued on her way to the kitchen to fetch Miss Jenkins.

Briony saw the half-smile on Daphne's face. "Oh, show the woman in and then go and tell Miss Jenkins that I want her here at once. Tell her it's urgent. And don't you dare go off and pretend you've forgotten or you can't find her or you'll be looking for another job by the week's end, d'you hear?"

"Madam, as if—"

"Oh, don't give me that humbug. I know what goes on in this house and I mean to change it, even if I have to have a complete new set of servants. Now, show Mrs Gould in and . . . well, bring tea or whatever it is these women expect."

It had been a nightmare, even with Lizzie to guide her, to keep up the formal conversation that strangers are expected to indulge in, made even worse by Mrs Gould's condescending and superior air. It was apparent that Mrs Gould thought that Mrs Cameron was far beneath her own station in life and as she sipped Mrs Cameron's tea and gazed round Mrs Cameron's drawing-room, looking for signs of neglect, Lizzie supposed, Lizzie herself wondered what the dickens the woman had come for. Neither she nor Briony knew that Mrs Gould had been forced to it by her husband who had to keep on the right side of Chad Cameron. Bernard Gould was a banker and if Chad Cameron was to withdraw his considerable funds from Bernard Gould's bank . . . well, surely Jessica could see what a predicament this would put him in, and so here she was, not making a friend of the dreadful girl but doing as her husband ordered her.

The courtesy call, which Lizzie told her she was meant to return, filling her with unimaginable horror, was repeated, not by Mrs Gould who knew the correct procedure, but by Mrs Seddon, by Mrs Addison who brought her lovely young daughter, Pansy, by Mrs Seddon with her married daughter Adeline at her side and by others, all eager to see what a pretty pass the usually smooth running of Longlake Edge had come to under the supervision of the new Mrs Cameron.

If they were surprised by the efficiency of the unobtrusive service performed by her parlour-maids they should not have been, for Daphne and Gladys had been trained by Sarah Cameron, whose ways had been continued by the resolute Lizzie Jenkins. Though Mrs Cameron had little to say her companion seemed to be *au fait* with the kind of conversation ladies indulged in and when, at the end of their visit, Miss Jenkins rang the bell for the maidservant to show them out they were thunderstruck, since this was, as they all knew, the correct and polite thing to do. And as for Mrs Cameron's afternoon gown, well, they could not fault it, nor the rest of her appearance. A lovely blue tarlatan that was so pale as to be almost silver, a tiny bodice shaped to her waist and flaring out over her hips in a basque. It had a V neckline revealing the creamy sheen of the skin at her throat, fastening down the front with a row of tiny pearl buttons. The sleeves were close gathered at the wrist and the skirt was fifteen feet round its hem. The blue turned her pansy eyes to a colour hard to describe and Mrs Addison was forced to admit that, though the girl who had stolen Chad Cameron from her own daughter was of the working classes, she looked very fine.

She wore a creamy silk on one occasion, a pale, pale barley-coloured muslin on another, a gauze of poppy red which was quite sublime, a duck-egg blue batiste and the ladies, when they had each one visited her as they had been told by their respective husbands, could talk of nothing else. The only one to call who Briony admitted she had any time for was Mrs Armstrong, the Vicar's wife, who was kind and gentle and easy to talk to, for she made it plain she was quite taken with Briony Cameron.

Chad was pleased with her, kissing her, his mouth warm and moist on hers hardly before Daphne had left the dining-room, carrying her off to their bedroom and making love to her with great enthusiasm, which he did every night anyway.

"They've not gone up already," Mrs Minty gasped, glancing surreptitiously in the direction of the door that led to Miss Jenkins's sitting-room. The housekeeper had taken over the comfortable room which had once been old Mrs Cameron's, the master's grandmother's, sewing-room. It had no personal belongings of her own in it, for she had brought none with her on her long walk from Carlisle to Moorend, but the room contained all that old Mrs Cameron had treasured. The walls were painted a pale grey and were lined with shelves that held books of household and domestic management and a number of pretty ornaments which her daughter-in-law and then her granddaughter had not cared for. There was always a cheerful fire in the black-leaded grate, for the room faced north-east. Two deeply cushioned wing armchairs stood one on either side of it, well used, for Briony often sat in there with her and there were cupboards containing a china tea service and a copper kettle in which water was boiled for tea. Briony had insisted on placing a picture or two on the walls and there were books, not just for practical use but for Lizzie's pleasure. It was an office as well as a sitting-room and in the middle stood a large table covered with a red plush cloth, with chairs about it, and in its centre there was always a bowl of flowers. It was here that Lizzie discussed accounts with the tradesmen; entered items of household expenditure in her enormous ledgers, those she begged Briony to peruse, gave orders to the maidservants and had interviewed Mrs Minty and Fanny, the maid of all work. Lizzie also ate her solitary meals at the table, for though Briony had protested bitterly Lizzie had refused to eat with her and Mr Cameron.

"Do you want your marriage to succeed, Briony?" she had asked sternly.

"Well . . ." Briony turned away from her, for to tell the truth she had not thought of it as being successful, only profitable to Danny.

"Of course you do, and in a household such as this the housekeeper does not eat with the family."

"You are my family. You and Danny and—"

"No, I am not."

"You are my friend."

"So is Sadie, but would you expect her to sit down to dine with Mr Cameron?"

Briony smiled. She loved Sadie dearly but she was realist enough to know that the very idea was preposterous. "But you are different to Sadie, Lizzie. You're more of a lady than I am."

"Rubbish! Anyway, I refuse to discuss it any further and I'm sure if you were to ask him Mr Cameron would agree. You are his wife and though he doesn't appear to be concerned at the moment, you will begin to have dinner parties. His friends and even his sister will be dining with you."

"Never! I've never heard anything so—"

"Miss Cameron is Mr Cameron's sister and will expect—"

"Don't talk daft. She'll not come here." And so far she had not done so though she had been seen in the garden talking to William Platt, the gardener, ordering him about, they supposed, as she had done when she had been mistress. He and Isaac, his lad, would be expected to see to her bit of garden and though he pulled a face when she had gone, he could not disobey her, could he, he had said angrily to Joe Blamire. She was the master's sister and the master paid his wages but didn't he have enough to do seeing to the vast ornamental and kitchen gardens of Longlake without fiddling about in that acre that surrounded Miss Cameron's house. Another man would have to be taken on, he grumbled, sitting down in a patch of sunshine to light his pipe, his lad squatting beside him, just as though, contrary to his words, they had all the time in the world.

But now, with the housekeeper safely tucked away in her sitting-room, and the master doing God knows what to his wife in the privacy of their bedroom, the maidservants cleared up the dining-room before sitting down to their own evening meal. They always ate whatever was left over from the dining-room and it was substantial, Mrs Minty saw to that, for she cooked enough to feed the five thousand despite what that there housekeeper said. She'd been told that Mr Cameron had a hearty appetite and his wife put away a fair bit, at least recently, and she'd have no one say that Flora Minty stinted on the food she put before her "family".

It was the next day, having seen Chad off to Liverpool where he had some business to attend to and where he was to stay overnight, sure in the knowledge that he was pleased with her and if he wasn't there was nothing he could do to stop her, she had ordered Joe to saddle Gypsy and ridden down to Moorend. She had nodded pleasantly at Len Stephens who was in the yard loading sacks on to his cart and when Betty Kean asked her to sit down and take tea she refused smilingly.

"Oh, no, Mrs Kean, I am here on business, not pleasure," and did not add that she had had enough of tea drinking to last her a lifetime. Besides which she did not fancy the idea of hospitality in the slovenly kitchen.

"Business, ma'am." Betty was confused. She could not get over this grand lady calling her "Mrs Kean" which she was, of course, but she was plain Betty to everyone else, including Mr Cameron, who had called a time or two. And as to business, whatever did she mean?

"Yes, Mrs Kean."

"Oh, Betty, please, ma'am."

"Very well, Betty, so if you will ask your husband . . . where is he, by the way?"

"Nay, ma'am, I'm not sure. 'E was 'ere a minnit since."

"Perhaps you could fetch the books to me then, er, Betty. I wish to see the figures."

"Figures, ma'am?" Betty's mouth hung open and the baby, which seemed to be permanently attached to her hip despite the one whose arrival was imminent, was shifted to the other as though that might help her mental processes which could not keep up with those of her visitor.

Briony sighed patiently. "Perhaps it might be better if you were to take me to your husband. I see that Len Stephens has gone." She glanced out into the yard where Farmer Stephens's cart could be seen disappearing through the gate, himself slapping the reins on the horse's rump. The second cart, one belonging to a man she didn't know, had drawn up to the ramp and the two boys were hoisting the sacks of corn the man had brought on to the stone ramp. Two wheelbarrows stood waiting ready to be wheeled up the ramp straight from the waggon. Once inside the mill the sacks of corn would be lifted by the sack hoist either to the stone floor, the first level where the millstones were located, or to the bin floor, the top floor of the mill for storage, the hoist being driven by water power. On the bin floor the corn would be stored in its sacks or emptied out into large wooden bins and when required for milling would be let out through spouts to the millstones on the floor below.

Briony's patience was wearing thin. She had not come here to take tea with Mrs Kean, or Betty as she had asked to be called, but to go over the books with her husband, to ascertain how much profit had been made in the three months he had been in charge of the mill. To collect the rent that was owing to her and to go over, inch by inch, the working of the mill to ensure that it was running as it had done in her father's day. She knew exactly what was to be done in each process, for if she had not taken part in the heavy work she had watched it and performed the lighter duties. The gearing that drove the millstones had to run at the correct speed and she herself needed to check that the new miller knew his job. So, where was he?

"Mrs Kean . . . Betty, I'll not detain you another moment," looking round her at the littered, somewhat grubby kitchen, at the struggling infant, at the enormous mound of the baby to come which she could see leaping about under Betty's apron. "I can see you are busy."

"Nay, Mrs Cameron." Betty put out a hand to detain this grand lady but before she knew what was happening Mrs Cameron had whisked across the kitchen and was up the stairs, *Betty's stairs*, and on to the stone floor, gathering all the detritus of milling on the hem of her lovely skirt. Betty admitted her kitchen and living quarters were a bit of a mess with seven children and one on the way and she could hardly be expected to clean the working mill which was just as bad, could she, and Mrs Cameron would ruin that lovely frock of hers.

Jacob was at the spouts where he was controlling both the quantity and quality of the meal that was being fed to the millstones. By turning the twist peg the amount of grain could be regulated and by varying the gap between the stones the texture of the meal could be altered. Depending on whether the meal was for flour or for animal feed, its texture would need to be fine or coarse. When the meal was ground it escaped down the spouts to the floor below to be collected in the traditional wooden meal ark and then be bagged in readiness for the owner to collect it.

He started quite violently when he saw her but she noticed he did not interrupt his work. He was covered from head to foot in a fine mist of flour, with bits of grain and even the rubbish which often comes with the corn from the fields and which is winnowed out by a sieve, a job that had once been hers. By now she was in the same state, even her hair and eyebrows whitened.

"Mrs Cameron, whatever be ye doin' 'ere?" he gasped. "'Tis no place fer a lady, ma'am. Why, look at yer, covered in—"

"It doesn't matter, Mr Kean. I won't keep you but a minute. If you could just give me the books, the accounting books, I'll take them home with me and look at them at my leisure. Tell me where you keep them and I'm sure your wife will let me have them. And then there is the rent."

"The books, ma'am? The rent? Why, Mr Cameron keeps 'em an' collects the rent. I've no 'ead fer figures, ma'am, an' I told 'im so but we're doin' grand, I can tell 'ee. Busy all day long an' . . ."

Briony could feel it welling up inside her, first the shock, the astonishment, then the thunderbolt of anger, the resentment, the sheer fury that for three months the man who was her husband had kept her at home fiddling with the stupid inanities of the world he meant her to live in while all the time he had been interfering in her *proper* life. The life she had planned for herself which was to keep this going, keep this mill working as it should be worked until Danny came home. If she could have managed to do it without him she would but her customers had not come. The men who had dealt with her father had inexplicably stayed away and into her mind crept a suspicion that . . . that her husband had had something to do with it. Suddenly they had all come back and really, should she not have known that he . . . *he* had been behind it. She'd been a bloody fool. An ignorant, naïve fool, but no more! Dear God, no more. This was Danny's mill that Mr Cameron had stolen, those were Danny's books and Danny's rent that had gone in *his* pocket but she'd be damned if she'd allow it to continue.

"Thank you, Mr Kean," she said haughtily to the confounded miller. "You have been most helpful."

"Mrs Cameron, you cannot possibly mean to wear such unsuitable garments. No lady would go about in—"

"I am no lady, Miss Avery," Briony told her through gritted teeth.

"But, madam, these clothes you are asking me to make are what a working girl would wear. A servant. Serviceable but not—"

"Miss Avery, are you to make these dresses and a cloak for me or must I go up the road to—"

"No, no, of course not, Mrs Cameron, but I'm sure your husband will be—"

"I do not care what my husband will be, Miss Avery. I am about to return to the work I performed before I was married and I cannot do that in this . . . this finery." She stared down contemptuously at the stylish riding habit she had put on this morning and which, after her visit to the mill, looked as though she had rolled about the barn in it. She had ridden like the wind up the road from Pooley Bridge to Penrith, frightening not only Gypsy on whose back she was not, as yet, an expert horsewoman, but the people she passed who stared after her in wonder. She lost her smart top hat which was picked up by a small boy who had capered about in it until it was snatched from his head by his mother who later sold it on a market stall.

"May I ask what . . . the nature of the work you mean to do, Mrs Cameron?" Miss Avery asked, meaning to send a message as soon as she could to Mr Cameron to come and fetch his wife who seemed to have run mad.

"I am a miller, Miss Avery." Mrs Cameron allowed herself to be led into the back room of the smart little shop where Miss Avery not only measured and fitted her customers but offered them coffee or tea, or even a glass of white wine if that was their fancy. A clever and successful woman was Miss Avery and she had no intention of losing the wife of the wealthy and influential Mr Cameron.

It was several weeks since Miss Avery had fitted Mrs Cameron into the well-tailored riding habit she had on and as she began the process of getting her out of it preparatory to measuring her for the amazing garments she had asked for, she noticed that the buttons pulled on the bodice and that the skirt had left a red mark round Mrs Cameron's waist.

"Is something the matter?" Mrs Cameron asked her, looking down as she stepped out of the skirt.

"Well . . ."

"Yes, what is it?" Mrs Cameron's voice was imperious, telling Miss Avery she was prepared to brook no further arguments.

"I had better measure your waist, Mrs Cameron," Miss Avery said warily. "It seems . . ."

"What is wrong with my waist?"

"Nothing, ma'am."

"Then get on with it."

"Nothing, except it is two inches bigger than it was when last I measured it."

"So?"

"Ma'am, I hesitate to ask but . . ."

"But what, for God's sake?"

"Are you perhaps . . . with child?"

"Don't be ridiculous, Miss Avery," she answered scathingly, but inside something began to shrivel and die as the dream she had cherished of running Danny's mill for him drifted away above Miss Avery's upturned, concerned face. With child! Was she to have a child? There had been nothing else since she had married that man last March and so . . . No . . . oh, no, not now, she couldn't be, she couldn't. She was putting on weight because of all the good food she now ate. That was it. How ridiculous Miss Avery was being and she'd tell her so.

"Don't be ridiculous, Miss Avery. Now, if you don't mind I'd like you to measure me for the dresses I have described and a good warm woollen cloak."

"Of course, Mrs Cameron."

"I shall send my groom to collect them . . . when?"

"Perhaps ten days, Mrs Cameron."

"Not before that, Miss Avery? I am eager to . . . well, never mind."

Miss Avery stood up, then, when she had done with her measuring, watched as Mrs Cameron rode away along the street, knowing that when the dresses were delivered to her within a few weeks they would not fasten round her waist and would be tight across the bodice.

——◆◆◆——

19

Sadie Evans peered through the window of her neat cottage, her face for a moment breaking into a pleased smile as she spied their Briony, as she still thought of her despite her raised status, coming at a gallop up the track from the road that wound round the lake, then she frowned, for the gallop and the furious expression on the lass's face heralded trouble. For a moment, a sad moment, she wondered where the compliant young girl who had once lived with her had gone, but then, wasn't she better off now that she had a bit of spirit, the spirit that had done its best to get out and yet remain hidden when Jethro Marsden had been alive.

She sighed deeply, then moved towards the fire where the kettle, which was constantly on the simmer, whispered steam. She reached for the brown teapot and after pouring some boiling water into it to warm the pot, took down the tea-caddy from the shelf above the fire. Swilling the water about the pot, she moved into the scullery and emptied it into the stone sink. Darting back into the kitchen she placed three good teaspoons of tea in the pot from the caddy, two for them and one for the pot, then stood it on the hearth to mash. She got out two creamware commemorative mugs, ones that the girl outside had brought her from Penrith, bless her good heart, each one bearing a picture of Queen Victora and Prince Albert on their wedding day in February. A set of four but she only used them for special occasions and this was one. Their Briony didn't get down to see her as often as she would have liked and she didn't blame her one bit, for the lass had her duties up at Longlake Edge where she was mistress. Besides, with her marriage their equal status in life had changed dramatically. Mind you, that young woman who was now housekeeper at Longlake had made a big difference in Sadie's life, thanks, she was certain, to their Briony. When Miss Sarah had moved to the Dower House, taking two maidservants and employing two more, Sadie had been expected to do all their laundry, as well as those who lived at the big house. Nine, counting Mr Cameron and Briony, which made fourteen with Miss Sarah's lot, and before you could say "knife" two more laundry-maids had been taken on at Longlake, Addy and Tilda, so with Jenny and Iris, Sadie's load had been considerably lightened. She really did no more than supervise, though the master insisted she still ironed the frills on his shirts. It meant she had more time to herself which she was glad of, since, though she admitted it to no one, she wasn't getting any younger.

Now, here was the lass evidently in some sort of temper by the look on her face as she flung herself vigorously from the back of the little horse and threw the reins in the general direction of the gatepost, opening the gate and plunging up the short path between the dazzling flowerbeds which were Sadie's pride and joy. There were butterflies, the names of which she didn't know, hovering about from flower to flower, and a great bumble-bee blundered against the glass of the window. She had meant to take her old cane chair out and sit for an hour in the sunshine but now that would have to wait. Iolo kept it so lovely, her little garden, and in this month of June it exploded with colour, the deep pink of begonia, the purple blue of Canterbury bells, carnations in pink and white and scarlet and the big yellow heads of daisies. There were always plenty to cut and they stood in bowls and glass jugs on her window sills and in the centre of her scrubbed table.

Without bothering to knock, Briony burst into the kitchen,

causing the tabby in the basket with her eternal litter of kittens to hiss warningly.

"Come in, lass," Sadie said mildly, reaching for the milk jug, "an' sit thi' down. Tea's mashin'. I've just medd a few scones."

"I've not come for scones, Sadie," Briony answered shortly, lashing her crop against her wide skirt. She threw herself down in Iolo's chair, putting her feet up on the stool, then immediately sprang up again and swirled about the room. The cat hissed again as Briony's skirt swept over her kittens and Sadie held her breath, for if the lass didn't settle it looked as though her lovely mugs might be sent flying to the floor.

"Well, 'appen tha'll tell me what tha' *'ave* come for an' just watch what tha're doin' wi' that skirt o' thine. Tha'll 'ave them flowers in't winder bottom over in a minnit."

She watched as Briony subsided obediently into the chair then passed her a mug of tea, waiting until the lass began to sip it before pouring her own.

She paused for a minute or two before she spoke.

"What's up?" she began, then reared back as Briony crashed her precious mug to the table.

"Everything."

"Nay, my lass, tha' mustn't say that. You wi' that grand 'usband an' nowt ter do all day but sit on tha' bum."

"That's just it. I don't want to sit on my bum. I want to work. I want to go down to the mill each day and make sure that that fool—"

"Nay, dos't mean Jacob? Tha' mustn't call 'im that. 'E works 'ard and I 'eard tell 'e were a good worker an' knows 'is job an' all, though she's not much of a one wi't scrubbing brush . . ."

"Well, maybe he does but I wanted to be absolutely sure of that so I rode there this morning to look at the books and where are they? Not there, I can tell you, oh, no."

"Then . . ."

"My dear husband has them, *and* the rent which he's been collecting these last three months from the miller. Moorend should belong to *my* family, to Danny and me and I should be the one to supervise its running, not Chad Cameron. How dare he, Sadie, how dare he and, not to put too fine a point on it I believe he deliberately made sure that there was no corn or wheat or anything brought to the mill while I was in charge of it. Now, suddenly, all the farmers and villagers are bringing their grain to be milled and the mill is flourishing."

"Well, what's wrong wi' that, my lass?" Sadie managed to interpose.

"I'll tell you what's wrong with it, Sadie, and I shall tell him as well when he gets back from Liverpool. I wouldn't have married him if I could have got the mill running without him. He promised his help, his money, anything I needed to keep the business viable until Danny came home and I agreed. I don't know what was in his mind. Why should he want to marry me so desperately that he had to lie and cheat? He could have had any of the fine ladies hereabouts so why should he pick me? I know he was sorry for us, for me and Danny when Faither leathered us and . . . and hurt Mother but to go to such extremes. I trusted him. I thought he was honest, now I find that . . . that . . . oh, Sadie, I can't forgive him."

She turned her face to the fire and Sadie could see tears trembling on her eyelashes and wondered why, if Briony was so wild and uncaring, so angry, so incensed at what she saw as her husband's betrayal she was so . . . so distressed.

She leaned forward, picking up one of the kittens that had escaped its mother, placing it back among the heaving bundles of fur. Her face was troubled. The room was suddenly still and quiet but for the crackle and splutter of the fire and the plaintive mewing of the kittens. The canary in the cage began to chirp and the tabby glanced up at it venomously as though for two pins she'd have the thing for a tasty snack.

"Did you hear me, Sadie?" Briony asked her.

"Aye, lass, I did."

"And you knew what he was about?"

"Not everythin'. I were *surprised*" – which was an under-statement – "when 'e wanted ter wed thi'." For gentlemen of Mr Cameron's stature did not marry the daughter of a miller. They had all in the cottages been flabbergasted, to tell the truth, for men in his circle of society were more likely to take a maid into their beds without the blessing of the Church. Many had and there were several lasses hereabouts lugging illegitimate children round the fells, looking for work or shelter. Still, this one had been lucky and it was a mystery to Sadie why she should be so outraged. Look at her, all done up in her grand riding habit, with a smart little mare to ride about on, who was at this moment eating her head off among Sadie's lupins. She had money to spend on whatever she wanted, a house full of servants to do her bidding and yet here she was bemoaning the fact that her husband, a handsome, well-set-up chap who was not just wealthy but generous with it and ready to give anyone a helping hand, had done his best to help her, for God's sake! As he was helping her brother in keeping the mill afloat when most men would have sold the place and pocketed the money.

"Well, is that all you have to say?" Briony demanded hotly, her tears gone, her face on fire with fury. Her astonishing lavender eyes snapped dangerously and her full mouth, the colour of a ripe strawberry, thinned to a mutinous line, all aimed at Sadie as though it were her fault.

"Nay, I could say a lot more only tha' wouldn't like it."

"Go on, say it. You can hardly deny that he dealt with me dishonestly."

"In what way, lass?"

"Well, first by telling the farmers to stay away so that I would have no work and then—"

"Tha' don't know that but if it's so it's not right," Sadie answered slowly. "But—"

"There are no buts and now it seems as though I am to be . . . to be . . ."

"What? What's ter do?"

"You mean on top of all this?" Briony dragged her hands through her disordered hair and Sadie wondered for a moment where the smart little top hat she usually wore when riding had got to. Her hair hung down her back so that she almost sat on it, a thick tangle of curls that would need a great deal of brushing to *un*tangle it.

Suddenly she sat back and once more turned her flushed face away from Sadie before she spoke.

"Sadie, I have heard . . . that is, when you and she were talking, not knowing I was listening and I wasn't really because it meant nothing to me."

"Aye . . ."

"You and Kate Benson. When she was . . . before Jacky was born; she didn't want another, she said and you said . . ."

For a sickening moment Sadie did not understand, then with an oath she sprang up and taking Briony by the shoulders dragged her to her feet. She shook her as a dog might shake a rag doll it is playing with, so that her head rolled on her neck.

"So that's it," she screeched. "That's what all this is leadin' up to. A babby an' tha' want me ter 'elp yer get rid. Eeh, madam, I've a good mind ter drag thi' up ter Longlake and tell that 'usband o' thine." She suddenly became still and her face was wary and afraid though she still held Briony by the arms. "Tha've not done owt, 'ave thi'? Tell me . . . tell me." And she began to shake her again but Briony dragged herself out of her reach, glaring at her from beneath her hair which fell about her like a cloak, while Sadie, her own hair escaping from its neat bun, falling about her inflamed face, glared back.

"I wouldn't be here if I had. D'you think if I could have got rid of it without anyone knowing—"

"Get rid of it. Tha' wicked little baggage. Dear God, I thought thi' were a decent lass. I thought thi' an' me were friends."

"I don't want a damn baby, especially *his* damn baby, not after the way—"

"Now you listen 'ere, lady. Let me hear one more word about gettin' rid an' I'll chain thi' ter me wrist fer the next, what, six, seven months. Dost know what can 'appen to a woman what tries ter interfere wi' nature? Oh, aye, I've 'eard of lasses what 'ave bled ter death an' others so badly 'urt they never recovered. Dirty old back-street women wi' a needle botchin' up a woman's insides. Dear Lord, that's a child inside thi'. *Your* child, an' Mr Cameron's and tha'll not murder it, not while I've breath in me body. Now, get thi' 'ome an' tell 'im. 'E'll be made up wi' it." Her voice softened and she ventured to take Briony's hand and was relieved when Briony allowed it. "Don't tha' see? 'E'll be that glad tha'll be able ter do as tha' likes wi' 'im. Get a good lass ter 'elp thi' an' then, when tha've given 'im a bairn, 'appen a son, 'e'll let tha' play wi't mill all the live long day."

Briony pulled her hand away sharply, her piteously downcast expression turning to indignation. "I'm *not* playing with it, Sadie Evans. I want to be part of it. I want to look after it for Danny. Make sure it's safe for him when he returns. Don't you see, if Danny hadn't been defending me he wouldn't be where he is now. If . . . if I'd let Father . . . such a little thing, really and if I'd known I would have let him."

She thought for a terrible moment that Sadie was going to knock her down. She raised her hand and her face twisted into a terrible mask of rage and disgust and when she managed to speak spittle sprayed from her mouth.

"Sweet Jesus Christ," she hissed, "'ave tha' any idea what tha're sayin'? Ter blame thissen fer what tha' pa did ter thi'. What about tha' ma? Danny wasn't just defendin' *you*."

"I know, I know." Briony's voice rose in a howl and next door Ethel Hodgson turned her head to look at the wall between her cottage and Sadie's. What the devil was going on? She'd seen that dratted animal munching its way along the fence, leaning over to wrench at the few flowers she herself had raised and she'd been in two minds whether to go next door and complain, only her Clem worked as a hedger and ditcher for Mr Cameron and she didn't want to antagonise his missis. She slipped to her front door and opened it the better to hear what was being said.

"Then if tha' knows what are thi' blamin' thissen for, tell me that?"

"Now that I'm . . . now that I understand what a man does to a woman I realise how easy it would have been, Sarah, to allow him."

"No, no, you don't know, lass, not really. What Mr Cameron does ter thi' in 'is bed is done wi' love. Nay, lass, don't look so surprised," as Briony turned wide, unbelieving eyes in her direction. "A man what loves a woman treats her wi' respect, gentle-like, especially a bit of a lass like *thi*'." Her own eyes turned away and gazed back at something she remembered sweetly. "Me an' my Dai . . . well, that's between me an' 'im but what tha' pa intended was black wicked, unnatural."

"But if I'd sat still and let him – Pa, I mean – Ma wouldn't have known . . . if I'd kept quiet. She wouldn't have hit him with the frying pan and he . . . Oh, Sadie, don't you see?" She was weeping broken-heartedly now and at once Sadie dragged her into her arms and held her tightly, her own eyes wet.

"So that's it, that's it, is it," she said over and over again, holding her lass and patting her, kissing her cheek passionately, remorse and understanding coming together until at last both of them were quiet. She let go of the girl she had loved as her own, bending to peer earnestly into her face then took her hand and sat her down in the chair, sitting down opposite her, still holding her hand between her own two.

"Listen ter me, lamb. Pin back tha' lug'oles" – smiling a little for that was what *her* mam used to say to her – "an' listen. That bugger what was tha' faither was the most evil of bastards. Ter put 'is 'ands on 'is own lass was the wickedest sin any man could commit an' 'e deserved ter die. I 'ope 'e rots in 'ell. I 'ope he roasts in the fiery pit fer all eternity an' what Danny did to 'im . . . well, if tha' Danny 'adn't done it, there's a score o' chaps would. My Iolo included."

"But . . ."

"Never mind but, lass. I know what tha's gonner say but it don't wash. If . . . if tha'd let 'im . . . 'andle yer, yer pa, I mean, as tha' seem ter think tha' should, next time it would've bin worse so it'd 've 'appened anyroad an' you p'raps in the family way wi' . . . Dear God, it don't bear thinkin' about so don't let me 'ear tha' sayin' what tha' said. It weren't tha' fault. None of it. Tha' pa killed tha' ma an' Danny killed tha' pa an' God knows he didn't deserve what 'e got but *it were nowt ter do wi' thi'*. Both you an' Danny were victims but Mr Cameron did everythin' 'e could ter 'elp the both o' yer. So think on."

Sadie leaned forward, her knees wide apart, her hands holding Briony's. "Look at me, lass, look at me." And when Briony raised her tear-dewed eyes to Sadie's, Sadie, satisfied with what she saw there, smiled, kissed her cheek and her forehead, then, all of a bustle, she stood up.

"Right, then us'll 'ave another drink o' tea an' then tha' shall go 'ome an' tell that 'usband o' thine the good news. An' don't you dare ride that animal back, d'yer 'ear. I'll be over termorrer an' if the place isn't buzzin' wi't good news an' 'is lordship struttin' about like a cock on a dungheap, thinkin' 'ow clever 'e is, then I'll know the reason why. Dost 'ear?"

Briony sighed. Most of what Sadie had said about Chad and the strange emotions she attributed to him about herself had gone in one ear and out of the other for the simple reason she didn't believe it. He had tricked her, trapped her for reasons best known to himself and she wouldn't, couldn't forgive him, but it seemed it did no good discussing it with Sadie or indeed with anyone. She was stuck, stuck with him and stuck with this child she was, apparently, to have. She knew inside where she seldom looked that she was not ready to be a mother. Mothers were like Sadie, or her own mother, placid, agreeable creatures with no thought in their heads but their homes, their children, and, though not in the case of her own mother, their husbands.

"Now think on," Sadie admonished as she kissed her soundly on her cheek, doing her best to smooth away the forlorn expression painted there. "As soon as tha' man—"

"He's not my man."

Sadie ignored the sad remark. ". . . comes 'ome ternight tha' must tell 'im the news."

"Tomorrow."

"What?"

"He comes home tomorrow." And from her expression one might have been forgiven for thinking some monster was coming home to climb into her bed.

"Well, then, termorrer. An' I expect ter see 'em all dancin' in't yard wi' tha' news. Now why don't tha' leave that 'orse . . . see, tie it properly ter't gatepost so it can't get me sweet william nor Ethel's peonies an' send Joe Blamire over ter fetch it."

"Don't you trust me, Sadie?"

"No, I don't, my lass. The minnit tha's in't wood tha'll be

heavin' thassen onter its back and gallopin' off on't dratted thing. Leave it 'ere fer Joe. I'll keep me eye on it."

Briony nodded resignedly and, still swishing her crop against her full riding skirt, which she had to loop over her arm in order to walk more easily, she climbed the rough path at the back of the cottages leading through the woods to the gate that opened into Chad's lower pastures. In-lands, they were called, the smaller and richer enclosures around the acres of garden that surrounded his house and where his flock lived in the worst depths of winter. She could hear men's laughter from the yard at the far side of the gardens where they were clipping sheep and further up the fell men were hay-making. Long shadows were beginning to stretch themselves across the steep sides of the fells, their subtle colourings changing with the fragrant breeze which was chasing the clouds across the late afternoon sky. The path, made by many feet, for this was the way the men who worked for Chad wended their way to their cottages after the day's work was done, was clear through the springing grass. Larks were singing above her head and late lambs danced and jumped across tussocks of grass. There was a faint murmuring of running becks and wind patterns formed on the waters of the lake, which she could see as she climbed the slight incline of the field. She loved this land of her birth but though her eyes were on it she saw nothing as she trailed blindly towards the place she must learn to call home. Higher up the bracken rippled and waved and through it she could just make out the head and shoulders of Iolo coming down from the fell. He saw her and waved and she waved back then began to hurry, for she was not in the mood for his good-natured pleasantries. He was more restrained with her now that she was his master's wife, as they all were, and again she deliberated on the awkwardness of her position, though it was more than that, the vacuum in which she found herself since she had become Mrs Chad

Cameron. Only Lizzie was the same and the circumstances in which they had become friends were, and always would be until Danny came home, a nightmare to her, but she was thankful that they had brought her such a good and true friend. Lizzie had settled down, at peace in her new life, thankful for it, and so had Thomas, for Billy was his idol and he had transferred his devoted dependence from his sister to the lad.

Yes, it seemed everyone was settled in their own special niche in life but, dear Lord, where was hers?

20

—◆—

"It seems we are to be parents," she declared baldly, speaking in the tone of someone who was announcing the menu for breakfast next day and for a moment he reacted as though that was what she *had* said. He turned and looked at her, his face devoid of expression for a fraction of a second then his eyes began to snap with joy and his teeth gleamed in his widely grinning face. Even then, as it was his nature, he could not quite accept what she had said without confirmation. He walked slowly across the carpet, his bare feet making a *shushing* sound in the deep pile, until he stood directly behind her, his reflection in her mirror hovering above hers. She was sitting at her dressing-table brushing her hair, long, deep strokes that lifted thick strands, snapping it round the brush, the light from the candles and the fire putting golden threads in it. She wore one of the many peignoirs Miss Avery had insisted upon, a filmy, lacy thing the colour of ivory with satin ribbons of pale gold holding it about her, but it revealed more than it hid. She wore it because she had been told – by Miss Avery – that this was what ladies wore in the privacy of their bedrooms with the man they married but it might have been sackcloth for all the pleasure she took in it. She knew nothing of ladies, or gentlemen, but if this was what was worn then she supposed she must wear it. It seemed to please Chad so she assumed Miss Avery was right.

She could see he didn't know what to do with this news she had just thrown into the arena, then wondered why she had used such a word, but then wasn't this marriage exactly that, an arena in which she and this man fought. He had returned from Liverpool this morning and it had been all she could do not to go at him at once with teeth and fingernails over the matter of the mill and his deceit, his dishonesty, his sharp practices with the farmers, and with her. Though he had not lied to her, for she had not even thought to ask him, he had deliberately schemed in order to have his way, which she supposed he was accustomed to getting and she would never forgive him. He had trapped her and now, with this thing growing inside her, she was doubly trapped, for what man will allow his wife to run her own business when she was carrying his child. Well, she told herself, that remained to be seen. She had performed her part of the bargain with those silly old women who had called on her; she had done her best to learn the rudiments of running his home, which seemed ludicrous when Lizzie did it so much better and this was how he had repaid her. He was a Judas and she could not forgive him.

"Briony . . ." He hesitated over her name. He was tense now, torn between elation, the feeling of male triumph and fulfilment which comes at the revelation that his masculinity was to be perpetuated, and a sudden realisation that her condition was not to her what it was to him. Her face was cold, set in lines of deep resentment and her eyes were hard. They looked as lavender might have looked had it bloomed in an iceberg and at the same time as though that lavender had been crushed underfoot.

He put his hands on her shoulders and though the grin of elation did its best to remain on his amber-tinted face he could feel it slipping as she shrugged away from him. She stood up and moved towards the bed, throwing off her peignoir to reveal an even scantier nightgown beneath it. At any other time he would have hardened immediately, indeed as he did every night in a prelude to their love-making, or rather *his* love-making, for as yet she could not be said to take an active part in it. Nevertheless he slipped out of the silk dressing-gown he wore and let it fall to the floor, advancing towards the bed totally naked, but her next words stopped him.

"This will make no difference to my plans," she said quietly, "despite your efforts to capsize them."

"Capsize them?" He pushed a trembling hand through the thick tumble of his hair, his eyes bewildered. "Plans?"

"You know full well what I mean, you bastard." Her voice was still quiet, almost conversational, as though she referred to nothing more important than the state of the weather. "I went to the mill yesterday and I'd be obliged if you would hand over the accounts which Jacob Kean told me you have in your possession. And also the three months' rent which I mean to put into an account in Danny's name."

"D'you mind telling me what the bloody hell you're talking about?"

"You know what I'm talking about." Hating him and yet unable to ignore the beauty of him. A fiercely masculine beauty, his body lean and symmetrical as she had seen it a hundred times or thereabouts in the months since their marriage, then was furious with herself for noticing such a thing at this crucial moment of their life. It was now that she must let him see that nothing he did, nothing that was to happen, meaning the child within her, would stop her from her goal. She would sink or swim in this venture she had taken up for her brother but if she sank, she would sink on her own.

"Tell me." His voice was almost lazy but his eyes were not.

"I already have. You have the accounts, the ledgers in which are written down the business done and the profits made at my family's mill and you have the money collected for the rent. I want it. I also happen to know, or have guessed, wondering why I didn't realise it before, that you have been directing the men who would have brought their wheat and corn to be milled at Moorend. You have forced them with your influence to take their trade elsewhere and then, when it suited you, told them to return." For a moment her voice faltered and was uncertain. "I . . . I really don't know why . . . Was it just to take my family's mill from us?" Then it strengthened, hardened. "But it doesn't matter, not now. You've weaved your spider's web of deceit for the last time. I mean to go each day to the mill and make absolutely sure that it is being run as I, and Danny, would want it to be run."

He straightened up and the expression on his face that had wavered between hope, joy, uncertainty and something that Briony certainly did not recognise, vanished. Whatever it was it drained away and a cold and savage rage took its place. He was not a man for revealing his emotions, which was one of the reasons Briony had not the slightest idea of what he felt in his heart for her, but now his feelings showed. They were not ones of love and as he leaned over her where she reclined on the pillows she fell back from him anxiously. He had placed a hand on each side of her body, his face so close to hers the golden glints in his eyes seemed to flash like the fireworks that had exploded in the sky on the day Her Majesty was married. His face was the colour and hardness of grey stone and there was a perilous white line about his mouth.

"Will you indeed, madam? With my child inside you did it not occur to you that I might have something to say about that? That, as your husband *and* in the eyes of the law your legal owner, I might have something to say on the matter? Well, I have and it is this. You wil' remain where you belong and that is in the home your husband provided for you. We shall have Doctor Travis here in the morning and you will stay in your bed until he gets here and if he says you may you will be allowed to walk in the gardens or go anywhere that I think fit and where I shall accompany you. The servants will be informed of this and you will be watched night and day and when I am not here you—"

She slapped him full in the face, a blow that rocked his head and swirled his thick hair about his skull, but he merely laughed.

"And as for that pretty mare I bought you she will be exercised by Joe or Ned and you will—"

He had her arms now, each one held above her head by the wrist but she spat in his face. "You can go to hell, you cheating bastard, and I hope you rot there."

"No doubt I will, my pet, but in the meanwhile remember that you are my wife and as such you will become—"

"I shall do as I please and that means looking after the mill for—"

"God in heaven, you are obsessed with that bloody mill and I've half a mind to get rid of the thing then perhaps I'll get a bit of peace."

She began to howl like an animal in pain and in the kitchen all went silent as those who had been about to go to their own beds looked fearfully at the ceiling and then at each other. Lizzie, sitting by her own fireside, leaped to her feet and would have rushed to the door, ready to climb the stairs two at a time, for it sounded as though Briony was in agony but then her husband was with her and what happened in the marriage bed was nothing to do with anyone but those in it. She stood, as they all did in the kitchen, as still as the garden statues about the terrace, listening for any other sounds to come from above but when no more was heard they pulled a face at one another, not wishing to discuss it, and continued on their way to their beds.

★   ★   ★

It was the following afternoon that Sarah Cameron heard that she was to be an aunt and Martha, who had heard it from Iris when she delivered the laundry to the kitchen door at the Dower House, wished she'd kept her mouth shut and let someone else give her the bad news for that, very obviously, was what it was. They were made up with it at the big house, Iris had said. The doctor had called, his visit somewhat a surprise to them all, for they hadn't known the mistress was poorly but it was all explained when the master came into the kitchen demanding champagne at eleven thirty in the morning, since there was something to celebrate, he told them. Champagne for every one of them as it was over thirty years since a baby had been born under this particular roof and he that particular baby. He had opened the back door and shouted for the men, fetching them all in to drink a glass, even William Platt's lad, Isaac, who was only twelve. Talk about a fuss. Talk about excitement with the mistress beside him, saying nothing but all tricked out in her lovely rose-coloured gown of zephyr, fine and silky which, now they had been told, they could see was tight on her. The doctor had been persuaded to take a glass and told them to expect a Christmas baby so she must have fallen on her first night. Mind, the mistress did look peaky and the master kept a tight hold on her arm but Iris supposed that was natural since this was his first child and he'd not want anything to happen to it, so what did Martha think to that. The only person the mistress spoke to, and who did not seem as excited as the rest of them, was Sadie who she'd worked with in the laundry and none of them heard what was said though Sadie did smile at her and hold her hand for a moment.

Martha had it in her mind to wish she'd stayed at Longlake Edge, for she'd been there when Mr Chad was born, she herself not much more than a young woman and she'd have liked to have been among it all when *his* child was born.

"I beg your pardon?" her mistress hissed when she was told, her face draining of every drop of colour so that even her lips were as white as bone.

"A babby, Miss Sarah." Martha stepped back slightly out of range, though of what she wasn't sure. "Mr Chad an' his wife are to have a babby," she quavered and was even more alarmed when Miss Sarah sprang to her feet and began to weave about the small but pretty dining-room as though she herself had partaken of Mr Chad's liberality with the champagne.

"You mean to tell me that that slut, that nasty, common little slut is already with child?" Her face quivered and her lip lifted in distaste. "I suppose I shouldn't be surprised since it's well known the lower classes have no restraint when it comes to the marriage bed." It was as though her brother had had no part in conceiving the child. "So, already she is filling my house with her miserable offspring. The place is to be overrun with snot-nosed guttersnipes making a pigsty of my family's beautiful home, smashing the furniture that generations have gathered and generally bringing their lower-class morals with them. No more than three months married and it has begun. She was probably with child before she led my brother by the nose up the aisle and, one wonders, was it his child? I shouldn't be surprised when it comes to find that it looks like the cowman or one of the grooms."

"Nay, Miss Sarah, never." The old woman was deeply shocked, remembering the shy, dainty, certainly *innocent* child who had come to be their mistress at Longlake Edge. Martha had never known a man's touch but that was not to say she didn't recognise a virtuous girl when she saw one and Briony Marsden, who had worked among them, had certainly been that.

Martha's words of reproof did not stop Sarah Cameron's

despairing venom and for half an hour she poured it out on to Martha who had no option but to listen.

She watched as her husband adjusted his crisply ironed cravat, ran his hand over his smoothly brushed hair, then, when he turned towards her where she still lay in their bed, pretended an interest in the pot of coffee Daphne had left by the bedside. She tried to pour herself a cup without sitting up, for she was completely naked beneath the sheets and had no intention of allowing him to see her, which was ridiculous for had he not just spent the night making love to her with such force and savagery her body felt bruised. If she had not already been with child she would have been persuaded to think he was determined to get her into that condition. She would not have been surprised to find blood on her thighs, as she had the first time he penetrated her, but she had not cried out, or made any objection. He was her husband; she belonged to him as he had so forcefully told her but that did not mean she was about to let him dictate to her. She was not to go beyond the walls of the garden, he had told her, and certainly her mare was out of bounds, but what difference did that make to her who, until two years ago had walked the length and breadth of the lakeside road, had climbed the fells and dragged a sledge with a load on it that a grown man would have found difficult.

"Let me help you with your coffee," he said with a certain irony in his voice as though he knew full well what she was about. He had during the night explored every inch of her smooth young body, turned it this way and that in the firelight, laid her down, sat her up, draped her here and there for his own pleasure and her efforts to hide modestly beneath the sheet seemed to amuse him.

He poured her a cup of coffee then handed it to her before leaning over and putting his lips to her cheek. She coolly accepted his kiss but did not return it.

"I'm to go to Penrith," he told her, reaching for his jacket, "but I'll be home for luncheon."

"I'll tell Cook."

"Shall I ask Lizzie to come up?"

She raised her shoulders in a shrug. "If you like."

"I thought you might want to discuss some household things with her."

"Not really. She is perfectly capable of doing *household things* without my help."

"Very well." He stood for a moment, his manner irresolute, which was unlike him but to tell the truth he had expected some kind of continued argument yesterday and again this morning but she had been perfectly controlled and he was not sure he liked it. Her rage had been expected, something with which he could cope but this cool indifference, this seeming obedience to his wishes, was not to be trusted. He had not yet spoken to the servants on the matter of guarding their mistress, for he was inclined to wait and see if her condition, one known to calm even the most hot-headed woman, might do just that and if it did he would have no need to restrain her from going down to that damn mill.

"Perhaps you might be free this afternoon?" he asked her formally, his voice cool, clipped.

She looked up at him in surprise. Free? What the devil did he mean by that? Free to do what and go where? She was his wife, he had just told her so, and belonged to him and from that he meant her to know that she was his to order here or there, even if he was not yet aware that she had no intention of obeying.

He stood with his back to the window, his dark face even further darkened by shadow. He smiled briefly though there was very little humour in it, watching her carefully, she thought.

"Why?" Her voice was barely short of being offensive.

"I'd be glad if you would come to my study."

"Why?" she said again. She drew the sheets even further under her chin, a somewhat defensive gesture which, though he did not remark on it, he noticed.

He looked at his watch and then back at her but she continued to study him as though this request were something she would have to consider carefully. She *had* made plans for today which naturally included a visit to the mill to question more closely that fool of a miller but she was not about to tell him. There were many things she would not tell him, not now, but he was evidently waiting for her reply.

"I am in something of a hurry, Briony," he reminded her.

But she was in no hurry. His curtly raised eyebrows tested his will against hers and she wanted to smile though, of course, she resisted the temptation to do so.

"Perhaps if I told you that it might be to your advantage to do as I ask." He turned away from her and from a silver box on the mantelshelf selected a cigar, lit it from the fire and remained with his back to her.

"Why?" she asked for the third time, maliciously, he was aware of that. Any small relationship they might have forged in the three months of their marriage was over, her manner told him, apart from that in the connubial bed. His male physical strength would make sure of that but in any other matter she was going to be as awkward as she knew how.

His voice was dry, somewhat disdainful but perfectly polite. "Just be there. Now, I have an appointment for which I'm already late. I hope to see you at luncheon."

It was a clear summer morning so, putting on her stout walking boots and the plainest gown she now possessed, a light barathea in a shade somewhere between sky blue and the green of mignonette, she stole out of the front door and ran down the gravel drive in the direction of the lake road.

"Where you off?" a stern voice asked her as she took a short cut across the immaculately shaved grass and when she turned guiltily there was William Platt. He was raking the lawn with a splayed instrument and beside him Isaac lowered the wheelbarrow he was pushing and viewed her with curiosity and admiration. They had all been told only yesterday that the mistress was in what Mrs Minty described as an "interesting condition" but though he ran his boy's eyes across the region where it would show up there was nothing to be seen as yet. He should know. He was the eldest of thirteen.

"Ah, good morning, William Platt," not even considering why the gardener should be given his full name. They all called him that and so did she. She did not even bother to question why he should feel it his right to enquire about her movements. He was authority and she had not been in her new position long enough to query that authority.

"I thought to take a walk by the lake. It's such a lovely day and so . . ."

"Not by thissen, tha're not, missis. Not now." Now that you're carrying the heir. Though the master, who had been known to William Platt since he was a lad himself, had not specifically asked them to watch out for this slip of a lass, it had been meant in his manner yesterday when they'd all had a sup of that there fizzy stuff.

"I'm not sure I like your tone, William Platt," she began, but the gardener pushed forward the lad.

"Lad's doin' nowt much so he can go wi' thi'. Well, not wi' thi', but just ter watch tha' don't fall, like. Off tha' go, lad. Watch out fer't missis." And she had no option but to suffer the boy slinking along several yards behind her, as much embarrassed as she was.

She strolled along the serene isolation of the shore, forgetting, after several minutes, the silent figure of the boy, who had the sense to keep well back. She went as far as

Castlehows Point, stopping frequently to stare out through the pale blue air, across pale silk water to the purple and brown misted heights of Barton Fell, continuing along a path edged with a profusion of lavender and clove-scented gillyflowers growing wild.

A sudden shout from the boy turned her back in his direction. He was pointing with great excitement to the sky and when she looked up, there, majestic in its beauty, effortlessly soaring on a handful of wind, was a bird of impressive proportions. As they watched it made some high-speed manoeuvre, diving for something only its keen sight could see.

"Bloody 'ell," the boy ejaculated, "tha' don't see many o' them to the pound." His mouth hung open as he still stared where the bird had been.

"What was it?" She watched with him.

"An eagle. Only a bloody golden eagle, that's what." Then remembering himself he slid away, waiting for her to follow him back to safety, which she did, as obedient as a child. For now!

She had been in his study only once before when she told him she was to work in the mill. Now he rose from behind his desk as she entered, indicating politely that she was to be seated. It looked exactly as it had done then, reflecting the influence of the man who sat opposite her, his work, his hobbies – which appeared to be shooting and fishing by the guns and rods that lined the walls – and was absolutely a male domain. Only the parlour-maids entered this room. The desk at its centre was large and there were many papers on it with books, ledgers, pens, an inkwell, two lamps, a penknife, a silver box with his usual cigars, and the most beautiful crystal paperweight she had ever seen. The light reflected from it was blue. It seemed to be full of jewels, fine points of light in sapphire, amber, amethyst and diamond, and she longed to pick it up and gloat over it but she continued to pretend an indifference she didn't feel. It was all immaculately tidy, as he was, and she marvelled at the fact that not once since she had met him had he looked in the slightest bit ruffled. Except for his hair when he made love to her! There were hunting prints on the wall and hundreds of books on the shelves and on a small table an enormous globe of the world. There was no fire in the fireplace but someone – Briony believed it might be Lizzie – had placed a great jug of dried flowers on the hearth.

She sat upright, her back not touching the chair. Her hair, which had hung down her back during her morning ramble with Isaac, was brushed back into a smooth coil on her neck. Her cheeks were somewhat flushed, for she had enjoyed her walk and eaten a good meal – somehow she found herself famished these days – and looked incredibly beautiful, bright and glowing against the darkness of the panelled walls. A window was open and the small breeze moved a wandering curl which had escaped her brush and Chad felt his heart move with loving pity for this self-willed young wife of his. He would have to curb her, of course, because of the child, but he meant to do it as gently as he knew how. If she would let him.

She turned an enquiring look in his direction, indifferent to whatever he might have to say, she would have him believe, but he could see her interest in the narrowing of her incredible eyes.

"I wanted to show you something." He spoke pleasantly but rather as if she had been a recent acquaintance and not the woman he had loved so fiercely the night before.

"Really?" She was considering a small yawn, deciding against it, but he noticed and did his best not to smile. He pushed a couple of leather-bound books towards her, ledgers or account books of some sort, then indicated with his hand that she was to look at them. There was also a small cash book on which she could see a name printed. Peering at it she saw, with amazement, that the name was that of her brother.

"Those are the account books I began when Jacob Kean took over as the miller at Moorend. He is not an accountant so I have kept them for him. When you read them, as I am inviting you to do, but only that" – his voice cool – "you will see that every entry is an account of the rents paid since Kean took over. And that" – indicating the small cash book – "is a bank account in the name of your brother at the Penrith bank. When you have balanced the ledgers and perused the cash book you will see that every penny is accounted for."

21

"Well, it all looks most satisfactory to me, Briony, and I'm at a loss to understand why you should question it. Jacob must have worked very hard, for those profits are excellent. He's made more in a month than a housemaid would earn in a year and I should know since I'm in charge of the household accounts. What is it that's bothering you? It's very obvious that something is."

Lizzie sat back in the chair which was drawn up to her sitting-room table, turning to regard the slender back of the girl who she found hard to call mistress. She was still a girl, despite her married state and her coming child. She was not much younger than Lizzie but her slight, small-boned figure, her soft, dewy freshness gave her the appearance of being barely beyond childhood.

Briony stood at the window looking out on to the herb garden which a former mistress at Longlake Edge had planted at the side of the house. The garden was surrounded by a high stone wall and contained a dozen beds divided by neatly raked gravel paths, each bed crammed with herbs which were not only decorative and of many colours, but a useful addition to cooking and for medicinal purposes. There was blue hyssop to be added to stews or dried for potpourri. Rue with greenish-yellow heads, French sorrel of pink to be added to soups or salads, purple sage, golden-lemon balm to be used for fragrant tea, white horehound, chamomile of a delicate ivory, tansy and sweet cecily and dozens of others, each bed hedged with the symmetrical and vibrant green of box. It was beautiful, a gentle kaleidoscope of colours as graceful and serene as the woman who had planned it decades ago, for Chad had shown Briony her portrait which hung on the landing at the top of the staircase. The aroma of the lemon balm drifted through the open window and she drew it into her lungs, wondering if the fragrance was as soothing as the tea was purported to be.

As she watched, William Platt, with Isaac a hand's breadth behind him, entered through an arched gate trundling their inevitable wheelbarrow piled high with numerous garden tools. William Platt selected a rake, handed it to Isaac and with a few words of what appeared to be instruction indicated that he was to rake the pathways. Then, when satisfied that Isaac was tackling the job as directed, he lit his pipe and strolled away in the direction from which he had come. Isaac, with the lethargy of youth when not watched, fiddled about for a few minutes, then, looking about him, sat down on a bench by the gate and turned his face upwards. The sun shone from a clear china-blue sky, the garden was sheltered and the boy settled back to enjoy the warmth. Briony had to smile, wondering whether to knock on the window and attract his attention. He was a nice lad. He had been sensitive to her needs the day before and had kept well behind her when she walked by the lake as though realising her desire to be alone, but he had had his orders, his demeanour had told her apologetically. But his enthusiasm over the eagle had been boy-like and had for the moment swept her own troubles aside. Nevertheless, if William Platt was to come back and find the silly lad lolling he would be sure to get into trouble.

Suddenly he spotted her. She was wearing white and was not hard to see between the heavy fall of the red woollen curtains. Instantly he sprang up and with a contrite grin of immense charm he picked up his rake and belaboured the gravel with great force. Not a moment too soon, for William Platt, as though hoping to catch him shirking, appeared at the gate, frowning and ready, should he be failing in his duties, to give him what for, no doubt accompanied by a box to his ears. The lad, turning for a moment in Briony's direction, winked conspiratorially. She smiled and was ready to wink back but Lizzie's voice behind her drew her back to her problems.

"Briony, are you listening to me?" Lizzie asked in a perplexed voice. "You ask me to study these ledgers and now you seem to have lost interest. You've gone over them—"

"Yes, I have and, as you say, they seem to be in order but . . ." How lovely it would be if there was no mill to trouble her, nothing but the garden, the house, the baby, the drifting day-to-day tranquillity of a lady of leisure to tax her mind. She had a strange feeling that though Chad had kept up the traditions that were the rule of polite society, the elite among whom he moved, the ones that his mother and then his sister had kept up, he did not really care for them himself. The constant entertaining and being entertained – not that he had insisted on that yet – which seemed to fill the days and evenings of the gentry hereabouts seemed to her to be merely a habit he had gone along with. How hard life had been, how cruel and merciless under her father's heel but now, if she should take what life – and Chad – offered her her days would be filled with the protection he could give her and their child. Children probably! Warm flower-scented summers, sparkling frost-enchanted winters in which to grow and dream, not of profit but of a future coloured with the joy, the safety, the comfort, the wellbeing of a childhood she had never known. If she gave it up, this obsession to run Danny's mill herself; if she let Chad continue to do it, since it seemed so far he had made a success of it. How pleasant it would be with no shadows like the one . . .

She clenched her fists and banged them forcefully on the

windowsill. Dear God, what was she thinking of? She had been about to brush aside this task she had, this duty, this sacred mission that she had vowed she would uphold until Danny came home and that meant making sure *herself* that the inheritance he should have had was intact. She could *not* brush it aside and merely put it in Chad's hands no matter how capable they seemed to be. What had happened to her? Was it the peace and beauty of the herb garden which, she realised, she had never entered nor seen except through this window, that had laid some sort of a spell on her? That and the impish laughter of the lad who was not many years younger than herself, the wink which had made her smile and given her a desire to wander out there into the sunshine and ask William Platt what all these lovely, colourful and aromatic herbs were called?

Lizzie looked at her in consternation, then sighed and stood up briskly. "Well, if you've nothing to do I have. The linen cupboards need sorting and—"

"No, really, Lizzie, I did want to discuss this with you and to ask your help to—"

"Yes?" Lizzie questioned suspiciously. "To what?"

Briony whisked round and her soft skirt drifted with her. It was girlish, the sort of dress an unmarried young woman might wear, with a wide sash of scarlet about the waist. She wore scarlet ribbons in her hair which was knotted carelessly at the back but from which curls escaped and fell about her face and neck. Lizzie could see that she had gained weight. Her breasts were fuller and the bodice strained across them and at the back, where it was buttoned from neck to waist, it pulled at the buttonholes. She would have to encourage Briony to drive into Penrith with herself as chaperone, companion, whatever Mr Cameron liked to call it, and let Miss Avery furnish her with a new wardrobe, and soon, for it was plain she would not be able to get into her gowns for much longer.

"Well?" she asked. Lizzie was wonderfully happy with her new position in life and had it not been for the worry of her father in the penal colony could have found no fault with the way things had turned out. She was a good organiser and was strict though fair with the servants. They had looked askance at first, for it was known she was a friend of the mistress but when they realised she was not about to take advantage of the fact, they had settled under her rule. Thomas was happy down at the mill under the kindly guidance of the miller and with the brotherly affection of Billy Williams, his previous dependence on her disappearing as his trust in his friends grew. Billy and Thomas, often with young Dicky and Isaac, would go off of a Sunday, wandering the fells, trapping rabbits for the pot, since Betty was always glad of something to augment her family's diet. A careless housewife but careful manager was Betty, which was probably one of the reasons the mill had shown such a good start. Thomas and Lizzie were twins, and now and again she was afraid that the other lads, though younger than him, might lead him into trouble but the local men, the shepherds and labourers who worked on Mr Cameron's farms, kept an eye on them, since Mr Cameron would not employ a lad who was likely to find mischief.

Briony sighed, moved across the room and sat down at the table, reaching for the ledgers and the small account book on which was printed the name Daniel Marsden. She smoothed her fingertips over the name and a small smile curled her lips, for it seemed the book gave her immense pleasure.

"Well, he certainly seems to have made a good beginning," she announced cautiously. "And this document tells me that the profit is now safe in a deposit in Danny's name."

"Then why the long face? You know that Mr Cameron wouldn't cheat you, don't you? Don't you?" Lizzie's voice became sharp. "Surely this has proved to you—"

"He *did* cheat me, Lizzie. He persuaded those who had corn

to grind to stay away and then, when he'd got his hands on the mill by marrying me advised them to bring their business there and that is why I don't trust him."

"But surely . . ." Lizzie hesitated. She had her own thoughts on why Mr Cameron had acted as he did and the answer was standing before her. How else was he to get this lovely young girl, a man so much older than herself, or so Briony would believe, to marry him? He had gone against his own family, his friends and acquaintances and men he did business with to win her, and surely to God it was as obvious to Briony as it was to her? "Look, I know he acted in a somewhat underhand way but surely these figures prove that—"

"I cannot trust him, Lizzie and so, as soon and as often as I can, I must get down to the mill to see what's going on and I shall need your help to do it. He hasn't said anything yet, to the servants, I mean, but he will to keep me under his eye. William Platt was ready to stop me yesterday and had the damn cheek to send young Isaac along to spy on me."

"Oh, come now, he was only protecting you, a pregnant woman."

"I'm barely pregnant, Lizzie. Six months to go and if I'm to be watched over and fussed over as though I were made of spun glass I shall go crazy. I understand I can't ride, but I can walk and if you were to come with me down to the mill and over to the farms to talk to the customers, to the villagers who send their corn and animal feed to—"

"And who is to run the house while I'm cavorting about the countryside?"

"Don't be daft. Mrs Minty can—"

"She is a cook and is paid as such. I have been appointed housekeeper and glad you were of it a few weeks ago so—"

"Please, Lizzie, help me or I swear I shall escape on my own and then who knows what could happen to me. I might fall or—"

"I will not be blackmailed."

The argument might have gone on and on, to the fascination of the kitchen staff who could hear every word through the closed door of the housekeeper's sitting-room which led into the kitchen. That there lass was set on having her own way and if the master found out what she was up to Miss Jenkins, as they had been instructed to call her, would be out on her ear. Mind you, Miss Jenkins was not some jumped-up baggage with ideas above her station but a lady who had seen better days and was now down on her luck. She knew what was what and if the day ever came when their young mistress was asked to entertain the master's old friends Miss Jenkins would tackle it with no trouble at all.

The arrival of the second post interrupted them in their stealthy attempt at eavesdropping and though Daphne would have liked to continue to hover by the door, ready to dash off to some pretended activity should it open, Gladys brought in a letter for the mistress which must be taken in. It was one of those that came now and then, all crumpled and damp-looking as though it had been in contact with water, which Daphne supposed it had considering where it came from. There was a lot of water between here and Australia! It also had various other things adhering to it which Daphne was not awfully sure she wanted to investigate, for God alone knew what grew, or crawled, in that vast land on the other side of the world. It looked quite ridiculous lying all tattered on the brightly polished silver salver on which she was expected to take in the mail.

She shrugged her shoulders at the others as she knocked at the sitting-room door.

The two women became silent, suddenly aware that their conversation might have been overheard and Briony put her hand to her mouth as they exchanged glances. She didn't want the maidservants to know what she had planned for the future.

"Come in," Lizzie said after a moment's hesitation.

Daphne bobbed a curtsey in their general direction and held out the salver.

"A letter for the mistress, if you please," she said, watching as Mrs Cameron snatched at it eagerly.

"It's from Danny, oh Lizzie, it's from Danny. It's been three months since I had one and that was written at Christmas." With frantic fingers she began to tear at the stiff paper then pulled herself together, trembling with nerves, treating it more delicately, for the thing was already fragile from its long journey. Daphne watched furtively, hoping they wouldn't notice her hesitating at the doorway, longing to have some titbit to tell the others, for the mistress was a paradox – though Daphne did not use the word – in these parts, but Miss Jenkins nodded at her and she had no choice but to leave, closing the door behind her.

For several long moments Briony studied the letter, ready to smile with joy, for Danny wrote a good hand, and descriptions of the work he did, the plants and flowers and birds that were so different to the ones he had left behind in England, the strange people who were indigenous to this beautiful land, captured her imagination. He worked on a farm owned by an English gentleman and the work suited him, it seemed, and because he could read and write he had been shown favour by his master. He and Mr Jenkins, who was very handy with a pen and could count in his head, a feat which impressed everyone, and who worked in the English gentleman's office, shared a small hut and were in the best of health, Danny had written, as had Mr Jenkins to his daughter.

But there was no letter to Lizzie today and, sadly, never would be again.

The blood drained from Briony's face as she lifted stricken eyes to her friend. The letter trembled violently in her left hand and she raised her right in the direction of her friend as if she were appealing to her for something. Her mouth opened and closed and tears began to form on her lower lashes but even before she could speak Lizzie tore the letter from her hand and began to read. There were no glowing descriptions of exotic flowers and birds in it, just the bald statement that Edwin Jenkins was dead. That he had died months ago, for the journey the letter had travelled was long. Her father had been dead since January and she had not known it. Briony had married and was to bear a child, she herself had become housekeeper and was, so to speak, in clover, as was Thomas, and all the while she had been gloating over their good fortune, good fortune come at last, her beloved father had been dead.

The letter dropped from her hand, whispering to the floor, coming to rest at Briony's feet. Briony bent down and picked it up, turning it over and over in her hand as though a thorough scrutiny might reveal something more, something they could understand. There were smudges on the writing, stains that had made the ink run and Briony knew instinctively that they were Danny's tears for the man who had been more than friend to him. He had given her brother affection, a man's affection he had never before known, the comfort of a friend when they had begun their incarceration in Carlisle goal. He had been teacher as well as friend and had helped Danny to accept his sentence and to look to the future and forget the past. They had survived together, begun their new life together, sharing their fears and when it had looked as though it would be got through, had rejoiced together.

Now the kind and gentle old man was gone and how was Danny to manage without him. She was horror-stricken by her own selfishness, for at least Danny was still alive but she could not help but admit that Danny was her first concern.

Lizzie began to weep, not noisily but as still and silent as the grave in which, one presumed, her father had been for the past five months. Would he have had a Christian burial or were convicted felons just tipped into any old hole that was handy? But even as these black thoughts came to her Briony knew that Danny would not have allowed it.

She knelt down at Lizzie's knee and took her hands in hers. She stroked them, then bent her head to put a kiss on the backs, her tears mingling with Lizzie's, saying nothing. After a while Lizzie fished in the pocket of her snowy-white apron over which dangled the symbol of her position in life: the housekeeper's chatelaine on which hung the keys of her kingdom. Keys to the storeroom, the wine cellar – in the absence of a butler – the silver closet. It did not only hold keys. There were other small, useful objects, a pincushion, scissors in a sheath, a thimble, all linked to a chain and hung from her belt. She took out a handkerchief, not the wispy sort of thing used by a lady but a big, white linen handkerchief that was not only as white as driven snow but a thing of practical usage. She wiped her eyes and scrubbed her face then blew her nose vigorously.

"I'm all right, Briony, please don't make any more fuss or I'll never stop crying. Though it sounds odd, I really did not expect to see my father again. He was an old man, frail and should have ended his days in peace and . . . and . . . Oh, get up, please get up and . . . Will you leave me alone for a while? If you would see to the lunch."

"Of course, darling." Though Briony hadn't the faintest idea how one went about such a thing. Her mother had taught her, with the few scrag ends of mutton at her disposal, how to cook a stew, a vegetable pasty, a potato pie, a dish of herrings purchased cheaply in Pooley Bridge, fruit tarts and such, but the serving of a meal fit to put before Chad Cameron was another matter altogether. Still, Mrs Minty would know, surely.

She closed the door softly behind her, standing for a moment against the door frame while the servants all stopped what they were doing and watched her, waiting for whatever it was she had to tell them. She had been crying, that was obvious, and with that mucky letter which had been put in her hand it could only be about that brother of hers.

She stirred and seemed to become suddenly aware of them. "Ah, Mrs Minty . . ."

"Yes, madam?" It took all Mrs Minty's resolution to call this child "madam", for Mrs Minty had worked for real gentry and by no stretch of the imagination could you call Mrs Cameron gentry. A nice little thing, and as refined in her ways as many of the *real* ladies Mrs Minty had served, but it was hard to take orders from her. Still, she was the master's wife and was to have his child and with herself getting on a bit and with jobs hard to find, despite her being a good cook, she minded her p's and q's.

"Miss Jenkins isn't well."

"Oh, I'm right sorry about that." Mrs Minty advanced to the centre of the room, wiping her hands on a clean bit of cloth. "Nothing serious I hope?" The others gathered about her the better to hear what might be wrong, for it must be something to do with that letter.

"No . . . well, yes. So I don't want her disturbed, is that clear?"

"Yes, madam, and what's to be done about luncheon?"

"Did Miss Jenkins discuss with you what was to be served?"

"No, madam, we hadn't got round to it, you see, what with . . ."

Briony was evidently not at all interested in what had held up the daily discussion regarding menus and her manner said so.

"What is there available?" she asked.

"There's a nice steak and kidney pie in the oven for the servants' dinner and a—"

"That will do. Mr Cameron will be home at midday and I'm sure steak and kidney will suit him fine. Thank you."

With a swirl of her gauzy white skirt she swept from the room, leaving the rest of them with their mouths open, for what were *they* to eat if their dinner was to be served to the master and mistress?

"Well, the nerve of it—" Mrs Minty began, but what she was about to add was cut off as the clatter of hooves in the yard told them that the master was home.

He found her in their bedroom weeping disconsolately, but as a man, a husband might do on finding his wife in such distress, he did not hurry across the room, take her in his arms and beg to know what was distressing her. He longed to, of course, but their relationship was not one in which he found himself able to do such a thing. He was a man of deep silences, a man of calmness, a man who had retreated into a distant part of himself when faced with the love he felt for this woman. He was a courteous man, a man of restrained cordiality and so he merely stood on the threshold of the room, the room in which he showed her a passion which astounded her and himself, and asked her politely what was wrong.

"You're not ill, are you?" And for a moment the strain on his face was evident, for this woman, this beloved woman carried his child.

"No, not me. Oh, Chad, it is so sad." She put her face in her hands and wept bitterly.

"What is?"

"There was a letter . . ."

"From your brother?" If it should be *about* her brother how was he to comfort her when the last person she wanted to hold her was Chad Cameron? His thoughts swung wildly from Lizzie on whom she relied and trusted as a friend, to Sadie, who was as dear to her as a mother and he was ready to ring the bell and send for one or the other.

"Yes, from Danny. It seems . . . oh, Chad, it seems the old gentleman is dead."

The relief eddied through his body and he almost began to smile, to move towards her with no idea of what he meant to do, but the complex tangle of love, of compassion he had always known for this young woman and the sad knowledge that she did not return it, compelled him to remain where he was. He watched her, cool-eyed, neutral, his speech clipped.

"I'm sorry, but you know he was frail and elderly. I'm surprised he survived the journey which I'm told is—" He stopped abruptly, for his wife's brother, God in heaven his own *brother-in-law*, had taken the hellish trip to the fate that he knew had not been deserved. When the lad came back – though he would no longer be a lad, even if he survived – he would make it up to him. In the meanwhile his inheritance was safe in his hands and with Briony carrying his child there would be no interference.

"Lizzie's resting but there's steak and kidney pie for lunch," she sniffled, this wife he loved so much that he physically hurt with it and again he wanted to smile, even laugh out loud.

"I'm glad you're managing without her," he told her gravely.

"But what is to happen to Danny, without the old man?"

He wanted to tell her that she was not to worry. That he would see to it. That her brother would not suffer, even that he would arrange to have him brought home, but he knew he could do none of these things and so, moving to stand beside her where she crouched in her chair, he put a gentle hand for a moment on her shoulder which she didn't notice, or if she did, was not concerned with it.

22

- - -

"Has Mr Cameron gone out, Ned?" Briony asked the groom who was currying Gypsy in the stable yard. The pale sunshine which glimmered about the edges of the clouds high above the stable roof caught the glowing chestnut coat of the placid little mare, polishing it so that, as Joe had remarked on passing, you could almost see your face in it. She stood patiently, her rear hoof lifted in a resting position, obviously relishing the gentle, loving hands that groomed her. They were all fond of her, since she had the sweetest nature and, the two grooms agreed, Mr Cameron certainly knew his horseflesh. She was a bit small for them, who were both big men, but young Charlie Sidebottom, the stable lad who was twelve and as light as a feather, rode her regularly to keep her exercised for Mrs Cameron. They threatened him with the hobs of hell if he should do anything to alarm or injure the pretty creature, meaning the mare – though Mrs Cameron was every bit as lovely – but he loved the animal as much as they did and rode her at a gentle pace.

Briony had sauntered out into the yard, doing her best as she passed through the kitchen to appear casual. She nodded at Mrs Minty who was stirring something on the kitchen range.

"Nice smell, Mrs Minty," she remarked.

"Soup fer lunch, madam. It's me peanam."

"Really. I shall look forward to it." Though she'd not the slightest notion what Mrs Minty had said. She knew that none of them would question her right to go where she pleased, not yet at least, but Mrs Minty, who was older and superior in rank to the rest and therefore perhaps might be inclined to be more outspoken, bobbed her frilled cap politely, watching her from the corner of her eye. Briony hoped to God she didn't meet Sadie, for Sadie *would* ask questions and if she didn't like the answers would demand what she was up to.

She smoothed the mare's neck and was delighted when the animal nuzzled her cheek. Ned watched and it was in his male mind that he wouldn't mind nuzzling the mistress's cheek, then wondered on the strangeness of calling this lovely young woman "mistress". Not so long ago he had sat beside her round the kitchen table with the other servants ploughing through the hefty and nourishing dinner Mrs Foster, who had gone to the Dower House with Miss Sarah, had put in front of them. Her mother and father had been dead, her brother over in Carlisle awaiting trial for murder and the child, for that was how she had seemed to him, to them all, had been as thin as a whisker and pale with not a word for the cat.

"She remembers me, Ned," she said with delight, as though it had been months instead of days since she had been up on Gypsy's back.

"Aye, lass," he said, grinning, the term "lass" coming more easily to his tongue than the formal address of "Mrs Cameron" which, by rights, he should use. "An' if tha' bring 'er an apple every day until tha' can ride 'er again, she'll never forget."

"Oh, Ned, of course, I'll go and get one now." And with no more ado, as if she were a child again, she sped back to the kitchen, flush-cheeked, her eyes a sparkling violet blue, grabbing an apple from the bowl on the dresser.

"For Gypsy," she explained breathlessly, as the maids all stopped what they were doing to watch her, all of them beginning to smile, for could you help it?

"Put it on the flat o' tha' hand, so, on tha' palm an' offer it to 'er," Ned explained and they both stood and watched the dainty animal crunch the apple between her strong white teeth.

"Eeh, tha' enjoyed that, didn't tha', lass?" Ned beamed, not sure whether he meant the mare or the woman.

"Anyway, as I was saying," Briony continued, as though the delightful moment had not interrupted the reason, the *real* reason for her visit to the yard. "Has Mr Cameron taken his horse, Ned?"

"Aye, missis, 'e 'as."

"Did he say where he was going?" Her face and voice were artless as she continued to rub Gypsy's nose.

If Ned thought it strange that the mistress found it necessary to question the groom on her husband's whereabouts, he did not query it. He was not, of course, to know of the conversation, or lack of it, that had taken place in the lovely bedroom at the front of the house last night.

If Briony had not been so distraught over the news that Lizzie's father was dead it is doubtful she would have addressed a word to him on the subject, on *any* subject, for the worm of betrayal, of humiliated distrust, squirmed inside her. She had always told herself that she did not love Chad Cameron, but she had liked him, respected him, believed that he had done his best for her and Danny. She had even, though she could not express it to herself, come to . . . well, she could hardly call it *welcome* his advances to her in their bed but she had become used to them, and him. She had found it rather comforting to sleep in his arms, to find his soothing presence beside her when her night dreams of Danny and her nightmares of Jethro had brought her sharply to wakefulness.

But now, with the revelation that he had been cheating her, it had turned around her trust in him until it was a spike in her heart. It hurt her quite dreadfully, she told herself, bewildered, and the truth of it had foundered what might have been a contented marriage on the rocks of mistrust. He had filled her with a painful anger that had turned her heart to stone. He had taken something from her with his deceit and now, with the baby growing inside her, he had the perfect excuse to keep her from what she saw as her work at the mill. She would never forgive him.

She had told him so icily, watching him in her mirror as he undressed, his back to her so that she did not see the expression on his lean face. He was a man with neat ways and even though he felt her words enter his heart like a serrated knife, turning cruelly, he continued to fold his clothes, placing his shirt and cravat into the laundry box from where Daphne or Gladys would take the day's laundry down to Sadie. He slept naked, for it was his belief that a man looked ridiculous in a nightshirt but before he turned to face her he shrugged into his silk dressing-gown.

"Am I to take it that you are not satisfied with the profit the mill is making?" His voice was as cold as hers.

"I'm not saying that."

"Then what are you saying?"

"The underhand way in which you have taken—"

He ran his hand across his brow as though the conversation were as tedious to him now as it had been on every one of the other occasions it had taken place.

"I believe you have told me that many times, Briony, and before you repeat it all again let me say this. I will not allow you to walk, ride, or even take the gig down to that mill. I am your husband. You are my wife and expecting my child. Until your brother comes home I will remain in charge of running it. Is that clear? You have seen the accounts. You have seen the amount of the funds put in the bank in your brother's name. That is all there is to it. Now I am tired and would like to get some sleep and, in your condition, I suggest you do the same."

They had slept back to back with a good twelve inches between them.

Ned reached for the brush with which Gypsy's mane and tail were untangled, making the soothing, clicking sounds he used with all the horses in his care. "Penrith, 'e said, an' ter give Sable a good groomin', as if I don't always."

"Of course, Ned, and when did he leave?" She hadn't heard her husband leave their bed this morning, nor the sounds of him dressing.

"Nay, lass, I'm not that sure. Early."

"Well, I'll be off too, I think, so will you get the gig ready." She again did her best to appear casual just as though the request was the most ordinary thing in the world, but at once Ned turned suspiciously, looking her up and down as if assessing where she might be off to and would the master like it. They all knew she was in the family way and should she be handling the gig in her condition? The master had said nothing to him about gigs, only about the mare which, naturally, he would not let her ride until the bairn arrived. It was a cool day, despite the bit of sunshine which did its best to fall about the yard. She was dressed in a practical outfit of barathea in a shade that matched her eyes. Not lavender and not blue but somewhere in between. A carriage dress, Miss Avery called it, though Ned was not to know that, only that she looked right bonny in it, noticing with half an eye that it wouldn't fit her for much longer. Still, he was not happy about it. She had a look about her he wasn't sure he liked, though ask him what it was and he couldn't have said.

"Well, Mr Chad said nowt about gig. Where tha' off to then?" speaking with the familiarity of a servant of long standing.

"I want to go into Penrith—"

"Nay, then I'll tekk thi'," he interrupted resolutely. "That there Roddy can pull a bit when 'e feels like it."

"No, Ned, it's not necessary. I'm to go to the dressmaker's for . . ." She glanced down in the general direction of her stomach and at once Ned understood. He turned a bright red and looked hurriedly away but his chin took a stubborn tilt.

"Nay, lass, 'tis a long haul to Penrith an' if master . . ."

She smiled. It was the smile that had felled Chad Cameron when they first met, settling about him, lifting his spirits, charming him, chaining him to her and though it did not have the same effect on Ned, who was quite satisfied with his pretty Jenny, he could not withstand it. Nevertheless, though he returned her smile he would not be moved.

"Just give Joe a shout will tha'? 'E's in't stable. 'E'll fetch Roddy from't paddock while I finish this lass an' then I'll . . ."

Briony wanted to stamp her foot and tell Ned Turnberry to mind his own business. That she was quite capable of driving to Penrith in the little gig but then, of course, she wasn't going to Penrith though she couldn't tell Ned, for then it would be all over the yard and the house that Mrs Cameron was off where she shouldn't. Not that they were privy to Chad's orders to her but they soon would be if he found out she had disobeyed him. There was only one person she could trust these days, only one person who understood her compulsion to check that the mill her father and grandfather had made so profitable was continuing to be so. No, that was not essentially true. The books Chad had shown her had within their pages the proof that *so far* Jacob Kean was doing well but there were so many other factors to be considered. She and Danny had been responsible for the cleanliness of the many working parts of the machinery; the way the grain was stored; the absolute necessity of ensuring that when the bins were emptied every particle of grain was removed. If any were left they might go mouldy and fresh grain poured into the bins could be contaminated. A dozen questions needed to be answered. A dozen functions in the mill needed to be checked and she was the only one, apart from Jacob himself – and who knew how careless he might turn out to be – who was qualified to check them. Good God, she had been at it for long enough, and under her father's cruel hand and experienced eye had learned more than Jacob Kean ever would. Only one person knew this and only one person understood.

"I won't be a minute, Ned. Get the gig ready if you please and I shall be back in a moment."

"I can't possibly come with you, Briony. I have the menus for the day to discuss with Mrs Minty and the household accounts to go over. Besides which, I don't feel—"

"Oh, darling, you can leave the menus to Mrs Minty. I honestly don't care what I have for luncheon and I'm sure Chad will eat whatever is put before him at dinner. Please, Lizzie."

"No, Briony. I am paid to look after this house and not to go gadding about with you here, there and everywhere. Besides . . ."

"Don't be silly, darling. Does it matter what you do to earn your wages? That stupid Ned is insisting that he drives the gig and all I want to do is . . . is go to Penrith." This last was a sudden inspiration, as were her next words. "You must agree I need new outfits or perhaps I could persuade Miss Avery to make me a corset then I can—"

"Dear God, Briony, although I am unmarried and have never had a child even I have heard that a corset is the last thing you should be wearing. Have you any idea of the damage you could do to the child?"

"Really, Lizzie!" Briony pulled her face into an expression of innocent bewilderment, though she knew from Sadie, who had given her what for when she had talked of "getting rid" as Sadie had called it, that women, fashionable ladies, had deformed the child inside them with tight corseting.

"Lord, Briony, I suppose I'd better come with you, if only for the sake of your health. Sensible, *loose* clothing is what Miss Avery must design for you and I need to make sure that is what you order, though I must admit I don't feel like making the journey today of all days. Still, I shall need a . . . a . . . mourning dress for Father."

Briony put her hand to her mouth, horror-stricken by her own thoughtlessness. "Lizzie, I'm so sorry, of course you must not come if—"

"No, I'll have a word with Mrs Minty and then I'll drive you into Penrith. It's the least I can do. If it hadn't been for you God only knows where me and Thomas would have ended up. And at least I can afford to purchase a decent gown. But there is something else."

She turned her back on Briony and gazed out of the window on to the herb garden.

"Yes, Lizzie, what is it?"

"Would you object to my writing to Daniel? He doesn't say what . . . what Father died of and, if you have no objection, I should like to write and ask him."

"Oh, darling, of course I wouldn't. We shall write together this very evening and Chad can get them away tomorrow."

The stable boy, Charlie Sidebottom, who was vigorously sweeping the yard, touched his finger to his thatch of hair as Mrs Cameron rode by him in the gig with Miss Jenkins at the reins. He was knocked sideways by the brilliance of the mistress's smile, though Ned, who watched them go, had an uneasy feeling he had been hoodwinked in some way.

"Nay, Mrs Cameron, but I can't do that. I'm right sorry but I've 'ad me orders an' really, don't tha' think it'd be best if tha' were ter go 'ome an' . . . well, wi' you in't family way . . ."

Jacob's voice tapered out in vast embarrassment and he did his best not to look at her slender waist where, as yet, he could see no sign of the child she was carrying.

Betty clutched her latest infant, whom she had patriotically named after their young Queen but called Vicky, to her enormous bosom which, Briony noticed with a shiver of distaste, was leaking with what she supposed was milk. Dear God, would she look like that when her child was born? she asked herself. Then was ready to smile at her own fastidiousness, for hadn't she been brought up in this mill which was not exactly Longlake Edge. Mind, Mother had been a demon for cleanliness about the house and had done her best to keep them all as dirt-free as she could in the circumstances, which could not be said of Betty. She supposed since her mother died and she had gone first to live with Sadie, then at Longlake where she had servants to keep her immaculate, she had grown used to discarding a garment the moment it was soiled. In fact she could not remember ever wearing an undergarment or nightgown more than once before it was whisked away to be washed. Daphne, who had always wanted to learn the trade of lady's maid and was eager to practise it, looked after her outer garments, and took care of Chad's jackets and breeches if a stitch was needed or a button sewn on and Dicky cleaned his boots, and hers, to a mirror-like shine.

"What are you trying to tell me, Mr Kean?" she asked him pleasantly, doing her best to pass the pair of them as they stood in the doorway. Lizzie, still perched disapprovingly on the seat of the gig, looked down at the group in the doorway to where Betty had summoned her husband. Betty was twice the size of Jacob and with the child in her arms was as solid and immovable as if the door were shut. The yard was busy with several waggons pulled up and waiting their turn to be unloaded of their grain-filled sacks and there were others evidently come to collect the meal or the flour they had delivered – as grain – earlier. Grain was measured by the bushel and a sack of flour weighed twenty stone and as Briony watched Thomas heaving them on to his shoulder, taking them to the sack hoist, she marvelled at the memory of herself and Danny as children, wondering how on earth they had ever coped with the weights. It was a miracle that they had not grown up with bones distorted or pulled from their sockets.

"Well, Mrs Cameron, I've got work ter do an' Betty 'ere's the same an' we've not time ter . . . besides, tha' shouldn't be 'ere." He eyed her elegant outfit which looked vastly out of place in the rough and tumble of the mill yard. She and Lizzie had indeed been to Penrith and had sat in Miss Avery's smart little salon drinking coffee among the other ladies of the neighbourhood who, drawn by the dressmaker's clever designs, her flair and her talent for recognising exactly what suited them, were beginning to consult her in droves. She could do a sketch from a vague idea they might have and with a few strokes of her pencil turn it into the exact outfit they had in mind. She knew about seed pearls and tulle frills, about embroidery and millinery and every garment from the skin outwards that a lady should need. Her salon was not large but it was exceedingly elegant, the walls painted a tranquil apple green picked out with gold. She had pale green hatboxes with her name on them and little green velvet chairs for her customers to sit on, where they sipped her coffee and hot chocolate and gossiped the day away while they spent their wealthy husbands' money. There were displays of shawls and fans, embroidered gloves, lace caps and collars, exquisite little things of ribbons and gauze that no lady could resist.

The ladies were not too sure that they cared to sit with a girl who had once worked in a corn mill and whose brother was a convicted murderer, though she was now richer than any of them and that broad-shouldered young amazon who was with her was no better. But since several of the ladies of polite society had already called on her they could do no more than bow in her direction.

Miss Avery, knowing Mrs Cameron's position, and her own, took her at once into a private fitting-room where Mrs Cameron was measured, taking not the slightest interest in what Miss Avery recommended in the way of concealing garments, telling her to choose what colours and materials she thought best and to send them to Longlake Edge when they were ready. Miss Jenkins was measured for a mourning dress of black silk which, she remarked, would do her for any occasion, since there would be no . . . no funeral, with a rather smart black bonnet of Miss Avery's choosing.

Within an hour they were at Moorend Mill.

"You didn't tell me we were to visit the mill, Briony, and I would prefer it if we went straight home. I'm sure your husband—"

"Oh, damn my husband, Lizzie, just drive into the yard."

"I see, this has all been a ruse to get me to drive you here so that—"

"Oh, stop it, Lizzie. If you're going to be so . . . Oh, God, I'm sorry, I shouldn't be quarrelling with you when you have just had such bad news but I can't—"

"Yes, you can. Mr Cameron is quite capable of—"

"Lizzie, I'm sorry but I must do this and besides" – her voice softened and she took Lizzie's big hand between her two small ones – "wouldn't this be a good time to tell Thomas? Not that any time is good but you know he'll be upset and while you speak to him, which you'll want to do on your own, I'll just have a word with Mr Kean." Thomas had seen his sister and had waved to her, still unaware that she had bad news for him, and even as she prepared herself for the task of telling him and for the distress that would ensue Briony had jumped down from the gig and was hammering on the kitchen door of the mill house.

She might have stood there arguing for the rest of the day with Jacob, who was proving more obstinate than she had bargained for, when the sound of a horse's hooves rang out above the clamour of the yard. They were not the slow steady clip-clop of a cart-horse, one of those that pulled the heavy waggons loaded with sacks of corn or grain. The protagonists in the doorway did not hear them, though others did, including Lizzie who had been just about to lead her brother into the barn where she would have some privacy to deal with his tears, for there would be bound to be some.

"Mr Cameron won't like it, if I was ter let tha' come ferretin' round the place, missis," Jacob was saying with the irritating patience of an obstinate man who knows he is in the right. "'E said particular—"

"Ferreting! *Ferreting!* I must remind you, Mr Kean, that this property belongs to my family and I am perfectly entitled to go over it whenever I please. You are merely a tenant so if you will step aside I wish to inspect the machinery and the corn bins. I happen to know, since I worked here for many years, that unless—"

Chad Cameron slowly got down from his horse and even then, in the hush that fell across the yard, she did not hear him come. A cart-horse nodded its head and its harness jingled musically. A blackbird sang its heart out in a nearby tree then took off in a whirr of graceful wings. The baby began to grizzle and her mother bounced her so violently on her hip the child's bonnet fell over her eyes. Lizzie thought her heart would stop in her fear for Briony.

Briony began to realise that something was diverting Jacob's attention, for he was looking over her shoulder, a smile beginning about his thin lips. Betty had her hand to her mouth but her eyes shone as though in expectation of a bit of excitement and before she turned she knew who was there.

She sighed deeply before she whirled to look into his face. His brown eyes were no longer brown but the dead dull colour of peat, slitted with rage and his mouth was hard and cruel.

"Get into the gig." He spoke like master to maid. Her stomach lurched uneasily, for though he was in full control of himself beneath that control was the scorching heat of his anger.

Still she tried to assert herself while all about them the men, the two women, stood frozen to the bit of ground they stood on.

"I have some business here, Chad," she managed to get out through her dry lips.

"No, you have not and if you don't get into the gig I shall throw you in."

"Chad . . ."

"Get into the gig. I shall drive."

"Your horse . . ."

"One of the men will return my horse."

"Lizzie needs to—"

"I shall have a word with Lizzie later. Now get into the gig."

She did as she was told but the expression on her face told him she would never forgive him for this, or indeed for anything.

23

"Where is she?" Mrs Minty's voice was fretful, for she knew they would all get it in the neck if her mistress was missing when the master got home. It wasn't fair. It wasn't right, but Mr Cameron had made it quite plain that he would hold them all responsible if it was found that she'd been down to that damned mill again. They had their work to do, hadn't they, she entreated the rest of the servants, and it was beyond reason to expect them to watch over her, to guard her, to keep her where she should be and that was in her own sitting-room or the confines of the garden. It wasn't their responsibility, was it, she asked plaintively and they all shook their heads and agreed that it wasn't.

"She were upstairs a minnit since," Gladys added. "Drinkin' 'er 'ot chocolate wi' 'er feet on't tuffet, nursin' that there animal an' I tell thi' if it widdles on't carpet again I'll wring its damned neck."

This was a regular complaint of both Daphne and Gladys, and the others, who weren't involved since they didn't work in the bedrooms, sighed wearily. "I reckon master thought it'd keep 'er company until bairn comes an' mebbe persuade 'er ter stop at 'ome where she belongs, which it don't 'cos she tekks it with 'er. I dunno." Gladys sighed reflectively. "I remember when she were 'ere as laundry-maid, dost remember, Daphne?" she went on, breathing heavily on a knife then polishing it on her apron before placing it on the tray she was setting up for the mistress's lunch. "She were the quietest little thing you ever did see, wi' them big blue eyes; well, more the colour of a sprig o' lavender, an' a face on 'er as pale as a snowdrop. Nowt ter say fer 'erself an' now would yer look at 'er, fat as butter an' a mouth on 'er like a fishwife. 'I'll go where I like,' she were screamin' at Mr Chad last night, 'an' no one'll stop me.' Well, we'll see about that, madam, 'e says."

"Now, Gladys, that's enough o' that," Mrs Minty told her. It was all very well to discuss the goings-on in this house among themselves but she drew the line at repeating what the mistress had said to the master, and vice versa. Their feelings towards the new Mrs Cameron were ambiguous – though that was not a word they would have used, not knowing its meaning – for she had once been one of themselves and now she shaped their lives. Keep them or sack them, if she wanted, and yet at the same time she was pleasant enough, making few demands on them. A slender wisp, or had been before the master got her with child, a graceful sprite as insubstantial as she was lovely, she drifted about the place as though she wouldn't dare open her mouth but, by God, she did, though not to them, or *at* them. It was the master who bore the full brunt of her displeasure, God love him, while it was Miss Jenkins who ruled the servants and she let nothing get past her.

They'd lost count of how many times the miller had been up to the house to complain to the master about the mistress interfering in the running of the mill, which, after all, since he paid the rent, was his concern, he was heard to say from the study where Daphne had shown him when he knocked on the kitchen door. Daphne had hung about in the corridor, ready to run for it if the door opened or that there Miss Jenkins should come along. She had heard the miller, who was a quiet sort of a man on the whole and wouldn't say boo to a goose, complain bitterly that he didn't think he could run the business efficiently with Mrs Cameron forever at his back, arguing with him over this and that, directing him in what, after all, was his business. The master had been most polite to Mr Kean, telling him – after about the third or fourth time the miller had whined about her – that it definitely wouldn't happen again. But short of locking her in her bedroom, what was he to do? Knowing her, as they all did too well by now, she'd probably climb down the massive horse chestnut tree which tapped on the window or get that there Isaac she'd taken a fancy to, to fetch her a ladder!

That's when, at the end of his tether they were all inclined to think, the master had brought her the puppy. And a flaming nuisance it was, too, both Daphne and Gladys, who had the cleaning up after it, agreed. Scruff, she called the thing, and it was a scruff, an' all. A Border terrier, the master claimed, with a rough coat which she was forever brushing, of a wheaten colour. *He* said it was a breed that was good with children, which made it suitable for when the infant arrived, but it certainly didn't keep her tied to her sitting-room. Here it was September and still she strode out with the dog prancing at her heels, flatly ignoring Joe or Ned when they pleaded with her to stay in the garden and they couldn't quite bring themselves to lay hands on her, going wherever she fancied, whenever she fancied it. The gig was out of bounds, Ned and Joe being threatened with the sack if they let her out in it, and so she put on her boots and wrapped herself in one of the outfits Miss Avery had made for her which concealed her thickening figure, and off she went.

"Mrs Cameron, will tha' not sit by't fire terday," Daphne wheedled her, longing to give the lass a good slap, for it wasn't so long ago when Mrs Cameron had run about at Daphne's command, or would have if she'd worked in the kitchen instead of the laundry.

"Whatever for?" Mrs Cameron, who used to be Briony Marsden, the miller's daughter, demanded haughtily.

"Well, it's goin' ter rain an' if tha' was ter get caught out in a downpour an' catched a chill the master'd be" – she almost said "bloody furious" which was how she herself felt – "not pleased, an' what with the babby comin' . . ."

"Not for months yet, Daphne, and I want a walk and so does Scruff, don't you, poppet?" Scruff's gender was not yet awfully clear to the servants, not that they cared, for whatever it was it made a mess, but as it jumped up, scrabbling at the mistress's skirt Daphne saw that it was male. It damn well would be, wouldn't it, she thought, Daphne's opinion of the male sex, whether animal or human, not being very high.

"Why don't tha' put tha' feet up, lass?" she pleaded, calling the mistress "lass" which sometimes did the trick but not today, and not on many another day as she and Scruff set off down the front drive and on to the road beside the lake. Very often, if William Platt happened to see her, he would send his lad, Isaac, scurrying after her to watch she didn't fall, or do something daft like trying to climb up Gowbarrow Fell, but most times it was the left turning to the mill at Moorend she took.

It was "back-end", as Sadie called the autumn and was absolutely pouring down, a hard-driving, hard-biting rain which soaked through Sadie's old shawl as she dashed across the yard to the back kitchen door. She liked to enquire after Briony and sometimes, if Lizzie was about, since Lizzie knew of Sadie's great affection for the lass, to the great consternation of the other servants, she was allowed up to Mrs Cameron's sitting-room for a bit of a clack. Briony may have gone up in the world but she was still "t' lass" to Sadie. Sadie was looking forward to the arrival of the baby and was convinced that it would be the makings of the girl who was her mistress. She'd be glad that Sadie had prevented her from getting "shut", as Sadie put it, and there'd be no more of this roaming about the countryside or, worse, interfering down at the mill. The master'd not put up with it for much longer; in fact Sadie was amazed he'd been so patient up to now.

"Do go up, Mrs Evans," Lizzie told her, regal in her black silk housekeeper's gown, her chatelaine clinking at her waist. "She'd be glad to see you, I'm sure. Perhaps you'd like to take a cup of tea up with you. It will warm you up."

Sadie knocked on Briony's door, balancing her cup of hot, sweet tea, satisfyingly strong, in her hand, entering at Briony's command and in a minute the pair of them, Sadie with her skirts pulled up to let the flames of the cheerful fire get to her old bones, were deep in conversation.

"Now then, 'ow are thi', little one?" smiling with great fondness on the girl she had taken to her heart.

"Not so little now, Sadie. Just look at me. Getting as big as the side of a house and how much longer I can stand it, I don't know."

And you'll be a damn sight bigger before the babe comes, Sadie thought, though she kept this to herself. She pushed the energetic puppy to one side with a gentle foot but the thing, as puppies do, took no notice, leaping up at her skirt repeatedly. With a sigh she picked him up and laid him in the wool-lined basket by the fire and, knowing proper authority when he met it, Scruff stayed where he was, his nose on the basket's side, his dark, intelligent eyes staring unblinkingly at her.

"How do you do that? He won't take any notice of me, though Chad can make him do as he's told when he—"

She stopped speaking abruptly as though the mention of her husband's name had come out unintentionally and was not a subject she cared for. She and Chad ate at the same table and when he spoke to her she answered, at least when the servants were about, but apart from that they rarely had any contact. She attacked him relentlessly on the matter of the mill and who should have the running of it – herself naturally – but he was immovable on the subject. Each time Jacob Kean came up from the mill to complain he would summon her to his study, neutral ground, she supposed, commanding her to sit down, which, to her own surprise, she did. He was completely self-controlled, not even raising his voice, cool and inflexible but each word he spoke cut through her like iced water. His lips hardly moved and his eyes were dark slits in the sombre room.

"Jacob Kean has just left and—"

"Sulking again, is he, because—"

"That's enough. I am not going to argue with you. I wish you to remain in this house," he proclaimed, as he always did but she interrupted him fiercely.

"I cannot do that, Chad. I feel that—"

"I no longer care how you think or feel. In fact you may think and feel exactly as you please. It's your behaviour that concerns me. You will do as you're told. You will be the wife of Chad Cameron and you will act as the wife of Chad Cameron should act. You will look after my house and when the child comes you will look after it as a mother should. Until that day you will be safe from my physical attentions. Do you understand? And you will not go to the mill. Do you hear? Now, I think that's all so—"

"No," she howled, "you can't dismiss me like that. You have to let me watch over Danny's mill. You have to stop treating me like a child."

"Then stop acting like one. Now, I have things to do." He opened a drawer and drew out a sheaf of papers as though to tell her that the interview was over, turning one over and then another.

"You can't stop me."

"But I can."

"And who will be my gaoler? You are not always at home to watch me and the servants daren't cross me."

He looked up at her and there was menace in his eyes. "I'm sure something can be arranged," he told her, then turned once more to his papers and she had no choice but to leave the room, her heart as heavy as lead. He slept in his dressing-room from that day onwards, to the servants' shocked astonishment, but Sadie, who had heard the gossip, said nothing of this.

"I've just come fer a bit of a fradge an' a warm at tha' fire. I'm soggin' wet through. It's welterin' down an' tha's in't best place terday, my lass."

Briony sighed heavily and her downcast face told its own story. "Oh, Sadie, when's this baby going to make its appearance? I'm bored to tears with my own company an' now this rain's keeping me in. Talk to me. Tell me what's happening in the village before I go mad with no one to talk to. Lizzie's always busy."

"Well, nothin' much changes in't cottages. Hilda Blackhall's 'avin' another an' where she's ter put it I don't know. 'Er place is like a rat's nest as it is wi' five young 'uns. I dunno, lasses terday don't know owt about keepin' their 'omes nice. An' it's not that there's no water ter keep a place clean what with yon taps Mr Cameron put in. They don't know 'ow lucky they are. I 'eard there's only one tap to a row o' cottages in Carlisle an' then it's only turned on fer an hour a day."

"Mmm . . ."

"Oh, an' yon Minnie from't kitchen's doin' 'er best ter ger 'er feet under my table."

"What do you mean?"

"Well, she's after our Iolo, in't she? Little madam."

"And isn't he interested? She's pretty enough."

Sadie bristled, for was there any woman in this world good enough for her Iolo? She'd had great hopes for the young woman sitting opposite her, and she knew Iolo had too, but her dream had come to nothing and it was hard to lower her standards to the kitchen-maid.

"Aye, pretty is as pretty does, an' she's a good clean girl but could I abide 'er in my kitchen, that's what I want ter know?"

For an hour Sadie managed to take Briony's mind off her brooding problem, both of them sighing over past troubles and laughing over shared memories, but it is doubtful they would have laughed so merrily if they had known where their master, for he was as much Briony's as Sadie's, was at that precise moment.

You could have knocked Martha down with a feather, she said to Mrs Foster, when, answering the peal of the doorbell at the Dower House, who should be standing on the scrupulously scrubbed step but the master.

"Good morning, Martha, and how are you today?"

She was so surprised she lost her voice for a moment, then he smiled and there was the lad she had virtually brought up, or so she liked to tell herself, his eyes a lovely velvet brown, with golden lights in them that told her he was pleased to see her.

"Eeh, master, what's ter do?" she asked him, for in the six months since they had moved to the Dower House she had only caught glimpses of him as he rode his great black horse out of the gate. "It's not babby, is it?" she cried, her hand to her mouth.

"No, everything is fine with . . . with Mrs Cameron, and yourself?"

"Well, thank you, sir. A bit of a twinge wi' me knees an' bits o' things . . ." Until she remembered who he was and here she was keeping him blathering on the doorstep.

"Is your mistress at home, Martha?" he asked her kindly

and she wondered how anyone with eyes in their head could ever think him cold, or arrogant.

"She's in't drawin'-room, sir."

"Will you tell her I'm here and would be obliged if she could spare me a moment."

Briony heard the commotion in the hall and wondered vaguely what was going on. She had been playing ball with Scruff, throwing it listlessly across the carpet and watching as the puppy scampered after it. He could not quite get the hang of the idea that he was to bring it back to her and kept throwing it in the air and tossing it in a corner, ignoring her commands to "bring it here". There had been a deal of scurrying about during the past hour, footsteps almost running along the passage beyond her sitting-room door, voices murmuring and what sounded like furniture being moved. A door banged and a voice told someone to be quiet but she was too melancholy to wander out and ask what was going on. What did she care if Gladys and Daphne had decided to spring-clean the place, though it was a strange time of the year to do so.

She had received a letter this morning from Danny and the tone of it had caused her some anxiety. It seemed he missed the old man, as he called him, and could not drag himself out of the pit of despair into which his death had cast him. He had no one to talk to, to have the lively discussions he and the old man had enjoyed, for his companions were rough, illiterate fellows who thought of nothing but women and drink, both of which were in short supply which made them dangerous. They were wary of him, since he was in favour with the owner of the property to whom they had been assigned. Always in his past letters there had run a thread of hope, a sense that he would get through this horror and come home to her and his mill, which, he knew, she was looking after for him. But now, faced with the formidable impediment of her husband

and the baby which was even now kicking vigorously inside her, how was she to watch over it for him?

God in heaven, what the devil was going on downstairs? She could hear voices raised, one of which sounded like Ned's. What was Ned doing at the front door? There was a sort of thudding noise as though something heavy had been dropped to the floor and Scruff lost interest in his ball, scampering to put his nose to the bottom of the door, where he sniffed and wagged his tail.

She picked him up and opened the door, moving along the passage to the head of the broad staircase, passing open bedroom doors, one of which had once been occupied by Chad's sister whom she had met only in the capacity of a servant. Miss Sarah, as the servants called her, had looked her over when Sadie had brought Briony into the laundry after Danny was taken to gaol. A supercilious look which told her that Chad's sister did not like being coerced into employing a girl she herself had not chosen. She had made the choice to move to the Dower House when Briony had married Chad, for reasons that were obvious, as Briony was not daft. Miss Sarah would not be usurped by a servant girl, a girl who was to take Miss Sarah's place in running Longlake, and so she had gone, but for some reason, as Briony peeped into her room, the door of which had always been kept shut, she saw boxes and wicker baskets, and in the hearth a cheerful fire blazed. Gladys was busy unpacking a box, giving the contents a shake and then hanging first one gown, then a second, in the wardrobe.

"What the devil's going on?" Briony managed to gasp, her face a picture of stunned astonishment. "Gladys, what are you doing, for goodness sake? Whose gowns are those? Have we got guests?" Beginning to smile, for who in this county would deign to be the house guest of Chad Cameron, the man who had married his laundry-maid?

"No, Mrs Cameron, not guests." Gladys's face was aflame with something Briony did not like.

"Then who?"

"It's nowt ter do wi' me, lass. Tha'd best get yerself downstairs."

"Downstairs? What for? What's going on, for heaven's sake and who is to . . . ?"

There was a clatter of feet on the outside steps at the front door and a voice told the owner of the feet to mind what he was doing with that box. "There are breakables in it so I would be obliged if you would treat it more carefully. See, put it there and then the maids can take it into the drawing-room and unpack it. That's if you have a decent housemaid capable of such a task. I suppose I shall have to start looking for trained, respectable servants. No, no! Carry that with more care, if you please, oh, and Daphne – at least you are still here – I will have a cup of tea in the drawing-room at once. Is there a fire lit? Well, thank heavens for small mercies."

The stillness and the silence that had fallen among the scurrying servants became obvious to the speaker and she turned irritably to see what had caused it. When she saw Briony coming slowly down the stairs, Sarah Cameron smiled, a smile that would not have gone amiss on the face of a cat that has just fallen in a pot of cream. Each woman waited for the other to speak. It was Briony who gave way first. She was white-lipped with anger but there was uncertainty in her voice as she spoke.

"What d'you think you're doing in my house?" she hissed. "Who said you could order the servants about as though they were your own? I'd be glad if you would take yourself off back to where you chose to live last March."

Sarah threw off her cloak and with a cold smile handed it to Daphne who took it automatically and even bobbed a curtsey. She began to move towards the drawing-room door which stood open invitingly, a cheerful fire blazing in the grate.

"I see my brother has not spoken to you then, and shouldn't that . . . that animal be in the yard. I don't care for dogs in the house."

They all gasped, Daphne, Gladys who was behind the mistress on the stairs, not wanting to miss the excitement, Ned and Iolo who were unloading the farm waggon which had brought Miss Sarah's things from the Dower House, and Joe who was about to drive the carriage that had brought Miss Sarah herself, round to the stable yard. The mistress's face was like the frosting on the cake Mrs Minty had just made and they all, every one of them, felt sorrow for the little thing, for there was no one in the world who could stand up to Miss Sarah, not even, it seemed, the master.

"What in hell's name are you talking about?" she said harshly.

"And let me get one thing straight from the beginning and that is I will not tolerate bad language in my presence though what else one could expect from—"

"I must ask you to leave now before I have you thrown out," Briony began, but Chad's sister had waited for this moment for too long to allow it to be cut short by this upstart who thought she could get the better of Sarah Cameron. When Chadwick had begged her to come home and take charge, not only of his home, but of his rebellious wife – and of his unborn child, who was the main reason for his climbdown, she was well aware of that – she had barely been able to contain her exultation. He had made it quite clear that this was to be of a short duration. Until the child was born, he said, when he was sure Briony would settle down to motherhood and forget the mill, but Sarah, once inside Longlake, had no intention of ever leaving it again. She had made a mistake in removing herself to the Dower House, in high dudgeon she now admitted to herself. She had missed the large and elegant house, the position in society it had given her, the entertaining, which was virtually impossible at the Dower House, the feeling of being a great hostess when her friends called. She could manage this slut, as she still called her, with one hand tied behind her back, and she could manage Chadwick, since he would be beholden to her.

She smiled as she continued on her way to the drawing-room. "Don't forget my tea, Daphne, then I will be up to check that the unpacking of my boxes is being done correctly. Well, don't just stand there, girl. Away to the kitchen and I'll see the cook right away. I might bring Mrs Foster back if this new woman doesn't suit."

Briony gently put Scruff into the arms of Ned who stood like a frozen pillar in the middle of the hall, his face almost as white as hers. Careful on her feet as an invalid, she followed her sister-in-law into the drawing-room. "Ask Miss Jenkins to come at once," she said over her shoulder to anyone who was listening, then, stiffening her back and squaring her shoulders, she prepared herself to tackle this appalling mischief which had grinned at her evilly before it struck her down.

24

For some strange reason Briony found herself compelled to fold her hands protectively about her belly where the baby stirred restlessly. It was as though already, in these first catastrophic moments, she recognised, with the instinct of a mother or mother-to-be, that this meant danger for her child.

She wanted to shout and scream and act like one of those women she had seen outside the George in Penrith clawing at one another in a drunken brawl. Anything to take that satisfied and superior expression from Sarah's face but as yet she was confused, more than confused, and before she gave Sarah the satisfaction of watching her make a fool of herself, she must remain calm and get to the bottom of this obvious mistake. Chad had done something, said something to this woman to make her believe she could march back into her old home and take over the servants, and herself, it seemed. But she must have support in this, for all of a sudden she felt weakened and only Sadie or Lizzie would stand by her. Sadie was out of the question. Sadie was a simple working woman without the cleverness with words to face up to this smug-faced woman who would simply reduce her to . . . well, no, nobody could reduce Sadie to anything but she could be *discharged* if she crossed swords with the confidently smiling woman who was seating herself with every sign of being totally at home in the pretty velvet-covered fireside chair in which Briony herself usually sat.

Briony turned with relief, though she did her best to hide it, as Lizzie walked into the room. Lizzie had that look on her face that Briony had seen before, a look that she showed to tradesmen who, thinking her a nobody in this house, tried to get the better of her.

She bowed her head politely in Sarah's direction then turned to Briony, the mistress of the house. "You wanted to see me, Briony?" She would have called her "Mrs Cameron" but Briony had forbidden it.

"Yes, Miss Cameron is under the impression that she is to be mistress here. That . . . that my husband has asked her to come back to Longlake Edge and take over the running of the house and I would like you to tell her, as I will tell her, that there is some mistake, that there is a misunderstanding."

Sarah, just as though she were alone in the room, reached out and rang the bell which summoned a parlour-maid, then sat back in her chair with her ladylike hands folded in her lap. When Gladys scurried into the room, sketching a curtsey in her direction, Sarah smiled coolly.

"I ordered tea five minutes ago, Gladys, and it has not yet arrived. I see that standards have slipped during the last six months but that will be dealt with shortly. Go and see where it is, if you please, and then send the cook . . . what is her name?"

"Mrs Minty, Miss Sarah." Gladys, with a sidelong look at Mrs Cameron – Briony, the master's wife – which asked plaintively what was she to do, sketched another curtsey.

"Mrs Minty. Well, ask Mrs Minty to come at once with her menus and—"

Briony, her mouth open, stared at her sister-in-law with consternation then suddenly snapped to life.

"What the blazes d'you think you're doing in my house?" Yes, *her* house, that's what it was. She had been mistress here for six months, by God. She was the wife of Chad

Cameron and though she did nothing that could vaguely be called domestic and had no need to, for Lizzie dealt with all that, *she* gave the orders. Or she could if she had the inclination. She hadn't done *much* ordering about since there had been nothing particular she wished to order. Gladys and Daphne carried on with their work in the drawing-room, the dining-room, all the downstairs rooms and the bedrooms. Minnie and Fanny presumably did as they were told under the auspices of Mrs Minty in the kitchen and scullery, and over it all Lizzie kept a careful watch. The outside men, under Chad's direction, performed their everyday tasks and there had been no need for Briony Marsden, Briony *Cameron*, to exert herself in any way. It all ran like clockwork with no complaint from the master of the house so what the devil was this shrew-faced woman doing sitting in *her* drawing-room giving orders to *her* parlour-maid?

"I am here at my brother's request, miss, and now, if you would excuse me, I would like to interview this Mrs . . . er . . . Minty to ascertain whether she will suit me."

"You will do no such thing, will she, Lizzie? Tell her, Lizzie. You employed Mrs Minty who had excellent references." She suddenly put her hand to her head, shaking it as though at the madness, the lunacy, not only of this woman who had taken over her drawing-room, but at herself for arguing with her.

Lizzie stood like a block of stone, her face drained of all colour, even her lips which opened on words that did not come. She knew what was happening here if Briony did not. She put out a pacifying hand to Briony for though no one, meaning Mr Cameron, had said a word to her, she knew full well, as Briony didn't seem to, that this woman would not be here unless she had been asked and the only person who had the authority to do such a thing was Chad Cameron. In a way she had seen this coming. Not *this* exactly, but something, for she knew, if Briony did not, that he was at the end of his patience. Briony must be checked. She was making a fool of him, hurrying at every opportunity down to the mill, interfering in the running of it, complaining to the miller that the stones that ground the meal were not being properly dressed, that the hopper, the square box that held the grain, and the shoe, the shute that conveyed the grain to the stones, were not clean, refusing to be checked, refusing to recognise that the mill was a profitable business under Mr Cameron's guidance and there was absolutely no need for her to be there. Briony had seen the figures in the ledgers and shown them to her, Lizzie. She had studied the amount of money that was being put each month in the account that had been opened in Danny Marsden's name in the bank at Penrith and yet, obsessively, she would not leave it alone. So, she was to be restrained and who else but this martinet smiling triumphantly in Briony's elegant drawing-room was able to do it? The servants had no power to contain her, other than coaxing, and that hadn't worked so it seemed he was taking a further step.

"Briony, do you not think that Mr Cameron—"

Briony flung off her hand and took a step towards the woman in the chair. "No, no, I will not have this intruder in my home." She turned violently on Daphne who had just crept in with a tea tray on which was daintily set out the tea that Miss Sarah had ordered. "Take that away at once," Briony shrilled. "I will not have my maids ordered about by another woman in *my* house." She was becoming hysterical, she knew it, wondering vaguely whether it was her condition that was causing it. Look at poor Daphne. She didn't know whether to go or come, or drop the tray, throw her snowy apron over her head and run screaming from the room.

"Put it here, Daphne," Miss Sarah told her and with great relief Daphne did so, almost falling over her own feet in her eagerness to be gone and bring her fellow servants up to date.

"Lizzie . . ." Briony turned about, her hands once again at her belly. "Fetch my husband at once. I swear I'll strike this woman if she doesn't leave my house. I must . . . he must deal with it." But, like Lizzie, some dawning horror was creeping over her and her hands shook across the folds of her concealing skirt.

"He's not at home, darling." Lizzie did her best to soothe her, cursing Chad Cameron for his unfeeling treatment of his pregnant wife, for who knew into what state this pandemonium might throw her.

"Ask the men where he might be. I must see him at once."

"I believe he said he was going to Carlisle," the woman in the chair said, sipping her tea as calmly as though she really were the mistress of this house, a mistress who was doing her best to deal with an unruly housemaid.

"Carlisle?"

"I believe so. Now, where is that woman? What was her name? Must I go to the kitchens to search for her? The menu for dinner must be seen to and I should perhaps make an inspection of the house before—"

"Do you want Mrs Cameron to have a miscarriage, madam?" Lizzie said curtly as Briony bent over, indeed almost *fell* over.

Sarah Cameron smiled. "I really don't care one way or the other. Now, I have things to do so if you and . . . this young woman would leave I would be obliged."

Lizzie put her to bed and debated wildly on whether it might be wise to send for Doctor Travis. Briony seemed dazed, staring into the layered muslin canopy that draped upwards to the ceiling at the head of the bed, saying nothing, her eyes wide and staring. Lizzie held her hand, then, not knowing what else to do, rang the bell and when Gladys knocked at the door,

slightly flushed and more than a little flustered, begged her
to run for Sadie.

"Sadie?"

"Yes, run and get Sadie and tell her to come up here. Oh,
and make some tea and—"

"Madam's in't kitchen." Daphne wanted to say "giving hell
to the servants" but thought better of it.

"Well?"

"I'm not so sure I should fetch tea."

Lizzie stared at her in amazement. "Don't be so silly. Mrs
Cameron could do with a cup of tea and so could I. You can
ask Sadie to bring it up if you're so reluctant."

"'Tisn't that, Miss Jenkins, but Miss Sarah—"

"Damn Miss Sarah. Now you either do as I say or I myself
will go down and tackle her. Do as you're told and as soon as
Mr Cameron comes in send him up here. And don't forget
Sadie."

"Oh, Miss Jenkins." For a minute Lizzie thought Daphne
was about to cry. She was amazed that though Sarah Cameron
had been here for no more than an hour she had the household
in a state of complete upheaval. Surely this was not what Chad
Cameron had in mind for his wife.

The tea was brought, all set out on a lace-covered tray, with
the silver teapot, milk jug and sugar bowl and the best china
tea service. There were ginger biscuits and slices of almond
cake and Lizzie suspected that Sarah was letting them know
that *she* knew how things were done in a properly run home
even if they didn't. Five minutes later Sadie sidled into the
room, looking fearfully behind her as though soldiers were
on her heels with orders to arrest her.

"I come up back stairs," she said breathlessly. "Minnie
slipped out an' told me. Said I'd bin asked for but madam
wouldn't allow it. I 'ad a good skenn round an' when it weer
clear I come roun't back. She's gorrem all backed up in't

kitchen like a bloody sergeant major hinspectin' the troops an' it took a bit o' nerve fer Minnie ter run fer me." It was evident that Minnie had gone up several notches in Sadie's eyes. "Ee', she's queer as Dick's 'atband, 'er," presumably meaning Sarah Cameron. "Now, what's ter do, lamb?" She moved lightly across the carpet and sank to her knees beside the bed. "Nay, 'tis no good skrikin'," lifting the weeping woman into her arms. "Sadie's 'ere, and Lizzie, an' if tha' think yon battle-axe'll get better o't three on us, then tha're not the lass I thought tha' were. See, sit up and drink tha' tea, an' I'll 'ave a sip an' all. I get right thirsty when me dander's up but us'll soon 'ave this lot sorted out, won't we, Lizzie. Just wait till master gets 'ome."

"But, Sadie, it seems Chad asked her to come here." Briony sniffed and sipped her tea, then wiped her nose with the back of her hand, infinitely pitiful, vulnerable as pregnant women are. Sadie regarded her compassionately, her seamed face sad. Whatever was to be done? How was the lass to get through this, because the woman downstairs would make what was already an almost impossible situation for Briony even more difficult. The lass had no real identity, that was the trouble. She was neither one thing nor the other. Oh, yes, she was the master's wife but she was also what the gentry called a "vulgar", come from the lower classes, the working classes, the daughter of a common working man. Nevertheless she had something about her that was as fine as many of her well-bred contemporaries but it made for confusion in her young life. For the first fifteen years she had lived with hardship in what almost amounted to squalor. Her own innate refinement, a discernment taught her by her mother, her intelligence and fastidiousness which had caught the eye of Chad Cameron would, given time, patience and determination, give her the incentive needed for her role in life. But now, at this precise moment, she didn't know herself what she was, who she was, or how to behave in the circumstances in which she now found herself. It was her own fault, of course. Or rather the fault of that mill she could not or would not leave alone. She had defied Chad Cameron time and time again, despite knowing her brother's inheritance was in good hands and now look where it had landed her.

"What am I to do?" she asked Sadie. "Tell me what to do."

"Nay, child, I can't tell thi'. Yer must do what tha' knows is best fer thissen an' fer't bairn. 'Appen if tha' 'adn't kept gallopin' down ter that mill – nay, don't go pullin' a face at me fer yer know it's true – tha' wouldn't be in this pickle. That woman wouldn't be sitting' in thy drawin'-room, orderin' *thy* servants about like they were 'er own. She wouldn't be in thy kitchen pokin' 'er nose in *thy* cupboards an' actin' like mistress of Longlake."

"This is Chad's fault, Sadie."

"No, it's not. It's thine. Stop at 'ome. Let 'im see tha' mean ter be mistress in tha' own 'ome then 'appen 'e'll—"

"But what about the mill?" Briony's voice rose in a wail and Lizzie sighed. Lizzie had the feeling that her own job was in jeopardy if Sarah Cameron took over the task of running this house. There was no need for a housekeeper and the only reason Lizzie was here was the fact that Briony would not face up to the task of learning her new place. Moorend Mill stood firmly between Briony and Chad Cameron and unless Briony, who had imagined, once she was Chad's wife, she could trip over there and see to the running of it whenever she had the fancy, was shown the error of her ways, and was made to give it up, there would be no peace in this household. A house cannot be tranquil with two mistresses and Chad Cameron should be aware of it. It was a measure of his desperation that he had brought in his sister who had shown clearly, at least to her and the other servants, that now she was in, she would stay in.

"Briony, you know that the mill is in good hands. Mr Cameron is a businessman, for God's sake, and will know to a nicety exactly how to make a profit *and* how to keep it in good heart until Danny returns. I should have thought that you, an intelligent woman, must see that. You have only yourself to blame that he has brought in his sister to—"

"Keep me imprisoned." Briony's voice was harsh and bitter.

"Yes, if you like. He cares about you—"

"No! He thinks I have his son in here," folding her hands across her belly and bending over, her face close to the quilted bedspread. "He cares nothing for me or he would allow me to—"

"Stop it! Stop it. Surely you can see that not only Mr Cameron but all of us are sick unto death of the mill and your hysterical and unreasonable attitude towards it."

"Lizzie!" Briony looked up at her, deeply shocked.

"'Tis true, child. Tha're a grown woman doin' a woman's job an' that's bein' a wife an' mother an' there's nowt else ter be said."

"So, you're all against me then?"

Sadie shook her head sadly, then hauled herself to her feet, turning to look at Lizzie as if to say what was to be done with the lass. It seemed it made no difference what anyone said to her, even those who loved her, so, as her old mam had often remarked, they might as well save their breath to cool their porridge.

"We're not against thi', lass, but tha've got ter face facts an' the facts is clear. Bide at 'ome an' 'ave tha' bairn. Be a good girl an' then, *then* 'appen maister'll let thi' . . . well, I dunno, tekk an interest in't mill. So stop bein' mardy. Don't tha' glare at me, lass, tha' know it's true. A spoiled child is what tha' are, isn't it so, Lizzie?" turning to the tall, straight-backed figure who stood quietly by the window. The puppy was jumping up at her skirt, ready for a game, too young to sense the tension in the room, but she seemed impervious to the animal, caught in some dilemma of her own and Sadie knew exactly what it was, for the pair of them were known to be friends of the mistress of this house.

"Lizzie?" she questioned.

"Yes, I'm here, but for how long I don't know."

The girl in the bed slowly raised her head and pushed back her hair. She narrowed her eyes as though a dazzle of light had just struck her and perhaps it had, for the woman downstairs had the power to affect more lives than just her own.

"Lizzie . . . Lizzie, what are you saying? You don't think she'll try to—"

"Oh, yes, Briony, she will indeed. She has no use of me, you see, and if Mr Cameron is serious about keeping you safely at home he will give her carte blanche to ensure you are *kept* at home! I would only complicate matters so . . ."

Briony leaped from the bed, her face a furious scarlet, her eyes snapping and her mouth open in what appeared to be a scream of rage though she uttered no sound. She flew across the bedroom, ignoring the small, romping dog who pranced and jumped in what he thought might prove to be a good game, and her arms came round her friend. Her chin barely reached Lizzie's shoulder but her whole manner said that she would defend this woman with every ounce of her being. Sadie wanted to laugh. It was like a slender gazelle, which she'd seen in a picture book of Iolo's, defending a lion but it did her heart good, for that nesh look, that dreadful look of delicate weakness and hopelessness, that heaviness of spirit which was unlike her had gone completely.

"Don't be daft, Lizzie. D'you think I would allow that? Dear God, if you go, then so do I! He can say what he likes and so can she but there is no way I would let you be taken from me. You are my . . . my sister, my beloved friend and . . ."

Sadie shook her head, for as usual the lass was going like a bull at a gate for what she believed in. What a child she was in many ways, up and down, mad as a wet hen one minute, then sad as a swan with a broken wing another, but ready to defend those she loved with a ferocious wildness that would let nothing stand in her way. By God, that woman downstairs had better watch out, for Briony Cameron was not as pathetic as Miss Sarah Cameron obviously thought she was. If Sadie could have looked into the future she would perhaps not have been so optimistic!

Chad Cameron returned home to the peace and quiet he had longed for ever since his young wife had told him of her pregnancy. There was a delicious aroma drifting from the kitchen and through the open doorway he could see Gladys and Daphne busying themselves at the dining-room table. A log fire leaped in the big grate in the hallway. Lamps had been lit, for it was the end of September and the nights had begun to draw in. There were flowers, enormous heads of chrysanthemums in bronze and gold and white on the hall table and he drew a deep sigh of satisfaction, for surely this meant that all had gone well today. Of course, all these things, the flowers, the fire, the lamps, had been the order of the day under the guidance of Lizzie Jenkins but there was something different this evening and he hoped in his heart that it meant what he longed for: that the mistress of the house was in charge.

"Is that you, dear?" a voice from the drawing-room asked him as he placed his hat and coat on the hall chair and he smiled as he moved towards the door. For that moment, stupidly, he realised later, he held in his heart's eye the peaceful picture of his sister and his wife sitting one on either side of the fireplace awaiting his arrival before going in to dinner. He knew he should have spoken to Briony of his intention to bring Sarah back to Longlake, just until the baby was born, naturally, before he left this morning. He had meant to but an urgent telegram regarding some business deal with which he was involved had called him to Carlisle and, knowing he was probably in for a trying argument with his young wife, he had postponed the confrontation and left in a tearing hurry. At least that's what he had told himself though he knew secretly he had been a coward. Given time, perhaps only a few hours, Briony, he was sure – though why he was sure he couldn't have said – would accept Sarah's . . . Sarah's help and guardianship – was that the word? – but if she didn't it couldn't be helped. She must be made to see that until she gave up this ridiculous obsession with the mill and settled down to her job as his wife and the mother of his child, she must be restrained from her madness, she must be *guarded* and only Sarah could be trusted to do just that.

Sarah was sitting where he had imagined her, a small glass of wine in her hand, but of Briony there was no sign and his heart sank though it was not evident from his expression.

"Good evening, Sarah," he said, his voice toneless, cool.

"Good evening, Chadwick. Do come to the fire. I'll ring for Daphne to pour you a brandy."

"There is no need, Sarah. I can pour my own drink." He moved towards the sideboard.

"Nonsense, my dear. One doesn't keep servants to idle about doing nothing but gossip, as I've found today."

"Really, I'm surprised. Miss Jenkins usually has them—"

"Miss Jenkins is no longer in charge, Chadwick. We have no need of a housekeeper now that I'm back so . . ."

Chad felt an icy trickle slide down his back and the hairs at the nape of his neck stirred as though a chill draught had touched him. He poured himself a brandy, waving away Gladys who had come running when Sarah rang the bell and Sarah frowned but leaned back in her chair.

"And where is Miss Jenkins, may I ask? And where, come to that, is my wife?"

Sarah winced and a deep look of disapproval tightened the corners of her mouth at the mention of the slut who was her brother's wife and the memory of the scene that had taken place earlier in the day. She sipped her wine as though it were vinegar. She had changed into her evening gown, an outdated thing of dark blue velvet and made a great show of glancing at his black frock coat and grey striped trousers, perfectly suitable for business but not for dining as she was accustomed.

"Perhaps we could discuss them – the two young women – over dinner, Chadwick. There is just time for you to change."

"Now would be a good time, Sarah. Where is Miss Jenkins?"

"She is in the kitchen where she is helping Mrs Foster. Yes, I would prefer to engage a cook I myself have chosen so for the time being—"

"And Briony?" He interrupted her rather rudely, she was inclined to think.

She took a sip of her wine before answering. "She has taken to her bed and I thought it best to leave her there for she was quite—"

But she was talking to her brother's back as he raced from the drawing-room and along the hallway towards the stairs, taking them two at a time.

She tutted, smoothing down the folds of her skirt, but there was a small, satisfied smile playing about her thin lips.

25

She was crouched in the low chair before the cheerfully leaping coal fire, her head bowed in what seemed utter dejection, the puppy on her lap, when he burst into the bedroom in a manner that was totally unlike him. Both she and the dog were startled. Scruff began to yap, but with a cry of rage Briony leaped to her feet, the puppy sliding from her knees, and, her face scarlet with rage, hurled herself across the room in Chad's direction.

She took him off guard and before he could defend himself her nails clawed three marks down each cheek.

"You bastard, you cowardly bastard. How dare you, how dare you bring that evil woman back into this house to create havoc among the servants, ordering them about, fetching her things, making herself comfortable in *my* drawing-room, treating me and Lizzie as though we were some indescribable things she had picked up on her shoes and barring the way to *my* friends so that they are forced to creep up the back stairs—"

"What are you talking about?" He had her by the wrists now, his face ashen, the bloody scratches her fingernails had left standing out like the daubs of paint a child might make on paper.

"And the worst of it is," she panted, struggling to get free, "is that you hadn't the nerve to tell me, to warn me, to discuss it with me. I am your wife and—"

"Ah, so you do admit to some place in this house, some

responsibility in that direction. I had thought your one concern was not our home but that mill which you can't leave
alone."

"So you thought to punish me, did you? To make me pay
for doing my best to keep my brother's inheritance intact?"

"Don't talk drivel. Your brother's inheritance is thriving
under *my* guidance and well you know it, but for some reason
you won't admit to it."

"I'm the one who should be guiding it." She was screaming
now and the puppy, finding the door open, ran through it in
terror, making for the safety of downstairs where he made
the mistake of turning into the drawing-room. Sarah eyed
it malevolently, then rang the bell and when Daphne, ready
to cover her ears to shut out the dreadful sounds that were
coming from upstairs, ran in, Sarah ordered her to pick up
the shivering puppy and deliver him into the hands of one of
the outside men. She would issue further orders regarding his
place later, she told the maid.

Upstairs, Chad stepped back from the virago who confronted him and though he himself was in a state of barely
controlled anger, inside, where truth lay, he knew he had
made an appalling mistake. What a bloody fool he had
been to imagine that this child bride of his would accept
the authority of his sister. That she would simply throw off
her resolve to look after the mill, to *interfere* in the mill and
meekly settle down to be his wife and the mother-to-be of
his child. But it was not that that was driving her to the edge
of madness so much as the dreadful fact that he had brought
in Sarah while her back was turned, so to speak. That he
had given Sarah permission to take over the running of
the house, or so it would appear to her, in a manner so
deceitful she would, she was telling him, never forget it.
He had given Sarah the right to guard – no, that was not
the word he had meant – to *imprison* Briony, was that it?

while he was away from the house since the servants had no control over her.

Damn it, he had to continue with his many business interests but that did not give him the right to treat her in this way and he was aware that she was justified in her resentment. Certainly she must be restricted from running down to the mill at every opportunity but surely there must be some other way of achieving it. He had wanted to protect her, to protect his unborn child, surely not an unrealistic desire for any husband or father, but he had made a bloody mess of it by not warning her about Sarah and giving her the chance to change her ways, at least until the infant was born. Was he out of his mind to think, as he had done as he entered the house, that Sarah and Briony would settle down like two cats in a basket, especially after all that Sarah had had to say on the subject of his marriage to Briony? The sad answer was yes. He must have been! Now look what he was faced with, he who had the reputation for the coolest head in the valley!

"Briony," he said gently, beginning again. "It was either this or lock you in your room. You're so headstrong, so absolutely—"

"*I must do it, I must!* Don't you see, it's my duty? I am to blame for Danny's—"

"What!"

"If I hadn't . . . if I had allowed Faither to . . . Danny did what he did because . . . please, Chad, please."

His face contracted in pain, realising what she was saying, and he put out his hands to grasp her shoulders, bending his head to look into her downcast face but she flinched away from him.

"What the devil are you saying?" His voice was harsh. But she had turned away, the violence in her gone, drooping away to the window where she gazed out into the blackness of the night, watching the moon dip in and out of the silvered clouds over the woodland. She was wounded, deeply hurt and for the moment the fight had gone out of her.

"Briony . . ."

"It doesn't matter."

"Yes, it does. Let's talk about it and then—"

"It's too late. The woman downstairs, with your help, has made it too late."

"It is only until the child is born," he continued, desperation in his voice.

"Is it?"

"I swear. I want you to rest and be safe. Can't you see, Sarah will—"

"Lizzie was—"

"You took no notice of Lizzie or—"

"And I am to obey your sister?"

"No, no, of course not but she will watch over you. Make sure you don't overtax yourself."

"At the mill, you mean."

"Yes." His voice was hard.

"Then there is no more to be said."

"No, I suppose not."

"Goodnight then."

"Won't you come down and have dinner?"

"With that woman at the table? I think not. Lizzie will bring me something on a tray."

He hesitated and had she turned and seen the expression on his face, the softness, the love, the weariness and worry and sorrow, the whole shape of their lives might have been altered.

"Very well, then I'll bid you goodnight."

The carriages began to arrive a few days later as it did not take long for news to spread, and the news that Sarah Cameron was back in residence at Longlake Edge caused a minor sensation. Was it true? they asked one another in the notes that were delivered from house to house. Ernestine Tyson, Jessica Gould, Madge Seddon and Nora Addison kept their grooms busy galloping to and fro with questions and answers and all four decided there was only one way to find out and that was to call.

Ernestine Tyson was the first to arrive, followed closely by Madge Seddon whose Adeline had been so unfortunately passed over by Chad Cameron in favour of the miller's daughter.

Sarah greeted them graciously, nodding to Daphne to bring tea, for though it was customary for a caller to remain no longer than fifteen minutes she had so much to impart now that she was back in her rightful position it would take a great deal more than that to tell them of it.

"Sarah, my dear, how lovely to see you and how wise of Chadwick to fetch you home where you belong. We had heard, as who has not, of the . . . the eccentricities of Chadwick's young wife" – the emphasis on the word "young", making it sound as though the extreme youthfulness of their hostess's sister-in-law was something of which to be ashamed – "but with you back at Longlake that will surely be rectified. Now, do tell us what has transpired."

The two women leaned forward, ready to be entertained by the misdeeds of the new Mrs Cameron, but the arrival of two more carriages and two more society ladies in the shape of Jessica Gould and Nora Addison and the sending for more tea checked the proceedings and it was not until the ladies were all comfortably settled, teacups to their lips, that Sarah, in one of the most satisfying moments of her life, began her account of the drama. It seemed that the comparatively new wife of Chadwick was not really up to running this great house, especially in view of her upbringing, which had been poor to say the least, and of her condition, if they took her meaning, which they did, and so Chadwick had been forced to turn to his sister for help. The young mother-to-be was not at all well and was being kept to her room, so for the moment, making it obvious that the moment would probably last for as long as she could manage it, she was to run Longlake as it was meant to be run. It had been so trying at the Dower House. They knew, she was sure, of her talent for entertaining and of Chadwick's need of her expertise in that direction. A man of business such as her brother was much in demand in good society, smiling round the fascinated group to let them see that they were included in that category, naturally, and it had been difficult, in view of . . . well, again they would know what she meant, to accept invitations. There had been no dinner parties, no entertaining, but she meant to put that right and was to give a small dinner party at the end of next week and hoped they would all be able to attend.

The housekeeper? Did they mean the woman whose father had shared a cell with the brother of . . . of course. Well, she could hardly be called a housekeeper, could she, since she had never been trained to run a house such as this one, glancing round smugly at the elegance of what she saw as her own drawing-room, but though the woman was really not needed since there was a sufficiency of servants now that she had brought back those who had gone with her to the Dower House, one couldn't turn the poor thing out to starve, could one. She did not mention that Chad had refused point-blank to get rid of the woman who was his wife's friend.

"She's been found a job in the kitchen. Maid of all work which seemed appropriate. I have taken over what she had turned into a housekeeper's room and shall use it as a sort of office. The only difficulty was the cook."

"The cook?" Nora Addison ventured.

"Yes, the one who was engaged in my absence, but I'm afraid she did not come up to my standards so I have given her a decent character, a month's wages and sent her on her way. She will find something, I'm sure. I told her to call on Mrs Armstrong who seems to know where posts may be obtained."

Sarah did not mention that Mrs Minty was in her fifties, an awkward age for a woman to find a new position. She did not mention that Chadwick knew nothing of the changes in the kitchen apart from the re-instatement of Mrs Foster, since it had not occurred to him, as it would not occur to any man, that there might be any. Nor did she tell them of the quite dreadful scene made by the slut when she had learned of it. The girl, informed by Daphne who had gone up with the coals for the fire, had run downstairs and burst into the kitchen like the ill-bred wanton she was. Sarah had them lined up, as Sadie had described the day before, while poor Mrs Minty, her face awash with frightened tears, had begged to be allowed to stay on in *any* capacity when the girl had thundered through the door from the hall and advanced on Sarah herself. She was still dressed in her nightgown, her feet bare, and Sarah had looked at her contemptuously, her lip curling, but then what else could you expect of a "vulgar"?

"What the devil d'you think you're doing?" she had hissed. "You have no right to turn Mrs Minty out and I shall tell Chad so when he comes home. No, stay there, Mrs Minty. You are *my* cook, engaged by *my* housekeeper and I shall—"

"Which housekeeper is that, my dear?" Sarah had asked silkily, ready to smile at the girl's sudden look of incomprehension.

"My . . . why, Miss Jenkins, of course. She is in charge of the kitchen."

"I don't think so, miss. We have no housekeeper here but we *do* have a scullery-maid by the name of Jenkins. She is just about to scrub out the scullery and pantry."

"What?" Briony had whirled about, her nightgown clinging

to the pronounced swelling of her belly and the new mistress was seen to grimace in distaste. "Lizzie, where are you, Lizzie? Dear God, what have you done with her? Lizzie . . ." Her voice had risen to a shriek and at the end of the line of servants, Minnie, who was known to be soft-hearted, had begun to weep.

"Stop that, you foolish girl," her new mistress had said sternly, her new mistress who used to be her old mistress and who had not forgotten that Minnie had chosen to stay at Longlake instead of accompanying her to the Dower House. Minnie had swallowed and stopped.

Lizzie, braving the storm that she knew would thunder over her, had stood up and moved slowly into the kitchen from the scullery. She wore a shapeless grey cotton dress which was far too short, wrinkled grey stockings and black boots. On her head was an enormous mob cap which completely covered her hair. It rested on her eyebrows, and about her waist was a sacking apron on which she was wiping her hands.

"It's all right, love," she had said steadily to Briony. "I'm all right. I have to work, you see, and this was all that was available."

"No. Oh, no, I won't have it, Lizzie. Take off those appalling garments and come up to my room. This . . . this woman might dictate to the rest, and I'm sorry for that, but I'll not have you working as skivvy. Not in my house."

"This is my brother's house, miss, and as his representative in it, I will say who is to work where. He has given me—"

"I don't give a damn what he has given you, you . . . you hell-hag, you will not reduce my friend to—"

"Briony, don't, please, don't make it worse. Mrs Minty is to go and I don't want to be next. God knows what she will tell Mr Cameron if you make matters worse and I need to be here . . . near you when—"

"How dare you speak like that, you sloven. Get back to your bucket."

"Lizzie, please, come up to my room and let us talk. This is a mistake and I will ask Mr Cameron to put it right."

"No, dearest." The other servants had gasped and Sarah Cameron's face took on the hue of a ripe plum. "Don't make it worse, for me or for yourself. Wait a while and see what is to happen. I am here. I have honest work. And then there is Thomas. I must have work near him."

"She has not threatened you with Thomas."

"No, she cannot but he is settled, happy at the mill and if I . . . if I left here . . . You must see, I cannot leave him alone, so, since I must have work this is as good as any."

Briony had wept broken-heartedly and it was then, though they did not know it at the time, that she began to break. The scene with Chad the night before had wounded her deeply but this was a mortal blow and in her vulnerable state she no longer had the strength to avoid it.

Sarah had smiled in triumph as Chadwick's wife turned away and, her nightgown trailing about her bare feet, moved towards the kitchen door.

"And how is dear Chadwick taking all this . . . upheaval?" Ernestine Tyson asked her now.

"Oh, there is no upheaval, my dear. A change of mistress for the time being while . . . until his child is born." Just as though the woman carrying it did not exist. Indeed had no part in it. "The house will run smoothly, for which he is thankful, and we will soon be entertaining on the old scale."

"And . . . his wife?"

"She is not well and will keep to her rooms and the security of the garden. That is what Chadwick wishes."

And it was noticed a week or two later that Mrs Cameron was indeed not well. She began to lose weight except for her hugely distended abdomen. Her arms and shoulders became thin so that the bloom she had gained in the first months of her pregnancy, her health and strength, the substance of her seemed to be absorbed into her monstrous belly. She was seen about the garden, uncertain of her balance so that William Platt ordered young Isaac to stay always at her side, even to offer her his arm, and it was noticed by the servants that she seemed more herself in his company. He talked to her of the birds that flew above the rooftops, pointing out the flocks of pretty chaffinches that nested in the oak tree at the back of the stables, their pink undersides flashing in the October sunshine, the tits, blue and grey, which searched for food in the orchard; the shapes of the clouds in which he could see horses galloping and ships sailing, sitting with her on the dry-stone wall to watch the rabbits foraging in the paddock, impervious to the dangerous hooves of the horses that grazed there.

She had taken the strange disappearance of her puppy very hard indeed, calling for him up and down the paddock and round the back of the stable block, with Ned and Joe and Charlie to help her. Old Duddy, though he hadn't much to say on the matter, made it his business to poke his nose down every rabbit hole, for the daft thing might have burrowed down in one. Daphne swore that she had handed the shivering bundle into Joe's hands on the night Miss Sarah came back and Joe admitted that that was so. He had put the little thing in the stable with Bart, Mr Chad's black labrador, made sure it was warm and fed, listened to it sadly as it cried dolefully for Mrs Cameron who had spoiled it, but the next day it was simply not there. Yes, it might have slithered through the space between the bottom of the door and the flags, for it was only a little scrap of a thing, but if that was the case where the devil had it got to? Mrs Cameron had been distraught, accusing Miss Sarah of getting rid of the puppy and though it seemed a silly and spiteful thing to do, the stable lads were of the opinion that she could be right.

Miss Sarah had laughed at the foolishness, the absurdity of the imputation against her good character, making out that the little mistress was off her head, but it was still a mystery to Joe how the small animal could have got through a bolted door!

"I'll get you another pup," the master had been heard to say but the mistress had turned from him and drifted away in that strange fashion she seemed to have developed, the fiery, defiant young lass they had known gone away. At least for now. They had all seen the deep scratches on the master's cheeks and knew their significance but the young woman who had put them there had had the stuffing knocked out of her but, please God, not for good.

Before she climbed the back stairs to the slit of a room in the roof she now shared with Fanny, Lizzie often slipped out to visit Sadie and the two of them wondered and worried over what was to become of the girl they both loved.

"I've never seen anyone so spent," Lizzie told Sadie. "She's like a bird in a cage, a wild bird that can no longer get out and hasn't even the strength to try."

"What's 'e doin' to 'er, lass? What's 'e think that bitch is up to? Can 'e not see fer 'imself?"

"He goes up to see her at the end of each day, Daphne tells me, but she won't talk to him, Sadie. It's my opinion that his sister lies to him. She's supposed to be back to watch over her but she takes no interest in Briony who spends most of her time in her room and when she does go into the garden she seems unable to take the shortest walk without clinging to Isaac's arm. A letter came from Daniel the other day but she barely read it and if I hadn't—" Lizzie stopped speaking abruptly and Sadie leaned forward to peer into the girl's suddenly flushed face.

"If tha' 'adn't what, lass?"

"Well, Daniel and I, since my father died, have been

corresponding. I asked Briony if she minded . . . well, I wanted to question him on the details of my father's death."

"Aye, tha' would want to know."

"Yes, well, it seems he was glad of someone to . . ."

"An' it's a right good job what wi' t'lass as she is."

"That's what I thought. I can reassure him and . . ."

"Nay, lass, tha' don't need ter explain ter me. All I want is fer someone ter keep their eye on that there bitch. Promise me tha'll try an' see our Briony."

"I will, Sadie. I promise."

She was as good as her word and on the afternoon that Miss Sarah set off in her carriage to return the calls her friends had made on her, Lizzie whipped off her apron and told the open-mouthed but approving servants that she was off up to see the mistress.

"But she be gone out, Miss Jenkins," young Fanny said, for she was still in a dither over who was in charge of her.

"I mean the real mistress, Fanny," Lizzie replied.

The bedroom, a lovely bay-windowed room, was bright with firelight. The mistress, for that was what she was, of Longlake Edge sat quietly, calmly before her fire, the dainty luncheon tray which Daphne had brought up for her barely touched on the table beside her. Daphne had got her out of bed, seen to her bathing, dressed her in the loose peignoir which she wore in the house, brushed her hair into a shining cloak down her back and tied ribbons to match to keep it from her face. She did not look well.

She did not turn to see who had come into her room but when Lizzie kneeled before her, taking her hands in her own, she smiled with pleasure.

"Lizzie . . . oh, Lizzie, where have you been?"

"Only downstairs, dearest. You have but to ring your bell and I'll be here in a minute."

"She wouldn't like it."

"Do we care, lass?" Lizzie grinned and was relieved when there was a glimmer of amusement in Briony's eye.

"Won't you come for a walk in the garden? The sun is shining and I hear that madam has gone visiting."

"Will you walk with me down to the mill?"

Lizzie sighed. "You know I can't do that, dearest. Your husband has given us all very strict instructions that you may go where you like in the grounds but not beyond. Madam was there when he said it, nodding sanctimoniously as though your health was her greatest concern and it seems he believes she is guarding you with her life, which is not true. But we all care about you, Briony and were it not for . . . well, I must keep this job, you know that or I would drive you myself in the gig. *She* would tell him, of course, if Jacob Keane didn't and you would be—"

"It doesn't matter, Lizzie. I'm not sure I could manage it anyway."

Lizzie searched her face in some alarm. "Are you not feeling well?"

"I feel a little dizzy when I stand and I have the strangest buzzing in my ears which makes walking uncertain. Perhaps later, or tomorrow."

"Let me send for Doctor Travis." She smoothed Briony's hands between her own, noticing for the first time that they were puffy, that her wedding ring was deeply imbedded in her flesh.

"No, really, I'll just rest today and then perhaps tomorrow . . ." Her voice trailed away and she turned to stare without interest into the fire. "If only Scruff was here. I miss him so, but if he were I should be afraid for him. That woman . . ."

"Oh, no, dear," doing her best to convince not only Briony, but herself, that the puppy's disappearance had nothing to do with Sarah Cameron.

"She killed him, Lizzie." It was said in a tone that was almost indifferent and a slither of fear crept into Lizzie's heart. "I don't know how but she killed him and sometimes I think she might kill me."

26

The first time she was locked in her room was the day after Sarah Cameron's dinner party.

It was the sound of laughter and music that dragged her up out of the pit of despondency in which she had wallowed ever since Chad had brought his sister back to Longlake. Chad had been in to her sitting-room as he usually did, speaking to her, saying something she had heard as though from a great distance, a muted sound as if she were inside a bubble which distorted the words, making them incomprehensible. She was not interested. He had gone away. Her tray had been brought up and placed on the round table beside the fire and Daphne, she supposed it was Daphne, had urged her to "eat up, there's a good lass" which she had tried to do since it was easier than refusing. The tray had gone and Daphne had brushed her hair, asking her solicitously if she would like to get into bed.

"No . . . no, perhaps later," she remembered answering, unable to make the decision, a condition that was becoming increasingly familiar to her.

"I'll come back in a bit then," Daphne had said and she had sunk once more into apathy.

The crunching of horses' hooves and carriage wheels on the gravel drive in front of the house filtered into her mind but there was nothing unusual in that, for the woman who was now in charge often drove off in her carriage, or the gig and there had been callers, or so she had been told by Daphne who was her only line of communication with the rest of the house. She remembered Lizzie coming and talking to her but that was a long time ago, she thought, or perhaps not. It might have been yesterday. She had lost track of time in this hazy world that was now hers.

It was someone playing the piano, a lilting melody that first turned her head in the direction of the door. A sound so sweet and haunting she felt herself begin to smile. It was a long time since she had heard music, a long time ago when she and Lizzie had discovered the grand piano in the drawing-room and Lizzie had sat down on the piano stool, lifted the lid and run her fingers along the keys.

"Can you play, Lizzie?" she had asked, enchanted.

"A little bit. My mother was the pianist in the family and she taught me." And for half an hour Lizzie had played a selection of lovely tunes, some jolly, making you want to dance, others gentle, almost sad, getting inside your head and your heart. But Lizzie had begun to cry as though the memory of those happier days had been too searing and Briony had gently taken her hands from the keys, closed the lid and led her dear friend upstairs where they had drunk coffee and talked of the future for which they both had such hopes.

With a struggle she heaved herself from her chair and, moving slowly on her swollen feet, clinging to the furniture until she had got her balance, she weaved her way to the bedroom door. Opening it, she followed the sound of the music but suddenly it stopped and the laughter she had heard earlier began again and, growing louder, there came the sound of people moving from one room to another. It floated up the stairs from the hallway, the deep tones of gentlemen and the lighter, well-bred voices of ladies. She heard Chad's voice, quiet, courteous, and the somewhat shrill pronunciation of his sister as she informed somebody that she was so glad to be "home", for winter in the Dower House would have been atrocious.

She did not actively decide to go downstairs and find out what was happening since, really, she had no interest but somehow her bare feet carried her, dreamlike, down the stairs, one hand on the banister, the other holding the diaphanous, floating edges of her peignoir about her. It was a soft shade of misted lavender blue, edged with satin in the same shade, tied loosely across the huge swell of her distended belly with wide satin ribbons. Her hair hung about her, falling across her shoulders and face, since Daphne, in her hurry to get back to her duties in the drawing-room, had forgotten the ribbon that held it. She looked like a crazy woman as she wavered into the dining-room and they all stared in horror, making no sound except Mrs Armstrong who put her hand to her mouth and moaned slightly. They could not believe this was the same exquisite creature Chad Cameron had led down the aisle, was it seven, eight months ago? Her skin had lost its lovely creamy glow and her eyes had sunk into her skull and the babble of voices, the genteel laughter that had ebbed about Sarah Cameron's dining table died away to frozen silence as she wandered into the room. She looked like a woman flickering an inch or two away from reality, no longer of this world and for a brief moment Chad Cameron could not move. Then, with a hoarse cry of pity, of appalled compassion, he sprang to his feet, knocking his chair backwards in his haste to get to her.

"Jesus God," he was heard to say before sweeping her up into his arms and carrying her out of the room. "Fetch Lizzie," he shouted over his shoulder to Daphne or Gladys who were serving the meal with the help of young Mabel, considerably startling them, and even then, when her husband had removed her and taken her to wherever it was they were keeping her, the guests could not bring themselves to speak. They darted glances at one another and at Sarah who recovered before any of them, for it occurred to her that this was a heaven-sent opportunity to strengthen her own position, not only in this household but in the eyes of her friends.

She sighed deeply and put her hand to her forehead. "I must beg your pardon," she began. "Now you all know how things stand at Longlake and why my brother had no alternative but to ask me to come back and run his home for him." She shook her head sadly. "The child is incapable of . . . well, you will see how things are. She is not . . . not well."

All the ladies began to speak at once, assuring her that they understood, that she was a saint to take over as she had done and that she must not give it another thought. The meal promised to be wonderful, as hers always were, they told her gushingly. Now she must not upset herself. They could see how difficult it was for her. Trying circumstances and if there was anything they could do to help her, to support her, she had only to ask.

The gentlemen, who had hastily averted their eyes from the peaked nipples of Chad Cameron's young wife which had been clearly visible through the thin stuff of her peignoir, kept silent, for what was there to say except, poor chap!

Daphne reported it all back to the kitchen, saying that Lizzie was wanted, to the consternation of Martha who, though she knew her mistress – the old one – was a tartar, she should not be discussed by these young maidservants. They were all agog when the scullery-maid, for that was her status, raced to the back door, opened it and screeched into the night for one of the grooms in case the doctor might be needed. Then they watched as Lizzie ran like the wind through the kitchen door and up the stairs, her face like granite, her breathing laboured, her eyes staring, for it seemed to them all their little mistress was going quite mad and her kitchen-maid with her.

Lizzie found him bending over the figure of his wife whom he had laid on the bed. She hesitated in the doorway, unwilling to disturb what looked like a tender moment between man and wife. Was this perhaps the start of a reconciliation? She was aware that this dinner party, surely in the worst of taste with the *real* mistress of the house so unwell, had not met with Chad Cameron's approval. Tales came out of the dining-room, which was the only place where the master and his sister met, that there had been arguments between them but Miss Sarah had had her way and the outcome had been disastrous. But perhaps not. Perhaps these two might find that they had something to share even if it was only the coming of their first child and she did not want to spoil it.

"You shouldn't have come down," he began, and Lizzie was sure he meant well by the remark which he had no chance to complete. Briony struggled to sit up and her husband reached out a hand to help her but she recoiled from his touch. Her face was still leaden but that vacant look which had plagued her ever since Sarah had returned, was gone.

"No, I suppose I shouldn't," she said crisply, "since I am nothing in this house. Less than the maidservants, in fact, who, I presume, knew you were to entertain guests tonight even if I didn't. No, don't touch me," as he would have put out a hand to her again. He recoiled as though faced with a dangerous cobra. "Now why don't you return to your guests. I promise I won't embarrass you again, at least not until this child is born when I mean to return to my proper place in life. I am trapped here, as you intended me to be trapped and I only hope this is a boy in here" – putting her hand on the mound of her belly – "for I have no intention of going through with it again. I mean to take over the mill. Oh, yes. Jacob Kean can go hang, and so can you. Now leave me alone."

"I don't think so, my dear." He stood up, that expression-less look on his face which showed none of the raging emotions inside. "At a risk of repeating myself you will go nowhere unless I allow it and everyone in this house is aware of it. Sarah—"

"—— Sarah," using an obscenity that made both Chad and Lizzie gasp. "I am mistress here."

"Really." And with that he left the room, brushing past Lizzie as though she were not there.

When the door had shut behind him she lay back, exhausted, turned clumsily on her side with her back to Lizzie, gasping with the effort, and began to weep. Lizzie ran to her and did her best to draw her into her arms but Briony resisted.

"Leave me be, Lizzie, please."

"But dearest, let me help."

"How?"

"Let me at least—"

"What? What the devil can you do? What can either of us do? You are nothing but a kitchen-maid, thanks to that bitch downstairs and I am nothing but a receptacle for the child."

"Which you will love when it arrives. You will be—"

"Nothing in this house. I am worth nothing in this house, child or no child. My life is down at Moorend where I want to be *useful*, running the mill and somehow saving it for my brother when he comes home. That is all I want. I have been tricked and betrayed."

"No, Briony, Chad thinks only of you. Keeping you safe. He . . . he loves you."

Awkwardly Briony turned towards her, on her face a look of bewildered amusement. She shook her head, tangling her hair on the lace-trimmed pillow, then began to laugh.

"Dear God, Lizzie, you live in a fairytale land, really you do, and I'm surprised that you should think such a thing after all that has happened to you and me."

"Why should he marry you then?"

"God knows why men do anything. It's a mystery to me. It surely can't just be that he wanted our mill. I'm young and capable of bearing him many children and I suppose he thought, being young, I would be easily led."

"My God, he made a mistake there, lass."

"Well, we'll see. Just let me have this baby and then we'll see."

She seemed better the next day as though the confrontation with her husband had put the spirit back into her, the defiance she had always shown, and though she could barely get out of her bed she rang for Daphne to get her dressed, her intention, she told her, to walk in the garden. Would Daphne warn Isaac that she might need his arm? She thought she might like to stroll down to the paddock and take an apple for Gypsy.

Daphne was in a state of high excitement, because the newspapers had reported that a daughter had been born to Her Majesty and it seemed to the servants that a great bond had been forged with the royal mother and child, for was not this family to be so rewarded in·the near future. A baby for Christmas, Doctor Travis had said and that was in five weeks' time, though the women of the household could not help but feel some anxiety whenever they caught a glimpse of their little mistress. Which wasn't often. It was weeks since she had been down to the gardens, for she was so heavy it seemed certain she would fall flat on her face, or rather her belly! She walked with difficulty and was forbidden to move out of her room unaided. But it seemed Doctor Travis was very pleased with her, or so it was said, though none of them knew exactly who had said it; and though her hugely swollen state alarmed them all, none of them, including the master, knew much about pregnancy or childbirth.

"I'll tell Isaac, lass," Daphne said over her shoulder as she left the room, for it was often hard to call this young woman "madam" and she didn't seem to object to the more familiar mode of address. The servants were becoming increasingly fond of her, and felt sorry for the way she was treated and the informal "lass" told her so. "Now don't tha' stir until I comes fer thi'."

It was a fine morning, cold but sunny, a good day for a saunter down the path that led to the paddock and Briony sat in the chair where Daphne had put her, her warm cloak of rich red wool, lined with pale grey chinchilla, lying on the bed where the maid had placed it.

Fifteen minutes went by and Briony began to fidget. For a start she wanted to relieve herself, which happened a lot these days, and the chair in which Daphne had left her, expecting to be back within minutes, was hard and uncomfortable. Where the devil had the girl got to? The day would be gone if she didn't get a move on, for already a few ominous clouds were gathering on the peak of Gowbarrow. Heaving herself from the chair, she moved heavily to the window, peering out towards the lake which had a grey shine to it and was beginning to ruffle as the wind caught it. Damn it, where was Daphne? She could see William Platt and Isaac far down the garden doing something with a bed of roses which had died down as the autumn passed. Isaac took the handles of the wheelbarrow and trundled it further down the lawn and William Platt followed. Damn it, why was the lad not up at the back kitchen door waiting for her or at least making his way along the winding path that led there?

Turning gracelessly, she moved across the deep carpet and reaching for the bell by the fireplace gave it a sharp tug, then lowered herself breathlessly into the fireside chair, the exercise exhausting her, it seemed, and waited for someone to answer it.

They stood about the kitchen like marionettes whose strings have been cut, Mrs Foster with a rolling pin in her hand, the pastry she had been about to roll out for what she called a "nice apple pie" – as if she made any other – in a smooth mound on the kitchen table. Minnie and Mabel were stripping Brussels sprouts, carefully putting a cross on each stalk as Mrs Foster directed, then dropping them into a bowl of cold water. Fanny, who had been sweeping the kitchen floor, stood at the open back door, the brush still in her hands and Lizzie, on her knees in the scullery, had her raw hands in a bucket of hot water. She was wondering why it was this woman had the knack of frightening these servants, of reducing them to the status of children in a schoolroom, but she supposed, like her, they had no power, no independence and were totally reliant on her, or at least her brother, for the very bread they ate and the roof under which they slept. She had the power to finish their lives if they displeased her. If it had not been for Briony and Thomas she herself would long ago have told her to go to hell, packed her bags and taken her chance in the world beyond Penrith, but that was it, she supposed. They none of them could please themselves, for there was always someone who depended on them, even if it was only themselves.

Hers was the only movement as she slowly got to her feet. Martha, in view of her age and long service, had taken it upon herself to sit down for a few minutes with a cup of tea, but as Lizzie rose to her feet, so did she. Daphne and Gladys hovered, there was no other word for it, by the door that led into the hallway, their eyes on the row of bells that was fixed to the wall above their heads. The one marked bedroom was jangling and Daphne put her hand to her mouth as Miss Sarah frowned ominously at her. Someone was whistling in the yard, the sound incongruous in the mounting tension of the kitchen.

"Madam, the bell is ringing." It was brave Daphne who spoke, knowing better than to use the words, "the *mistress's* bell is ringing."

"I can see that, Daphne, and I will go and find out what

she wants. There is no need for any of you to attend her. The master has put her in my charge since the . . . unfortunate episode last night. You will understand, I'm sure."

Oh, yes, they all understood. The little lass had shown this woman up, she had created a terrible situation the night before by floating into the dining-room in her night attire when there were *guests* and it had been most embarrassing for the master's sister, they all knew that. But surely the master would not be so cruel as to put that poor child in this woman's care? She was already unwell. Daphne had told them that you only had to look at her swollen hands and puffy ankles to see that and really should not the doctor be called to look at her? What was the master thinking of, and him usually so kind? The mistress, the *real* mistress had not been herself for weeks, drifting about like someone lost in a fog, calm, senseless really and not at all like the vivid, hopeful young woman they had first known. Daphne, who had had more to do with her than any of them, acting as her maid these last months, was longing to get back to her, for it was almost half an hour now since she had left her sitting in her chair waiting for Isaac to accompany her on her walk. How far she'd get was another matter but they were all out there watching over her, Isaac and William Platt, Joe and Ned and Charlie and she'd come to no harm. They'd carry her home if needs be.

"Miss Sarah," she ventured, braving the woman's anger. "She be on 'er own an' wonderin' . . . 'appen she'll tekk it into 'er 'ead ter come downstairs an' if she was ter fall . . ."

"No, she won't fall, Daphne, not on the stairs, for I have the key to her room and following the master's instructions" – which was a bald lie – "she will remain there safely."

The silence was awful, appalled, but not for long.

"You can't keep her locked up," the well-bred voice of the scullery-maid told her mistress. "Do you want to send her out of her mind?"

"She already is as far as I am concerned and if—"

But the scullery-maid was halfway across the kitchen and took no notice. They watched her, Minnie, as was her wont, beginning to cry, for she felt so sorry for the poor little mistress and was deadly afraid of the old one.

"Go to her if you will, miss, but you cannot enter her room for I have the only key. And let me say it will be the last thing you do in this house, for I shall make it my business to see you are discharged and believe me you will find no jobs open to you in this neighbourhood. Do I make myself understood? Now, I shall go up and find out what the . . . the girl wants and you, Daphne, will come with me and see to her needs while I am there. She will not suffer, I can promise you. She will be warm, well fed and will come to no harm but she must be confined for her own sake. We cannot have her wandering about, perhaps harming herself, can we?" And certainly not showing me and my family up in front of my friends who are bound to call this afternoon, if only to find out what steps had been taken to confine the witless wife of Chad Cameron, and though she did not voice this last they all knew what she meant.

Under her smiling, contemptuous eye Daphne helped her young mistress to the water closet which was, thankfully, in the extremely modern bathroom Chad Cameron had had installed in the small dressing-room off the bedroom before he had married Briony Marsden. It was all done in black and white with a white enamelled bath to which the maids brought hot water heated in the kitchen. There were brass taps from which came cold water, tall cupboards containing enormous white fluffy towels, a washbasin known as a lavatory basin, again with brass taps, over which hung a large mirror with an etched border. There were table toilet areas all with matching borders which were echoed in the wall tiles and the stained-glass windows were draped in net curtains. The room was tiled in white with black and white linoleum tiles on the floor and it was, perhaps, the room that had most impressed young Briony Marsden. There were coloured bath soaps, sweet-smelling as any flower, a great variety of which were in evidence about the room in vases and bowls, with sponges, pumice stones and loofahs.

"Why is this woman here, Daphne?" Mrs Cameron asked her tremulously, clinging to the maid's arm and really, Daphne told them all later, she wanted to take her mistress in her arms and cry with her, and for her.

"Put her in her chair, Daphne," Miss Sarah said shortly. "I have no time to be wasting up here. Really, my brother has no idea. And does she want anything else?"

"I want to go—"

"You are to go nowhere, miss. Now, ask her if she wants . . ."

Daphne, who had painfully lowered her mistress to her chair by the fire, knelt at her feet, struggling with her, for her mistress did not want to sit down. She wanted to go out down to the paddock, she kept saying.

"Will I fetch thi' a cup o' 'ot chocolate, lass?" she asked gently.

"No, you won't, Daphne. I wish to walk."

"Oh, lass, can't tha' see—"

"That's enough, Daphne. I've never seen such histrionics in all my life. Now you can leave us, that's if . . . this young woman has nothing further she wants."

"I want to walk."

"Yes, so you said but I'm afraid that's not possible in your condition. Surely you realise that after your performance last night."

"Daphne, will you bring Lizzie to me, please." For even yet Briony had not realised the seriousness of her prison.

"There'll be none of that, miss. None of my servants has the time to be running here and there after you. Now I must go and so must you, Daphne. If this young woman wants anything tell her to ring her bell and if she does you are to come to me. I have the key to her room and will supervise her requirements."

"But, madam, I don't think she should be left on 'er own, not like she is, an' wit door locked. What if tha' were out an' . . ."

Sarah sighed dramatically and in her chair Briony felt reality, which had stayed with her for so short a time, begin to slip away again. She could hear *her* voice saying something about "mind your tongue, girl" and the sound of a key turning in a lock then it was quiet. She remained quite motionless, trying, in the most appalling silence of her life, to fight her way back to reality through the thundering waves which were once again swamping her mind but it was impossible, so she sank slowly beneath them where it was peaceful and safe.

"You have looked in on her, Chadwick?" Daphne heard her mistress say at the dinner table that evening, sympathy which she knew to be false in her voice.

"Yes, she seems . . . tranquil."

"Good, good. We had a little trouble this morning when she wanted to go out which, naturally, in her condition would not be safe."

"Trouble?"

"Oh, not trouble exactly. Daphne and I quietened her, didn't we, Daphne?" The mistress's cool blue eyes fell on her warningly.

"Yes, madam." Daphne's voice was stony and she avoided her master's gaze. He was, as always, immaculate, the sombre neutral shades of his evening dress unruffled, his face registering no surprise, no alarm. His eyelids lowered very briefly but not before Daphne from the corner of her eye had seen the agony in his. The key, of course, had been nowhere in evidence when he had entered his wife's room, for was it not in the mistress's pocket where Daphne had watched her put it.

He turned away and considered the bowl of soup that Gladys had just placed before him.

"Thank you, Sarah. I . . . well, thank you."

"Chadwick, dear, you must not worry, nor do I need thanks. I am here to help, you know that. Now, my dear, drink your soup."

27

―――◆―――

"Look, Daphne, I know you see her all the time and you tell me she's fine but what you mean is she's . . . she's not *ill*, physically, and I'm not even convinced of that, but what I really want to find out is what her mental state is. If you will just look the other way."

"I don't know what yer mean, Lizzie Jenkins. Look t'other way, what do that mean?"

"While they're at dinner, Mr Cameron and *her*, with the bedroom door unlocked, which it must be if Mr Cameron's at home for she'd not dare to keep her a prisoner while he's in the house, I could slip up and have a word with her. Dear God, it's been a fortnight now and no one but you has seen her."

Daphne bristled. "An' are yer sayin' I'm not able ter see to 'er?"

"No, I'm aware that you take her food up and she eats it, some of it, that you bathe her and dress her and make her comfortable but you tell us she doesn't speak to you so how can you ascertain her condition, what's in her mind? What the devil does she *do* all day with no one to talk to?"

"*I* talk to 'er."

"But she doesn't answer?"

"Well, no she don't," Daphne conceded, "but that—"

"It means she is not herself, Daphne."

"Master goes in."

Lizzie made a sardonic noise in the back of her throat. "And are you there?"

"Sometimes." Daphne was really on the defensive now, for no one could care for anyone as Daphne cared for the little mistress. Spoon-fed her sometimes she did, just to make sure she got a bit of broth down her, or one of Mrs Foster's delicious egg custards while the old mistress stood over her impatiently, tapping her foot and giving every impression that if Daphne didn't look lively she'd drag her out and leave the lass to her own devices.

"And does he speak to her? Engage her in any conversation?"

Daphne looked astonished. "Conversation?"

"Yes, does he talk to her about everyday things like where he's been and . . . and how her day has been, what she has done?"

"Eeh, I dunno."

"And does she answer him, that's if he does?"

"Well, no, she don't even look at him," Daphne finally admitted, which she thought was not right, for the poor man was doing his best. He must be worried out of his mind at the state of her, as they all were, but what could they do against that she-devil who had been put in charge of her? William Platt regularly handed in flowers for her and the grooms never failed to ask after her. Daphne did her best, running to Miss Sarah a dozen times a day on some pretext to get in to see her little mistress, keeping an eye on her, even if the old mistress did tell her off something fierce, but she could do no more, could she?

"They're killing her between them," Lizzie began, while all about her the servants watched her apprehensively, gaping and exchanging anxious glances, for it was December now and the baby was due by Christmas, or so old Doctor Travis had said.

"Nay, never." Daphne was shocked, putting her hand to her mouth, tears of pity for the lass trembling on her eyelashes.

This baby was eagerly awaited, at least by them, and every last one of them had been sewing and knitting tiny garments, even those who had no talent for it. There was a room at the top of the house which had been the Cameron children's nursery and was to be so again and in it was a cradle that Lizzie had refurbished with spotted net draperies. Sadie had washed and ironed the nursery linen and had even embroidered hearts and flowers and birds on the baby blankets and sheets. Mabel and Minnie had scrubbed it out from floor to ceiling but it was twenty-five years since a child had occupied it and it needed more. As far as cleanliness was concerned, it was all ready for the new infant, but, they said sadly, when was the mistress to take an interest in the room where her child would live? New mothers, or rather mothers-to-be were usually made up with ideas for nursery themes on the walls, fresh paint, shelves for nursery books, rows of soft toys and rugs for the floor. A nursemaid and a wet nurse should have been engaged but it seemed it had not occurred to either of the prospective parents, and certainly not to its aunt, to prepare for its arrival.

"Are they at their meal now, Daphne?" Lizzie asked, lowering her voice to a whisper as though those in the dining-room might hear her.

"She is. He's in't study 'avin' summat on a tray. Said he were busy," Daphne whispered back.

"Where's she up to?"

"She's just started on the lamb."

"I'm going up."

"Dear Lord, Lizzie, please. It's more'n me job's worth." Daphne was ready to weep.

"She'll not know. Anyway she'll not come up if she's eating. I'll only be a minute."

Briony was sitting by the fire, as placid as a mother cat in a warm basket. She was neat and tidy, her hair brushed and caught back with a blue ribbon to match her rich blue velvet robe. It was very full but did little to conceal the massive swell of her belly. She had her feet on a small velvet stool where, Lizzie suspected, Daphne had put them and where, she felt, Briony would leave them, and herself, until someone came to put her somewhere else. On the table beside her was a tray, daintily set with a white lace cloth on which sat a half-finished bowl of soup. The plate beside it was hidden by a well-polished silver cover. When she lifted the cover the plate beneath held several thin slices of lamb, tiny roasted potatoes, dainty florets of cauliflower, freshly picked and cooked peas and in a silver covered jug an appetising gravy made from the meat's juices. All very nourishing, beautifully presented and tempting enough to seduce any appetite. It had not been touched.

Lizzie placed her hand on Briony's shoulder, leaving it there for a moment in dismay, for it was so thin. Like the frail bones of a bird beneath the warm velvet and quite appalling in comparison to the bulge where her child heaved, lively as an eel beneath water, thought Lizzie, breathing a prayer of thanks. Briony did not look up at her touch.

"I've popped in to see you, dearest," Lizzie said quietly, again as though the woman downstairs could hear her. "Briony, it's me, Lizzie. How are you feeling? Won't you turn and greet me? She's at dinner." Wondering if Briony knew who she meant in her senseless state, but very gradually Briony turned and looked up into Lizzie's face.

"Lizzie?"

"Yes, darling, it's me. We have none of us seen you for so long I thought it was high time I came up. I know *she* won't like it but sod her, as Ned says," and was relieved when Briony smiled. "I know that's rude but sometimes it's the only way to say what you mean, don't you think?"

"Lizzie . . ."

Lizzie kneeled down on the floor, holding Briony's hands in hers. They were lifeless at first as though human contact was something to which she had become unaccustomed then they began to cling. Her eyes glowed into Lizzie's and though she knew full well that Daphne did her best for Briony, Lizzie was aware that Sarah Cameron would make sure that nothing of any interest would be spoken between them. Besides which, Daphne would be inhibited by the old mistress's presence. Starved of company, starved of words, starved of love or of friendship, no wonder this child, for really, was she any more than that, had retreated into a world of her own. She had lived in a hell of the worst kind for most of her life and now, when she might have known peace and happiness, her own wilfulness and the downright cruelty of her sister-in-law, not to mention the lack of perception and arrogance of her husband, had forced her to this.

"You do not look well, dearest. I shall send Joe for Doctor Travis and that bloody woman can go hang. There, you see, you have me swearing again. Let me fetch your husband."

"No, Lizzie, no. I don't want him here. You stay with me. You and Sadie are all I need."

"But Daphne is kind to you even if—"

"Daphne? I'm not sure who—"

"Daphne is your maid, dearest. She looks after you."

"Does she? Oh, yes."

"Will you eat your meal now, my love? You must keep up your strength and then tomorrow I will ask Mr Cameron – Chad – if you may go into the garden."

"You will do no such thing, girl," an icy voice from the doorway said. "And if I find you up here again I will discharge you on the spot. Look at you, you are a disgrace. How dare you come into this part of the house dressed like that. A sacking apron—"

"I didn't have time to change, besides which—"

"That is enough. Now get back to your scullery and send up Daphne to get this girl to bed."

"I will get her to bed. There is no need to send for Daphne."

Sarah Cameron swelled up like a garden toad, her face the colour of a plum. "How dare you question my orders," she hissed. "I am mistress here—"

"Aye, but for how long? When this child is born and Briony is herself again, how long do you think you will remain here? Why Chad allows it is beyond me and I've a good mind to go now and tell him what you do to this poor child." But even as she spoke she knew she had gone too far. Her anger and pity had driven her to speak her mind but, oh, God, she was going to pay for it. Sarah Cameron's expression told her that, and not only herself but Briony as well. The plum colour of apoplectic rage had drained away, leaving the flesh of Sarah's face as bleached as marble and as cold, and her lips thinned to such an extent she could barely speak.

"You are finished here."

"I mean to speak to Chad, Mr Cameron, since I can't believe he knows—"

"Are you indeed? We'll see about that." Sarah stepped forward and pulled the bell that summoned the servants. As she reached over the leaden-faced pregnant woman in the chair, Briony flinched away from her and Lizzie had the horrid thought that this woman, surely mad, could have struck her sister-in-law, for her fear was very evident.

She did not move fast enough, she realised that later. Before she could get to the door and run screaming for Chad – would he believe her, sweet Jesus, would be believe her? – Daphne hovered in the doorway.

"Fetch Gladys," was all that Sarah said but with those words Lizzie knew she was to be forcibly removed from the premises. The two maidservants were strong – they had to be

to get through the housework which was theirs for twelve or
so long hours a day – and between them, though she herself
was no lightweight, they were equal to the task of propelling
her down the stairs, through the kitchen and out into the yard
where, no doubt, the men would be ordered to see her off the
property. Well, so be it, but it made no difference. This mad
woman would be defeated one way or another. She would
stay with Sadie tonight and then tomorrow she would wait
for Chad at the gate at the bottom of the drive and tell him
the whole story. Surely to God he would realise she was telling
the truth. She couldn't believe that she hadn't been to see him
before, presented him with the facts about his lunatic sister
who was doing her best to drive his young, vulnerable wife out
of her mind. He hadn't helped, and neither had Briony with
her mad obsession with the mill, but it must all be brought
out into the open, and tomorrow morning before it was light
she would position herself at the bottom of the drive where
she could accost Chad Cameron.

"One sound from you, madam, and you will be out of
this neighbourhood so fast you will scarce have time to
draw breath and so will that idiot brother of yours, do you
hear and where else will he get work? You, no doubt, will
find something, scrubbing or such, and I'll even give you
a reference if I have your word you will keep that wicked
mouth of yours shut. Ah, here are Daphne and Gladys." She
whirled about and smiled at the two terrified housemaids.
"This woman is to leave Longlake Edge at once. Is that
understood? When she is in the yard one of you is to go
and get her things and she is not to be allowed to enter this
house again. Is that clear? Good, then off you go."

She had gone when Chad answered the timid knock at his
study door, taking the telegram from Daphne's hand with an
absent-minded nod. He did not even look up from his desk

or he might have noticed the drawn, frightened look about his maidservant's face. She bobbed a curtsey and closed the door quietly behind her, hurrying back to the kitchen where half the younger servants were in tears and the other half grim-faced and unable to meet each other's eyes.

He found his sister sitting placidly with his wife, her embroidery in her hands, though Briony as usual did nothing but gaze into the fire. He wondered as he entered the room whether he might get her another puppy, or maybe a kitten, for her hands were so empty and still and he remembered how she used to play with . . . what had she called him? Scruff, that was it. He studied her passivity, his heart turning over in his breast. Even though she could not be said to have any expression, or even movement, she was an enchantment, a bewitchment to him and he wondered desolately if he would ever recover from what seemed almost like an illness. He had been like this, taking no pleasure from much in life, not even his businesses and the challenge they had once given him, ever since she had revealed to him that she was pregnant and what's more hated the very thought of it, and, he supposed, him for getting her in the condition. She had been so exquisite, so dainty and slender, so graceful, and would be again, he knew, but she looked quite grotesque sitting there, her head appearing to be too small for the size of her body. He felt a prick of unease, for surely the way she was, the way she looked couldn't be right, couldn't be normal. Doctor Travis appeared to think she was well and he, who knew nothing of such things, could hardly argue with him, could he?

He picked up a small ornament from the satinwood side table that stood against the wall, and fingered it absently. It was a pearlware potpourri vase covered with hand-painted flowers and from it drifted a delicate fragrance. He lifted it to his nose and sniffed, then slowly replaced it on the table, unaware that his sister was watching him carefully.

"How is she?" he asked, though he could see very well that she was not as she should be, but still it pleased him that his sister had taken the trouble to sit with her.

"I think she'll do very well, my dear. She has eaten her meal and I was just about to call Daphne to help me get her to bed."

"You are very good to her, Sarah. I really don't know what I would have done without you."

"Who else could you have turned to, Chadwick?"

"But should she be so quiet? I worry that she does not get out more. Just a short walk would do her good, I believe. I think when I get back I will encourage her to stroll with me in the garden."

"You are going away, my dear?" A smile began to form about her lips.

"Yes." He held out the telegram in his hand. "Not for long, a couple of days at the most, but I must go this evening. Some business in Liverpool that needs my urgent attention. I'll leave you my address so that if . . ." He waved a hand in Briony's direction. "I wouldn't dream of going but there are two or three weeks yet to . . ."

"Of course. I understand, but you must not worry. I am here and if it should be necessary I will send one of the grooms for Doctor Travis and get a telegram off to you at once. Now go and pack."

Lizzie was at the gate before the dark December night had even begun to lighten, urged on by Sadie who, if she had had her way would have gone storming up to Longlake with a pitchfork, demanding entrance to her lamb! Sadie had been furious, frightened, then furious again followed by tearful at what was happening to the lass and what had been done to Lizzie, but she knew absolutely that when Lizzie had spoken to Mr Cameron, opened his eyes to the situation, he would put everything right. He was not a wicked man, though it might seem so, just misguided in his trust of his sister. He would allow her and Lizzie to take care of Briony in her last days of pregnancy, she was sure of it, and when the babe was here he and Briony would make a go of it. And Briony, with her child in her arms would forget that damned mill and leave it all for her husband to look after. So Sadie comforted herself during that fitful night. She was up with Lizzie, watching sorrowfully but with hope as Lizzie made her way down the track towards the road beside the lake.

Lizzie wasn't sure that Chad Cameron was to go out on this day but there weren't many mornings when his handsome ebony mare did not set off in some direction. She berated herself that she couldn't quite get up the nerve to go boldly to the back door and knock, demanding to see him, but there were so many lives, and livings, who depended on this house and she was frightened to set the cat among the pigeons, so to speak, and perhaps get one of them into trouble. Work was hard to come by, decent work, that is, and if, through her determination to see Chad Cameron, to reveal to him what his sister was doing to his wife, one of the grooms, the stable lads, the housemaids should be unintentionally involved who knew what might happen.

There had been a slight frost during the night, a crackle of silvery white lying thinly on the ground and delicately painting the trees and shrubs. The sky was lightening over High Raise, the purple blue of the night turning gradually to lemon and green then more swiftly to a delicate winter pink as the sun lifted itself over the fells. It was bitterly cold and though Lizzie was wrapped in her own good warm cloak with Sadie's shawl tied about her, since neither woman knew how long she might have to wait, she could feel the chill settle in her bones. She dared not stamp about too much, or walk to the lake and back to get her circulation on the move lest Chad Cameron should

come through the gate and be missed. Birds began their early
morning song and a carter, staring at her curiously, passed on
his way to Pooley Bridge. She had no watch, for such luxuries
had all gone in the early days of her mother's illness, but she
knew the servants must be up at Longlake, going about their
morning chores. Her feet were so cold she could not feel them
and was suddenly afraid that if she moved from the gate where
she clung she might fall over and be unable to rise.

For four hours she waited and when, at last, she saw signs
of movement in the shape of William Platt and Isaac, William
Platt stopping to light his pipe, she could have cried with relief.
She waved feebly, trying to attract their attention, but they
had stopped to study a plant which seemed to give William
Platt some anxiety. She dared not shout for fear of capturing
the attention of . . . well, of the creature of darkness who had
them all in her clutches. Dear God, how dramatic she sounded
but it was true, may she rot in hell. Why, oh why, wouldn't
William Platt or Isaac look in her direction? What on earth
could be so interesting – and at this time of year when the
garden slept – that kept them bent over that particular bed
with their backs to her?

Suddenly from round the corner of the house raced the
black, shining shape of Chad Cameron's dog, making joyfully
for the gardener and his lad, with Joe in hot pursuit. The
groom was shouting something, probably rude, Lizzie had
time to think, and both figures straightened up, turning to
the sound. The dog, escaping from the yard, bounded in an
ecstasy of welcome towards them, his rear end corkscrewing
with joy, then, just as suddenly, he swerved and galloped
past the formal, well-pruned rose beds where William Platt
and Isaac stared with astonishment. Down the lawns he
went, the grass falling in smooth, terraced levels to the open
wrought-iron gate where she hovered and which led on to
the road. He almost knocked her over as he jumped up to

greet her, knowing her from the days when she had moved efficiently about the house in her duties.

"Eeh, lass," William Platt said anxiously as he reached her, his broad red face not knowing what expression to assume. He was breathing hard after running down the slopes after the dog, as was Joe who was also cursing under his breath, the only one enjoying the moment being Isaac. "What tha' doin' 'ere at this time o't mornin'? Tha' look fair clemmed. See," to the dog, "be'ave thissen. Get 'old of 'im, Joe."

"Bloody daft beggar," Joe declared, then, seeing Lizzie, begged her pardon, for despite her demotion in the house she was still a lady. He grabbed the dog and began to haul him away from her. He had heard of the rumpus at the house yesterday, as it seemed William Platt and Isaac had not, and had he not seen her himself, dragging off with her bundle of belongings, making for Sadie's she had shouted to him, in case she was wanted, he supposed.

"I'm looking for Mr Cameron, Joe. Do you know if he's about? I'd like a word if you could manage it without Miss Sarah knowing. I'd come up to the house but I've been . . . discharged and I don't want to get anyone into trouble."

"Eeh, nay, lass," William Platt muttered, clenching his teeth about the stem of his pipe and shaking his head, for they all knew which way the wind blew at Longlake. That poor little girl with her belly out to here and that old . . .

Joe held Bart's collar, doing his best to restrain him, to drag him back towards the stable yard. The dog, as though sensing bad manners were out of place at the moment, obediently lay down.

"I'm sorry, lass, but the master's gone," Joe told her apologetically, for he knew what she was up to.

"*Gone!* But I've been out here half the night and didn't see him."

"'E left last night. I drove 'im ter't station ter catch train ter . . . Liverpool, I think 'e sed 'e were goin'. Back day after termorrer. Nay, Miss Lizzie, what's ter do?" The dog was forgotten as all three men surged towards her when she reeled against the gate.

28

It was Dicky who first heard the cry. Dicky slept in a small cupboard-like space under the back stairs, a cosy place entered by a door from the passage that led to the master's study. There were shelves at one end on which Dicky kept the objects that are treasured by a boy of his age: bits and pieces he had picked up on the fells, an eagle's feather, a curiously shaped stone, a couple of bird's eggs, a book which Iolo had given him, for though neither he nor the cowman could read there were some wonderful pictures in it. There was a change of underclothes which were put on when those he wore were washed each week, and a couple of pairs of warm, woollen socks, knitted for him by Sadie. He had come from an overcrowded cottage up near Tirril but at Longlake he had been taught to be a clean lad, a tidy lad and the bedding in the little cupboard, also changed each week, was folded away every day. He loved his small, private space, did Dicky and considered himself a lucky fellow to have such a decent job and place and the good food he ate three times a day. His brother Billy who worked at Moorend Mill was not quite so lucky, for he slept in a barn and was not so warmly clad but he was well fed and seemed happy enough. Their mam was forever thanking the fates that had put two of her many children in such a good position in life.

They had all gone up, the maidservants whose boots he cleaned, whose orders he obeyed and whose errands he cheerfully ran, and the house was quiet. He had found a nest of mice in the far paddock that day and, praying the women would not see it, had picked out one of the babies to keep as a pet but the thing, away from its mother, was not doing so well, even on the saucer of milk he had stolen from the kitchen and which he was persuading the tiny creature to drink. He had a candle, which he was not supposed to light under the stairs, and when the cry echoed from somewhere in the house he instantly snuffed it out, then waited for some movement from upstairs but nothing happened, nothing stirred. He was about to light it again with one of the matches he was definitely not supposed to have when he heard the cry once more. He felt the hairs on his arms and the back of his neck prickle and rise and was about to burrow, him and his mouse, under the covers when something in the nature of the cry made him open the door to his cupboard and listen more intently. There it was again, faint and fearful, it seemed to him.

"'Ere, that sounded like mistress," he said to the half-dead mouse. "Get yer in there while I go an' see what's up," shoving the mouse in a small box, then, pulling on his breeches, the only part of his clothing he removed in bed, he crept out into the passage and made his way to the wide front hall. There was no light but he was young and had good eyes and could make out where he was. The furniture stood in deep shadows and the clock ticked sonorously as he stood at the bottom of the stairs, then, greatly daring, for he had never been further than the kitchen, he tiptoed up the stairs, ready to dart back if anyone should challenge him. Behind one door he could hear the sound of wobbly snores and a grunt or two but the rest of the doors stood silently open all except one. He stopped there and put his head on one side, beginning to believe that he had imagined the two cries, when from behind it there was a sort of rustling noise, a sound of a gasping breath, then a faint voice said two words.

"Oh, please . . ."

Dicky nearly wet his pants, or so he told a fascinated Joe and
Ned and Charlie later, much later, but resisting the temptation
to run like hell for the safety of his retreat under the stairs and
the company of his new pet, he sank down and, putting his
lips to the faintly lighted crack at the bottom of the door he
whispered to whoever it was who had called.

"Is . . . is summat up?"

"Oh, please . . ."

"'Tis Dicky."

"Oh, please help me."

"Eeh, what am I ter do?" He felt ready to cry, for it
surely must be the little mistress on the other side of the
door but if there was one thing he dared not do that was
fetch the old mistress, for, like them all, she frightened him
to death.

"Lizzie?" the voice gasped.

"Miss Lizzie's gone, missis."

"Oh, please . . ."

He knew the door would be locked, for they talked of
nothing else in the kitchen, but despite this he tried it. It
was locked and the woman on the other side of the door was
beginning to moan in the most dreadful way.

Dicky stood up and moved this way and that, hesitating,
frightened, wishing to God he'd never heard the sound that
was coming from the other side of the door. It was like an
animal in pain and Dicky loved animals. Oh, Jesus . . .

With a great sob of terror, for he was mortally afraid of
losing his job, he raced up the servants stairs and hammered
on the first door he came to.

It took Daphne a good ten minutes to wake Sarah Cameron
while, in the wide passage from which all the family's bedrooms led, the rest of the maidservants milled about and
clutched one another. They made soothing noises to the

woman who was locked behind the door and who was making appalling noises of her own.

"Madam, we need t' key ter't mistress's bedroom," Daphne was pleading. "It sounds as if 'er time's come, madam. Shall I send fer't doctor? Oh, please, madam, can we not have't key? Gladys 'as gone down ter put water on ter boil. She's early, an' wi't master not 'ere . . ."

Daphne continued to babble at the old mistress's door, determined if the blasted woman didn't respond soon to send for Joe and Ned to break it down. Surely no woman could sleep through the noise that was beginning to rage through the house, what with the women calling to one another, with Joe shouting up the stairs to ask if he was needed and the general flurry of activity that comes at a time like this. But when the door finally opened a fraction and Miss Sarah peered through the crack her face was screwed into that familar, impatient expression they all knew. Her pale hair hung in two long, thin plaits over the flat bodice of her flannel nightgown.

"Good heavens, girl, what is all this commotion?"

"'Tis little mistress, madam."

"Who?"

"The babby be comin'."

The door opened wider and despite her resolution Daphne stepped back a little, for though she had never yet done so, Miss Sarah looked as if she might be tempted to aim a blow at the maidservant's head.

"Nonsense, girl, there are more than three weeks to go, or so the doctor informed us and I'm sure he knows best." She made as though she were about to close her door. "Now, all of you get back to your beds and let me hear no more of this nonsense."

"Please, oh, please, madam." Daphne was becoming frantic and the old mistress eyed her with distaste, ready to shut her door in the face of the housemaid's impertinence but, greatly daring, Daphne put her foot in the opening of the door. Her face was white with fear but wore an expression of obstinacy that said, no matter what the consequences, she was not about to abandon her young mistress. The doctor must be sent for, surely this mad woman must realise that but the mad woman was struggling to close her door, hissing her venomous displeasure. Just as suddenly Daphne withdrew her foot, letting the door close, then turned to Minnie who bravely stood behind her.

"Run fer Joe, Minnie. Tell 'im ter fetch an axe."

"An axe?" Minnie quavered.

"An axe, tha' knows what an axe is, don't yer, an' Ned must ride like 'ell fer't doctor. Send Charlie fer Lizzie an' Sadie an' . . . Oh, I dunno, just go, lass, an' the quicker the better."

She was in labour the whole of that night, the next day and the night after. Miss Cameron was vague as to where her brother might be when pressed by the doctor, for really Mrs Cameron should have her husband at least within call, he told her fretfully. His nurse was in attendance and all that could be done for the labouring woman was being done. Her pains were very close together and clearly very sharp, he added, and his patient's sister-in-law pulled a face as though in disgust, her main concern seeming to be the state of Mrs Cameron's bedroom door which hung in a shattered state from its hinges.

The kettle was continually on the boil that first night, the servants sitting or standing about the kitchen waiting for news. Mrs Foster, all of a doo-dah, as she called it, pushed the sleeves of her nightgown up and turned to making a few scones, to soothe her nerves, she said. There was nothing to do but wait, Doctor Travis told the circle of anxious servants who began to hang about in the front hall. He was easy and reassuring. This was one job that could not be done without some pain, he told them, but it was clear they were not reassured, for was not the sight of Miss Sarah's face at breakfast enough to scare the pants off anyone. She didn't seem to care about what was going on above her head, complaining over the poor state of the porridge and that the mushrooms were not fit to be eaten. The toast was burned and the coffee cold and she really would have to start looking for new staff if this sad state of affairs went on.

Lizzie and Sadie sat beside Briony, ignoring the irritation of the nurse brought in by Doctor Travis, doing their best to encourage her, holding her hands until their own were sore and swollen with her vice-like grip, their faces showing signs of lack of sleep, of strain, of helplessness. Meanwhile in her drawing-room the old mistress rang for tea, or coffee, or whatever fancy took her, *her* face registering astonishment at all the fuss.

The next morning Chad Cameron returned home to chaos and confusion, to several differing accounts of what had happened in his absence and to the worried face of Doctor Travis who, being elderly and somewhat out of touch with the latest midwifery techniques, was out of his depth. His wife, barely recognisable and barely conscious, lay panting on her bed, her pains so rapid and so severe she could hardly draw breath between them, her cheeks sunk into dark hollows, black rings around her eyes. Lizzie wept quietly beside her and Sadie sagged against the wall, her face turned towards it.

"Leave us," their master whispered to them, sinking to his knees beside his wife's bed, doing his best to get her whimpering, twisting body into his arms, turning his face from the impatient nurse who was of the opinion that all husbands should be kept from a lying-in. But within half an hour a younger man, a colleague of Doctor Travis, arrived, fetched by Joe, his businesslike air telling those who still huddled at the foot of the stairs that now things would get going and giving them comfort. Miss Cameron, who was about to sit down to luncheon, rang her bell imperiously and when it was answered told Gladys to ask the master to come and see her.

"I think 'e's busy, madam," Gladys said through gritted teeth.

"That is for him to decide, you insolent girl. And where is Daphne?"

"She be busy an' all."

"How dare you speak to me like that. Fetch Mr Cameron at once."

Gladys slid from the room and informed those in the kitchen that she'd swing for that bloody woman and if the bell rang again Dicky could answer it for all she cared.

Lizzie and Sadie, banished to the kitchen, sat with their heads in their hands, cups of tea before them, teetering on the edge of despair, while the women, and the men at the back door, begged for news but they had none to impart.

"'Tis not going well, is it?" old Martha quavered, smoothing her apron over her own sterile stomach, her lovely vision of the new baby, with her to oversee its progress, slipping away with every hour. It was not unusual for a first baby to take a long time to arrive but thirty-six hours was more than any lass could survive and the little mistress was not strong, not now. Martha had pictured herself sitting before the fire with the new nursemaid, whoever she might be, in what she knew would be a decently refurbished nursery, the master's child in her arms, out of reach of the old mistress who wouldn't dream of climbing the stairs. But the picture was fading and as it did tears slipped down her cheeks along the deep furrows age had put there.

"They're giving her something," Lizzie muttered from beneath the fall of her disordered hair.

"Givin' 'er somethin'. What does that mean?" Minnie asked in a trembling voice.

"I don't know, Minnie. They say she will sleep for a while. If she has a little rest perhaps . . ." Suddenly she sprang to her feet, violently pushing back her chair. Terror gripped her and her need to be near Briony, even if it was merely hovering on the top hallway, overtook her.

Chad Cameron stood just outside the bedroom door, his face pressed to the wall. He still wore his travelling cape and boots. She put her hand on his shoulder but he didn't move nor even look round to see who had touched him.

"Mr Cameron, Chad . . ."

"They say there is a danger to her heart; the strain. Doctor Monroe wants to use forceps since he is of the opinion she has suffered enough."

"And so she has, Chad."

"But the damage to . . . to the child, the skull. It seems it must be my choice who lives or dies."

"And what do you want, Chad? You are the father and must—"

"I want her to live."

"And the child?"

"I don't care about the child. Only her. He, the doctor, tells me she is young enough to bear it, that I am allowing my . . . my devotion to the mother to move me; that is how they talk, Lizzie. The child might be a son, my son and heir; as if I give a damn for that. She is the only one I care about."

"Then tell them to do it, Chad. She will die if they don't, if they don't stop her agony."

"I love her so much, Lizzie."

"I know, my dear, and when she is recovered you must tell her."

"She doesn't want me, she never wanted me. Only that damn mill."

"Never mind the mill, Chad. Go in and tell them to do it. She is well loved and if she should die . . ."

They administered the blessed laudanum with Lizzie kneeling at the bedside to hold Briony's hand, in the absence of her husband who seemed rooted to the spot beyond the broken door.

"Not long now, dearest, not long now." She smoothed back the wild tangle of hair plastered to Briony's skull, its darkness made even darker with sweat. Her lips were flecked and bitten. She was immersed in pain, nothing left of her bright, defiant nature, her individuality, just a female body labouring in agony.

Her children, a boy and a girl, were delivered almost at once, the thin wail of the newborn echoing across the room, along the hallway and down the stairs to where every one of the indoor servants, including Dicky, who felt he had played an important part in the birth, were congregated. They turned to one another, the sound releasing their tears, which ran down every face, even Dicky's, in sheer thankfulness, and the commands of the old mistress to return at once to their duties were totally ignored.

"I will not have this in my home," she told them shrilly, but they continued to stand patiently waiting for news, not of the birth which they now knew had taken place but of their mistress's condition. She could rest now, they told one another. The cradle from the nursery would be brought downstairs and put beside her bed and they would pamper her, spoil her, surround her with flowers and gifts as new mothers ought to be. The baby would be admired, cherished, marvelled over and the house would be alight with the joy a child brings. Now that she was safely delivered surely the master would get rid of the harridan who had made their lives miserable for the past couple of months. Listen to her now, caterwauling her displeasure, but they remained where they were, waiting for Lizzie, who would surely come down and tell them the sex of the child, not that it mattered, at least to them, as long as the little mistress was all right.

Lizzie came jerkily down the stairs, then sank slowly on to the bottom step while they crowded about her and in the background the woman who had once been mistress began to shriek of dire punishments, of dismissals and retributions that would follow this mutiny.

Sadie sank down beside Lizzie, her heart drumming inside her breast, for there was something wrong here, some dreadful thing that would surely hurt her badly. She put her arm about Lizzie's shoulder.

"Tell us, lass."

"Never mind that, you vile creature. Look at her; there is blood on her apron and I will not stand these sluttish ways," Sarah Cameron screeched in the background.

"Tell us."

Lizzie raised her head and a small smile lit her drawn features. "Twins . . . twins, she's had twins. Both well."

Minnie threw her apron over her head and wept her joy, and Dicky began a little dance, for wasn't he the clever one, taking part in the birth of not one child but two.

"What?" Daphne managed to say, shaking Lizzie's arm.

"A boy and a girl."

"Eeh, never, one of each; no wonder she were so big, the little treasure."

"I knew it, size of 'er."

"An' 'er no bigger than two pennorth o' copper."

"See, Dicky, run an' tell Joe an' Ned an' the rest."

"*I will not have this commotion in my house. Get back to your duties at once or I shall have my brother dismiss the lot of you.*"

"An't mistress? Is she . . . ?" It was Martha who spoke the dread words, for none of them had wanted to be the one to . . . well, to ask the question.

"She's badly, in't she?" Sadie was the one to speak.

"Yes." The word was like a slap in the face for the excited women and when the master came down the stairs, his face like grey dust, his eyes lifeless, his mouth working in a way that reminded Sadie of a boy doing his best not to weep, they fell silent.

"Sir . . ."

"Chadwick, will you tell these insolent women to get back to their work. I am ready to eat lunch and I'm sure you must be hungry after your journey."

"My wife is sleeping," he said to no one in particular.

"Good, then perhaps we can get back to normal and after we have eaten I would be glad of a word regarding these servants who labour under the misapprehension that they might do as they please just because . . . They have refused to—"

"Sarah, I'd be glad of a moment; my wife—"

"Surely the fuss is all over and we can—"

"*Fuss!* Sarah, she has just given birth to twins. Surely a little fuss is in order?"

At once Sarah Cameron realised her mistake. For the moment, in her fury at the way these women had disobeyed her, had continued to disobey her in showing their devotion to the girl upstairs, had even broken down the door which she had kept locked, she had quite forgotten the charade she kept up in Chadwick's presence. She must quickly think up some reason for the broken door, which she realised Chadwick had not yet noticed, but she was confident that she would smooth it all over and despite the squalling brat – *brats, twins for God's sake* – upstairs, continue the pleasant life she meant to keep for herself at Longlake Edge. The girl was easily controlled, the last few weeks had proved that, and with a bit of diplomacy and the certainty that the girl would be fully occupied in the nursery, she herself would run the house as it had always been run.

"Of course, my dear, she has undergone a great ordeal and needs her rest, as you do, as we all do. It has been a most difficult time but . . . well, twins, what a great joy they will be to you, and to us all. Now, tell me what you wish me to do, but first let me get the servants back to the kitchen," turning to smile benevolently at the open-mouthed women who clustered about them. "Off you go, there is nothing more to be done but wait for news from upstairs and the moment we hear that . . . that . . . your mistress" – dear heaven, how hard that word was to get out – "is progressing as we all hope she will, the master or I will come and let you know. Won't we, my dear?" She turned to her brother, allying herself to him for them all to see. "And Blackhall had better be fetched to see to the door which seems to have been damaged in the . . ."

But Chad Cameron had more on his mind than a damaged door. He could not erase the picture from his mind's eye of the silent, skeletal figure on the bed in her pretty bedroom. In her pretty misted rose, misted green and cream bedroom that he had chosen for her, the delicate rose and cream quilt placed carefully across her quiet body which barely raised it from the bed. The nurse had tidied her, tying back her lank hair, but nothing could be done to hide the skull-like face on the pillow. His children, who he had hardly glanced at, had been whisked away by Sadie who told him that he must get a wet nurse at once, for they were such little scraps and it was plain their mother could do nothing for them. Yes, the broken door was not on his mind as he ran his hand distractedly through his hair, which was just as well for Sarah. His normally sharp attention to everything about him was sadly blunted. He wanted to run upstairs, take the barely living figure on the bed and hold her in his arms, pump his own strength, his will, his resolution into her frail body. The doctor was still there, reluctant to leave her in case of . . . well, he could only call it a deterioration in her condition. She was hanging on by a fingernail and if Mr Cameron could think of anything that might bring her back from the wastes in which she wandered he would be thankful. Of course, when she had regained her strength the children would be her salvation, for it was his experience that a mother . . . well, he was sure Mr Cameron would see what he was getting at. Now, that woman who would keep trying to get to Mrs Cameron, was she perhaps a relative? She was most insistent and his nurse, who was most competent, was not happy about it.

"Who?" he had said, looking down on the sunken face of his wife, his heart breaking with love and despair.

"The tall woman."

"Who?" he had asked again, unable to tear his eyes away from his love.

"She is outside the door now, Mr Cameron, and I'm afraid I don't care to have my nurse interfered with. Mrs Cameron will not do well if she is not cared for by an experienced midwife."

Chad had turned blindly to stare uncomprehendingly at the doctor, his eyes blank, then looked at the door, just beyond the door where, if she had not been at Briony's bedside, Lizzie had waited for thirty-six hours.

"Lizzie?" he questioned.

"Is that her name? Well I must ask you—"

"No, you must not. She is my wife's friend and is to be admitted whenever my wife needs her. Is that clear?"

"Mr Cameron, I must insist—"

"No, you must not. Let her in. She is to have a bed beside my wife's."

"Mr Cameron," the doctor had protested, but Lizzie had flown thankfully to Briony's side and now, with his sister watching him with what he imagined was compassion, he made his way unsteadily to his study.

29

She opened her eyes and sighed deeply just as she did every morning on waking. She looked up into the misted muslin draperies above the bed, deciding there must be a window open, for they moved slightly as though in a stray draught. She was warm, comfortable and yet her body felt weak and drained in some odd way as though she had used all her strength running up and down Gowbarrow Fell or performed one of the gargantuan tasks her father had set her when she was a child.

The last memory disturbed her and she stirred a little under the covers then, very slowly, which seemed to be all she was capable of at that moment, she turned her head. There was a chair close by her bed, the low velvet chair she herself sat in before her fire and in it, lolling awkwardly, was her husband. He was asleep, his head to one side in what looked to be a very uncomfortable position. His clothing was crumpled, his ruffled shirt open at the neck, his jacket and cravat discarded and he was not at all his usual well-groomed self. His face was gaunt, tired, his cheeks fallen in, his long, thick eyelashes shadowing the deep sockets about his eyes. She frowned. Had he been ill and if so what was he doing perched on a chair beside her bed?

A sound from somewhere in the room startled her and she moved her head on the pillow, but again it was surprisingly difficult and she wondered why. There was a woman in an enormous, immaculately white apron, a starched white cap on her head, just about to move through the connecting doorway into the bathroom, a bowl in her hand. Briony frowned. Who on earth was she? And what was Chad doing sitting by her bed? He looked as though he hadn't changed his clothes for days which was so unlike him.

The woman came out of the bathroom – was she a nurse? she looked like one – and put the bowl, a pretty basin patterned in shades of misted pink, pale green and cream like the rest of the bedroom, on a stand, placing the matching jug inside it.

The sound of the bowl chinking against the jug reached the sleeping man at her side and slowly, as though he rose from a deep, deep pit, he awoke, opening his eyes, looking about him, confused, she thought, wondering where he was and what he was doing here. Then at once he turned his gaze on her and she was bemused by the concerned anguish that darkened his already dark eyes. She smiled at him and was amazed when tears sprang to his eyes, hanging on his eyelashes, tears that he brushed hastily away with the back of his hand. He hitched closer to her, then put out a hand as though to take hers which were trapped beneath the coverlet. Struggling to get them free, for it seemed to her Chad wanted to clasp them, she found to her consternation she didn't seem to have the strength to release them. Chad didn't seem to mind. He gently turned back the quilt and took one in both of his, lifting it to his lips. Looking deeply into her eyes he kissed the back, then, turning it over, smoothed his lips against the pulse that fluttered in her wrist. She could feel the whiskers on his chin prickling her flesh and a small sensation which started somewhere inside her was very pleasant.

"Darling," he whispered so that the woman by the wash-stand could not hear. She was ready to come across, Briony thought, and interfere, say something disapproving, but Chad turned on her, violently waving her away, and she stopped abruptly. He turned back to herself and smiled and in his

eyes was a warm, deep glow of something which she liked
though she didn't know why. She had always felt safe with
Chad, she supposed that was it, right from that first moment
when he had stood up to her father in the mill yard. She had
always trusted him, known that no matter what happened
he would be there to protect her. There was something at
the edge of her consciousness, something that troubled her
but she couldn't quite catch it and was too tired to try. She
wished she didn't feel so . . . so weak. She would have liked
to put her hand up to Chad's cheek, cup it, have him turn
his mouth into her palm as she remembered he had done in
the past, but it seemed the raising of it was beyond her.

"You've come back to us," he murmured. "My Briony,
my dearest Briony." He smoothed her hair back from her
forehead and his hand was trembling, and it was then she
began to understand that some dreadful thing had happened
to this man, for his suffering was very evident. She tried
again to reach out and touch him but it was as though
she were strapped to this bed, tied hand and foot, unable
to move except when he helped her. Her body felt buffeted,
as though she had been thrown here and there by a strong
wind, torn up and flung against hard objects that had bruised
and injured her and yet she could not remember anything . . .
or, well, there was some fearful thing, or *person* hovering in
her memory; a locked door, fear, pain; and yet Chad was
here, lifting her, despite the protests of the woman in white,
into his arms and against his chest where she settled and the
black memory drifted away.

"Don't go, don't leave me," she said to the man who held
her, wondering why it was so difficult to speak and why her
voice was so croaky.

"I won't, little love, but let me give you a drink. Mrs Foster
sent up some iced lemonade."

"Mr Cameron, I don't think," a voice beyond Chad's broad

back protested, but he reached for a glass, one with a spout and tenderly, carefully, placed the spout between Briony's lips and she drank slowly the most delicious drink she had ever tasted. He wiped her mouth gently on a napkin, then put his arms about her again and she felt herself drift off into a dreamless sleep. For a second her eyes sprang open, focusing on his strong, brown throat. "Don't leave me," she said again.

"I will never leave you, my love, never." Reassured, she fell asleep.

"Send for the doctor," he whispered over his shoulder to the nurse who still hovered anxiously, "and tell Miss Jenkins to come up."

"Sir, I don't think we are ready for visitors yet."

"Don't be bloody stupid, woman. Lizzie isn't a visitor. Ring the bell and ask her to come up. She's been waiting for this day for a long time, as have we all. Now, do as you're told."

He cradled his sleeping wife to him and when Lizzie Jenkins knocked on the door he indicated with a nod of his head that the nurse was to open it. Still she demurred, but Mr Cameron could be very obstinate as she knew to her cost and with a sigh she opened the door.

Lizzie, looking as strained as he did, crept across the carpet and sank down on the opposite side of the bed. She put out a careful hand and without disturbing the sleeping woman, or the man in whose arms she slept, placed it on Briony's forehead.

"She's a lot cooler. The fever seems to be abating."

"Mr Cameron, I really must protest. The patient should be laid down until—"

"My wife is perfectly safe where she is, Nurse. She would not sleep otherwise. I'll wait until Doctor Monroe is here, then . . ."

He turned back to his wife, putting his lips to her brow and again a small smile lifted the corner of her mouth. Lizzie saw it and was amazed. She watched the couple who, for the past few months, had barely spoken to each other and when they did it was only to quarrel and now here was Briony sleeping peacefully in her husband's arms. In the weeks since the birth of the twins she had awakened before and had been fed, changed, bathed, but she had been semi-conscious, unaware of her surroundings and of those who cared for her. Now she was looking better, gaunt still and pale, but with a certain undertint to her flesh which had been missing for so long. And she knew them!

They had believed she would die. The house had been in mourning as though already the death had occurred of its little mistress. The babies had not, at first, done well and could you wonder after the nightmare of their birth. The two tiny infants still bore the faint marks on their frail skulls of the forceps that had been used to deliver them, but thankfully the doctor had told them that they would fade. And it had taken two days to find a suitable wet nurse. The servants had been at their wits' end, for it seemed that not only were they to lose their young mistress but the two babies as well. Those in the kitchen and out in the yard were the only ones to be concerned, or so it appeared to them, for Miss Sarah carried on with her social gadding, calling on her friends and having them call on her as though there were nothing amiss at Longlake. Mr Cameron and Lizzie barely vacated the sickroom so it was left to Sadie, who knew every woman in the district and, more to the point, every woman who had just given birth, to find a suitable young woman.

Up in the nursery there was now the plump, placid wife of one of Chad Cameron's shepherds, suckling not only her own fat boy, her first child which was a blessing, born on the same day as Briony's twins, but the twins as well. She was at it night and day, she said cheerfully, but she didn't care. She had nothing to do but sit by the fire, eating her head off, a baby at her breast, sometimes two, one to each side, waited on hand and foot by the eager maidservants who fought with one another on who was to take up the never-ending trays of food she required! A grand holiday it was, and she and her Eddie would be glad of the extra coins Mr Cameron poured into her hand. She'd never seen a man so grateful and all for a mouthful of milk. But they had begun to thrive, those two little scraps, though as yet their mam, and scarcely their pa, had been up to see them.

Jinny Harrop, the shepherd's wife, and the new nursemaids, two of them again employed in a great hurry, got on like a house on fire. That battle-axe who was Mr Cameron's sister had done her best to oppose Mrs Evans on every damn thing she could but Mr Cameron, it was reported, had stood his ground and allowed Mrs Evans and Miss Jenkins to make their own choice: two young lasses not yet in their twenties but their families were well known to Mrs Evans. Both girls were the eldest of a large family which were the best sort in Mrs Evans's opinion, for, having helped to bring up an assortment of younger brothers and sisters, who would know better than they how to go about it. Cheerful, country girls from decent families who had settled in grand, in Jinny's opinion, considering the rush that had been necessary. Mrs Evans and Miss Jenkins had managed for the first forty-eight hours, with plenty of help from the kitchen, but now they were like a basket of kittens, she and Nan and Beth with the three babies all coming on a treat, though that Miss Cameron had complained, it had been reported to them, that there was too much laughter floating down from the nursery floor. And what was wrong with a good laugh? they asked one another. Not only did it do them good but it was known that children thrived where there was a cheerful atmosphere!

"She's . . . she's going to be all right, isn't she, Chad?" Lizzie whispered.

"We'll know better when the doctor gets here, but at least she knew me."

"Thank God . . . oh, thank God! Did she mention the children?"

"No, not yet. She scarcely knew where she was but she recognised me."

"When will you mention it?" Which seemed a strange thing to say, just as though they were speaking of a new piece of furniture that had arrived, or an addition to the stable. Briony had been far away from them for such a long time. She had given birth and lost herself in a fever, not, thank God, puerperal fever, for Doctor Monroe was an enlightened medical man with radical ideas regarding hygiene, but some common fever which had caused a dangerously high temperature and hallucinations. Now she was sleeping naturally, but she would have to be a great deal stronger before they could burden her with worries about her babies. Let it come back to her gradually in its own good time.

In those first weeks Lizzie herself had looked as though she'd been through some storm, just as Chad did, her hair tied back in a careless ribbon and falling down her back in a lank tangle. She had done no more than rinse her hands and face, flinging her exhausted body on any handy bed in the servants' quarters to sleep fitfully, restlessly, waking after no more than an hour. She couldn't remember when she had last eaten a proper, what Mrs Foster called a "sit-down" meal, though she had begged Chad a dozen times to try the soup or the broth Cook sent up. He was thin, haggard, but she knew that until Briony was totally recovered he would neglect himself, his business, his appearance and the cards of congratulations that had come with every post, for it was not often a man was blessed with two children at the same time, and one of them a son!

She put out a hand and rested it on his. He looked up, startled for a moment, then he smiled as they resumed their vigilant watch over the woman they both loved.

It was dark when next she came to herself and this time her head was clearer. The woman in the white apron – she thought she *must* be a nurse – was still fiddling about with something in the background, but this time it was Sadie who sat beside her, her head nodding, her eyes half closed, her snowy white mob cap tipped slightly askew over her forehead.

She lay beneath her warm quilt in her pretty bedroom and smiled dreamily, wondering why Sadie sat beside her bed. She was not to know of the storm that had raged in the servants' quarters over Chad Cameron's determination to supply every comfort and support that his beloved wife might need and he believed Sadie Evans to be one of them.

"I cannot possibly manage without my laundry-maid," Sarah had told Chadwick, reasonably enough, she thought, but Chad was no longer the reasonable gentleman – by which she meant he was prone to argue with her – that he had been before the birth of his children.

"I believe there are five of them in the laundry at the moment, Sarah. Surely five laundry-maids are enough for a household of this size. We seem to have a surplus of maids, not only in the laundry, but in the kitchen." Which was true since Sarah had brought back those she had taken to the Dower House. Only poor Mrs Minty had been considered surplus to requirements as two cooks in one kitchen was a situation for disaster. Fortunately, at Lizzie's intervention, the vicar's wife had found the cook a nice position with an elderly widower and, as Mrs Minty said several times a day to the kitchen-maid who waited on her, she felt she was in clover, especially at her age.

"They are all needed, Chadwick, particularly since the arrival of your . . . of the children. Those nursemaids and the wet nurse produce more washing than the rest of the household put together. I have never seen such a basket of laundry as comes down from the nursery several times a day."

"I believe young babies soil their clothing."

"Please, Chadwick, there is no need to go into detail." Sarah's mouth crimped in distaste. It had not taken long for her to realise that she was in no fear of being challenged over her treatment of her brother's wife before the birth of the twins and consequently it had not taken her long to become herself again, her true self, though she was careful still of what she said about his wife, since he appeared to dote on her. But the girl lay in her bed, no opposition to Sarah's running of the house, and as long as the brats remained in the nursery and out of her sight she was able to resume her position as mistress of Longlake Edge.

Daphne had been inclined to take the sulks for hadn't the little mistress been in *her* charge for weeks before her confinement and she believed that her care should have continued. She had fought the old mistress tooth and nail on the night the little mistress had begun her labour and though she could not quite bring herself to tell the master about the locked door, since she had been threatened with dismissal should she do so, she did think her support might have been taken into consideration. She did not put it quite in those words to the master, for Daphne was an uneducated farm labourer's daughter but she had had high hopes of becoming the little mistress's personal maid one day and the master had agreed, though he had looked as though he could have done without this farrago just at the moment. When the mistress was herself again, he had said vaguely and she had had to be satisfied with that.

The christening of the twins had taken place two weeks after they were born, for though they were gaining weight at Jinny Harrop's breast it was felt, considering their poor beginning and their size, which was still very small, it might be as well to give them names and for them to be received into the Church, so to speak.

It was Sarah, the undoubted mistress of Longlake now, who arranged the service, who made out the invitation list, small but important, who decided who were to be godparents and who suggested their names, their father being too preoccupied with the health of their mother to give his full attention to the event. They were his children, certainly, the boy the heir to his great estate but until Briony was out of danger it seemed he hadn't the patience nor the time to become involved.

"What do you think to Robert and Margaret, Chadwick? They are family names after all and very suitable. Father was Robert and Grandmother was Margaret so with your approval . . ."

"Whatever you say, Sarah," he had answered, his foot on the bottom stair, his eyes lifting to the bedroom where his wife lay in a comatose state.

"In view of their . . . delicacy, Chadwick, it should be soon."

"Of course," barely turning to her as he climbed the stairs two at a time.

Briony smiled at the sight of Sadie then did her best to raise a hand, but again it was fastened securely beneath the bedcovers and no matter how she struggled she just didn't seem to have the strength to release it. She lay for several minutes, barely moving, for the last thing she wanted was the nurse to come bustling officiously across. She was sure Sadie must be tired and, besides, there was a memory niggling at the back of her mind and she wanted to study it, to take it out, turn it over and slowly digest what she would find.

Her hands, which were folded neatly beneath the bedclothes, rested on her stomach and slowly, as memories drifted one by one through her mind, a much clearer mind than when she last awoke, she realised, her hands began to move. They smoothed across the soft material of her nightgown, from the slight hollow beneath her ribs to the sharp points of her hip bones, then up again and where they had been exploring was a flatness, a lean concavity that didn't seem quite right to her. For a moment the reason for it escaped her. Again she ran her hands delicately across her belly and as she did so her heart began to quicken, to beat faster and panic set in. Where was the huge mound that she had hauled about with her for weeks, months? Dear God, what had happened to . . . It was all so mixed up in her head, the pain . . . no, the *agony*, the struggling; hands on her, things tearing at her, a woman screaming, a man's soothing voice; where was he? He had made her feel safe. Where?

Turning her head she began to whimper in Sadie's direction and at once, despite her age and aching weariness, Sadie shot up in her chair though Briony's voice had been no more than a whisper. The nurse hurried across, ready to push the visitor aside but she should have known better, for Sadie was not a woman *anyone* could push aside, let alone this interfering busybody. As the nurse said bitterly to the doctor later, she felt herself to be unnecessary in this household, for there was always some servant trying to do her job!

"Sadie . . ."

Sadie pushed back the coverlet, to the nurse's chagrin, and took Briony's limp hands in hers. "Yes, my lamb, Sadie's 'ere."

"What? Where . . . the child?"

Sadie smiled, then leaned forward to place a fond kiss on Briony's forehead. She brushed back the still lank hair from her brow and her smile broadened. Well, it was more of a grin than a smile and Briony found herself responding to it.

"Tha've a son, my lass!" Sadie gloated.

"A son?"

"Aye, an' a daughter an' all."

"A daughter . . . twins?"

"Really, Mrs Evans, I don't think it is up to you to divulge—" the nurse said indignantly but she might as well not have existed.

"When, Sadie?" Briony's voice was still faint but her hands clutched at Sadie's with surprising strength.

"Four weeks, now, lass."

"Four weeks?"

"Aye, tha've bin right poorly."

"The . . . the babies, they are . . . well?"

"Oh, aye, thrivin' an' just wantin' a scen at their mam. I'll get the lass ter bring 'em down."

"Now, Mrs Evans, I must insist that you allow me to decide."

"And Chad, is he . . . ?"

"I'll send fer 'im."

"But not *her*, please."

"No, not 'er. See, Nurse, ring that bell an' send someone ter fetch maister."

"Really . . ."

"Never mind *reely*. Just do as tha're told. Mrs Cameron wants ter see 'er 'usband *an'* 'er bairns, which is only right an' proper."

He moved quietly across the room and stood at her bedside. He was dressed in his immaculate business suit of dark frock coat, grey pinstripe trousers, snowy shirt and cravat. His hair was smoothly brushed and his boots gleamed with a high polish in the fire's glow. In fact just as she was used to seeing him. During her illness she had imagined, or dreamed, the man who had held her and kissed her and soothed her. If he had existed at all he was long gone and here in his place was her husband, the cool, impersonal, courteous Chad Cameron.

He looked down at her and smiled, the polite smile a visitor might give an invalid and behind him hovered two young women she had never seen before, both with a swaddled bundle in their arms.

"Briony, my dear, you are better, I see, or so Doctor Monroe tells me, and no doubt eager to see your son and daughter. They tell me they are doing well and so, with Nurse's permission, they have come to visit you." Again he smiled his cool smile, turning back to the two beaming young women.

Something inside her broke. She didn't know what it was, only that it hurt her quite badly. She had given birth to the two carefully wrapped children behind him, a son for which she supposed he must be pleased, and, for good measure, a daughter, both of them strangers to her, as he was a stranger to her. She had known him in several guises: as a man of business who had taken over her brother's mill; as a man of detached kindliness, of resolve and efficiency when it was needed at the court and the gaol; as a fair employer; as a man of purpose who, for reasons best known to himself, which he was *keeping* to himself, had required her for his wife. She had known him in her bed where he was, she supposed, an experienced lover. And yet teasing her memory was a sweetness, a tender dream of something that had soothed and comforted her when she needed it. A warmth, a feeling of utter safety, of love, yes, of love! Of a haven so wondrous, a resting place of hope and peace it had held her in its shelter waiting for this moment.

But it had been no more than a shadow without substance, a figment of her imagination and the loss of it was more than she could bear.

Barely glancing at the two nursemaids who were obviously immensely disappointed not to mention bewildered at being ignored, for in their experience a new mother cannot wait to get a glimpse of her baby, she turned her back on the lot of them and closed her eyes.

"I'm very tired," she murmured, pulling up the quilt so that her tears were hidden.

30

"She takes no interest, Doctor Monroe. She – we – have two beautiful children in the nursery and she acts as though they belong to someone else. Very politely she admires them, nodding her head, but when pressed to nurse them, as politely refuses, saying she would be sure to drop them or . . . The nursemaids think . . . Well, it doesn't matter what they think but frankly I don't know what to do. They need their mother and I need—"

"Your children to have a mother?"

"Yes." Chad Cameron stood with his back to the doctor, looking out over the garden which was beginning to show tender signs of the coming spring. William Platt and his lad had been busy planting spring bulbs at the "back-end" and the curved beds edging each lawned terrace stretched down to the lake. They were filled with colour, for William Platt saw no reason why every garden should not yield as much beauty and enjoyment during the early months of the year as in the summer and autumn. From January when the snowdrop and winter aconite timidly offered their simple charm until May when the ranunculus and anemone appeared, the whole tribe of spring-flowering plants delighted the eye with their varied beauty. There were daffodils. There were tulips, flauntingly scarlet, virginally white, cheerfully yellow. Crocus had taken their turn, followed by the lovely scilla, blooming next to the dog's-tooth violet, the colour of which reminded Chad of his wife's eyes. Hyacinth, planted early and anemone planted late, exploded together in a ribbon of colour with the yellow of alyssum and the deep purple of arabis, but Chad's unfocused eyes saw nothing but the slender figure of the young woman who romped with a puppy at the edge of the lake.

"You can see she has regained her physical health."

"Aye, she's blooming, there's no doubt about it." The young doctor who had undoubtedly saved the lives of Chad Cameron's wife and children spoke from the depths of the comfortable chair in Chad's study to where he had been shown. A tray with a pot of coffee, cups and saucers and a plate of Mrs Foster's delicious macaroons had been placed on the desk and the doctor poured himself another cup, stirring in a teaspoon of sugar.

"May I ask if ye've . . . resumed your marital relationship? I don't mean to pry, but as a doctor I feel I must—"

"No!" The word snapped bitterly from between Chad's lips which had been clamped about a cigar. He replaced it and dragged its smoke into his lungs, then blew it out where it drifted to the ceiling.

"Why not, Mr Cameron?"

Chad turned violently and for a moment Doctor Monroe flinched, for it was his belief he had never seen such suffering on a man's face.

"D'you think I want to put her through that again? Get her with child?" Chad snarled. "Sweet Christ, man, she nearly died, and in agony. I am not a beast, Doctor, but a man with, I hope, some thought for—"

"I see." The doctor's face was soft with compassion and a certain respect, for he had known many men, supposed gentlemen, who bedded with their wives a bare week or two after the birth of a child, giving thought only to their own needs and none for the woman's health, nor her birth injuries. It had been very evident to Doctor Monroe, who deeply loved his own new wife, that this man felt the same

about the woman who had nearly died giving birth to his son
and daughter. His actions during his wife's labour and for days
afterwards had shown clearly what she meant to him, but there
was something very wrong in this household and for the life of
him he couldn't put a finger on what it might be. It was not
natural for a young mother to evince such little interest in her
child, her children, particularly the first, but there she was in
the garden larking about with a spaniel puppy as though she
were a child herself. True, she had suffered greatly during
the birth and afterwards had been gravely ill. For nearly a
month she had been in what might be called another world,
that first bond a mother makes with her infant sadly lacking.
Was that it? He was a young doctor with many what might
be called *radical* notions and though he knew nothing about
the human mind, very few in the profession did, there was
something sadly amiss with Mrs Cameron's. He had seen
patients who had suffered a great shock, a fright, some terrible
event which had sent them reeling into a dazed state but surely
Mrs Cameron, who was loved and petted by everyone in this
house, could not be such as they?

"Perhaps I made a mistake in giving her the dog." Chad
Cameron spoke softly to the window pane.

"Pardon?" Alec Monroe was mystified.

"Had I not given her the puppy might she not have taken
more interest in her children?"

"I hardly think that could be the case, sir. No woman puts
a dog before—"

"She had a dog, you see, which she was fond of but it
mysteriously disappeared. It upset her so I thought that . . ."

"Mr Cameron, I have spoken to your wife, as you know,
examined her and I can find nothing wrong with her. She
is a healthy young woman now that she has recovered from
her confinement. As to her . . . well, her . . . I hardly know
what to call it. Indifference seems too strong a word but if

she were persuaded to spend time with her babies, perhaps with you . . ."

Chad Cameron laughed, a harsh sound with no humour in it. "Doctor Monroe, you have been most kind, most assiduous in your care for my wife and children but well, perhaps . . . You are newly married, I believe." He turned and smiled, a smile of such kindness, sweetness, Alec Monroe would have said, and such humour, he was quite bewildered by the change in him.

"That is so." He stood up, placing his cup and saucer on the desk.

"I would be glad, and so would my wife, for she needs *young* company, if you would dine with us. Perhaps next week. My sister, who, as you know, or perhaps you don't, entertains her friends often and dines with them, I happen to know will be . . . this might seem strange, but she is to dine out next Wednesday. Perhaps you and Mrs Monroe would be free . . ."

If Alec Monroe thought the inference that while the cat's away – Chad Cameron's sister – the mice – Cameron and his wife – would play, to be very strange, he made no show of it.

"We would be delighted. We have not been long in Pooley Bridge and my wife is . . . would be glad to know yours. Thank you."

Instead of ringing for Daphne Chad showed his visitor out himself, walking with him to the front of the house where Ned was waiting with the doctor's grey. Chad held out his hand and the doctor took it, then, mounting his horse, he cantered off in the direction of the open gate. Briony turned at the sound of the horse's hooves on the gravel, waving cheerfully, and Alec Monroe marvelled at the apparent ease of the young woman who played so happily with her dog and yet found no time to do the same with her three-month-old babies.

★　　★　　★

Briony watched Doctor Monroe's grey canter through the
gateway then lifted the puppy, which had flopped on to the
grass beside her, into her arms and buried her face in its silky
coat. It was a beautiful golden tawny brown with long, flat ears
and amber eyes which were intelligent and gentle. It licked her
face ecstatically and she laughed out loud, telling it to behave,
then began to walk slowly back towards the house, the puppy
squirming in her arms, then settling companionably against
her breast. She called it Silky and it had been her constant
companion ever since Chad had dropped it on her bed several
weeks ago.

"It's not Scruff who was a boy and this is a girl but I
thought you might care for it. For her." Without a word he
had turned and walked out again, leaving her staring after him
in consternation, at the same time doing her best to avoid the
excited nipping of sharp teeth and the slobbering of a smooth
tongue.

They were like that, she and Chad. Polite, friendly even,
cool when alone, smiling at one another in the presence of
others, particularly Sarah who was in no hurry, it seemed,
to return to the Dower House now that Longlake was again
running smoothly and effortlessly under her care. Sadie had
returned to the laundry where she did little more than train
and supervise the laundry-maids under her, Briony made sure
of that, though she was always aware that Sarah did not care
for what she saw as her interference. It was the one stipulation
Briony had insisted upon, for Sadie had taken the place of
her mother and one did not have one's mother slaving in a
laundry. For the rest, let Sarah do what she wanted. Briony
didn't care.

She could hear voices coming from round the side of the
house, and laughter, coupled with the deeper tones of William
Platt and those of the irrepressible Isaac and though she did
her best to avoid them, for she knew who was about to trundle

round the corner on to the front lawn, she was too late. A strange contraption was first to appear, a sort of small carriage, or a cart which was supposed to be pulled by a pony. *Miss* Cameron had decreed that this cart, which had been used for both herself and Mr Cameron, was quite adequate. It had been adjusted by one of the men so that instead of being pulled, a handle had been attached so that it might be pushed by one of the nursery-maids. In it were the babies and Briony would have given a year of her life to turn aside, hurry off in the opposite direction, but Nan and Beth were waving to her, William Platt was staring in what seemed to be deep disapproval and Isaac was ready to break into a run, only his obligation to William Platt's authority stopping him from doing so.

"Mrs Cameron," Nan exclaimed as the group hurried over. "We was 'opin' ter catch thi'. We saw thi' from't nursery winder, didn't we, Beth?"

"We did that, so I said ter Nan, there's Mrs Cameron in't garden. Seein' as 'ow it's a fine day let's get these two inter't cart then 'appen we'll catch 'er. They're dyin' fer a look at their mam, aren't thi', me lambs?" bending to peer at the two rosy faces side by side on their pillow, smiling fondly at them and ready to let Mrs Cameron do the same, since she had not been up to the nursery for almost a week. They had heard that the gentry did not treat their offspring as they did and as far as they were concerned Mrs Cameron, as the wife of the master, was classed as gentry. Mind you, though they had had no previous experience of looking after children apart from their own brothers and sisters, they had expected their mistress to show more interest in her own, even if it was only for the hour they had heard was allotted to them at bedtime. Mrs Cameron had been very ill, close to dying, it had been rumoured, after the babies' birth so perhaps that accounted for it, but here she was, bonny as a freshly blooming rose and just as vigorous and could any mother resist the beauty and charm of Robbie and Maggie, as they secretly called the twins. Well, Robert and Margaret was a bit stiff and starchy for two little mites such as these.

William Platt stood to attention to one side of the cart, his hoe held like a musket at his side, his expression telling Briony that he did not care for her neglect of these two Cameron children, these two bairns who belonged, not just to the master and mistress of Longlake, but to all those who lived and worked on the estate. Every soul on it was interested, concerned, in fact doted on them and Mrs Cameron's treatment of them was not approved of.

She drew a deep breath and looked down into the padded, well-tucked-in depth of the cart, meeting the solemn round-eyed gaze of her children. Her children, or so they had told her. *Dear sweet God, her children.* Her own flesh and blood, the babies who had torn their way out of her, yelling their displeasure, she remembered that now, and who, for God's own sweet reason, she could feel nothing for. Why, if they were her children, come from *her* womb, bone of her bone, did she not feel the maternal bond that she had believed, and knew to be the truth, all mothers feel? Why was she not drawn to them? They were beautiful. They had her eyes, she could see that, a lovely lavender blue set in a fan of dark lashes and on their heads, curling softly from beneath exquisitely embroidered bonnets, Chad's dark hair. They were not identical but they were very alike. Rounded rosy cheeks, rosebud mouths which tried a tentative smile at the unfamiliar face above them, and a smudge of a nose with plump, starfish hands waving like sea anemones above the quilt covering them. They were hers, hers and Chad's, and though she had not the faintest idea what he thought of them – since when did he and she ever speak of anything important? – to her they might have belonged to any of the men and women who worked on Chad's land.

"What lovely children," she would have said, smiling, if their parents had been Jenny and Ned Turnberry, Kate and Ernie Benson, Dorry Blamire and her Joe. She would say it and mean it, but for some strange and frightening reason they awoke nothing in her. In their own mother! She could look at them, admire them, but to touch them, pick them out of their nest and hold them was beyond her. She didn't know why, she only knew it was so.

"They're doing well, then?" she managed to blurt out, causing great offence, not only to Nan and Beth, but to William Platt and Isaac who had both considered her to be a worthwhile person. They had taken a great liking to her when she used to come out into the garden, showing a keen interest in their planting and designs. Recently, since her bairns were born, the lass had known great suffering, so they had been indulgent of her, understanding, or so they thought, her reluctance to take up her duties as a mother. Even before her confinement the old witch in the house had given her a hard time, locking her in her room, so they had heard, which was enough to upset the strongest constitution. Nasty, malicious ways she had, the old mistress, but now, here was the young one, well and restored to full health with no reason whatsoever to turn from these bonny bairns, and yet she acted as if they were nothing to do with her!

"Well, I must be off," she told them, her face expressionless, turning away from the cart and striding off across the lawn, the blasted dog in her arms getting more attention from her than the babies in the carriage. *Her* babies.

"Well!" Nan said, her face as red as the tulips in the bed at her back. "What dost tha' mekk o' that?" She turned an honestly bewildered face to Beth, for who could possibly resist the charms of the two cherubs in the cart? They were loved by all the servants and even their pa came up to the nursery and, gingerly at first, picked up one and then the other, holding each one out, hands under their armpits, inspecting them. As he grew more confident he had taken to nursing them, one on each arm, and, when he thought no one was looking, smiling into each absorbed face and even trying out a word or two. It was lovely to see him and if only the mistress would do the same.

"Nay," Beth answered, shaking her head sadly. William Platt was so upset he began to dig furiously with his hoe, upending several tulips before he realised what he was about and all Isaac could do was gaze almost tearfully after the little mistress as she sped through the gate that led to the track and the cottages at the bottom of the slope.

Lizzie had four well-scrubbed children sitting around her kitchen table when Briony burst in to the cottage. It had not occurred to her to knock, or even to consider whether Lizzie might be occupied when she had run full tilt, not *to* Lizzie but *from* the children in the cart.

Sarah's return to Longlake had pleased no one, not its master, her brother, not its mistress, her sister-in-law, and certainly not the servants who, though there were too many of them for the jobs on hand, seemed to work even harder than they had ever done. Only one person had benefited: Lizzie Jenkins! That was not to say she had been unhappy in her position as housekeeper to Mrs Cameron but what she did now gave her immense satisfaction, and, perhaps more importantly, a home of her own.

Theresa and Bert Newby, the latest of Chad Cameron's employees to live in the row of cottages, had upped sticks, or so Sadie put it, after five minutes, again Sadie's words, and returned to Theresa's mam's place near Greystokes. Theresa, it seemed, couldn't function without her mam at her side and so she and poor suffering Bert had given notice and, packing a borrowed handcart with their bits and pieces, their two children, had returned to Teresa's mam!

For a week the cottage remained empty and when, to the open-mouthed astonishment of the rest of the cottagers, Miss Jenkins had moved in, you could have knocked them down with a feather, or so Dorry Blamire said.

"Oh, aye," Sadie preened, she'd known all about it, for Mr Cameron had informed her, the very words she used implying that she and the master were close friends, and what's more Miss Jenkins was to turn the place into a school! That's right, a school and any of them who wanted their offspring to learn to read and write had only to apply to Miss Jenkins.

There were not many, at least from among the cottagers. What was the use of schooling to a lad who was to be a shepherd, a waller and ditcher, a cowman, a farm labourer? And as for the lasses, they could work as dairy-maids, kitchen-maids, laundry-maids and any other labouring job open to them without benefit of the written word, bringing in a few bob a week. They were children for a few years only, then, at the age of nine or ten were put out to work at nearby farms or one of the big houses along the lake, but those too young for such activities might as well spend a few hours out from under their feet, their mothers pronounced.

Flo Blamire, six years old, Jess Turnberry and Annie Kean, the same age, and Maudie Kean, who was eight and a bit simple, were slumped lethargically at the table, slates at the ready, attempting to follow the incomprehensible squiggles "Miss" was marking on a blackboard. They were very obviously there on sufferance, their own. These were Lizzie's day pupils, but on most evenings she attempted to teach the rudiments of reading, writing and "sums" to a much more enthusiastic set of pupils, those who *wanted* to learn. Isaac, the gardener's lad, Billy Williams who naturally brought along

Lizzie's brother Thomas who went everywhere with him and, strangely, twenty-two-year-old Iolo Evans. Sadie couldn't get over it and was ready to shed a tear over the fact that her Dai hadn't lived to see the miracle of their Iolo finding his way round a blessed book. And the best thing of all was that it was all free, not even the penny or tuppence charged by the "ragged schools".

Lizzie's cottage was a replica of Sadie's, of them all, with a large kitchen parlour, a scullery, a winding stair that led to two bedrooms, all furnished with the discarded contents of Longlake attics. What a fuss that had caused, for every damn thing Lizzie and Joe, who was giving her a hand, brought down from the attics Miss Sarah made a great fuss about, declaring she couldn't possibly part with this or that or the other bit of rubbish but finally, after Chad had intervened, Lizzie's small home was ready and if love, elbow grease and beeswax could be said to make a home, Lizzie's was luxurious.

She turned from her blackboard now and her face creased into a frown. She was always pleased to see Briony, particularly after the horrors of the last three or four months, but the mistress of Longlake seemed to think that Lizzie was always immediately available whenever Briony felt the need to walk over. It caused not exactly chaos in the classroom, for chaos was something Lizzie would not allow, but the four girls immediately turned towards the visitor expecting a halt to the boredom they so evidently felt. Lizzie was aware that there was no scholar among these children but she had high hopes for her evening pupils – apart from Thomas – who were all attending because they *wanted* to.

"Oh, Lizzie, I'm sorry, I forgot it was lesson time. I really only wanted to . . . well, never mind, I can come back when you're not busy."

Lizzie sighed. The puppy, after a nap in her mistress's arms on the walk down from Longlake, began to stir, twitching her silky ears and her silky tail in anticipation of a bit of fun. She began to struggle to get at the four children who had surged towards her. Foolishly, Briony put her down on the flagged floor and at once all four girls, who were well used to farm dogs, sheep dogs, working dogs, all of which were trained not to play, but to do a job and certainly not to have games with children, began to fight one another over who was to be first to clutch the eager puppy in their arms. She leaped and yipped and licked and nipped to their delighted screams and again Lizzie sighed. To be truthful she was glad of a break from the nerve-grinding job of trying to get a bit of information into these reluctant scholars, so she smiled at Briony, shaking her head as though in defeat.

"Go and make us some tea while I sort this lot out. Now, Maudie, at your age you should have more sense than to . . . Now see what the dratted thing's done. Jess, let go of the other end of the rug or the thing will have it in shreds. No, *no*, Annie, don't let it bite your ribbon or your mother will expect me to buy you a new one. Put the thing down."

"She's not a thing or an it," came an irritated voice from the scullery where Briony was setting out the teacups. "She's called Silky."

"Well, *Silky* then. Put her down and off you go home and be here at nine in the morning, d'you hear?"

"Yes, miss." Reluctantly, with many a backward glance at the puppy who was chewing the corner of Lizzie's rag rug, the one she had made for the hearth at Moorend Mill, they left, banging the door behind them.

For several minutes, during which the puppy fell abruptly asleep again, as puppies and babies do, Briony and Lizzie drank their tea, staring contemplatively into the glowing heart of Lizzie's fire. The room and the simple action of drinking tea, which reminded her of Sadie and Sadie's kitchen, soothed

Briony and the hectic tension of her walk over from Longlake gradually drifted away. She knew it would come back, it always did, but for now she was with one of the two people in the world who could bring her peace and some measure of self-worth. Lizzie loved her. Sadie loved her, both of them without judging her. They did not understand her, least of all Sadie who was a mother herself, but they were patient, allowing her to come to that place where they were both convinced she would finally arrive. But . . . but if only she felt the same.

Her breath shuddered from her in a long-drawn-out sigh.

"Oh, Lizzie, what am I going to do?"

31

She was in the nursery when the door opened and Chad entered. He hesitated on the threshold, evidently surprised to see her, then the expression she knew so well crossed his face and she shivered somewhere inside. A cool, appraising expression that caused her heart to beat heavily. It felt bruised and she put her hand to it as though in comfort, not understanding why he should have this effect on her.

The large room was sombre, the walls painted a practical dark green so that it would not show marks, for children were known to have dirty hands. The floor was bare linoleum, well scrubbed and polished, with a large pine table in the centre and before the cheerfully crackling applewood fire, which gave out a heady fragrance, were three sturdy rocking-chairs in which the nursery-maids and Jinny Harrop nursed the three babies. Thrown in front of the fireplace was a large rag rug, on which, surprisingly, a pretty grey kitten lay sleeping. Off the room were a couple of others, the night nursery where the twins slept and the bedroom Nan and Beth shared. Jinny walked home in the early evening, carting her heavy boy with her since she was not needed and her Eddie did like his "conjugals". She was, in fact, pretty sure she was already pregnant with her second! There were toys on the table, toys Briony had not noticed on her previous visits, woollen rabbits and teddy bears, mechanical soldiers and several books made of fabric, well chewed she noticed, wondering who had put them there, then instantly knew, for who else, besides the servants, would care about the babies? There was a guard before the fire over which several tiny garments aired.

She had been making her usual polite enquiries as to the health of Rob and wee Maggie, as they seemed to be called, and had been told somewhat stiffly that the "bairns" were doing well, eating from a spoon the sloppy mixture which it seemed babies progressed to when they were being weaned and had begun to sleep all through the night.

"Is that good?" she had asked hesitantly and was assured that at four months it was *very* good. Jinny had stood up when the mistress entered the room, clasping her own squirming boy to her breast but the twins slept peacefully in separate cradles. She looked down at them, marvelling at their infant beauty. Their skin was clear and smooth with good health, rounded pink cheeks and sweet little rosebud mouths which sucked even as they slept. They had noses that were no more than an unformed blob and though their long-lashed eyes were closed she knew they were the clear lavender blue of her own. Their hair was becoming thick and curly, glossy and dark. They were her children, hers and Chad's, the result of the rather pleasing hours she and he had spent in their deep marriage bed, but if her life had depended on it she could not bring herself to pick them up.

"Good, good," she murmured, turning away and it was then that Chad came into the room.

"Good morning," he remarked to no one in particular and all three servants bobbed a curtsey, smiling, pleased to see him. He walked over to the cradles and glanced at his son and daughter and Briony was bemused by the tender smile that lifted the corners of his well-shaped mouth. She stood on the square of linoleum to which, it appeared, she had become rooted. He seemed to forget she was there, putting out a finger to touch each velvet cheek then turning to Nan who hovered at his back.

"They slept well?" he enquired solicitously.

"Oh, aye, sir, though I reckon they've both got a tooth ready to come through."

He looked pleased, not understanding the fretful days and nights that were ahead, not only for his children but for those who cared for them, but Nan, who was experienced in such matters, frowned and shook her head.

"They'll know about it then, sir."

His look of pleasure gave way to one of alarm. "In what way, Nan?"

"Eeh, them teeth give 'em 'gyp, sir. Me mam used ter say, comin' an' goin', teeth're a right beggar an' seein' as 'ow she'd nine of us she should know."

"Indeed, and did she have a palliative?"

"Pardon?" Nan looked bewildered.

"A cure, something to help the pain."

"Oh, aye, never fear, sir. She always had summat ter rub on their little gums."

Chad sighed in relief. "Thank goodness for that. Now, if there is anything they need just let me know. I'll be up later. Send Beth to tell me when they're awake and fed, then . . ."

He had another long, lingering look at his children, then as though suddenly becoming aware of Briony's presence, he turned to her politely.

"Can you spare a moment, Briony? In my study?"

She awoke from her trance with a small start, realising that she had been watching him with her mouth hanging open and her eyes wide with astonishment. He was looking dispassionately at her, his eyebrows raised in a question, waiting politely for her answer.

"Yes, of course," she faltered, moving towards the door which he held open for her. She was aware with some part of her brain not totally absorbed with Chad Cameron, that Nan and Beth were exchanging glances. That same part of her was also struggling with the mesmerising awareness that her husband, who was looking at her so coolly, was quite bewilderingly attractive this morning. He was dressed as usual for a day's business, wherever that might take him, immaculate in his well-pressed suit, his polished boots and the snowy fall of his cravat. He did not use the pomade gentlemen usually smoothed on their hair so though his had been neatly brushed it had already begun to fall in a most endearing way over his forehead, thick, vigorous and curling. As she passed him she could smell the scent of him which she realised had become familiar to her in over a year of marriage. A scent of lavender, of cigars and of the cologne he patted on to his freshly shaved cheeks.

"I'll order some coffee," he said when they were in his study, reaching for the bell, "or would you prefer tea," turning to her in that excessively correct fashion he had adopted since the birth of the twins.

"Thank you, coffee will be fine," she responded in like manner. Dear God, what was happening to them? Why, why, did he treat her as though she were some unexpected guest in his house to whom he owed the courtesy one showed a guest? What was wrong? She had turned away from him, she was aware of that, when she realised she was pregnant; or had he turned from her, perhaps in abhorrence at the thought of making love to a woman with a child in her belly, even though the child was his? He had possessed her every night and sometimes during the day in the first months of their marriage, making love to her with a fierce passion, and sometimes with a tender gentleness that had bewildered her, but he had made it perfectly plain that he desired her, needed her, *demanded* her in his bed, for she was his wife. He had dominated her, enthralled her, she realised that, reduced her to the purring, stretching fluidity of a satisfied cat and she had made no demur for it had been satisfying. She had not loved him, she had told him that a dozen times but she had eventually and definitely not been averse to being *loved* by him. He had wanted her for a wife which had amazed not only her but everyone in the district, but he was Chad Cameron who felt no need to explain himself or his actions to anyone, least of all her. She had married him for only one reason and that was to keep the mill for Danny, but now, when it had all come to an end she admitted she missed it, and him. He had made her laugh when thoughts of Danny had dragged her down. He had cherished her, protected her – except against his own sister, a voice in her head reminded her – given her a life of luxurious ease and then turned away as though the experiment no longer interested him.

And yet . . . and yet there was a memory in her head drifting like mist over the mountains which lifted and fell as mist does. It was of his arms about her, his cheek pressed against her hair, his words speaking her name, calling her his dearest . . . dearest – or was it his darling? – his voice telling her he would never leave her and yet he had. He had gone away and left this stranger, this ever so courteous stranger in his place and she didn't know how to bring back that man, she realised now, who had made her feel safe, had protected Danny's interests, had given her friend Lizzie a home and a position in life, had even secured work of a kind for Lizzie's brother, who would never have found it elsewhere. He was a kind, generous man who hid it all under the austere exterior he showed to the world, and to her. He was looking at her now, a question on his otherwise expressionless face, a raised eyebrow asking her something. It was only to ascertain whether she would like to be seated!

"Thank you," she answered him, smoothing down the apple-green skirt of her gown.

The coffee came, brought by an inquisitive Daphne who could not wait to get back to the kitchen to tell the rest that

the master and mistress were having coffee in his study and
what could it mean? They had all noticed that their master
and mistress no longer shared a bed, for how could it possibly
be kept secret. The little mistress drifted through her days
doing God knows what, going God knows where, while the
old mistress ruled the house with a rod of iron, totally usurping
the little mistress who didn't seem to care. She wasn't right in
the head, they had all agreed on that, believing that the shock
of the bairns' birth had upset some delicate mechanism in her
brain and where was it all to lead? they asked one another.
So perhaps, they whispered when Daphne brought back the
news that they were *talking* in the master's study heralded a
change. Please God for the better!

"I thought you might like to see these," Chad was saying,
his manner cool. He had lit a cigar and was sitting totally
relaxed, leaning back in his chair. He had a sheaf of papers
and what looked like a ledger on his desk which he picked
up and handed to her and which she took with slightly
trembling fingers. She didn't know what to expect but his
well-bred smile seemed to say this was something she might
be pleased with.

"What is it?"

"Don't you recognise the name on the ledger?"

She placed her coffee cup on its saucer on the desk and
looked down at the ledger on which was printed in gold
lettering as though he wanted her to realise the importance
of it, the name *Daniel Marsden*. She glanced up at him, not
knowing what to do next.

"Don't tell me you have forgotten the . . . er, arguments
we had last year about your brother's affairs. I told you—"

"Yes, yes, but such a lot has happened." Dear God, was
she losing not only her mind but her memory? She wrote
to Danny as she had promised and now and again a letter
reached her, travel-stained but readable and she remembered

Lizzie telling her that she too had written to and received letters from Danny. She seldom thought about the mill now in the shadowed world in which she had lived for the past six months but it seemed her husband had, for there on the page she opened was an account of her brother's holdings and on the last one was the amount of money at Danny's disposal should he return home this very day. It was a sizeable sum!

"What?" she stammered, looking up at Chad, catching the tail-end of an expression she couldn't quite grasp, nor recognise.

"With the rent from the mill, paid very regularly by Jacob Kean, I have taken it upon myself to make a few investments on Danny's behalf. Shipping mostly, which is fast growing, a few shares in a mine I myself am concerned with over Coniston way, the railways which are overtaking shipping investments, so when Danny returns he will be a moderately wealthy young man. The mill will be his, should he want to return to the job of milling, or there will be other opportunities open to him. I thought you might like to know."

He smiled through the smoke from his cigar, a lazy smile that gave away nothing of his feelings nor the almost over-whelming emotion her young beauty, her open-mouthed astonishment and growing delight aroused in him. There was a saying that every flower blooms in its season, some early, some late, but his wife, the woman he loved so intensely it took all his strength not to leap across his desk and drag her into his arms, was blooming now. She must be . . . what? Nineteen? Twenty? He was not sure. It was almost four years since he had first come across her in the yard of the mill and she would have been about fifteen, he supposed, at the time. He didn't know when her birthday was, for she had never revealed it. Did she know herself now that her mother was dead? For surely birthdays had never been celebrated under Jethro Marsden's rule. She moved in a world of her own, her spirit quenched, a world in which he and their children did not exist. Throughout the winter months she had sat alone for hours on end, he was told, on the wide windowsill of her sitting-room, gazing pensively out over the frozen garden and only recently had ventured out with the spaniel puppy he had given her. He didn't like it but more than anything he didn't like the casual way she treated her babies' existence. The trouble was he didn't know what to do about it. Perhaps the invitation to Doctor Monroe and his wife for dinner might effect some sort of . . . well, he didn't know what to call it but anything he could do to bring her back to the defiant and troublesome creature she once had been was worth trying. Should he tell her of a plan he had in mind regarding her brother or should he keep it to himself, for it was not certain that it would come to fruition? If it failed might it not send her spinning totally off the edge of the world?

He stood up, telling her that the discussion was at an end and obediently she rose to her feet, amazing him with her quiet acquiesence. She placed the documents on the edge of the desk, then looked up at him and smiled, not the vivid thing it had once been but a smile none the less.

"Thank you, Chad, thank you." Then she turned and slipped from the room.

"He's made Danny a small fortune, Lizzie, and if he goes on as he is doing by the time Danny returns he'll be able to do what rich young men do. Become one of the leisured classes."

"Get away with you, Briony. Can you imagine Danny riding to hounds, playing cards and . . . well, I'm not awfully sure what these rakes do with themselves to pass the time but I'm sure Danny will not be one of them. He said in his last letter that he means to build up the business, which already is thriving. He seems to be settling over there and at one point I was afraid he might decide to stay. He is trusted by those he works for and is well thought of. The system of transportation seems to be nearing its end, since those who have settled in colonial lands say they do not want them filled with convicts. They are to try a different—"

"You would be troubled if Danny didn't come home, Lizzie?" Briony interrupted. There was a puzzled look on her face, which deepened as Lizzie blushed a furious scarlet.

"Of course, sweetheart, I know you would be broken-hearted if—"

"I'm talking about *you*, Lizzie. I know you and Danny have corresponded, have done for a while, and it sounds to me—"

"What? Danny and I have become friends in our letters. If I have helped to make his exile more . . . less . . . less terrible then I am pleased but . . ."

"Lizzie, darling, if there is something growing between you and Danny I could not be more delighted, really. But it is such a long time to . . . to when he comes home. He has been gone for almost two years and it seems a lifetime and still he has five more to go."

"That doesn't matter, at least to me and, besides, you are making more of this than there is. Nothing has been said, or rather written. I'm just happy if I am making his sentence more bearable. That is all. But this news of Mr Cameron's will be of great satisfaction to him. I suppose over there it will be a distant thing but to know that when he comes home he will have such a wonderful future waiting for him must help enormously. Don't you think so?" Lizzie dropped the bodice on which she was sewing a button to her lap and gazed dreamily into the fire as though already perceiving that future, perhaps not only for Danny but for herself, then turned a rapturous smile on Briony who sat on the other side of the hearth in Lizzie's kitchen. The boys had gone, Iolo, Billy,

Isaac and Thomas, shouting and jostling and laughing into the darkening night, and the two friends were sharing the inevitable cup of tea before Briony began her walk home. Silky lay twitching on her lap, chasing rabbits in his puppy dreams and the freshly cut peonies Briony had brought over, white, yellow, pink and red, which Lizzie had arranged in a vase, filled the room with fragrance.

"Mr Cameron is the kindest man I know," Lizzie continued quietly, picking up her sewing. "What he has done for you and me, for Danny and Thomas and the children who are learning to read and write, and indeed for many men who are down on their luck is quite incredible. Not many men of his rank would have—"

"I know. I have just come to realise it, Lizzie. I have been . . . I have not understood how it is with him and now, when I do, it seems it is too late."

"What does that mean, for God's sake? Are you actually admitting to some feelings for him?"

"It doesn't matter what I feel. He no longer cares. Last night we had Doctor Monroe and his wife to dine with us. *She* was out" – and Lizzie knew exactly who *she* was – "so there were just the four of us. He was pleasant, good-humoured and so attentive to Mrs Monroe, I actually felt . . . felt . . ."

"Jealous." Lizzie leaned forward eagerly.

"Of course not, but I thought how nice it was, how good it might have been if . . ."

"If Miss Cameron had left you alone to get on with it. You might not have made much of a housekeeper but you and Chad would have had a great deal of fun while you tried. Oh, Briony, go home. Tell him what you have just told me. Try and—"

"And what? He has made it possible for Danny to start a new life when he comes home but now that he has the children, a son, he no longer needs me."

"Rubbish. I saw him when it was thought you might die. He was distraught. Can you not . . . well, I am a spinster, I have never known a man, but I'm damn sure if I had what you've got I'd fight bloody hard to keep it."

"*Lizzie!*" Briony had begun to laugh.

"And there must be a way, known to a lot of women, or so I have heard, of tempting a man into their bed."

"*Lizzie Jenkins*, you are incorrigible but—"

"Darling, try. Let him know that you have feelings, and you have or you would not be talking to me like this. Now go home and . . . well, I hardly dare say it, but . . . but *seduce him*."

"Lizzie, what would I do without you? You came into my life—"

"And you into mine and now we are getting silly" – by which she meant sentimental – "so go home and do as I say."

It was full dark when she waved goodbye to Lizzie. The puppy ran about eagerly, sniffing here and there but returning constantly to her side, since she was not awfully sure she liked the close-growing trunks of the trees that pressed up to the path, nor the almost wavering blackness of the night. The wind sighed through the leaves that stirred above her head. Several times she turned and looked back along the faint line of the path, standing, her nose quivering, growling softly in her throat before scampering to catch up with her mistress, and the man who followed held his breath. The puppy had caught his scent on the wind but fortunately, being still a baby, was not game enough to turn and protect his mistress.

Briony felt a sudden urge to hurry and she realised with amazement it was to get home to Chad! The conversation she had had with Lizzie was fresh and disturbing in her mind and at the same time excitement stirred in her. Perhaps Lizzie was right. Lizzie was what Briony called a discerning person, a woman who was quick to read a flaw, or a rare excellence in another's character and her approval of Chad was very evident. Could she be right in her assessment that Chad would, respond, indeed might welcome any overture that she, Briony, might make towards him? Certain actions on his part, for instance the way he seemed to be devoted to the twins, had put him in a new light, not that he had ever been less than kind to herself or indeed to anyone that she knew of. And also there was that flash of cognisance regarding his tenderness, his care, his words on the night she had been so ill. "I will never leave you," he had said, *promised*, and the memory of it seemed to have burned itself into her mind, for she had never forgotten it. Months had gone by and he had shown nothing but a polite concern for her, as he would for a total stranger, but nevertheless something in her had been awakened and would not let her be. Had she really fallen in love with her own husband? she asked herself, gasping as she broke into a run. She must hurry home and find out. See if Lizzie's suggestion, laughingly made . . . *seduce* him. What if he should turn away in disgust? God in heaven, could she bear it? She must, she must. She was on a journey and Chad was at the end of it. She had become resigned to the fact that Danny's mill was in the best of hands and all she had done by her actions of last year when she had insisted on going over there and mithering the life out of Jacob Kean was to aggravate him, and Chad. So, she must tell him so, tell him that she had changed.

She entered the house by the back door, as always, and the servants, who were busy clearing up after the evening meal, were not surprised. They had become used to her ways by now.

"Good evening, Miss Briony," Daphne chirped, sketching a small curtsey, continuing to give the kitchen table a good going over, as Mrs Foster insisted. They all called her Miss

Briony now. Madam, or Mrs Cameron was beyond them, since once she had been "Jethro Marsden's lass", Briony Marsden, and even just Briony when she had worked alongside them a year or two back.

"Good evening, Daphne." Daphne noticed the mud on the hem of her lovely silk gown and stuck to her dainty beige kid boots. She and Daphne had resumed their mistress and lady's maid relationship, though neither of them was terribly sure how it worked but it seemed to suit them. Daphne looked after her clothes, brushed her hair, ran her bath and generally "messed about", as a rather jealous Gladys put it, in Briony's bedroom. The gown and the boots would be part of it in the morning!

"Is the master in his study?" Briony continued, striding towards the door that led into the wide front hallway. Silky temporarily deserted her, for she had learned there were delicious titbits to be had in the kitchen, sidling towards Mrs Foster, her short tail going ten to the dozen.

"No, Miss Briony, 'e's out. Didn't eat 'is dinner and the mistress were that—"

"That's enough, Daphne," Mrs Foster said icily.

Briony stopped abruptly, her hand, which had been reaching for the door handle, falling uselessly to her side.

"Did he say when he would be back?"

They exchanged startled glances with one another, for this was something new. The little mistress asking for the master. Was it something to do with the talk they had shared in the study or . . . well, what?

"No, Miss Briony," Cook said, glaring at the others, for it was none of their business.

For some reason the little mistress's shoulders slumped and they watched her sadly as she left the kitchen.

In the yard Chad Cameron leaned against the wall, unconcerned with the mud on *his* boots, his head bowed, then, without disturbing the stable lads, quietly entered the stable, saddled his mare and led her out on to the grass that lined the stable yard. When he was far enough away to be unheard he leaped into the saddle and galloped off along the dark lakeside road towards Pooley Bridge.

32

It was the first time she had taken Gypsy out since long before the twins were born and Joe was not at all pleased.

"I'll go wi' thi', lass," he told her firmly, though he had more than enough to do as it was without traipsing about the fells with the little mistress.

"No, you won't. Just saddle Gypsy and get on with what you were doing. I'll be perfectly all right. I won't go far, Joe, I promise. Just to Pooley Bridge and back on the road. I need to buy something . . . something for Lizzie. And I might stop in and see Mrs Monroe." This was a bit of spur-of-the-moment inspiration, since Joe had taken charge of Doctor and Mrs Monroe's gig when they had dined at Longlake and, knowing of them, was satisfied with her explanation. ·

"Well, thi' be careful, dost 'ear," he grumbled. "Just remember tha've not bin on that mare fer many a long month. Aye, I know she's gentle as a lamb but she's not bin out much except in't paddock so just tekk care. Now think on."

She wore her riding habit though she had refused to put her hat on, much to Daphne's distress who was a worse perfectionist than any "proper" lady's maid in dressing her mistress. A lady didn't go out without a hat but, tutting her disapproval, she made do with twisting Briony's hair into a neat coil at the crown of her head and tying it with a ribbon of blue to match her habit. Under the skirt Briony had on her breeches which meant she had no need of the side-saddle Joe had begged her to use.

She walked the mare for several hundred yards then urged her into a trot then a canter until she reached the village, enjoying herself enormously when she realised she had not forgotten all that Joe had taught her. She nodded to one or two surprised ladies as she walked sedately through the village, then, skirting the northern end of the lake on to a deserted lane, put the mare to a canter again, then a gallop. Leaving the more or less smooth lane that ran beside the lake she began to climb, the lake a mirror of pure silver at her back, its encircling fells outlined in it, the air crystal clear, the whole giving the impression that the nearest gathering was at least a hundred miles away. Pure solitude in the bare heights and wooded hollows of this land she loved. There were thriving communities about her, hill farms and cottages and the great houses of the wealthy but they were all hidden as she went up and up. The only signs of life were the placidly chewing ewes feeding on the ripening grass. Their newly born lambs capered beside them, looking astonished when mother moved on, racing to catch up with that friendly teat, tails moving frenziedly when they caught it. Herdwick sheep were small, agile, wiry, goat-like in their movements and it was said that no others could possibly survive the harsh winters of Lakeland.

A shepherd with his setting-off crook in his hand, two sheepdogs beside him, paws raised as they awaited his whistle, watched her go by, amazement on his weathered face. She called out to him, commenting on the soft blue day, but he merely hunched his shoulders, touched his crook to his battered hat and moved on, his expression clearly saying there was nothing so daft in this world than a bloody woman.

Pooley Bridge, Howtown, the lovely bay of Sharrow, Glenridding and Patterdale across the water were dominated by the grandeur of Helvellyn but she was making for Arthur's Pike. It was over seventeen hundred feet high, a bare, empty land save for the heather, the ling and bilberry-edge, the warmth of the sun drawing out the scent of the heather, the peat and the thyme through which she rode. Arthur's Pike was the northerly termination of the long High Street Range, craggy and rough; the steep flank that fell to Ullswater had acres of tumbled boulders strewn across it, testifying to the harshness of the cliffs and the force of the numerous becks in flood. She knew that not only Joe, but her husband would have a fit if they knew she was up here on her own.

But somehow she felt a desperate need to be alone. To be away from all the expectations of those with whom she lived. They all carried the belief that she should be, or do what *they* thought was right, was correct, was the way of things in their world. They loved her, at least Sadie and Lizzie did, and wanted only what was best for her. A woman lived her life according to the circumstances in which that life had put her and there was a code that must be respected. She was not *normal*, their manner towards her told her and she was ready to agree with that. They believed her illness after her children were born had caused it and she supposed there was a lot of truth in that, but there was something else in her world that was off kilter and she must find some quiet place of solitude where she could think about it, dig deep into her mind, and in the peace and calm of this high place decide what it was and how to put it right. In the last few days she had found that her feelings for Chad, which might previously have been described as indifferent, had altered subtly. She had found herself watching him as he crossed the yard, elegant and graceful, to where Joe held his ebony mare; the way he lifted himself into the saddle, the good-humoured smile which tilted the corner of his mouth, his voice deep and masculine as he gave Joe a last-minute order. She had listened for his step along the wide, deep-carpeted corridor outside her bedroom door and, from far away on the nursery floor, heard the sound of his laughter, the knife slice inside her telling her he was with his children, the children she could not bring herself to love.

She reached the grassy undulation that led up to the summit of Arthur's Pike. It was a day of sunshine and shadows and above the deep trench of Ullswater she could see the full ranges of Helvellyn. The water of the lake was like silk, a rippling silk as the clouds passed across it from west to east. She reined in Gypsy and slid from her back, letting the mare drift across the grass, bending her fine head to crop. It was only a short walk to the summit, crowned by a large cairn in its centre, but she headed for a path of sorts which skirted the precipice looking out over the water.

For several minutes she simply stood, hands on her hips, staring with narrowed eyes across the high, magnificent vista that was strung out on the opposite side of the lake. The deep wooded areas of ash and oak, the patchwork of vivid greens closer to the water, enclosed by ribbons of dry-stone walling, the moving grey-white dots which were sheep. A farmhouse or cottage with drifting grey smoke wisping from chimneys, the tiny figure of a farmwife in her yard.

She sighed in deep content, meaning to sit with her back to a mossy, grey pitted boulder while she emptied her mind of all that troubled her. Perhaps unravel it so that it might make some sense to her, when the sudden whinnying of her mare turned her abruptly to stare in her direction and she was surprised to see her greet another horse, the pair of them rubbing noses in a friendly way.

She stared, ready to rub her eyes, for surely she was dreaming. The horse, a mare, was as black as ebony, as black as Chad's lovely animal and evidently was well known to Gypsy; even as her dreaming mind noted these strange facts her heart tripped and began to beat faster. What was Chad's horse doing up here peacefully cropping the grass, for God's sake, and where was Chad? It was not tethered and having greeted Gypsy the two animals grazed quietly side by side, the only sound their strong teeth tearing at the grass. Slowly she walked across the plateau, approaching Chad's animal with care, for she was a highly bred mare and inclined to be flighty with anyone but her master and Joe. Putting her hand to the mare's neck, she patted it, relieved when the animal allowed it.

"What the dickens are you doing up here, and where's Chad?" she asked, foolishly she knew, but the mare, after throwing her a wide-eyed look of what might, in a human, have been concern, continued to graze.

Briony turned around, her wide riding skirt swinging out and slightly disturbing the horses. Round she went, north, south, east and west, looking across rolling fells, woodland, fields, water, distant farms and wandering sheep, just as though she might spy her husband striding up a slope or down a path of scree, perhaps climbing a wall, but there was nothing to be seen other than the bare, beautiful, empty landscape. Her heart was beating like a drum, for she well knew that Chad would not simply abandon this expensive piece of horseflesh, even if that was all Sable was to him . . . which she wasn't. He was genuinely fond of the handsome animal and would do nothing to jeopardise her safety.

She whirled again and the horses threw up their heads, eyeing her and moving nervously.

"Chad," she shouted and the echo of his name was flung back at her, travelling from peak to peak as it went and returned.

"Chad, where the devil are you, Chad?" And again her voice seemed to travel to Pooley Bridge and back and far down the fell to where the shepherd's dog was herding the sheep through a gate. It raised its sleek head and looked up towards Arthur's Pike, then, drawn by the shepherd's whistle, continued with its job.

Briony walked slowly to the rough path on the edge of the plateau, peering down the steep, boulder-strewn slope but there was nothing. No sign of Chad nor indeed of anything bar the wandering flocks of ewes and their lambs. She began to walk the track, holding up her cumbersome skirt which trailed about her feet until, impatient with the damn thing which she hadn't wanted to put on anyway, she unbuttoned it and threw it to the side of the path. Carefully she walked, easier now without the constriction of her skirt, following the summit round its edge until she had done the full circuit. She called his name, her voice sounding hoarse and afraid even to her own ears as she walked. She wanted to run, to *hurry*, for it seemed to her that this needed urgency but the path was scattered with loose rocks and the knowledge that she might turn her ankle, or worse, go over the edge, made her careful.

Twice she did the circuit of the edge of the summit, her breath heaving in her chest, her heart hammering in her chest, breath and heart ready to strangle her.

"Oh, Chad, where are you, where are you, my love . . . my love?" And as though those last two words had opened something in her that had been tightly furled for a very long time, something that led her eyes to where he lay, she saw him halfway down the steep slope just below where she had stood dreaming across the lake towards Gowbarrow Fell. Lying beside him, guarding him, his head on his paws, was Bart.

"Chad, Chad!" she screamed. The horses reared and flung their heads about, then, as one, they took off down the path along which they had both come. She didn't notice them go, since her whole being was concentrated on the man on the rock-littered slope. "I'm coming . . . Chad," she shrieked and with no thought for care, for caution, without thinking at all, she began to scramble down the slope between towering rock walls, boulders as tall as a man, heather and gorse which tore at her, bouncing almost from rock to rock, as he must have done, her terror-stricken mind told her. What had he done? How had he, a man who had lived and worked and climbed in these fells since he was a lad, come to have fallen in the first place? Had Sable, frightened of the height, the precipice, fidgety and nervous, thrown him over her head, over the edge? Dear sweet Jesus, please . . . please, not now, not now when I have finally found him don't let me lose him. Don't let him be dead.

He was wedged against a hard and ancient rock, thrown there millions of years ago, contorted by earth movement but which had weathered, as those about him had, into somewhat lumpy, grass-covered, lichen-covered humps. There were, nevertheless, sharp corners to it, deep fissures and both his legs were caught in one, flung up in a grotesque fashion, like a doll discarded by a child. His arms and body, his head, which was bloody beneath his hair at the base of his skull, lay on the tufted grass. Bart raised his head and whined.

Fearfully she approached him, her wild dash halted, not by fear of him or what his injuries might be, but that he would be dead.

"Chad, my darling . . . Chad, please . . ." She dashed the flowing tears from her face, scarcely realising that she was weeping broken-heartedly, then knelt down carefully as though she might disturb the ground he lay on and further injure him. Putting out a hand, she gently touched his face which was warm. Her fingers delicately reached beneath his chin where – she didn't know how she knew – there should be a pulse and when she felt it fluttering, her weeping became even more intense. Bart licked her hand in great thankfulness, she thought, but he did not move from his master's side.

"Thank God. Thank you, sweet Jesus," she muttered, bending to kiss Chad's face, her tears splashing on his skin. She was wasting precious moments, she knew that as she was doing it, raining kisses on his face, her body convulsed with her sobs, then, again with great fear, she turned her attention to his legs. His breeches had been torn and through the jagged rents across his thighs and shins she could clearly see white bone protruding through his flesh. Blood, shattered bone, torn flesh and then there was the blood that stained the grass beneath his head so what damage was there hidden in his thick hair? Whatever it was she must get help; but, raising her head and staring wildly about her at the empty landscape, from where? She wanted to stop here, lift his beloved head into her lap, nurse it, and him, kiss him and hold him in her arms, guard him as Bart was doing, but the hard kernel of strength and common sense that Jethro Marsden had unknowingly bred in her struggled to the surface. She didn't want to leave him here alone. In fact she couldn't bear it but what else was she to do?

"Darling . . . darling," she said to the unconscious man, "I won't be long. I must go for help. A farm, further along. You see I can't manage you on my own. I don't want to leave you . . . but Bart will stay with you." Dear God in heaven, what did she think she was doing, wasting time talking to an unconscious man, explaining to him where she was going and why?

She kissed him again, this time on his mouth, a soft kiss in which all her love was contained and miraculously the corners of his mouth turned up in a sweet smile though he was still insensible. With a last desperate look at him she began to climb back up the slope towards the summit of Arthur's Pike. The grass was still damp from the early morning dew, for this side of the fell was in shadow, and there were stones broken from the outcropping of rocks which slid and skidded under her feet. She wished she'd had the presence of mind to fetch down her skirt to cover Chad with and as she climbed, sweating and panting, she agonised on whether, after reaching the summit, she should climb down again and wrap him up in it. Or would it be quicker and less dangerous – what if she should fall and finish up with Chad? – just to get on Gypsy's back and ride down the fell to the nearest farm, wherever that might be? When she got to the top she would stand for a moment and stare out into the valley to see where the nearest chimney smoke was. A man could surely be found to ride like the wind for Longlake, or perhaps first for Doctor Monroe. Would his gig be able to get up here? Some vehicle would be needed, or would he be best on his horse?

All these thoughts, which had been whirling round in her head on the treacherous climb to the top, disappeared like mist in a wind when she finally climbed painfully on to the rough track. She was panting and heaving like an old woman, longing just to lie there and get her wind but she forced herself to her feet and turned in the direction of the horses.

The horses were not there. For a second she stopped, aghast, her heart ready to burst with the exertion and the shock of finding them gone, then she began to run towards the cairn in the centre of the summit, shouting and screaming her terror. Perhaps they had moved round to the other side but though she slid round the cairn, searching the plateau for Gypsy and Sable she could see at once they were no longer where she had left them.

"Gypsy, Sable, where the bloody hell are you?" she shrieked as though they were naughty children who were playing a trick on her. She ran like the wind to the path along which she and Gypsy had climbed no more than an hour since but there was no sign of either horse. She could barely breathe, her chest was so sore and rasping with the effort of her climb. She was hot, so hot and sweaty that without a thought she undid the dozen buttons down the bodice of her riding habit and flung it from her, standing for a bare moment in her pretty, frilled chemise, her arms and much of her bosom bare, before

starting the descent towards the lake. The path was no more
than a sheep trod, rough and overgrown here and there, the
burgeoning heather and gorse doing its best to snag her. But
in her breeches and fine lawn chemise she found she could
run and run, going downwards, the muscles in the backs of
her legs straining and cracking, her breathing laboured, her
face scarlet and dripping with sweat. All thought but the one
that told her that Chad might be dying, already dead was gone
from her seething mind.

Several minutes later as she tripped over a rock and measured her length, leaping up again at once, she realised she
had forgotten to search the slopes of the fells for signs of
smoke. She was just going *down* with no idea where the
nearest habitation might be, her instinct moving her to the
lake where surely, surely there would be a farm labourer, a
shepherd, someone to help her. But she couldn't just keep
running, hoping for some miracle to put an obliging farmhand
in her path. She must pull herself together, stop the panic that
was bubbling in her brain and think . . . *think*. Look, use her
head and her eyes, stop this headlong descent to God knew
where. Stand, calm down, look about her, for she could hardly
spot chimney smoke when she was in a mad dash, her eyes
looking where to put her feet, could she?

Deliberately she forced herself to stop, though her instincts,
her love, shouted at her to keep on the move, for every second
was of the utmost importance. She leaned her back for a
blessed moment against a tall boulder, spots dancing in front
of her eyes, then, drawing in a deep breath, she looked out
over the sea of heather, the rocks, the huddled sheep, the
dry-stone walls which meant she was coming to lower ground
and stared into the distance.

She saw it at once to her right. A chimney from which
smoke drifted. No buildings which must mean the farm
or cottage lay beyond the hill revealing just the chimney,

but where there was smoke would be people and without giving herself another second to take a breath she began her downward passage again, leaving the sheep trod, moving to the right through the rough, newly growing heather which tore her flesh until it ran with blood.

The farmer's wife was to say time and time again, thrilled to be the centre of such an eager audience, that she nearly fell in the pig trough into which she had been peacefully tipping the kitchen scraps when the apparition, that was the word she used, shot into her farmyard. For a moment she fell back, tripping on an inquisitive hen as the apparition began to babble but when, finally, she recognised that this was a woman, bloody and nearly naked, she didn't stop to ask unnecessary questions. She herself screamed at the top of her voice for one of the farm men to come to her aid, for surely the lass must have been attacked by wild beasts, while she did her best to persuade the gabbling spectre into her farm kitchen, for it was not decent for the men to see her as she was. When the young woman, who, amazingly, turned out to be the wife of Chad Cameron, had managed to get her tale out, she realised she might just as well not have bothered. Mrs Cameron refused absolutely to be tucked decently into the chimney corner but set off, just as she was, ready to lead the men to where, it seemed, Mr Cameron had met with an accident.

"See, lass, put this shawl round thi'," the farmer's wife begged her, for the men who had run to her call were eyeing her in a way the farmer's wife didn't like.

"Send for Doctor Monroe," she was screaming as she turned and began the climb back to where her husband lay.

"Where?"

"To Arthur's Pike."

"Tha've run from Arthur's Pike?" the farmer's wife asked in astonishment but she got no answer. She stood at her gate while the man who cared for her husband's farm horses clambered on one and set off at a rare old lick for Pooley Bridge, and her husband, who was nearly as excited as she was, followed on the heels of Mrs Cameron, followed himself by a shepherd, a cowman and the man who did dry-stone walling for all the farmers hereabouts. Sighing, for she would have liked to have gone with them, she returned to her kitchen where she proceeded to set out clean sheets, and everything she, as a farmer's wife, kept ready for accidents. The kettle and several pans were filled with water and put on the fire to boil and while she waited, too charged up with the unexpected event to get back to her duties, she had a cup of tea.

Twenty minutes later she was at her gate to watch Doctor Monroe who she had heard was right good with things medical, gallop past with their horse lad not far behind. Eeh, it was as good as a parade, she told her cronies later, enjoying it all enormously, but she was not quite so sanguine later when the poor broken body of Mr Chad Cameron was brought into her kitchen on a farm gate, his wife cowering at his side, and no sign of her own good shawl which she had so kindly lent her.

Joe and Ned were having a brew themselves, sitting in the sunlight, their backs against the stable wall, their pipes drawing nicely, when Sable and Gypsy galloped up the track and, had the yard gate not been open, would, Joe was convinced, have crashed into it in their panic.

"Bloody 'ell," Ned said, his best pipe falling from between his teeth and smashing to smithereens on the cobbles. The two horses were in a lathered panic, hard to catch as they smashed round the yard. The kitchen staff, drawn to the door by the commotion, cowered back and Minnie, as usual, began to cry, for she was always the one to think the worst. She was right this time and the two grooms were white-faced and sweating by the time they had calmed the mares and persuaded them, trembling still, into their peaceful stalls.

"See, Charlie," Ned was shouting at the gape-jawed stable lad, "run an' fetch every man tha' can find." Charlie was halfway to the gate as the rest of Ned's instructions followed him. "Tell 'em ter come 'ere at once, any of 'em . . . all of 'em. Sweet Jesus, what the 'ell's 'appened ter't master?"

"An' mistress?"

"She said as 'ow she were only goin' ter Pooley Bridge."

"An' yer believed 'er, yer bloody fool."

"'Ow was I ter know?"

"Yer daft bloody fool. Now we'd best get doctor just in case."

"Oh, great God in 'eaven . . ."

33

The trouble began barely five minutes after Chad was carried carefully into Longlake Edge, still on the farm gate but well wrapped about with the blankets the farmer's wife had *loaned*; she made that clear, for she and Fred couldn't afford to go throwing their hard-earned cash about. Several, the wool come from the backs of their own flock, were folded and laid out to pad beneath Mr Cameron's back and head. After Doctor Monroe had temporarily tended to his broken legs, he was carried by six men, Doctor Monroe walking backwards in front to guide them, to his home across the water. Mrs Cameron, still in a state of indecent undress, hovered beside him like some pale, demented ghost, her hands fluttering towards her husband in the most heartbreaking way. The dog, which refused absolutely to leave his master's side, circled the little group anxiously.

Sarah Cameron was waiting at the top of the steps at the front door of Longlake Edge, tall, regal, and very evidently ready to take charge, and everyone, from the men who carried the injured man, the servants who lingered in the hallway wanting to help, Doctor Monroe and Sarah herself were confounded when the demented figure of Mrs Cameron sprang forward and opened her arms wide as though to defend her husband.

"Don't you dare touch him," she hissed malevolently. "I will take care of him."

Sarah gave her a contemptuous look, eyeing distastefully her appalling state of dishabille, her expression clearly conveying her belief that what else could you expect from this insane person, then stepped forward to guide the men with the stretcher. "Don't be ridiculous, girl," she proclaimed. "Now move out of the way and allow my brother to be taken to his room, and someone get that dog out of here. Take him to the yard where he belongs."

"I will say where the dog belongs and I would be obliged if you would remember that though he may be your brother he is *my* husband so get out of my way and let the doctor tend to him."

"I beg your pardon."

"But I don't beg yours so kindly allow—"

"Ladies, ladies, please," the harrowed doctor intervened. "Let us first see to Mr Cameron and" – eyeing the stairs that led to the upper hall – "I don't think we're going to be able to get him up there. Is there a room downstairs? It would be easier to fetch a bed down than to get Mr Cameron up."

The men carrying the gate breathed a sigh of relief, for they too had been wondering how they were to negotiate the gate and the quiet figure of the man on it up to his bedroom. He lay swaddled about with Mrs Benson's blankets, his face white to the lips, his closed eyes deep in black sockets. No one knew how long he had been lying injured on Arthur's Pike though Joe had been asked to saddle Sable very early, he was heard to say, almost before it was light, for he'd had to get out of his bed to do it. The weather was mild for April which was a blessing, since it was not unusual to have snow in the Lake District, even this late in the year, but the little mistress hadn't found him until noon.

"If we moved his desk out a bed could be placed in his study. It's quiet there and yet easily accessible to the servants. I myself will need only a truckle bed and the proximity to the kitchen will mean . . ."

Sarah stepped forward, her head high, her back straight, her manner stating quite clearly that she was mistress here and had been for over a decade. True, she had spent a month or two at the Dower House when her demented brother had so disastrously married this trollop – look at the way she was dressed, for heaven's sake – but it was to her the servants turned for instruction and the doctor must be prepared to do the same.

But she had not yet taken Doctor Monroe's measure. Indeed she was about to send one of the grooms to summon Doctor Travis who had attended the Cameron family for more years than she could remember, since she did not know this jumped-up young man. She was rendered speechless – for a moment – when he brushed her carelessly to one side.

"Right, take him to his study. This way. Thank ye and place the gate verra carefully on his desk, but dinna lift him off. I'll examine him just where he is and make my judgement about what should be done for him. Mrs Cameron, if you'd lead the way."

"Just a moment, young man. I'll thank you to remember that I am in charge of this house as my brother will tell you when he . . . he recovers."

"Which he willna do if you continue to interrupt, madam. Your brother has severe injuries and will need very careful nursing."

"Which I will provide. A nurse will be employed—"

"Please, if you wish your brother to mend you will get out of our way and let us attempt it."

Briony could feel the strength that had ebbed and flowed ever since she had found Chad on the fellside run fiercely through her veins as she considered what was needed. Not for the treatment of Chad's injuries, Doctor Monroe would see to that and ask for what he required, but for the nursing and care that was necessary and everything that must be done before that. She sent Joe and Ned speeding up the stairs, both of them ignoring Miss Cameron's hysterical command to ride at once for Doctor Travis. They were to dismantle the master's bed and fetch it downstairs to the hallway with the mattress where they were to await further instructions. Clean sheets, pillowcases, blankets, quilts were all to be made ready, the maids squabbling with one another on who was to do it, until she quietened and calmed them with a gesture which told them who was in charge. A fire was to be lit in the study and Gladys was to stand by in the passage leading to the study to relay any orders the doctor might have for the kitchen. Only when the farm gate with Chad strapped to it was placed gently on the desk did she she move to stand beside the doctor awaiting her orders.

There was much coming and going with hot water, *boiling* water, kept to that temperature on the fire, Charlie galloping off to the doctor's surgery in Pooley Bridge with a list of his requirements to Mrs Monroe which he was to wait for: splints, bandages, alcohol, dressings, instruments – since he had brought only the bare necessities – what he called an *antiseptic* spray; his wife would know what it was, devised and used, he said later, by a man named Joseph Lister and which would undoubtedly save many lives.

Chad Cameron was to owe his life to Alec Monroe – and Joseph Lister – for the young doctor was one of the new progressive men well versed in the latest techniques in medicine and, more importantly, hygiene. He had qualified at the prestigious University of Edinburgh and had spent the three years since crafting his trade, as he called it, in the great hospitals, the Edinburgh Royal Infirmary, which was described as a teaching hospital, and for twelve months the Allgemeines Krankenhaus in Vienna which provided teaching for medical students and doctors newly qualified.

"We must have another woman to help us," he told the still strangely attired but steady Mrs Cameron, "but not . . ." He paused delicately.

"I understand, Doctor," Briony answered quietly and, putting her head out of the study door where Joe and Ned were standing guard, particularly against the old mistress who still insisted on entering, Lizzie was sent for. She was there within seconds, for who in the row of cottages didn't know that Mr Cameron had been injured and who among them did not long to help him. Sarah could be heard screeching, as the door opened to let Lizzie in, that she would send for the constable if she was not allowed entrance to tend to her own brother. It was an insult to the name of Cameron to be forced to let trash in the form of these two low-bred women nurse one of her own family and it was not to be borne and quite simply she would not— Her voice was cut off as the study door was closed on it.

The three of them, with Joe to help with the lifting, Iolo who was strong and steady taking his place at the study door, undressed Chad Cameron, carefully removing every article of his bloodstained clothing until he lay, still on poor Mrs Benson's ruined blankets, completely naked.

"I like to see what I'm doing," the doctor said absently.

Chad's cheek was gashed to the bone, one eye was blackened and there was grit embedded in his chin where he had evidently hit something on his downward journey. The breath escaped in and out of his lungs in a tortured scrape which seemed to Briony to indicate that his ribs must be broken but he was not dead!

Doctor Monroe removed a wooden tube with a rubber ring at one end from his box. He placed the plain end on Chad's chest and the other tipped with rubber against his own ear. He raised his hand for complete quiet as he listened, then sighed before replacing the object in its box. Gingerly he placed a hand here and there on Chad's bruised and bloody body. The removal of his clothing had revealed the true extent of his injuries, for in his plunge down the slope he had hit a number of rocks and boulders.

"Mmm," he murmured, more to himself, Briony could tell. She looked at the lean, hard body, the graceful, elegant body of her husband, the body which had loved hers so well, and to which, she knew now, hers had answered. Wide at the shoulder, narrow in the hips, his stomach taut and flat, his manhood nestling, small and vulnerable, in the thicket of crisp hair between his legs. A dark, powerful, beautiful male body but powerful no longer, his hard chest rising and falling shallowly, rapidly. With remembered passion she pictured the complex pattern of bone and muscle beneath his skin, the tight clenching of his jaw in moments of his own pleasure, the harsh hands and limbs of his conquest of her body and then the warmth of him, the cherishing of her. And now it was shattered and could Doctor Monroe put it together again so that she could, at last, tell him of her own passion, for him and for their life together?

She and Lizzie bathed him and soothed his contusions with the contents of what the doctor called a phenol spray and applied dressings, at his instructions, soaked in phenol. With the gentle but strong hands of a woman, Alec Monroe set the bones in both legs above and below the knee, sewing up the wounds and again applying dressings soaked in phenol round the splints.

"And that is all we can do now. Thank the good Lord he's unconscious," he murmured as he carefully washed his own hands and all his instruments in a solution of the phenol, then put the instruments in boiling water before draining and wrapping them carefully in gauze. "We must get him into bed now while he remains so. Tell those men of yours to come in. Will that desk shift, do you think?"

"If not then the men can smash it up and throw it out of the window."

Alec Monroe smiled for the first time since he had looked at the broken body of Chad Cameron, eyeing the small, tenacious woman who stood before him. Also for the first time he noticed her strange state of undress. She was wearing breeches and what was evidently an undergarment of some sort, sleeveless, low-necked, very pretty but revealing more than ladies usually revealed. It was spattered with blood and dirt, as was her face and her hair hung in rat's-tails about her face. She noticed his smile and looked down ruefully at herself.

"I know I look a sight but I ran down the fells, you see, and I couldn't do it all togged up in a riding habit. I had to get help," she said simply, turning to gaze yearningly at the man on the desk. "There was no one else."

Alec wondered at the change in this young woman with whom he and his wife had dined only a few days ago. Then she had been exquisitely turned out, quiet, scarcely joining in the polite dinner conversation which her husband had done his best to keep up. She had smiled when spoken to and been perfectly amiable but her presence had been like that of a lovely ghost. He had attended the birth of her twins and had seen her in the most dire straits any woman can be in and had been troubled by her failure to return to the real world after her adversity. Vague she had been, dazed, stunned and in what he had come to believe was a state of shock. He had said so to her husband, but four months was a long time to remain that way and he had begun to worry that she was permanently damaged by something that had happened in her past. It was not just the harrowing experience of her babies' birth, he suspected, but other events he knew nothing of, at least in detail. Now would you look at her, brisk, efficient, clear-headed, issuing orders to the servants, helping steadily in the repairing of her injured husband, longing to hang over him, touch him, inclined to stroke his cheek and even kiss him in a passion of love, and yet going about the business of ensuring his comfort, his treatment and his recovery with a look about her that said she would do it, or die in the attempt. And fight that termagant of a sister every step of the way!

The moment she stepped out of the study and into the passage she was attacked, not quite physically but with such force she had to step behind one of the men to protect herself. She did not flinch though.

"I insist on seeing my brother at once," Miss Cameron shrieked. She was genuinely concerned, Alec Monroe could see that, but stronger than her concern was her fury at being excluded from the sickroom. And by the young woman she evidently believed was beneath her and, what's more, incapable, not only of nursing Chad Cameron, but of running his home. "You have no right to keep me from him. I must insist upon being allowed to send for my own doctor and a nurse, of course, an experienced woman who knows how to—"

"There is no need, Sarah. I intend to nurse him myself with Lizzie's help and Doctor Monroe is the best in the valley. He is—"

"I do not care to be told what he is." She eyed Alec with the contempt she thought he deserved. "Doctor Travis has been our physician for many years."

"Exactly, and is an old man whereas Doctor Monroe is young and though he has not had the experience perhaps that Doctor Travis has he knows the latest methods of treatment for broken limbs."

"Broken limbs?"

"Yes, Chad came off his horse and has broken both his legs and possibly some ribs."

"How on earth did he do that, for heaven's sake?" Just

as though the very idea of an accomplished horseman like her brother falling off his horse was ridiculous and, what's more, if he had it must be the fault of this stupid girl who was obviously exaggerating the seriousness of her brother's injuries. "Anyway, I don't know why I am standing here arguing with you. I shall see for myself. Please stand aside, and as for you men" – turning to glare at Iolo, Ned and Joe – "get back to the stables where you belong and don't come into the house until I myself send for you."

"Sarah, I'm afraid I must ask you to go to your room and stay there until Doctor Monroe gives you permission to visit Chad."

"*I beg your pardon!*"

"He is still unconscious and while he remains so it is Doctor Monroe's intention to move him into his bed which Joe and Ned and Iolo are about to put up. His desk must be removed and—"

"How dare you speak to me like that in front of the servants and in my own house."

"*No*, Sarah, my servants, my house, mine and my husband's. I am mistress here and if you don't care for that you must return to the Dower House. Now, if you will stand aside I must go and wash and change. Lizzie will stay with Doctor Monroe until I return which will be in five minutes' time so there is no need for you to hang about."

"*Hang about!* Why, you ill-bred hussy, how dare you speak to me like that. Get out of my way."

"I'm warning you, Sarah, if you are not out of this passage in the next three minutes I shall ask Joe and Ned to remove you forcibly. I don't care where you go just as long as you're no longer blocking the way to my husband's sickroom."

She pushed past her open-mouthed sister-in-law and the three men who had just been summoned into the study by the doctor to dismantle Chad Cameron's enormous desk and reassemble the bed they had brought down. Doctor Monroe stood in the doorway while they did it, one eye on his patient who showed no sign of recovering consciousness and who was being carefully watched over by the tall, broad-shouldered woman who apparently had Briony Cameron's full confidence, the other on the infuriated woman in the passage who evidently could still not believe the way she had been treated.

"Well, would tha' believe it?" Daphne was saying to the equally open-mouthed maids in the kitchen. "If I 'adn't 'eard it wi' me own ears I wouldn't 'ave believed it. 'Tis like a kitten turnin' on a tiger, an' gettin' the best of it."

"Eeh, but the poor master," Gladys whispered dramatically. Gladys had been one of the servants hanging about in the hallway when the master had been brought in and had described the state of him to the others. All wrapped up like a parcel but his poor face, all bloody and torn, and as for the little mistress, what on earth had she been doing to fetch up in her undergarments, tell her that? Them horses had come in to the yard in a rare old state so what had happened up there on the fells?

Joe and Ned rode up there the following day, Briony was not sure why and was not sure that she cared, but they seemed to think some explanation was needed as to why their master, the best horseman they knew, had fallen off his mare and down the bloody fell. Sable had not been injured so it was obvious *she* had not come a cropper. The mistress told them that the mare had been peacefully cropping the grass when she rode up so what could have caused him to tumble like that? It was as though they blamed themselves despite the little mistress's repeated reassurances that it wasn't so. It was they who looked after the master's animals, they said stubbornly, but they were forced to admit they could see nothing that could have tipped the master down that steep slope which had so damaged his body.

She or Lizzie sat by his side day and night, watching him grow gaunt, grey, haggard, waiting for him to regain consciousness, and each day Alec Monroe came to see him, sometimes twice a day which, though his presence was reassuring, frightened Briony even more. The grey doughy look of his skin which was stretched across his increasingly prominent cheekbones was gradually beginning to flush and she knew Alec Monroe was worried. She had watched him bite his thumbnail and after several days of observing him when he examined Chad she had realised that he did it unknowingly when he was troubled.

"What is it, Alec?" she asked him, unaware that not only was he worried about Chad but about her, for she had lost weight through not sleeping, not eating properly though Mrs Foster sent in nourishing little delicacies to tempt her appetite. Lizzie and she fought tooth and nail, she because she refused to leave her husband's side and Lizzie because she insisted she must rest.

"He has a fever. One of his injuries must be infected," Alec told her now and so, a week after the accident, the bandages were removed and Chad's body was subjected to a minute scrutiny to ascertain where, in the many wounds and contusions on his increasingly thin and ravaged body, the infection might be. None was immediately evident so the phenol dressings were reapplied after a careful sponging down.

In the passage beyond the study door which was kept locked now after she had tried to force her way in, Sarah still roamed restlessly. Doctor Monroe had allowed her in for a few minutes on the second day, since, after all, he was her brother but she had been so appalled at what she considered his medical mistreatment, screaming that she would have Doctor Travis come at once, causing a commotion that had instruments, vases of flowers sent in by William Platt, a blue and white invalid's spout cup and various other objects flying in a crash about the room. Had she not been physically restrained by Lizzie she would have flung herself across Chad's body in her hysteria.

On the eighth day, as Briony hung over him, her elbows on the bed, her face a scant inch from his, his eyes opened and stared, without recognition, into hers.

Her heart stopped then leaped like a salmon in a river, knocking badly against her ribs and for a moment she didn't know what to do. Stay here and kiss him, murmur his name, ring the bell for Lizzie, shout for someone to send for Alec or simply get down on her knees and say a prayer to that God she believed quite definitely did not exist? With her eyes still on him, not daring to look away, she felt for the bell and when Lizzie was beside her indicated Chad's open eyes.

"Send for Alec," she whispered. His lips were cracked and peeling but when she placed the spout of the cup against them they opened and a trickle of cooled water ran down his throat. He was in a sense still semi-conscious, his strength still waning, and though she was not aware of it, Alec was. His eyes stared fixedly into the distance as if seeing something denied the others, then gradually closed as he turned his head away, the first time he had moved, moaning a little.

She sat by the bed and for the first time a dull despair trickled through her and when Alec touched her arm and begged her to go and get some rest, she shook her head for she must be here when . . . when . . .

"I'll stay with him," he said firmly but in a fit of fury she shook off his hand and would not move. Once or twice Chad's eyes half opened but were fixed in a fever stare, a daze where shadows writhed. She smoothed the hair back from his forehead and behind her Alec Monroe and Lizzie watched compassionately as Chad Cameron began to die and his wife with him. Alec knew that even the strongest body could not endure the consuming ravages of high fever for more than a day or two and this man had no strength left.

"Chad, darling, dearest love, please don't leave me. You know I cannot live without you . . . no, perhaps you don't, for I never said so, but I've found that it's true." The warm air about them was still as though nothing should interrupt the flow of words that washed over the stricken man. "I had a choice once, beloved, but now I have none. If you go what shall I do? I know that we must part one day, that is what happens, but please, Chad, don't let it be now. Not when we, and the children, your children and mine, need you so."

Suddenly she whipped round and spoke urgently to Lizzie. "Fetch the children. Bring them here."

"Briony, dearest, he's unconscious, he won't know them."

"He will. If he no longer cares . . . cares about me, he loves his children. I've heard him laughing with them. Fetch them, Lizzie. It can do him no harm now."

The two babies, bright-eyed with interest, round-eyed with curiosity, were brought in, one to each of Lizzie's arms. They had just awakened and were beginning to make those incomprehensible sounds that infants make, blowing bubbles as they made them. They were round and plump and infinitely appealing, so that even Doctor Monroe smiled.

"See, Chad, it's Rob and Maggie come to see you. Won't you speak to them, look at them?" And though Chad stirred and moaned a little he did not turn.

They had all gone, babies, Alec and Lizzie, for what else could they do for the weeping woman but leave her alone with her dying husband, when a small movement of his hand caused her to turn her head to look at it. It twitched then slowly turned with its back to the blanket on which it lay, palm upwards. She put her hand in it and with a weak movement the fingers curled about hers.

34

His face was gaunt and shadowed with illness but peaceful, the lines about his mouth smoothed out and his golden-brown eyes clear and lucid.

"Briony . . . ?" His voice was hoarse, questioning as though he had to make quite sure that the woman who had laid her lips gently on his was really her.

"Yes, my love, I'm here." Her eyes, brilliant with unshed tears, which emphasised their incredible lavender blue, glowed into his and her hand smoothed the rough, uncombed darkness of his hair. For the first time she noticed the strands of grey in them and her heart tightened with pain, for she knew that she had put them there. He had sweated in the night, a healing sweat that had broken the fever, leaving him weak, drained, but was the start of his mending.

"Where the . . . the devil am I?"

"You're with me; with me, that's where you are." The words conveyed not his physical whereabouts but something else entirely and though he was bewildered by it she knew he understood. She bent and kissed him again, a long, tender, caressing kiss, enfolding his lips with hers as once he had done to her and he groaned.

"I don't seem to have . . . to have the strength to respond . . . as I would wish to." But he was smiling, a lopsided smile that lifted one corner of his cracked lips, and without thinking she put her tongue to them and licked them gently, the moisture from her mouth ready to soothe his.

"God in heaven." His hand, which was still feebly holding hers, did its best to lift itself to her cheek but it could do no more than twitch. "Am I dreaming? Just when it seems . . . it would be welcome to us . . . to us both I'm too bloody weak to . . ."

"It doesn't matter."

"It does to me, lass; but where . . ."

"We're here together in your study."

"My study!"

"You've had an accident, my dearest, dearest Chad. Oh, how I love saying that."

"What?"

"Dearest, you are my dearest."

"How? Bloody hell, last time . . . I spoke to you, you hated the sight . . . of me."

"Now I love you."

"Tell me . . ."

"What, that I love you?"

"Yes, that."

"I can't explain it. I only know that when I saw you lying on the fell my whole world seemed to tilt and though I didn't consciously think of it, since I was too busy climbing down to you, some part of me was aware – I didn't know if you were dead or alive, you see – that I couldn't manage without you in it. I didn't want to even imagine it . . ."

"Thank God for the bloody adder."

"The adder?" Her face was a picture of amazement.

"Yes. It was beneath a rock and when . . . it rose and struck at . . . at Sable, she reared and . . . well, I don't remember anything . . . after that." He was becoming breathless and she could see that even this short conversation was tiring him. His eyes were closing in sleep, a natural sleep.

"I'll have another of those . . . kisses," he murmured and he smiled but the slight grip he had on her hand tightened.

She kissed him then reached out to ring the bell.

"Well, it's about time an' all," Sadie said, wiping her eyes on her apron. She had been taking a few minutes' break from her duties in the laundry, drinking the hot, deep brown liquid which passed for tea in the Longlake kitchen, when Daphne burst in to tell them that the master had woken up and spoken clearly to the little mistress.

"Mind, 'e'd gone off again when I got there but mistress were cryin' an' 'oldin' 'is 'and an' . . . well, kissin' 'is face and she ses 'Daphne, 'e's come back to us', an' I've ter send Ned fer't doctor, an' she were cryin' an' sorta laughin' at same time."

"Eeh, bless the Lord."

"Run an' tell Ned, Dicky, an' stop prancin' round like damn monkeys," for the whole room had burst into an excited babble of noise and jigging about as though it were a party.

"I can't believe it."

"'Tis true, I tell thi'."

"After all this time."

"Will 'is legs be all right, dost think?"

"'Ow the dickens should I know?"

"'Appen little mistress'll get a bit o' rest now. She's done nowt but catnap."

There was a sudden silence then and all movement ceased as the realisation of what must be done hit them. They exchanged troubled glances then hesitantly Gladys spoke.

"Should we tell Miss Sarah? That maister's back, like."

"Miss Briony said nowt about it."

"But . . ."

"It's nowt ter do wi' us, Gladys. She just said run fer't doctor and that's what Ned's doin'. It's up to 'er."

"What about . . . the other?"

"An' that's none of our business neither. It's downright

wicked what she's done but she's mistress 'ere, at least until Miss Briony—"

"We should tell 'er, Miss Briony, I mean."

"Would *you* like to?" Daphne glared at Gladys and the soft-hearted Minnie snivelled.

"She'll find out soon enough."

"Aye . . ." Sadly.

His recovery was rapid since he was a normally healthy young man. He slept a good deal and when he awoke he expected to find her there and if she wasn't he was testy, irritable, demanding she be found and brought to him at once. He was as thin as a rail and when the invalid food Alec Monroe had prescribed for him was put before him he pushed it away.

"I don't want this slop! I need food, real food. Tell that bloody woman in the kitchen to fetch me something I can get my teeth into and then when I've eaten I want you to come and lie down next to me and tell me again how much you love me and, if it can be managed, which being a clever woman I'm sure you will contrive, I mean to make love to you."

"Chad." She laughed. "Don't you think it's a bit soon for—"

"No, I don't, and if we don't try, how will we know? I am unhappily aware that these bloody legs are still somewhat immovable but if you were to help me we could—"

"Darling, darling, Alec would have a fit."

"I don't want to make love with Alec. It's you I need, desperately. Do you know how long it's been since—"

"Yes, I'm sorry, but I'm well now and so will you be soon and until then—"

"Bugger it, come here."

"Chad . . ."

"Briony, I love you."

"I love you too."

"Then come here."

He was naked which was his normal custom, but Daphne and Gladys found it shocking though naturally they saw nothing of him but his bare shoulders. It was Alec's suggestion since it was so much easier to tend his healing injuries without troubling him with the removal of a nightshirt. When the bed was changed or he needed his private functions seen to, Joe, who had proved a gentle and understanding helper, was summoned, though it was Briony who attended to the bathing of his body.

"Take off that thing you're wearing." His eyes gleamed in anticipation.

"The maids might—"

"Lock the door."

"Chad!"

"Did you or did you not promise to obey me when we married?"

"Yes, but—"

"Then obey me."

He wriggled as far as he could in the bed and she slid naked in beside him. His breathing was uneven but it was not with cold, or weakness.

"Jesus, it feels good to hold you."

"Are you sure I'm not—"

"I'll tell you if . . . but it might be helpful if you were to kneel over me . . . there, with your hair falling; now sit back."

He studied the quick rise and fall of her peaked breasts, his fingers brushing the almond buds of her nipples, the flat white silkiness of her stomach which had been full and rounded when last he saw it, the dark spring of curls at its base. His hands and eyes wandered to the point of her shoulder, her clenched rounded chin, the deep, unfocused blue of her eyes and slowly he began to move his hips, taking her with him in the rhythmic dance of love.

With his guidance she had lowered herself on to him. His penetration of her was deep, slow, tender and then fierce. His hands were firm on her buttocks. It was a delicate balancing act between his desire and his weakness but when he came to a shuddering climax she was not far behind him, her body arching backwards in an overflowing of joy in which they both moved, a slow-moving stream in which they both drowned and then slowly rose to the surface.

They lay in one another's arms, equal now in their loving, content, smiling, ignoring Daphne's discreet knock at the locked door and when Daphne returned to the kitchen, her face beaming, to tell them the master and little mistress were . . . well, being a decent young woman who had never known a man's touch, she was not sure how to phrase it, somehow they all knew what she meant.

Sadie was there and as they all blushed, none of them being married, she grinned delightedly.

"They'll be fine now," she told them, drinking deeply, not just of the strong tea but of the joy of remembrance of how it could be. "Another babby in nine months, tha' mark my words."

Daphne and Gladys brought the twins down each day to see their papa, standing to watch as he held first one and then the other, then, as he grew stronger, both together on his bed. They were solemn with him, piercing him with the fixed stare of children, their thumbs plugged firmly into their rosy mouths. They could sit up now, with the help of a suitably placed cushion, beautiful children with a tumble of dark glossy curls, rosy, rounded cheeks, their mother's eyes, and he loved them as he loved their mother, but he made no move to include her in the play he did his best to introduce. One step at a time, was his maxim at this juncture, for he was still enchanted with their new-found and shared love. Briony would sit before the fire, half turned away from the scene on the bed and the troubled glances of the two maids, but even after all this time she found she could still pretend that these two babies were nothing to do with her. It was not even a pretence for that was how she felt! She had even stopped wondering at it. She was just one of those women empty of all maternal feelings and there was no use trying to force them as she had done at first in her visits to the nursery.

After ten minutes of attempting to form some sort of connection between his children and himself, with the maids awkwardly standing by and his wife seemingly impervious to the babies' charms, just as though she were a visitor, a visitor who was entitled to admire them from afar, he would reluctantly indicate to the maids to return them to the nursery.

Sarah visited once a day, refusing politely to sit down, enquiring after his health and his progress, studiously ignoring Briony, her face averted from the truckle bed on which Briony had at first slept.

"Your friends are all asking after you, Chadwick, and wonder when they might visit. I told them that your doctor is in charge and since I am not acquainted with him I cannot say."

"I don't think he's up to visitors yet, Sarah."

Sarah turned icily cold eyes on Briony, studied her for a moment in surprise as though the china dog in the hearth had spoken, then turned back to Chad.

"Is there anything I can do, my dear? As you probably know I have been kept from you against my will but you have only to ask." Her expression said that if she had been in charge and Doctor Travis attending him he would have been up and about by now.

"Thank you, Sarah, but my wife is looking after me and Doctor Monroe is pleased with my progress."

"Hmm! Well, I am expecting some friends later so I will leave you."

Chad had been confined to the study, and Briony with him for five weeks, but was ready now to be lifted into a chair if he felt up to it, Alec said. It was a fine day, a June day with a pale blue sky stretching across the unruffled waters of the lake. William Platt had handed in a great basket of roses for the master which Briony had arranged in a haphazard way, since, as she said herself, she was neither domesticated nor artistic, and the fragrance filled the room. Out in the garden there were beds of them, and all the summer flowers William Platt and Isaac took such pride in. Perhaps soon she and Chad would be able to get about in the gig, visit Lizzie and even the mill, for Alec had brought two walking sticks with arm rests which, when he was on his feet, would enable Chad to be even more independent.

They made love in one way and another almost every day and as Sadie reported to the others, for she had been allowed in to see him, the pair of them looked as bonny as only a good loving could make them. She made them blush sometimes, with her candour, especially with young Dicky smirking in the scullery, but the growing happiness of the master and mistress crept into the kitchen. Shining eyes the pair of them had, Sadie told them, a tendency to touch one another even in company and it did her old heart good to see it.

"Why don't you get a couple of the men to lift you out on to the terrace, Chad?" Alec asked him after he had examined the splints on his legs that day. "I'm of the opinion these splints will be off in a week or two and you need to ease yourself slowly into the great outdoors."

And so Briony had gone upstairs to change into a summer gown, a pretty gown, for she was sure Chad must be sick to death of seeing her in this old working thing. She smiled. They would sit on the terrace and look out over William Platt's beautiful garden and perhaps the sun would put a bit of colour into Chad's pale face.

The babies were crying on the top floor as she went up the back stairs but she took no notice, for Nan and Beth were there and would tend to them. They were, she had been told, good babies, sweet-natured and even-tempered except when they were teething which she supposed they were at the moment. She hadn't made one of her dutiful visits to the nursery since Chad's accident. After all she saw them when they were brought down to the study.

She chose a white muslin gown with a broad sash of scarlet satin and after shrugging herself into it since it would only take time to summon Daphne, she brushed her hair loose, threaded a scarlet ribbon through it, then hurried out of her room and along the wide hallway to the back stairs which was the quickest way to the study. She couldn't wait to get back to Chad. To let him see her in her lovely gown, besides which it was a hardship to her to be parted from him for even a few minutes. She smiled as she started down the stairs, wondering what had happened to that girl who had thought of nothing but the mill at Moorend, the girl who had been tied by bands of steel to her past life, to Danny and his transportation, to his return and her need to preserve his life for him when he did. Then Chad had been nothing but a hand in a pocket full of money to make this come true, and though she was still concerned that Danny's life should be waiting for him when he did come back, now *her* life lay waiting for her downstairs.

She was halfway down the stairs, her heels clattering on the oil cloth when the sound of the babies' continued crying brought her to a hesitant stop. She had heard them before, many times, but barely a moment after they began, their cries were cut off as either Nan or Beth picked them up. Now they went on and on and though she did her best to ignore it, something, God knows what, for it had never done so before, tugged at the area in her chest where her heart lay. Dear God, why didn't those two women attend to their charges? What the devil were they up to? Sitting on their behinds drinking tea, she shouldn't wonder, but that wasn't like them. They loved the babies and . . . and . . . sweet heaven . . .

Without conscious thought she found herself turning on the stairs and when she reached the top turning again to go up those that led to the nursery. The door was closed but the sound of heartbreaking crying was louder.

She almost whirled about and went down again, for she really didn't want to be involved with this. Besides, Chad was waiting for her and the lovely prospect of getting out of the sickroom with him called out to her. But somehow she found she couldn't move. They were her flesh, bone of her bone, blood of her blood but they weren't her children, not really, were they?

Then who the devil's are they? a small voice said inside her and for the first time she listened to it.

Opening the door, she walked in. The window was tightly closed and the first thing she noticed was the stink of urine. Of wet napkins. Not that she had ever had anything to do with it, changing Rob or Maggie. For a moment a great confusion reigned in her head, for she had called them by their names instead of the babies, the twins. She didn't recognise herself but she did recognise the smell.

Both babies were flopping about in their cradles, doing their best to sit up, clutching the sides with chubby, desperate hands and wailing, not a wail of temper or woe but of despair, of fear, the sound a child makes when it is on the edge of hysteria.

For a moment she couldn't understand it. Both babies, when they saw her, held up their arms to her, she who was almost a stranger to them, which seemed to indicate to her that they were so distraught any friendly face would do, even hers.

"What is it?" she asked them, moving slowly over to the

cradles and looking down at them. They were the first words she had ever spoken to her own children and they both stopped crying though their hiccupping sobs continued from about their thumbs which they had plugged into their mouths for comfort.

A movement behind her made her whirl about and a woman rose to her feet from the nursery chair where she had been seated. There was a magazine in her hand, one she had evidently been reading.

"Good morning, madam," she said, quite unruffled, it seemed, not only by Briony's appearance but by the babies' wailing.

"Who the devil are you?" Briony snapped and the woman took a startled step backwards. "And where are Nan and Beth? What the devil's going on here? Why are these babies crying?"

"Madam, since your husband was taken ill—"

"Never mind that. Kindly fetch Nan and Beth and by God I warn you that not only you but both of them will feel the edge of my tongue when—"

"You must be Mrs Cameron. My name is Nurse Cartmell."

"I know who I am but your presence here is a total mystery to me and why—"

"Madam, if you would just let me explain."

"You'd best be quick about it, for when my husband hears of this . . ." She was quivering with rage and with something else that she could not name. The babies kept drawing her eyes to them. Their own were enormous, filled with fat tears and they seemed to cower back each time the woman spoke. She was tall, thin, dressed all in black with a spotlessly white apron and a cap which covered her iron-grey hair. She looked spiky, narrow, sharp-cornered, as though her embrace might hurt, but then from the look of her she had never embraced anyone in her life.

"I am the new nanny, Madam. The others, two of them, have gone. I was told they were too lax." She sniffed and hitched her arms about her non-existent bosom. "Miss Cameron told me—"

"Miss Cameron?" Briony's voice was dangerous and the woman took another step backwards.

"They . . . the children," giving the heavy-eyed babies a cool nod. "Well, Miss Cameron told me that she was afraid the children were being spoiled, besides which she was afraid they would pick up the rough speech of their previous nurses. Working-class women, I believe. And they lifted them from their cradles the moment they cried, which is not good for them. They have to cry sometimes."

"Is that so?"

"It exercises their lungs, you see." Nurse Cartmell seemed to have regained her equilibrium, unaware of the menacing expression on Mrs Cameron's face. "They cry in temper and soon find that by crying they will quickly have their wishes gratified. Also I'm a firm believer in routine. They are fed at certain times, changed at certain times, sleep when they are put down and are not picked up in between. They must learn, you see. I have been a nanny for many years in the best households and come with the highest references."

"Well, you'll get none from me when you leave so I suggest you pack your things and ask one of the grooms to take you to the station in Penrith."

The woman gasped. "But I was just about to change them, Mrs Cameron," as though that might appease this dangerously threatening woman.

"Don't you touch those children or I will knock you to the floor."

"Madam!" The woman was aghast, her expression saying she had never been spoken to like that in her life, but what could you expect from a woman of the lower orders as Miss Cameron had told her she was.

"Where are the children's napkins and clean clothes?"

"Mrs Cameron, please reconsider. Miss Cameron will not be at all pleased to hear that you have taken it upon yourself to dismiss me."

"Miss Cameron is not the mistress of this house. I am, and I'm telling you to leave before I have you thrown out. Now, where are the napkins?"

Chad was sitting impatiently in the chair where Joe and Ned had placed him. The two men stood awkwardly by the open window and it was very evident that all three were wondering what the devil she was up to. Surely it didn't take this long to change into a frock, but then women were a rare breed and who were they to challenge them?

When she walked through the open door, a child dangling under each arm, the pair of them big-eyed but quiet, both Joe and Ned swore they thought Mr Chad was going to get up and walk towards her.

"These babies need changing so I suggest we do one each. Have you any idea how to go about it, Chad, because I haven't? That bloody woman upstairs gave me these things."

"What bloody woman?" Chad spluttered.

"The bloody woman your bloody sister employed to look after our children and when they are changed, since they are wringing wet, and somewhat sweeter smelling, though I should really leave them as they are – wouldn't you like to see Sarah's face if I did – I intend to go to the drawing-room, taking them with me, tell her what I think of her and ask her how soon she can be out of my house. I don't care who she has visiting."

"Can I come?" he said, grinning.

"Of course. Now which one will you have? I think we'd

better put them on the bed. There, oh, I've got Rob. Look at that dear little . . . what d'you call it?"

"Its correct name is a penis."

"A penis, really? Isn't it the dearest little thing you ever saw? Now can you manage Maggie?" While the two grooms, red-faced and grinning, slid from the room, since they knew they weren't needed here.

35

Daphne never got tired of repeating what she had been privy to in the elegant drawing-room of Longlake Edge on that day. Wherever she went she was asked to describe it all over again, since the whole valley had heard parts of it by the end of the week and she was more than willing to fill in the bits they had missed. Mrs Foster, the head of the kitchen by reason of her position as cook, had half-heartedly told her she was not to gossip about her employers, but it made no difference, for when an explosive event such as this had taken place, one having far-reaching results that affected them all, how could it be ignored? It was the only subject discussed in every household, from the big houses that lined the lake to the fell farms and cottages that were scattered from Pooley Bridge to Patterdale.

Daphne was about to hand a delicate china cup of tea that Miss Sarah had just poured out to Mrs Seddon who was describing her niece's wedding which she had attended in Gloucester when the door was flung open and the procession marched in. She could only call it a procession and if the Penrith Brass Band had followed on playing a stirring tune she could not have been more confounded. The cup and saucer wavered in her hand, her mouth fell open, she distinctly heard the bone in her jaw click and Mrs Addison, who was seated next to Mrs Seddon on the settee, fell back in astonishment.

Briony felt a distinct inclination to laugh and had she not been so infuriated might have done so. She was still not exactly sure *why* she felt so maddened. Until half an hour ago she had scarcely been aware of the two babies. Oh, she had seen them about, even made an effort to trudge reluctantly up the nursery stairs to have a look at them, since she had been well aware that it was expected of her. But for all the emotion, real emotion they aroused in her they might have been the offspring of one of the servants, or the women in the cottages beside the ones lived in by Lizzie and Sadie. Pretty babies, for sure, throwing their heads back and smiling widely, showing their shining pink gums to anyone who spoke to them. Just as these two had smiled hesitantly at her as she laid them on Chad's bed. They had watched her with grave curiosity, still as little mice caught in the open by the cat and when she spoke, both of them jumped, startled. Their faces had been flushed by their crying and slightly sweated but they had borne with equanimity the somewhat rough handling she and Chad had subjected them to as they were changed from their wet garments and napkins into some baby clothes she had found airing by the fire.

Silky, grown from a puppy to a young dog now and who had lived in the study with her and Chad ever since Chad's accident, had been as fascinated as she was, sniffing at the babies with evident interest. She herself had studied first one and then the other with bewildering delight, the fury she had known swamped by something else. She could not say exactly that she loved them, for she hardly knew them but she did feel a great need to *protect* them. Her hand moved of its own accord to smooth the tumble of dark curls that capped each neat skull and all the time she had been conscious of Chad's eyes on her. When they were both presentable Chad's hand had come out to her and she had taken it.

"Well done," he had said, gently, the expression in his eyes soft and loving, immeasurably moved.

Holding his hand for a moment, sharing the blossoming

pleasure, she rang the bell and when Gladys came running, sent for Ned and Joe.

"Are you ready, Chad?" she had asked when he was seated in his chair and the men, clearly fascinated, had set themselves to lift him, since he was a heavy man.

"And willing, my darling," he had answered her, nodding to the mystified Ned and Joe to pick up his chair with him in it. On his lap was cradled his small daughter.

"I've a bloody good mind to try out those crutch things Alec brought over," he grumbled, more for effect than anything, for the feel of the solemn infant on his knee was very pleasant.

"You'll do no such thing, d'you hear?"

"Yes, Nurse! Now I wonder how one makes them laugh?" gazing into the face that was staring, wide-eyed, into his.

"I'm sure we'll find out."

Sarah Cameron's own face was a joy to behold, or so Daphne told the others, though not in those exact words, when the little mistress strode into the immaculate drawing-room, one of the babies on her hip, already, it seemed, experienced in the method used by most mothers when carrying a young child. Her eyes moved in confoundment from Briony to the chair in which her brother sat, carried by the two grooms, both with their sleeves rolled up to reveal their brown, sweated arms. He had the second baby on his lap. The drawing-room, essentially Sarah's room since she had been its chatelaine for many years, was large and airy but it no longer seemed so when invaded by a woman, two babies, three men, one in a chair, and a prancing, excited young dog.

Like the rest of the occupants of the room, Sarah's mouth fell open and her eyes blinked slowly from one intruder to the next, halting for a moment on the placid babies, dropping, appalled, to the stableyard muck which still clung to the grooms' sturdy boots and was depositing itself on her fine carpet, then finally coming to rest on her brother, who was smiling as placidly as the infants. She had time to notice that beside the dog, even the damned cat, which she herself had banned from the nursery, had attached itself to the retinue, sinuously rubbing against the skirt of Mrs Addison's expensive silk gown. Her two callers had the same expression of horrified amazement on their faces as did their hostess. In the doorway behind Chad, grim-faced and tight-lipped but determined to be heard, was Nanny Cartmell.

"What . . . ?" was all Sarah managed to say, her face turning from the pale hue of shock to the vivid red of fury, but it was nothing compared to Briony's. Sarah was infuriated but she was a lady with other ladies in her drawing-room, while Briony was not and she had no scruples about offending anyone, the more the better in her opinion.

"Yes, you may ask 'what', Sarah Cameron. I did myself when I came across this harridan" – turning to look over her shoulder at the nanny, whom she had just noticed standing to attention like a guardsman behind her – "in my children's nursery. She was calmly reading a magazine by the fire while Rob and Maggie—"

"Rob and Maggie?" Sarah repeated incredulously.

"That is what we call them, my husband and I, but that is beside the point. They were both deeply distressed, cry-ing—"

"It does a child good to cry."

"How would you know that since you have never raised a child? And how dare you interfere with my children while my back was turned? They were well and happy with Nan and Beth."

"Two working-class women."

"Like myself."

"Exactly, and they were teaching my niece and nephew—"

"They were not there to teach them anything, but to love them and care for them."

"In lieu of their mother?" Sarah sneered.

"Yes, I'm ashamed to say, but that is not the issue here. I will not have that bloody woman in my house, let alone my nursery. You have terrorised the servants to such an extent they didn't dare tell me that you had got rid of Nan and Beth and put that monster in their place. I have been preoccupied, true, with my husband's illness but things are to be different from now on. Chad and I . . ." She turned a brilliant smile on her husband but Sarah Cameron was recovering from her shock and though she did not care to have what she called "dirty linen" washed in public she was not about to let her friends see her overridden by this intruder, as she thought of her brother's wife, into her home and her world.

She turned icily to Chad. "Are you to allow this . . . this slut to insult me in my own house?"

"No, Sarah," Briony cut in quietly, conscious that the raised voices, the terrible atmosphere of hate and resentment was beginning to upset her children. *Yes, her children.* "This is not your house. I am mistress here. My orders will be obeyed, not yours. I will employ or discharge servants and that woman who is waiting at my back to complain to you of my action had better be out of *my* house within the hour. Daphne," turning to the paralysed parlour-maid.

"Yes, ma'am?" Daphne squeaked.

"Run and tell one of the men to saddle a horse and see if they can persuade Beth and Nan to come back. In the meantime Sadie . . . yes, I think Sadie and I will look after the children."

Amazingly, she looked down into her son's alarmed face and kissed him, smiling reassurance.

Sarah stood up and swung round to her brother. "Chad, have you nothing to say to this deranged woman?"

"Be very careful, Sarah. Briony is my wife and the mother of my children *and* she is mistress of Longlake." Joe and Ned had set the chair down and were hesitating in the doorway from where the discharged nanny had vanished, waiting awkwardly to see if anything else was required of them. "She has my full backing in this."

"*Your backing!* You are to allow her to speak to me like this in my own drawing-room in front of my friends?"

"When will you accept that this is not your drawing-room? This is not your house. You have no place here, so I suggest you pack your things and take yourself back to the Dower House—"

Briony interrupted hotly, all the damped-down emotion of the last few months rioting gloriously to the surface. "There is no room for two mistresses in one house. Even Mrs Seddon will agree with that, won't you, Mrs Seddon?"

Mrs Seddon, thus appealed to, made a strangled sound in the back of her throat, desperately trying to push the cat, which seemed to have taken a great fancy to her, away from her skirt. The dog was worrying the frill on the settee and she had time to wonder what this house would come to when poor Sarah left. Bedlam, was her guess. She wore a tall flowerpot-shaped hat with an upright feather which swayed as she moved and young Robbie Cameron, sitting comfortably on his mother's hip, stared at it with open-mouthed admiration.

"I . . . I think it might be as well if Mrs Addison and I . . . if we took our leave, Sarah," she mumbled. "It is getting late . . ."

The two ladies sprang to their feet, pushing past their hostess with little concern for manners, ignoring Daphne who had returned to report to the little mistress that Charlie was riding hell for leather to get Nan and Beth.

"Sadie's 'ere, ma'am," and dying to get her hands on the

little lambs and carry them off to the kitchen where the rest of the maidservants were gathered excitedly. It was weeks since anyone but that there stuck-up cow had clapped eyes on them and they were anxious to inspect any damage she might have caused.

"See Mrs Seddon and Mrs Addison out, will you, Daphne, and then you and Sadie can take Rob and Maggie—"

"Rob and Maggie, indeed. I've never heard anything so low and common in my life. They were christened Robert and Margaret."

"While I was ill and had no say in the matter, but the next, if she's a girl, will be named after *my* mother. Her name will be Emily and a boy . . . well, my husband will have the naming of him. I believe it will be in spring though Doctor Monroe will be able to tell us more exactly."

The concerted gasp that echoed about the room turned the secret smile on Briony's face to a wide grin, for the implication of the remark was made very evident. The master had damaged his head and his ribs; had lain in a state of unconsciousness for many days; both his legs had been broken but it seemed it had not prevented him and the little mistress from . . . well . . .

They all began to smile, all but one, that is. Chad held out his hands. His daughter had been gathered lovingly into Sadie's eager grasp, so with a great shout he placed his hands on the arms of the chair and did his best to stand up. At once the two men were at his side, as was his wife, pressing him back in the chair, begging him not to be daft, sir, but Briony understood and with a lovely gesture kneeled at his side.

"I'm sorry, my darling. It was not the best way to tell you but it just came out when . . . when she . . . I've only just realised. Perhaps I should have waited."

Sarah was disgusted. Appalled, she straightened her back and grimaced, for she too had understood what the slut had just told them. Strangely, despite all that had happened, she had not yet realised that she was standing on the edge of a precipice and that, should she not draw back, she would be over. She was of the opinion, as she had been all her life, that a stronger will than hers did not exist and that with a few well-chosen words she would have this low-born wife of Chad's reduced to her proper place in this house and that place was not as its mistress. That her brother, as he had done for most of his life, would allow her her way and that this brouhaha would soon be sorted out. She was livid that her two friends had felt the need to withdraw but she did not blame them. With the lack of the good manners she herself had been taught and which this slut lacked, what else could one expect?

She lifted her imperious head. "It seems that once more your wife has disgraced herself and in front of my friends and the servants which I find quite abhorrent. I shall go to my room and I hope that by the time I come down for dinner there will be some order in this house. I have never known such ill-bred—"

Briony rose to her feet and advanced on her sister-in-law with such loathing, with such an obvious desire to harm Sarah Cameron, even the animals could sense it, darting under the valance of the settee. Alarmed, both Ned and Joe moved to take her arms but she threw them off.

"Oh, don't worry, I'm not going to harm her, though I would like to knock her teeth down her throat."

"Really, did you ever hear—"

"Yes, Sarah, really," Briony hissed menacingly. "Now, I won't say this again but if you and that nanny you hired are not gone from my house by nightfall I shall have Joe and Ned throw you out. Go upstairs and pack what you need for the night. Take what servants you require to put the Dower House in order and get yourself down there. Those servants who wish to may stay with you, though I think you might find there aren't many, but those who don't will be assured that their jobs are still here."

"Chad . . ." Sarah turned appealingly to her brother, disbelief and a growing fear on her face.

"I advise you to do as she says, Sarah. This is her home and she is entitled to have in it whom she pleases. It seems she does not wish to have you and I'm inclined to agree with her."

"I will not be spoken to like this."

"Please leave, Sarah. You have done enough harm to my wife and my children and I will have no more. Be thankful that I am to allow you the tenancy of the Dower House. Now" – turning to Ned – "ask Gladys to accompany Miss Cameron to her room and help her to pack, and then I think you may carry me up to my wife's bedroom, oh, and bring those crutches."

They spent the summer in the grounds of Longlake, down by the lakeside, driving the pony and trap which Ned had found for them in Penrith. It was like a small box on wheels with seats into which the children might be strapped, pulled by the placid Roddy, easy for either Chad or Briony, as she grew bigger, to drive. They saw no one but their friends the Monroes and Lizzie, spending hours on their own, getting to know one another and their two children. The babies were careful with them at first, especially Briony whom they hardly knew, but by the end of August they were holding out their arms to her to be picked up, welcoming her with their infant babble. A new perambulator was ordered, for it seemed it might have good use made of it, and their parents pushed them up the track as far as the paddock, Chad making good progress on his crutches, to see the horses who came to the fence to be fed an apple or two. They struggled down to the lake, keeping to Chad's pace, where he threw stones into the water to the children's delight, fed the ducks which came clamouring for bread, stopping to kiss one another so that William Platt was frequently embarrassed by the sight of them in one another's arms, though Isaac didn't seem to mind. Well, Mrs Cameron was pretty enough for any man to kiss, wasn't she, he remarked, earning himself a cuff on the ear! The long sloping lawns were not ideal for the use of crutches but Chad Cameron persisted, saying that when Rob and Maggie hauled themselves to their feet and took their first steps, he meant to be doing the same.

It was a lovely summer, days on end of arching blue skies across which the golden orb of the sun sailed serenely, and with William Platt and Isaac on hand to supervise it all the garden, as did the little mistress and her children, blossomed and grew. The lawns were cut and watered early in the day, the edges neatened and the beds themselves were that summer a magnificent blaze of colour just as though to make up for the dark days behind them. Lupins of every shade nodded their stately heads in the direction of the two inquisitive babies who began to crawl at eight months. They scuttled off the rug their parents put down for them, making with unerring direction for the brightness of the flowers, putting anything in their mouths that interested them from daisies to worms. Their plump dimpled hands reached for French marigolds, their faces as golden as the sun itself, for sweet william, larkspur and stock from the palest pink to the deepest red.

Nobody called, though there was a constant coming and going at the Dower House where Sarah had set up her court, employing a brand-new cook and kitchen-maid, two parlour-maids and a man to tend her garden. She gave small dinner parties, those at Longlake heard, where the conversation dwelled on the mystery of how Chad Cameron kept his business affairs in order when he did nothing but loll about all day with his young family. Take your eye off business for a moment and chaos reigned, the gentlemen who were in it said, and how long could he continue to live in the style to which he was accustomed, they asked one another, going on the way he did?

They sat for hours during the summer and well into the unseasonably warm autumn days round the white wrought-iron table in comfortable white wicker chairs put out there each morning by the continually smiling maidservants, all vying with one another to wait on Mr and Mrs Cameron, to be included in the joy, the laughter, the sheer amazement of seeing the master, who should surely be back at work now that he could get about, sitting placidly holding his wife's hand or nursing one or other of his children. Nan and Beth were back but really, they complained to the other servants, they might just as well not have bothered, for the master and mistress did most of their work for them! The nursery, which had been done over in bright colours, white paintwork, pictures, books, a score or more of toys scattered on the vivid rugs, for the master and mistress did not insist on tidiness, was a joy to work in. At least they got their hands on the babies of an evening, they said, for the master and mistress retired to their bedroom after their meal and if Miss Briony had not already been with child, it was pound to a penny the master would most certainly have got one on her in the ensuing months.

It was December when, yawning luxuriously until his jaw cracked, Chad Cameron turned to his wife who was curled beside him in their big bed and announced that it was about time she went about her duties which she had sadly neglected during the last few months.

Briony lifted her head from his shoulder and peered at him in the warm, leaping light from the crackling fire. Her hair was tumbled about her head, falling across her eyes and she sat up and pushed it out of the way. The sheet fell forward to reveal her breasts which were growing fuller as her pregnancy progressed. Chad's eyes drifted to them and so did his hand, holding the pleasing weight of one in his palm, ready to start again the lovely hour they had just spent on waking.

She slapped it away. "Never mind that, Chad Cameron. What do you mean, my duties?"

"Don't tell me you have forgotten the interminable arguments I had forced on me last year regarding your responsibility to your brother's mill." He grinned lazily and reached once more for her breast.

"Stop it. No more until you tell me exactly what you mean."

"Then can I do this . . . and this," his hand doing things that made her gasp and at the same time inclined her to giggle.

"I'm getting out of this bed unless you explain."

He put a solemn expression on his face. "Very well, if you insist but won't you just allow me to . . ."

"Chad . . . Chad, will you be serious for a minute." And Daphne, who had been about to knock on their door with their morning tea, hastily retreated, reporting to the servants in exasperation that "they were at it again"!

Chad relented and drew her into his arms, holding her against his chest and for a moment they were quiet. Soon they would go up to the nursery to say good morning to their children but for now he became serious.

"I want you to take the gig and go down to the mill to collect the rents. Jacob Kean has rather taken advantage of my accident and has got behind with his payments."

Briony shot up, again brushing the tangled hair out of her eyes. "Has he indeed?"

"He has, and it is up to you to get down there and sort it out. No, my darling, not right this minute," as she was ready to scramble from the bed. "I realise that I was not fair in denying you the right to oversee the running of the mill but this is my Christmas present to you. I have another one but I shall wait until it arrives before . . . oh, very well, go, for God's sake and tell Jacob Kean that he's . . . I'm sorry, I'm sorry," as she turned on him, her eyebrows raised in haughty displeasure. "Do as you think fit, my darling, but be home soon. You know how I fret when we're apart." He was grinning but they both knew there was truth in his rueful remark.

Jacob Kean had a strange look about him – almost shy – when she came to the door of his bagging and drive floor an hour later. She had driven the gig with the preening Daphne beside her, for though he might allow her to take in hand the question of outstanding rents and the inspection of the mill, her besotted husband was not prepared to let her do it unchaperoned. Eyeing her swollen belly and muttering in an aside to his open-mouthed Betty that it must be true about the reconciliation between Mr and Mrs Cameron, Jacob met her obsequiously at the door.

"I've been meaning to get over wi' rents, Mrs Cameron," were the first words he spoke. "We 'eard as 'ow Mr Cameron met wi' an accident but tell 'im—" But Briony brushed him to one side and strode through the mill door looking speculatively about her, then out again into the yard, followed by Jacob.

"There's no need for me to tell him anything, Mr Kean. I shall be running the mill from now on. I have the books here," indicating the ledgers and account books she had under her arm. "You are six months behind with your rent so I have come to collect it. You seem to be busy," nodding at Thomas and Billy who were manhandling sacks of milled grain on to a cart.

"Well, business an't been that good, Mrs Cameron but—"

"That is not what I heard so my rents, please, Mr Kean, or would you like to terminate your lease of the mill?"

"Eeh no, Mrs Cameron." Jacob Kean was clearly horrified. "But could I fetch it up later in't week? I don't keep that much money on't premises."

"Mr Kean, I am running a business here and I cannot . . ." But Mr Kean seemed to be no longer listening to her but was smiling over her shoulder at something that had caught his attention.

She whirled about, her full skirts swirling round her ankles and Daphne, who had been standing protectively beside her, for who knew what might happen among all this machinery, whirled with her.

There was a tall young man standing in the gateway. He was lean, sinewy, his face a deep brown as though he had known suns far stronger than the one that shone this December day in the land of the lakes. He was dressed decently but soberly in the fashion of the previous decade, a plain brown collarless jacket with breeches to match, a white shirt, also without a collar, gaiters and stout boots. In his neck was a neckerchief of pale blue, the only note of colour in his outfit.

He began to walk towards her, moving slowly, carefully and as he drew near her heart performed a terrifying yet joyful thump in her chest, a resounding thump that set the child inside her moving to its beat.

She took a step, then another, her arms lifting, then her voice was raised in a paeon of wonderment and poor Daphne nearly fainted, for her little mistress began to run. Run with her belly bobbing up and down and what Mr Cameron would say when he heard she shuddered to think.

"Danny . . . Danny . . . Danny." Miss Briony was screaming, ledgers and account books all over the place while Mr and Mrs Kean, unaware that their days of easy money were over, smiled and nodded in amazement.

"How? How?" Briony shrieked in her brother's ear, his

arms about her, his face buried in her neck, his tears mingling with hers.

"Mr Cameron did it, I dunno how. Transmutation, they call it. Dear Lord, Bri, dear Lord. And Bri, he's given me the mill back and a great lot of money . . ."

He'd done it again, given her something and then taken it away but it didn't seem to matter. With his wealth and influence he had found a way to bring Danny home and at the same time given her exactly what she had longed for; placed her exactly where he had always wanted her to be. For just over three years, ever since the day her father had been killed and Danny taken away they had fought one another for what *they* had wanted but it didn't seem to matter any more. There would be difficulties but she was aware now that difficulties could be surmounted, problems solved, mountains climbed, then, when the summit was reached, as they had reached this one, must be guarded, cultivated, nourished. He had got what he had always wanted, as he usually did, but then so had she. Her beloved brother was in her arms and waiting for her impatiently in their home was the man she loved and who loved her. So what did it matter how they had arrived at this precious place. It only mattered that they had!